THE
THORNS
REMAIN

Also by JJA Harwood

The Shadow in the Glass

THORNS REMAIN

JJA HARWOOD

MAGPIE

Magpie Books
An imprint of HarperCollins*Publishers* Ltd
1 London Bridge Street
London SE1 9GF

www.harpercollins.co.uk

HarperCollins*Publishers*
Macken House
39/40 Mayor Street Upper
Dublin 1
D01 C9W8
Ireland

First published by HarperCollins*Publishers* 2023

Copyright © JJA Harwood 2023

JJA Harwood asserts the moral right to be identified
as the author of this work

A catalogue record for this book is available from the British Library

ISBN: 978-0-00-860316-8

Typeset by Palimpsest Book Production Ltd, Falkirk, Stirlingshire

Printed and bound in the U.S.A. by Lake Book Manufacturing, LLC

To Rae, Ellie, and Moz for all their love and support,
and for never once being afraid to say,
'Make it gayer, you coward.'

The roses fall; the thorns remain.

PROVERB

Prologue

The sun was shining on the day that the village of Brudonnock disappeared. The sky was a blazing blue, bright as topaz, and no one walked beneath it. The wind trailed its fingers through the forest, rustling through birch leaves and pine needles. The smithy ticked quietly as it cooled; spiders crawled across the kirk door.

Even the forest was quiet. No deer calves stumbled through the bracken, no wood pigeons cooed among the trees. The vast shape of Ben Macdui wavered like an uneasy shadow in the distance. It, too, was silent. Waiting.

It was not waiting for long.

Slowly, a figure came into view, limping along the dusty Aberdeen road. It picked its way across the path, shoes in hand. Long, curly, mushroom-brown hair shifted in the breeze, and a long skirt swept up clouds of dust in its wake. The girl came closer – hungry, sunburned, swaying – and shaded her eyes, staring at the village.

Even from the path, she knew that something was wrong.

She put her shoes on and half-ran, half-stumbled back into

1

the village. She skidded to a halt, dust billowing around her ankles, sweat trickling down her spine. Her eyes darted around, taking in the closed windows, the locked doors, the unused chimneys, and dread started to trickle into her mind.

They couldn't be gone. Not all of them.

She knocked on the kirk door and got no answer. She peered inside the smithy and saw nothing there. She tore off the lid of the old well, and then the new – nothing there. Her mother's cottage – but there she could only stand outside, staring at the darkened windows, while fear caught her by the heart and squeezed.

She ran between the crofts, yelling at the top of her voice, and as her feet skittered across the dirt all she could think was *you bastard, you bastard, you bastard* until it ran through her mind like a prayer.

Sweating and shaking, she staggered against the side of the new well and collapsed onto the ground. Panic billowed around her. Didn't she still have time? Wasn't there still a chance? There had to be. She dug the heels of her hands into her eyes; this was no time to lose her head.

She almost laughed at that.

She slapped herself across the face and gripped great handfuls of her hair, forcing herself to concentrate. 'Think,' she said, because there was nobody to hear her talking to herself now, 'where could they have—'

Water stirred in the well at her back. She froze. The sound echoed up the long, thin walls, gurgling and splashing, and drawing closer. If she listened carefully, the steady *slap* of the water might have sounded like hands, or hooves, splashing against the wet stone.

The water sloshed over the sides of the well, trickling down her back. She did not turn around. Once, she might have done, but now she feared what she might see.

Water dripped over her shoulder, into her hair. She heard it lapping and gurgling as the thing in the well leaned forward and leaned close to her ear. It spoke in a voice like stones dropping into water. A familiar voice, but one she'd only heard screaming.

'You know where they are, Moira Jean.'

Moira Jean kept herself still. The sun seared her skin. She would have liked nothing better than to have splashed some of the cool, clear water on her face, but now she knew better. Now she knew what lurked in the water, in the woods, and at the bottom of wells.

'That I do,' she said.

PART ONE

PART ONE

Six weeks earlier

The letter came when Moira Jean was in the fields, with the rest of the villagers. Dove-grey clouds tumbled across the sky, and a wind that still carried the tang of snow tugged loose locks of her hair. But she did not feel the cold. She'd just dragged the plough up the length of the north field, and she was red-faced and sweating. It had to be done. The horses had all been requisitioned in the war, and Mr Brodie wouldn't lend them a cow in calving season. All the villagers who could drag the plough had to take a turn with it, and now that Moira Jean's turn was done she could flop into the dirt at the edge of the field and groan. They were all waiting there, wincing and stretching out their shoulders, and Moira Jean wondered if she could put off her second shift by volunteering to get everyone a drink.

Shoulders throbbing, Moira Jean unhitched the plough and handed it over to Callum Selkirk. It clinked against the medal she'd pinned to her shirt; she knew it was foolish to wear it into the fields but she couldn't help it. The little bronze disc winked up at her in a brief burst of sunlight, and for a moment she remembered a gap-toothed smile and strong, scarred hands. She shook the thought away before it could show, and helped Callum fasten the leather straps across his shoulders; since

7

he'd lost his eye, he struggled with buckles sometimes. 'Mind the edge of the old field,' she said, nodding to a long ridge of earth that cut across one corner – all that remained of the long, thin strips of farmland that had belonged to the village before Brudonnock. 'I nearly pitched over.'

Callum let out a dismissive snort and rubbed an old scar on his chin as his brother, Jim, and their neighbour, Fiona MacGregor, settled the plough into place behind him. 'Now tell me this, Moira Jean,' he said, in the tone of voice he used when he was starting to get political, 'why can't we use the fields that were here before? There's no need to tear up what worked for centuries. Why'd some rich landowner think he knew better than the people who—'

Moira Jean gave him her most disarming smile. If she let him get started, they'd be here all day. 'Only the rich can afford to be daft. On you go, now.'

That was when the letter arrived.

Duncan McLeod brought it up to the fields, struggling up the path on his crutch. He was waving the letter over his head as he went, shouting, and nearly slipped in the mud when his stiff, wasted leg caught the edge of the old field. Fiona went to him at once; her mother, Mrs MacGregor, watched her go with a calculating look on her face. Moira Jean followed, rolling her shoulders.

'Duncan?' Fiona was asking, 'What is it?'

Duncan flapped the letter at her, wheezing. 'It's from the Fitzherberts!'

Callum nearly dropped the plough. Fiona put her hands over her mouth. Silence snapped out across the field like the crack of a whip. Her tiredness forgotten, Moira Jean sprinted over.

'What does it say?' she gasped.

'It's addressed to the estate manager . . .' Duncan said, his voice trailing away. There was no estate manager. Mr MacCallan's legs had been blown off at Verdun, and the Fitzherberts still hadn't hired a replacement. They hadn't hired any replacements, even though the estate had half as many hands as it had before the war, and last year's terrible winter.

Their tenancies were up for renewal; Moira Jean tried for a smile. A sick curiosity was filling her up. 'Well, you're not waiting for the new one to turn up before you open it, are you?'

'Just a moment, Moira Jean,' Fiona said sharply. She was looking at Duncan's twisted leg, at his trembling hands, at the damp auburn hair plastered to his sweat-slicked face. She hauled a bucket over and turned it upside down, placing it on the ground. 'Sit down, Duncan. We've time for you to catch your breath.'

Fiona took his arm and helped him sit on the upturned bucket. Moira Jean held his crutch for him, feeling a twinge of guilt. She couldn't stop staring at the letter; she'd barely registered the state Duncan was in. Her eyes flicked to Fiona's hands, strong and sure, and she looked away quickly.

'Thank you,' Duncan said, when he'd got his breath back. 'Shall I . . .'

'Whenever you're ready,' Fiona said, smiling. Moira Jean didn't know how she wasn't shrieking, *For God's sake, Duncan, read the damn letter*, but she tried not to let her nerves show on her face. Her hand found the cold medal, heavy on her palm. The rest of the villagers had already gathered around, placing anxious hands on each other's shoulders as Duncan opened the envelope.

He unfolded the paper. Over her shoulder, Moira Jean could

feel the presence of Drewitts, the Fitzherberts' palatial house at the heart of their country estate. Its clean, white walls would be gleaming in the spring sunshine, like an egg she could never crack open.

Duncan read quickly, his eyes flicking from line to line. Nerves mounted in the pit of Moira Jean's stomach. Her mother wrapped an arm around her waist, and whispered, 'Don't you worry, hen. We'll be—'

Duncan's thin face split into a grin. He laughed, quick and breathless and full of relief. 'Another year!'

Moira Jean relaxed. Her mother murmured, 'Oh, thank God.' Duncan's mother, Mrs McLeod, gave him a kiss on the cheek; Callum's father, Mr Selkirk, slapped him on the back, his booming laugh echoing across the field. Fiona threw her arms around another neighbour, Martha Galbraith, and Moira Jean suppressed a little twinge of jealousy.

Mr Galbraith, Martha's father, stumped over, leaning on his walking stick. His knuckles were white on the handle of his cane. 'And we're all on the list, lad?' He and his daughter were Travellers, settled in Brudonnock for the past few years, and the old man always worried they would be the first to be turned out.

Duncan nodded. 'Everyone in the village. Even An—'

Moira Jean stiffened. Her mother turned to look at her, eyes flicking to the medal. Fiona saw too, her quick, green eyes missing nothing. Before Duncan could say anything else, she asked 'Does it say if they're coming back?'

'I . . . no. Not in the letter, anyway.'

'Good!' said Callum, who'd finally got himself out of the plough harness. 'We don't need them.'

There was a tightness around Duncan's jaw now. Moira Jean

plastered on a smile and clapped her hands, before anyone could comment on it. 'Let's celebrate!' she said, craving something else to talk about. 'I'll away and see what Mrs McGillycuddy has in the pantry.'

'Moira Jean!' her mother scolded. 'You're not to bother the housekeeper for the sake of a few biscuits!'

'Aye,' said Mr Selkirk, nudging Moira Jean and grinning, 'ask her what's in the wine cellar instead.'

Everyone laughed, except for Mrs MacGregor. Duncan motioned for his crutch; Moira Jean handed it to him and helped him stand. It was easy, Duncan had always been small and slight.

'I think something could be spared,' he said, 'Mrs McGillycuddy's been going over the books with me. It can't be much, not until after the harvest's in, but she'll not begrudge you a wee dram to keep out the cold.'

'And I'm *so* cold,' said Moira Jean, immediately. The villagers laughed again. 'Duncan, let me see you back down to Drewitts.'

'I'll help,' said Martha, fishing her glasses out of the pocket of her skirt and putting them back on. 'You'll want a hand carrying everything back with you, Moira Jean.'

They set off back down the hill together, leaving Callum to struggle back into the plough harness with the help of Fiona and Jim. Satisfied, Moira Jean rolled her sore shoulders; at last, there was something to look forward to. They said nothing until the north field was well out of earshot, and the cattle pastures unfurled behind them like rolls of green velvet. The high, white walls of Drewitts came into view as they rounded a corner in the path, shining in the morning light. The village of Brudonnock lay just beyond, neat and clean, as if it had

11

been put on display. The last remains of the old village – a ruined croft on the hillside – stared down at them, like a crow perched on a rooftop.

'All right,' said Duncan, when they were sure they could not be heard. 'I don't need both of you to help me down the path. Where are you going?'

Moira Jean laid a hand over heart, pantomiming sincerity. '*Me*? Why, I'm away to ask Mrs McGillycuddy if she might spare a wee bite to eat for the poor farmhands, slaving away in the fields—'

'Moira Jean.'

'*Slaving away in the fields*, I said. So famished and thirsty are we, *so* very famished, that even the merest crumb of—'

Duncan turned to Martha. 'And are you poetically famished as well?'

'No. I'm away to the library.' They laughed. Martha flushed. 'It's cold up there!' she said. 'It's windy and I want to sit inside and read.'

Moira Jean sighed. 'Aye. By a fire. And with some tea – and scones!'

'And a wee cat to fuss over,' said Martha, wistfully.

'Mrs McGillycuddy's not got a cat, has she?'

'Well, no. But she should get one.'

'She *should*! A wee grey one that'll let us play with it . . .'

Duncan nudged Moira Jean with his shoulder. 'You'll not have time to play with it. *You're* one of the poor wee farmhands, slaving away in the fields . . .'

Moira Jean snorted. 'Catch me going back up there now. That plough's heavy.'

* * *

12

Moira Jean snatched five blissful minutes in the kitchen at Drewitts. Surrounded by gleaming copper pans and bundles of dried herbs, she stood in front of the range and spun Mrs McGillycuddy a line about how hungry everyone was, and how terribly cold it was up in the north field, and how only oatcakes with jam would give them the strength they needed to keep ploughing. Martha managed ten minutes, because she didn't keep bringing up jam. She was able to slip into the house on some pretext while Mrs McGillycuddy shooed Moira Jean out the door with a promise to bring them all lunch.

Moira Jean tramped back up the hillside, having only stolen one biscuit. She felt this was very restrained of her – the little theft was the only exciting thing that she'd done all day – and huddled against the side of the cowshed so she could enjoy it out of the wind. As she ate, wind tugging her curls out of place, she watched the village. Brudonnock was a clutch of near-identical cottages petering out towards the slope of the Aberdeen road. Half of the houses were empty. Thatched rooves rustled quietly in the wind, and the hiss of the straw and thrush-song was all she could hear. There was no shop, no social club, no public house that she could sneak off to. There was a small kirk and a smaller schoolroom, which was mostly used to dry and store the villagers' peat now there were no more children. There were two wells: one new and one old and overgrown, and a small forge, where Fiona's brother, Malcolm MacGregor, spent his days smacking hammers together or something. Moira Jean spent most of her time in the fields or in the dairy; she wasn't clear on the finer points of what a blacksmith did.

Moira Jean could name every member of every family who lived in every cottage – even the ones who were no longer there. She knew who had the biggest mixing bowl, who would kill a spider for her if her mother wasn't there, who would turn a blind eye to a discreet nap in a bothy and who would turn her in. If she leaned too far over the rim of the well, a dozen different hands would try to pull her back. The village was as soft and familiar as an old blanket, and it was only since the war that she had started to notice how faded and worn it was becoming. Knowing that they were all safe for another year was like a weight had been lifted from her shoulders; she didn't realize how much of a burden the worry had been until it was gone.

Malcolm came out of the forge, blond and bearded, a ladder tucked under one massive arm. He waved when he saw her, and Moira Jean waved back, hoping he wouldn't notice the shortbread from this distance. He propped a ladder against the Galbraiths' front door, climbed it, and began prising off the horseshoe nailed on the lintel; times were too hard for superstition, and there never seemed to be enough iron. The sight of him made Moira Jean reach for her medal again. He'd told her he wouldn't need it – although it was a little heavier than Callum's and Duncan's and might have had a trace of iron in it, it was mostly bronze – but it made her feel better to have it in her hand. She wasn't ready to part with it.

Moments later, there was a shriek. Moira Jean nearly dropped her shortbread. Old Mrs Iverach was hobbling towards Malcolm, yelling something in Gaelic and waving her walking stick. But Malcolm did not notice her. He was hard of hearing, so Mrs Iverach had to move around into his line of sight to get his attention.

'Good morning, Mrs—'

14

'What are you *doing*, Malcolm MacGregor? Get down from there!'

'Ah, it's not so high. I'll be all right.'

Mrs Iverach made a noise of disgust at the back of her throat. 'Not you! You leave that iron be!'

Malcolm climbed down the ladder. 'I asked, Mr Galbraith said I could—'

'Oh, I'll be having words with Billy Galbraith,' Mrs Iverach muttered, 'never you mind about that. But you're to let that iron alone, you hear? You've no idea what you're doing.'

'All right, Mrs Iverach. Will you not step up to Drewitts for a spell? Mrs McGillycuddy said she'd want your help in the kitchen.'

This was a tactic Moira Jean was familiar with. Mrs Iverach had odd habits. She left saucers of milk outside her door, which froze over in winter and stank up the village in summer. She loaded up her doors and windows with willow twigs, and shrieked whenever anyone came near them. She refused to wear green, and every harvest wove together a horrible straw doll which sat in her window for a year and gave Moira Jean nightmares. And every time Malcolm had to pull a horseshoe off someone's door, Mrs Iverach would come barrelling out of her cottage, demanding that he stop. After the first time, they'd all agreed that they'd send her up to Drewitts on a pretext and let Malcolm get back to work once she was out of sight. Moira Jean's mother had told her that, in her youth, Mrs Iverach had been moved along by countless landlords clearing their lands of tenants. The old lady never talked about it, but everyone in the village knew it had left its mark on her. It was better to humour her superstitions, Moira Jean's mother had explained, if they gave her some comfort.

Moira Jean took another bite of shortbread and watched them go. Malcolm was walking at half his usual pace, Mrs Iverach's withered hand clinging to his arm. Malcolm was nearly twice her size. He listened to her patiently as he escorted her up to the kitchens, and Moira Jean had to smile at the sight. With buttery shortbread crumbling on her tongue and spring sunshine on her hair, smiling came easily. Their homes would remain theirs for another year, there were carts on the Aberdeen road again, and when the seeds were sown, she could look for work. She could go to Aviemore, or Inverness, or Glasgow, or – anywhere. They'd had the papers from Stronach, the next village over, and everyone said the 'flu would have burned itself out by the summer. She could *find* somewhere with shops and social clubs and public houses, somewhere vibrant and loud – and, she realized, as she watched Malcolm humouring Mrs Iverach until he could get back to work – somewhere full of strangers.

A memory stirred. Angus, smiling, taking her hand. 'Anywhere you like, Moira Jean. I'll not mind, as long as you're there.'

She shook her head. The old, hollow feeling had opened itself up inside her; she crammed the rest of the shortbread into her mouth to see if that would fix it. Unfortunately, that was when Martha saw her.

'Are you—'

'No,' Moira Jean said, spraying crumbs everywhere.

Martha glanced over her shoulder. Despite the wind, her hair was still in a neat, dark bun, and Moira Jean felt a twinge of envy. 'Did you get one for me?'

Moira Jean shook her head.

Martha groaned. 'You're terrible! And you've sugar all round your mouth.'

16

Moira Jean wiped her lips. 'Better?'

'Well, your ma won't notice.'

The two of them dawdled back up to the north field, pretending that the wind had slowed them down. Unfortunately, it wasn't that windy any more, so everyone knew they were lying. But by the time they reached the north field, the sibling rivalry between Callum and Jim had almost finished off the ploughing, so nobody minded.

Mrs McGillycuddy brought them lunch: oatcakes, cheese and a pail of milk, fresh from the dairy. Mrs Iverach came too, and poured a splash of whisky into every cup, 'to keep off the chill'. They huddled at the edge of the field with the rest of the villagers, gossiping with Mrs McLeod and Mrs MacGregor, while Callum and Jim finished the last of the ploughing and Mr Selkirk bragged about his sons to anyone who would listen. 'Good lads,' he kept repeating, 'it's good to have them both back where they belong.' By three in the afternoon, they were done, and as they all trudged back down to the village, Moira Jean tried not to think of how much smaller the crowd was than it had been two years ago, before –

Desperate for a distraction, she nudged the person walking next to her. It was Jim Selkirk, and because he was fourteen, he went bright red.

'Here,' she whispered, 'does your da have the still working again?'

'I . . . I don't . . . it's a secret, Moira Jean,' Jim stammered.

She rolled her eyes. 'Aye, a secret from the Fitzherberts. Go on and get your brother if you'll not tell me.'

Jim glanced at Callum. He was chatting with Fiona, who was looking extremely pretty. The wind and the work had

17

turned her cheeks a delicate pink, and her blonde hair gleamed. Jim blushed; Moira Jean cleared her throat.

'Pinch some of his whisky,' she hissed, forcing herself to focus. 'Let's all have a wee drink in the woods tonight.'

'I don't know . . .' Jim mumbled, chewing on his bottom lip.

'Ah, come on,' Moira Jean said, ruffling his dark hair. 'We've earned a break and we've something to celebrate. No one'll mind.'

Duncan stumped forward to catch up with them, slightly breathless. 'What's this about celebrating?'

'We're away to the woods for a drink tonight. Jim'll raid the still for us.'

'Moira *Jean*!' Jim protested. Further down the path, her mother turned to look up at them. Jim lowered his voice. 'I've not said I'll do it!'

'What's this?' Martha asked. 'Are we having a party?'

'Aye, in the woods. You're both coming?'

Martha made a thoughtful noise and scrunched up her face, the way she always did when she was trying to remember something. It made her glasses wriggle. 'I suppose it'll be fine if we're outside,' she mused. 'There was something in the *Lancet* about fresh air keeping off the 'flu.'

Moira Jean's jaw tightened. All at once the world seemed closer, tighter. How had she forgotten so quickly?

'We'll not have to worry about that,' Duncan said. 'Mr Munro brought the letter over and he said it's all fizzling out, and he was in Aberdeen just yesterday.'

Martha beamed. 'It is? Oh, that's something to celebrate all right. I'll write to Ma, tell her she can come through in the summer. Count me in; I'll be over when Da's asleep.'

'Me too.'

18

Callum ambled over, with Fiona in tow. The two of them were resolutely not holding hands. 'What're you blethering on about?'

'We're away to the woods for a drink tonight,' said Martha. 'Moira Jean said – Moira Jean?'

Lost in thought, the smile had slipped from Moira Jean's face. She hoisted it back into place. 'Aye, we're all going. Here, Callum, get us some bottles out of your da's still. Jim says he—'

'I didn't say *anything*!' Jim protested. 'I didn't say I *would* do it, and I didn't say I *wouldn't* do it, either! God!'

He stomped away from Moira Jean, his arms folded. Callum laughed, and Moira Jean joined in. She didn't quite feel it, but hoped she would, if she laughed long enough.

'We'll be there, with the whisky,' Callum said. 'We'll have to wait for Da to fall asleep first, mind.'

Moira Jean snorted. 'You've met my mother, Callum. What d'you think I'll be doing?'

When her mother was sleeping, Moira Jean counted to one hundred, then slipped on her boots and crept out the door. It felt like she'd been waiting for hours. Her mother had bustled around their little cottage, asking very carefully worded questions and deliberately not looking at the wooden chest shoved out of sight on top of Moira Jean's box bed. Moira Jean bustled around too, straightening and folding things just to keep her hands busy. If she kept moving, her thoughts wouldn't settle into old patterns.

The cottage Moira Jean shared with her mother was one large room with a vast fireplace built into the northern wall, with a dresser alongside it and a narrow table and chairs opposite that. Built into the back wall were two box beds;

enclosed in enormous wooden chests with wide doors set into their frames, they could have been taken for cupboards when they were closed. It was not exactly conducive to sneaking; with every step, Moira Jean waited for her mother to fling open the door of her box bed and yell until Moira Jean slunk back inside.

The front door closed behind her with a gentle *click*. Moira Jean froze, waiting for a noise, but there was nothing from inside the cottage. All she could hear was the rustling of the wind in the leaves, smelling of snow and damp pine. Moira Jean picked her way through the village, holding her skirts high above the mud, squinting at the path down to the Aberdeen road. Her friends were waiting for her on the other side, just visible in the light of the crescent moon. When they saw her coming, they turned and headed into the trees. Callum led the way, staggering over pine roots and swearing. Jim followed, giggling; she could smell the whisky on him from here. Then came Fiona and Martha, arguing in fierce whispers, Fiona's blonde head bent close to Martha's ear. Duncan laboured along in their wake, his hand white-knuckled on the grip of his crutch. Moira Jean watched them go, half-wondering if she should slow her pace until they drifted off without her. There was a quietness to them that had not been there the year before. No one was moving between the pairs, weaving individual conversations together with a laugh and an easy smile, making them all forget that they'd been doing the same tasks for days and would do them again tomorrow.

Angus was not there.

The thought sliced into her, hands twitching on the hem of her shawl. She wasn't going to think about him.

20

Duncan looked over his shoulder, grinning at her. 'Shift yourself, Moira Jean!' He nodded at his bad leg. 'You're slower than me!'

Moira Jean sparked into life. Shoving thoughts of Angus away, she matched his grin with a wink. 'I'm enjoying the view.'

Duncan laughed, his cheeks flushed. 'You're to walk in front of me on the way back, then.'

Moira Jean ducked under a branch and caught up with him while Callum and Jim crowed. 'I know you, Duncan McLeod. You'll not be able to see straight by then.'

They all laughed, and Moira Jean laughed too. It was easier when she laughed.

She let the others go a little further and lowered her voice. 'You've not heard from Edgar?'

The corners of Duncan's mouth tightened. 'He'll not see me. Not since—' He gestured at his leg. 'I thought I'd away and see him, before harvest. If Ma's sewing brings in more than five pounds, she'll not need me to stay and work here. I . . . I heard he was wounded.'

'So were *you*.'

'Moira Jean . . .'

Moira Jean remembered Edgar Fitzherbert's smooth, white hands and unlined face and felt a sharp stab of anger. She took Duncan's free arm and tutted, but said nothing more. Duncan still hated it when she called Edgar names, even though there was nothing else worth saying about him.

Eventually the pines thinned and they came to a clearing with a small, bare hillock in the centre. Fiona and Martha, still arguing, gathered dry pine roots and juniper twigs and soon they had a fire. Whenever she spoke, Fiona's mouth always formed each word clearly, a habit she'd learned so that her brother Malcolm would be able to understand her. Moira Jean always found it difficult to stop looking at it. From the back of the group, Moira Jean could tell that Fiona and Martha were arguing about whether hotel work was safe again. She blushed. It felt a little like eavesdropping.

Callum pulled out several bottles of young whisky from his jacket and passed them around. Fiona looked worried. She was chewing on her bottom lip. Moira Jean looked away; her face was red enough. 'Won't your Da notice when he cracks open the barrels?' Fiona asked.

Callum grinned at her. 'He'll not mind. And if he does, I'll tell him it's the angels' share.'

Jim, already drunk, burst out laughing. Callum lifted the bottle out of his hands, Jim tried to snatch it back and caught the edge of Callum's eyepatch, so they immediately fell into a scrap. It was better to let them get on with it, so Fiona and Martha started arguing with Duncan about whether Inverness or Aberdeen would be a better place for them to make something of themselves, now that the 'flu had died down. It was a familiar discussion, and one she'd once relished. Fiona said that there was more work to be had in the Edinburgh hotels, and Callum and Jim, having got the fight out of their system, said they'd rather take their chances in the Glasgow shipyards than make a living being professionally smarmy.

'That's a fine plan,' Martha scoffed, taking another swig, 'if you're of a mind to fall in a kiln and burn to death—'

Callum snorted. 'Who d'*you* know who's burned to death in a kiln?'

'I read about it, it can happen—'

Fiona took a bottle from Jim. 'I'll take an Edinburgh hotel over a shipyard any day. More sunshine down there.'

'And evening classes,' said Martha, 'and lectures, and libraries, and—'

'Aye,' said Callum, 'and more disease, and overcrowding, and nothing for the common man to—'

Duncan groaned. 'You've been after those bloody pamphlets again.'

Callum gestured for the bottle. 'So you'd trust the care of yourself and your family to some swish bastard down in London? If you want to get on in life, you've no business putting your faith in the rich. Bastards, every man jack of them.'

Duncan took another swig and said nothing.

'It's the working man,' Callum went on, 'that must look out for—'

Jim let out a high-pitched giggle. 'The working man,' he said, and collapsed into laughter again.

'Would you give it a rest with the red stuff, Callum?' said Martha.

Callum opened his mouth to reply, but Fiona cut across him. 'What do you think, Moira Jean? Inverness or Aberdeen?'

Moira Jean flinched. She'd been foolish, and let herself settle, the whirlpool of her thoughts circling around familiar depths. Sharing all the plans she'd once had would be like setting a paper boat onto the Atlantic and watching it sink. She had been staring into the fire, only half-listening, and she was not ready for them all to be looking at her. She had let the cocksure tilt of her chin droop, let the challenge fade from her eyes and now they could all see that she had been made hollow. Lesser.

Jim burst into another fit of giggles. 'Moira Jean, Aberdeen,' he said, 'Moira Jean, Aberdeen. Moira Jean, Aberdeen. Moira Jean—'

A memory stirred. Angus, smiling, his voice slightly slurred. *'Moira Jean, your eyes are green, you are the queen of Aberdeen—'*

Her hand strayed to the medal without thinking about it. They all saw. Pity crept into their faces.

Callum smacked his brother on the back of the head. 'Pack that in!'

Jim went for him again and under cover of the fight, Moira Jean put herself back together. She smiled, raised her head, sat up straight. She papered over the cracks and now, the hollow centre of her was hidden from view.

'Inverness,' she said.

She would not be pitied.

She took a swig of whisky and spat it into the fire. The flames flared up with a hiss and they all flinched back. Moira Jean gave her most devilish grin and winked at Martha. 'There's your Glasgow kiln,' she said.

They all laughed, and no one laughed louder than she did. They passed the bottles around and took turns spitting into the fire, and Jim nearly burned his eyebrows off, and Duncan brought out a bundle of oatcakes and passed them around. They found mushrooms at the edge of the clearing and tried to fry them on a large, flat rock – it didn't work, but they ate them anyway. Flushed with whisky, Moira Jean told Fiona that they would taste better with a bit of fried slug jelly to go with them, just to make Fiona squeal.

There was an itch under Moira Jean's skin. It was not enough. She needed more.

Moira Jean presided over a spitting contest and got the hem of her skirts thoroughly drenched. She persuaded Martha to let her try on her glasses, and tried to pull her most academic face. She got Jim to throw oatcakes over the fire and tried to catch them in her mouth; they burned her tongue and dropped into the flames but she did not care. She teased Callum relentlessly, calling him 'Comrade' and trying to do a Russian accent, and then flirted with him a little so he'd know she didn't mean any of it. She flirted with Duncan, too, and he flirted back because there'd been enough talk about him and Edgar already and Moira Jean knew it was all true.

It was still not enough. It had to be louder, faster, brighter – bigger than the cold core of her. She needed more.

Callum and Fiona were sitting next to each other now. His hand was very close to hers, and she was looking at him in a way that suggested all his hopes would come true. Angus had looked at Moira Jean like that, once—

Moira Jean jumped to her feet. 'Let's have a dance,' she said. 'Someone give us a tune.'

Duncan rolled his eyes at her. 'You've not been working hard enough, Moira Jean, if you've energy for dancing.'

Moira Jean laughed, but it was still not enough, it would never be enough. 'How could you not want a dance on a night like this?' she said, gesturing at the stars, half-hidden in the smoke. 'So clear and fair – just like your voice, Fiona. Give us a song and we'll have a wee dance.'

Fiona blushed a little. 'You've no need to make a fuss.'

'I mean it! You're far and away the best singer here. Why not give us a tune?'

Lying flat on the ground, Jim began to tap out a steady beat with a stick. 'Give us "Keep the Home Fires Burning",' said Martha.

Moira Jean's mouth tightened. 'Not that one,' she said, trying to keep her voice easy, 'let's have something with bones in it.'

'Auld Lang Syne?'

She laughed. 'It's not a bloody wake!'

'*You* pick a song, then,' Martha grumbled.

Someone began tapping out another rhythm on top of Jim's beat.

'I've not said I'll sing it, mind,' Fiona protested. 'I'll not get a dance if I've to sing for the lot of you.'

'Ah, but you're so much better than the rest of us!' said Moira Jean, as the others began to plead too. 'Finish off those bottles and I'll take over, but only if you swear you'll not remember a word.'

Eventually they flattered Fiona into submission and she lurched to her feet, blushing. Jim banged his stick on the floor to speed up the beat and Fiona launched into 'Johnny Lad'. They danced around the fire, laughing and staggering into each other, and no one laughed harder or danced faster than Moira Jean. Her feet ached, the hem of her skirts was singed and her throat was sore but still she dragged the others up to dance. With Jim's beat echoing around the clearing and Fiona's song in her ears, she did not need to make herself laugh any more. The music and the effort and the whisky were filling up the hollow place inside her and when she smiled and spun, she meant it.

The song ended, and Callum hauled his brother upright and started singing 'Nancy Whisky'. They clapped out the beat as Jim tried to dance, swaying and staggering, and Moira Jean jumped over the fire and snatched up his hands to steady him, laughing. They danced around the clearing, Jim bright red and staring at his feet, the beat and the other, stranger rhythm pulsing in Moira Jean's veins. It curled and coiled around the beat and she matched it step for step, a lightness swelling in her chest that she had not known in months. Jim staggered back and she grabbed Callum instead, never losing a moment. They whirled around the clearing, clapped their hands and stamped their feet, and as the sound of the pipes wove around the beat Moira Jean felt the music close its fingers around her heart. It tugged at something inside her chest and she could not help but follow it. This was what she had been missing. The empty place inside her was forgotten – how could she be empty with music fizzing through her veins?

She frowned. Who had brought pipes?

But now the beat was getting faster, and the pipes wound around the rhythm like snakes, and all her friends were on their feet, laughing and dancing. Fiona and Callum, Duncan and Martha, Jim and—

Moira Jean stared. She missed her step.

Jim was dancing with a stranger. A tall, slender, graceful stranger – but, as she tried to focus, a headache began to build behind her eyes and she had to look away.

She could not hear the beat now. She felt it instead, thumping through her veins in place of a heartbeat. Was the strange rhythm actually being played, or was it just the patterns of many stamping feet and clapping hands? The more she thought about it, the more she realized she did not recognize the sound at all. One moment it sounded like a wooden stick against a tree, the next it seemed sharper, like two rocks being smashed together, and the next it could have been a drum, but none of them had brought one.

She shook her head. It was starting to hurt, now.

Callum pulled her forwards and the music grew louder. It flooded through her like a storm, wild and lovely, and she could not have stopped stamping and kicking her feet even if she'd wanted to. She spun faster and faster and faces whirled by in a blur. The clearing was full now – hadn't there only been six of them, before? – and everyone was dancing. Jim, lurching towards a woman she did not know. Duncan, his crutch on the floor, his twisted foot bleeding. Callum, staring transported at . . .

Something cold cut through the music. Moira Jean turned back to look at her dance partner. Her head began to ache. She knew it was Callum. Of course it was Callum, she told herself, hadn't she known Callum all her life? Of course this was him. He had the same dark eyes, dark hair, and—

Her head pulsed as she tried to focus. Dark eyes and dark hair was not enough to go on. Callum had a missing tooth just behind a canine, he had a scar on his chin, he wore an eyepatch over his left eye, lost at Amiens. The Callum across the clearing had the eyepatch – she could see it as he spun, while the Callum in front of her pulled on her hand.

Moira Jean yanked her hands away. She squeezed her eyes shut and clasped her hands to her chest, the medal cold against her fingers.

She opened her eyes.

It was not Callum.

For a moment something like her friend's face flickered in front of her. But it was a more beautiful face than the one she knew – perfect, unmarred and strangely lit from within. Then, it disappeared.

Faces flickered in front of her. An owl with a curved beak stretching too far down its face. Something with skin like pine bark and a mouth that would not close. A man with antlers sprouting from the place where his eyes should be. Horror surged through her. She turned to run, but her way was blocked by dancers – monstrous dancers whose bodies changed shape so fast they seemed to flicker. A woman with long strings of ivy falling from her mouth. A shambling, shapeless thing made of willow leaves. Something stuck between the shape of a fox and the shape of a man. Their ever-changing hands were rested on her friends' shoulders, clasped around their waists, and curled around their fingers, but still they smiled, and still they danced.

Fear clawed at her from the inside. Her friends couldn't see them. They didn't know what they were.

Moira Jean pushed her way through the dancers. Hands, talons, twigs and claws caught in her hair and scratched at her clothes. How many of them were coming after her? Moira Jean shook her head, desperate to shake off her fear. It didn't matter. She had to get to her friends.

Fiona was closest. Moira Jean grabbed her arm and tried to wrench her away from the thing she was dancing with – *don't look at it*, she thought, fear burning through her, *don't look at it*. Fiona just laughed, her eyes vacant, and spun herself out of Moira Jean's grip. She tried Duncan next, but his bad foot was bleeding and even the pain could not bring him to his senses. All around her, her empty-eyed friends were smiling and dancing with monsters, their laughter hollow, their smiles slack.

'Wake up!' she screamed, 'For God's sake, wake up!'

They ignored her.

The things did not.

The music grew louder – but it wasn't music, now. It was a shrieking, wailing mass of noise and she was the only one who could hear it. The beat pulsed underneath her boots like a living heart. Moira Jean ran for the edge of the clearing but something was snaking around her ankles – an adder, brambles, or strings of ivy, she could not tell. She struggled against it, heart pounding. It locked itself around her knees. She fell. Terror screamed through every nerve in her body. She crashed to the ground, teeth jarring, and curled herself into a ball, clutching Angus's medal and waiting for the end.

The music stopped. The things wound around her legs vanished.

Moira Jean stayed huddled on the ground, shaking with fear. Something rustled in the trees. An owl hooted overhead and her eyes flew open.

The clearing was empty.

She sat up, still trembling. The moon shone high overhead. The fire they had built had gone out.

Moira Jean was totally and completely alone.

Moira Jean started awake. She sat bolt upright, covered in sweat, her heart pounding – and promptly threw up over the side of the bed. Her head ached like something was about to burst out of it.

'You've surfaced, then.'

Moira Jean groaned and wiped her mouth with the back of her hand. She was home, in her own narrow box bed, and her mother was looking at her through the open door of the bed with her arms folded. Moira Jean was still wearing yesterday's clothes; the medal dug into the palm of her hand.

'What time is it?'

'Past eight o'clock. Half an hour longer and I'd have had you in the water trough. Now get dressed.'

'Jesus, Ma! Why didn't you tell me it was so late?'

Her mother pointed a finger at her. She was a small woman

30

with kind eyes and neatly greying hair, but there was a tone to her voice that Moira Jean knew not to trifle with. 'I'll not have blasphemy and vomiting in the same morning, Moira Jean. You're lucky I put out a bucket. Now get up and get that cleaned.'

Moira Jean heaved herself out of bed, her head throbbing. Even her eyes ached—

A man with antlers where his eyes should be—

Moira Jean started. She shook her head, wincing, and banished the image. She'd had too much to drink, it had given her the strangest dreams. Leaning against the box beds, she felt thoroughly sorry for herself. The night before she'd left a trail of muddy footprints leading straight to her bed – ashy, muddy footprints, because she'd strayed too close to the fire. Moira Jean's face burned. She could've set her skirts alight.

Out of the corner of her eye, Moira Jean could see the chest, perched on top of her box bed. The lid was just visible over the frame of the bed. Moira Jean's head was pounding, her stomach roiling, her legs aching – she couldn't deal with the memories now. She picked up the broom and used the handle to poke the chest back out of sight.

Then, she set to work. Moving around felt like a curse, but the familiar rhythm of housework helped her set her thoughts aside. She cleaned up the mess she'd made and fumbled herself out of her clothes, very glad that her brothers and sisters, who'd all left home, were not around to tease her or make loud noises. Her skirts were covered in dirt, she supposed she must have fallen—

Things winding themselves around her ankles—

Moira Jean dropped her drugget skirt. She was imagining things. Barely one dram of whisky and she was jumping at

31

shadows. She changed her blouse, shift and petticoats and laced up her stays in a foul mood. She'd torn holes in both her stockings – *more bloody work*, she thought, as she screwed them up into a ball – and brushed her skirts and boots back into life muttering about bloody Jim Selkirk and his bloody whisky. Dressed, she felt slightly more human, even if she did catch herself swaying on the spot.

Her mother laughed when she saw her. 'Would you look at the state of you!'

Moira Jean tried to wrestle her hair into a bun, wiry brown curls exploding out in all directions. She was sure it looked like brambles. 'Alastair was worse. And Hamish.'

'And you teased your brothers every time. I've a mind to write and tell them, let them get revenge.' She brandished a letter with a smile. 'Alastair's just sent me some more ticket money, I ought to write and thank him for it . . .'

'No! Ma, they'll not let up until next year—'

'And it's no more than you deserve, after what you put them through.' She smiled, the lines around her eyes etched deep. 'You'd a good time then, love?'

Moira Jean felt the weight of the medal against her chest. The pin sat against her breastbone like a claw trying to poke its way through. Moira Jean said nothing. To speak would be to crack herself open, and she did not know if she could put herself back together again.

Her mother sighed. The light streaming through the door made all her grey hairs shine. She turned away, and put Alastair's money in an old tobacco tin labelled 'Canada' on the dresser.

'Go on and gather some pine roots, hen,' her mother said. 'You'll want the fresh air.'

She handed Moira Jean a bundle of oat cakes and a slice of cheese, with strict instructions that she wasn't to bring them back up again. Moira Jean staggered out of their cottage, glaring at the sunshine, and dragged herself up the hillside the moment her mother went back inside. The pine roots could wait; a nap would set her to rights. She slumped onto a patch of scrubby yellow grass and stared down at Brudonnock, praying her mother wasn't going to come out of the cottage any time soon.

Brudonnock seemed smaller than ever from the hillside. The cottages were clean and well-kept – the Fitzherberts liked a pretty village – but they were tiny. From this distance they looked more like a ring of identical mushrooms sprouting up through the grass, and the two wells like a couple of molehills, the old one covered over and half-forgotten. Only Drewitts did not seem small, looming over the village like a cloud threatening rain. The estate had stood empty since the war, and now that the tenancies had been renewed, Moira Jean was fine with that. If the shooting season didn't call the family back soon, Drewitts would be sold, and she and all her neighbours would be turned out of their homes. But they were secure for another year, whether the family came back or not, so there was no need for Edgar Fitzherbert to show his rotten face in Brudonnock ever again.

The old village had once been higher up the hill, according to Mrs Iverach. Not that the old lady had visited; she told everyone, loudly, that she'd never once associated with the folk that had been cleared out of old Brudonnock, before Drewitts was built. The old croft was all that was left of it now – that, and the edges of the old pastures, buried under the lines of the north field. Sometimes, she wondered if the old houses had all been built to the same pattern as her own, or if the old villagers had felt as frustrated as she did on long evenings with little to do, but mostly Moira Jean tried not to think about it too much. There were still scorch marks on the walls of the old croft, and a frantic look in Mrs Iverach's eyes whenever anyone mentioned it.

On the other side of the Aberdeen road was the forest. When she closed her eyes, Moira Jean could almost forget it was there. The noise of the village almost drowned out the rustling leaves. Hammers clanged and metal hissed and spat in the smithy, cows lowed, sheep bleated and, on the other side of the hill, someone was whistling for a dog. But then a cloud skittered across the sky and the scent of juniper and pine came to her on the wind.

This was what had called the Fitzherberts north some sixty years before: the promise of cheap land, proud stags and fat partridges. This was what would call them back. Little had changed in sixty years: the same houses still stood, the same trees still grew, the same families still sweated in the fields. Even after four years of being stripped back by the Canadian Forestry Corps, the forest was still magnificent. Larch and birch and pine crowded together, sure and strong, and the clean, fresh scent of the trees had tangled in Moira Jean's hair ever since she could remember.

Moira Jean lay back on the scrubby grass and sighed. The cold, clean smell of the forest emerging from winter soothed the rough edges of her hangover. A gentle breeze played with her hair. The familiar rhythm of the year was starting back up again – calving season, lambing season, sowing season – the same rhythm she'd known all her life. Moving through the same old dance one more time was like trying to put on clothes she knew would not fit. There had to be something else, something that would give her colour and life and meaning.

Last year, there had been.

A memory bubbled up to the surface. She'd been lying on the hillside, eyes closed, the sun on her face. She'd been trying not to laugh. Angus had laid down beside her, propped up on one elbow, winding one of her curls around a finger while he fumbled for his pocket knife. 'Just a wee something to remember you by,' he'd said, 'you'll hardly know it's gone.'

She'd aimed a playful kick at his feet. 'You'd better not forget me, Angus Dunbar.'

'As if I could.' He'd leaned down, and just as she was tilting her face to his, ready for the kiss, the lock of her hair was sliced away. The kiss didn't come. Instead, Angus swore, and then said, 'Did I ever tell you how bonny you'd look with short hair?'

The memory was so real. She could almost see him – dark-haired, dark-eyed, with a gap between his two front teeth and a smile that always quirked up higher on one side of his face. For a moment, she could have sworn she felt his familiar bulk lying beside her, shielding her from the wind. But when she reached out, there was only scrubby grass and loose grey rocks underneath her fingers.

She shook the thought away. There was no point in dwelling on it. She had her future to think of, and she'd better decide what to do with it before her mother went off to join her aunt in Canada. Her siblings had all found something to do with themselves; so could she. She could join her sister Aileen in her shiny new London Post Office, or traipse across the country with the Ordnance Survey like Hamish, or sail away for a fresh start in Canada as her aunt had done. There was nothing keeping her here. The rest of her family had left Brudonnock one by one and found jobs and spouses and plans. She'd had those things herself once, and relished the finding of them. But the thought of starting her search again was exhausting, and there was nothing she needed to look for in Brudonnock.

'Moira Jean!'

Moira Jean flinched and sat up so quickly that her head pounded. The shout rang across the hillside, maternal disapproval echoing all the way down the Aberdeen road. Her mother was glaring at her from several feet below, hands on hips.

'Did I say you could laze around on the hillside? Shift yourself and do something useful!'

Moira Jean resumed her nap out of her mother's line of sight, scarfed down her oat cakes and cheese and grabbed a few token handfuls of pine roots from the edge of the forest so it looked as if she'd tried. Her mother was not fooled. She cuffed Moira Jean around the back of the head and sent her to draw some water.

No matter which way she held it, the rim of the pail bumped into Moira Jean's leg as she walked. Their cottage was at the higher end of the village, looking down onto the Aberdeen road. She trudged past the stone cottages, knees aching. The inhabited ones were trim and clean, with vegetable gardens cleared for planting and chickens scratching in the dirt. Each one was built to the same standard, but they'd made them their own: Mrs MacGregor with her awful patchwork curtains, Mr Selkirk with Callum's regimental crest carved into the lintel, Mrs Iverach with a saucer of milk set on the doorstep. The empty ones stood like abandoned snail shells, thatch overgrown, wooden doors swollen in the rain and weeds creeping closer to the doorstep. The old worry wormed its way back into her head. What would happen if the Fitzherberts decided that pretty villages were not worth the expense?

She resisted the urge to make a rude gesture at Drewitts; Mrs McGillycuddy would complain if she saw. She passed the old well, the cover half-overgrown, and the kirk, clean and cold in the spring sunlight. The sight of the neatly tended kirkyard behind it put a catch in her throat. Old, weathered gravestones clustered against simple wooden crosses, still drooping in the earth after months of waiting for the masons to carve proper headstones. How long was it going to be before Angus—

Moira Jean pinched herself on the arm. She wasn't going to think about Angus. There was work to be done. She had to muck out the chickens, sort through their seeds to find what could be planted, and borrow a newspaper to see if there'd be work worth having in the summer. She'd be no use if she was distracted. She had to pull herself together.

But there was the Dunbars' old cottage, gloomy and dark in the corner of her eye.

She'd been avoiding it ever since she'd had the news, and the sight of it was like a slap. Lichen covered the doorstep. Moss grew in all the crannies in the stone walls. The thatch on the roof was patchy and straggly, gnawed by squirrels and rats or stolen to line magpies' nests. Her throat was suddenly tight. Angus had thatched that roof himself. They'd been thirteen, and Angus had dangled off the ladder one-handed to try and impress her. But she'd wanted to impress him too and had scrambled up the ladder, throwing a handful of straw at him as she went, and the rest of that afternoon had been lost to a thatch fight. They dared each other to the brink of stupidity, climbing higher and higher, and never once had Moira Jean thought that she might fall. She stared up at the ridge of the roof, willing herself to see Angus's dark curls peeking up over the straw.

She knew she wasn't going to.

Anger flashed through her like lightning. She wiped her eyes, roughly. It was stupid to cry over an empty house, she told herself. Brudonnock was full of empty houses. One more didn't matter.

She turned her back on the cottage, her mouth set into a hard line. A magpie flew overhead, aiming for the thatch, and before she knew it she had swung the bucket up, ready to throw it. She stopped, her heart pounding, her hands balled into fists. What was she doing?

Moira Jean lowered the bucket. 'Bastard,' she said to the magpie.

'Moira Jean! Does your mother know you talk like that?'

Moira Jean jumped and spun around. Mrs McGillycuddy was standing behind her. She was a short, stocky woman of about forty, with a lined face and ash-blonde hair that was always in a perfect bun. She was glaring at Moira Jean through her little round glasses, clutching a shawl of the Fitzherbert family tartan.

'Sorry, Mrs McGillycuddy,' said Moira Jean. 'I was only scaring away a bird.'

'You'll scare off more than birds with language like that,' she said with a sniff. She glanced towards the abandoned cottage. 'Still, I daresay I'll not tell your mother if you'll bring up some water to Drewitts for me.'

Moira Jean knew, with absolute certainty, that Mrs

McGillycuddy would be waiting to catch her swearing again for the rest of time. 'That's no trouble at all. I was going down to the well myself.'

Mrs McGillycuddy went to fetch the buckets from Drewitts. Next to the housekeeper, who was always so neat and clean, Moira Jean became extremely aware of the grass and soil staining the back of her blouse, the amorphous mass of freckles all over her skin, and her brown, curly hair already exploding out of its bun. Also, she was sure that Mrs McGillycuddy knew that she was hungover.

Moira Jean drew a bucket of water for her mother and ran back home with it, wrestling her hair back into place the moment she was out of sight. When she came back, Mrs McGillycuddy was waiting with two big enamel buckets; Moira Jean filled them and began to haul them back towards the house. They were very heavy, and soon all the muscles in her freckled forearms were sore. As they walked uphill, Moira Jean silently cursed whoever had decided to build Drewitts on a slope.

Soon, they passed from the worn dirt of Brudonnock to the gravel paths and manicured lawns of Drewitts. As she got closer, Moira Jean noticed they were not quite as manicured as they had used to be: having spent the previous day ploughing fields, the weeds in the empty flowerbeds leapt out at her even from this distance. She was not surprised. The undergardener had been killed at Passchendaele, and would not be replaced until Mr Cameron, the head gardener, felt it was safe to interview people again. He had tuberculosis, and was terrified of catching the 'flu. He wouldn't even come into the Drewitts kitchen for his dinner; Mrs McGillycuddy had to leave all his meals outside his shed on a tray.

Mrs McGillycuddy led Moira Jean round to the servants' entrance – even with the family gone for nearly five years, they could not use the front door – and Moira Jean brought the buckets into the vast kitchen. It was twice as big as her cottage, and that wasn't even counting the pantry. But it was dark, and the copper pans hanging on the walls were clouded with dust.

'Bless you, Moira Jean,' said Mrs McGillycuddy. 'I'll have some work for you here when the seeds are sown. I could use another pair of hands about the place.'

Moira Jean raised her eyebrows. She'd done duty as a housemaid before – every woman in Brudonnock had to work for Drewitts in some capacity, when the Fitzherberts came to stay – but she hadn't been very good at it. She'd trod mud into the carpets, dropped one of the enormous copper pans, and kept getting things caught on the antlers of the mounted deer heads whenever she'd tried to dust them. After one disastrous incident when a thirteen-year-old Moira Jean hadn't been able to keep a straight face listening to the Fitzherberts' after-dinner conversation, Mrs McGillycuddy had told her that she was best suited to outdoor work. These days, the housekeeper usually relied on Fiona.

Still, money was money. 'I'm sure I'm glad to hear it,' said Moira Jean. 'Are the family coming back?'

Mrs McGillycuddy looked away. 'That remains to be seen. But with Fiona still in Edinburgh I'll want your help for the spring clean.'

Moira Jean frowned. 'But Mrs McGillycuddy, Fiona's not in Edinburgh. She's here. She helped plough the fields yesterday.'

'None of that, Moira Jean,' said Mrs McGillycuddy, rapping her knuckles on the vast kitchen table. 'I saw you out in the fields yesterday, same as everyone else in the village, so I know for a fact Fiona wasn't there. I know you like a laugh, but if you must play your silly tricks on people, pick someone who didn't bring you lunch. On you go, now.'

Moira Jean left, bemused. She supposed that in the crowd of villagers clamouring for their lunch, Mrs McGillycuddy might not have picked out Fiona's face. But there were only a dozen people in Brudonnock, and whenever anyone left it was all the village talked about. It was an odd thing to forget. If Mrs McGillycuddy had been a little older, Moira Jean would have dismissed it as the housekeeper's memory faltering.

Moira Jean stumped back down towards the village, pinching the bridge of her nose. There was a headache building behind her eyes.

Moira Jean would have liked nothing better than to get back into her bed and bury herself under layers of woollen blankets. Her head was pounding, and if she could have passed the rest of the day simply eating and sleeping she would've considered herself a lucky woman.

No chance of that.

One of their chickens had got out and was after Mr Galbraith's onions; he shouted at Moira Jean from his doorstep and waved his walking stick as she chased the chicken around his vegetable patch. In the afternoon she had to give Mrs McLeod back her sewing machine, which Moira Jean's mother had borrowed – she'd hoped to catch Duncan there, but he was nowhere to be seen. Then it was back home, where Moira Jean's mother was pinning on her hat, getting ready for a house call.

'I'm away to Stronach tonight, Mrs Macanroy's time has come on early. Now, you're to check on Mrs Iverach before your supper, and I've said you'll be along to Mr Selkirk's tomorrow to help him with his fence, so don't forget. You're not to take any of his whisky home with you, even if he offers.'

Moira Jean snorted and collapsed into a rickety wooden chair. 'No chance of that.' Then, she frowned. Callum and Jim were Mr Selkirk's two sons; why did he need *her* help?

'Ma—' she began.

Her mother picked up her call-out bag. It was a vast leather doctor's bag; she had been a nurse before she married Moira Jean's father and came to Brudonnock. 'Make it quick, love.'

'It's not important,' said Moira Jean. 'Just wondering how Callum and Jim managed to weasel out of that one.'

Her mother fixed her with a very stern look. 'That is hardly appropriate, Moira Jean.'

'What?'

'I've no time for this,' her mother snapped. 'Just you have a care how you speak to Mr Selkirk. In fact, you can go round there tonight and bring him supper. Lord knows the poor man needs a wee bit of kindness.'

'What?'

But she was already out the door. Moira Jean watched her go from the doorway, her heavy doctor's bag still visible even when she was almost at the horizon.

Something was not right.

The Selkirks had made it through the war and the 'flu. Why would *they* need a little kindness, when so many other families in Brudonnock were far worse off? The kirkyard was so much fuller than it had been, but it was not full of Selkirks. What had her mother meant?

Moira Jean examined the light beyond the window critically. They had no clock, but she knew it would be dark in a couple of hours: the shadows were creeping towards her doorstep and the sky was starting to soften. A dutiful daughter would do as her mother asked and check on Mr Selkirk about now, to see if he wanted a meal, and seeing as it was on her mother's orders, it definitely wouldn't be being nosy.

She set off.

Mr Selkirk's cottage was at the other end of the village, closer to the Aberdeen road. Moira Jean traipsed down the slope, gritting her teeth against the noise of ringing hammers as she went past the smithy. The Selkirks' house looked like every other house in Brudonnock: long and low, with a thatched roof and stone walls – only Callum's regimental crest, burned into the door, marked it out from its neighbours.

She knocked on the door. Mr Selkirk opened it, and she was shocked to see how thin and lined his face was. Surely it hadn't been so careworn yesterday. She looked into his eyes. It seemed as if something had been pressed out of them. A chill crept up Moira Jean's spine. A day in the sun could not do that.

'Moira Jean?' He sounded confused. No, not confused – lost, which was worse.

'Ma's away to Mrs Macanroy's tonight; she asked me to see if you wanted a bit of supper.'

Mr Selkirk ran a hand over his face. 'I'm not hungry.'

Moira Jean tried to smile. 'Ma's been telling you about all those dumplings I burned, hasn't she? I've come a fair way since then, I promise—'

'I said I'm not hungry, Moira Jean!'

His hands were clenched, his eyes were glassy with tears. Too late, Moira Jean realized her mouth had fallen open. She closed it, but shame had already crept onto Mr Selkirk's face.

43

'I know you mean well, Moira Jean,' he mumbled. 'But . . . I've word from the hospital. Jim, he's . . .'

Mr Selkirk swallowed frantically. He shook his head. He shut the door. Moira Jean stood on the step, bewildered.

It didn't make any sense. How could Jim be in the hospital? Moira Jean's mother was the closest thing to a doctor that Brudonnock had. The nearest hospital was in Inverness – more than a day's walk away, and costing more than any farmhand could afford. How could Jim be there, when she had seen him just last night?

Uncertainty prickled across Moira Jean's skin. She wanted to look over her shoulder, but when she did, there was nothing there. She stood on Mr Selkirk's doorstep for a moment longer, chewing on a thumbnail, listening to weeping on the other side. One person weeping.

Dread mounting in her stomach, she backed away. Was it 'flu? She took another step back – but that didn't make sense, either. Mr Selkirk wouldn't have been able to get him up to Inverness and back, with no horse and cart in the village.

A sense of wrongness burrowed into her bones. There was no way Jim could be in Inverness. And there was no way that Fiona could be in Edinburgh, either – that was miles away, and she wouldn't have left in the morning without saying goodbye. But where were they? And, she realized, she hadn't seen Duncan, or Callum, or Martha all day. Surely they couldn't have gone too.

Moira Jean walked back up the hill. She felt as though she was walking across the deck of a ship, waiting for the ground to tilt beneath her feet. Her friends had been here. They should *still* be here. But they were nowhere to be seen, and nobody seemed to be worried.

Where were they?

Without really meaning to go there, she found herself outside Mrs Iverach's door. A horseshoe was nailed to the lintel – Malcolm hadn't got his hands on that one yet – and the little saucer of milk outside her door had been licked clean. Moira Jean brightened; Mrs Iverach had finally tempted in a cat.

She knocked on the door. Moments later, Mrs Iverach opened it. Just shy of ninety, she was the oldest person Moira Jean had ever met, never took her white linen mutch off her head, and barely came up to Moira Jean's elbow. She blinked up at Moira Jean and her wrinkled face split into a smile.

'Moira Jean! Did your ma send you along?'

'Aye, she said to see if you wanted anything.'

'She's a good woman,' said Mrs Iverach. 'Would you run up to the dairy for me? That saucer needs refilled.'

Moira Jean tried to peer around Mrs Iverach's shoulder. 'He must be fair famished if he got through all of that! Can I see him?'

Mrs Iverach frowned. 'See who?'

'Your cat.'

The old lady laughed. 'I've no cat here, lass!'

'Then who's the milk for?'

Mrs Iverach's laughter vanished. 'Never you mind,' she snapped. 'Just you away to the dairy for me.'

Too late, Moira Jean remembered what her mother had said; Mrs Iverach's mind was not what it was. Best to let the subject drop. 'Mr Brodie knows what you want, does he?'

'Oh, aye,' said Mrs Iverach, relaxing a little. 'He's a good lad. And when you've done that, you can fetch young Callum and tell him I'll want his help planting my garden.'

'I'll – have you seen him?'

'Not today. I'll wager he's still suffering after the din you bairns made in the woods last night.'

Moira Jean flushed. 'You heard that?'

'You're lucky your Ma's a heavy sleeper.'

'Mrs Iverach, I'm so sorry—'

'Apologizing again, Moira Jean? What've you done now?'

Moira Jean turned. Mrs MacGregor was walking towards them, a basket of pine roots tucked under her arm. She was trying to look disapproving, but there was a smug tilt to the corner of her mouth.

'I've not done anything—' Moira Jean began, but at this point, it didn't matter. Mrs MacGregor had already started.

'Let me talk to her ma for you, Mrs Iverach,' she said, 'Alma knows Moira Jean needs a firm hand, even if she'll not administer one herself. I said to her, "that lass has always been a wild one, Alma, not like my Fiona," and not that she'd say a word against you, Moira Jean, but she did give me to understand that—'

'Aye, and you can send Fiona along as well,' Mrs Iverach interrupted. 'She's a bonny singer, I'll not deny it, but nothing's bonny when it's keeping me awake.'

Mrs MacGregor frowned. 'What do you mean?'

'She was with the others, last night.'

'I – oh. Oh, I see.' Her tone changed, became slow and syrupy-sweet. 'Fiona's in Edinburgh, Mrs Iverach. She's been there for a few months now.'

Mrs Iverach folded her arms. 'Don't you try and tell me otherwise, Nellie MacGregor. I saw her here, yesterday, with my own eyes.'

Mrs MacGregor's smile was set in place. 'All right. If you say she was here, then she was here.'

Mrs Iverach's jaw tightened. 'Less of that tone,' she snapped, and slammed the door in Mrs MacGregor's face.

Mrs MacGregor made an outraged noise. '*Well*,' she said, shifting her basket a little higher, 'far be it from be to speak ill of an invalid, but—'

'I can still hear you, Nellie!' Mrs Iverach called through the door.

Mrs MacGregor blushed. Ruffled, she rounded on Moira Jean. 'I don't know why *you've* not gone to Edinburgh,' she snapped. Moira Jean flushed and looked away; if everything had gone to plan, she *would* be in Edinburgh. Mrs MacGregor ignored her discomfort and kept talking. 'Don't you want to make something of yourself? You can't be a drain on your poor ma forever, you know. Here,' she said, thrusting the basket at Moira Jean. 'You're the only young person in Brudonnock, you may as well make yourself useful. And you ought to run up to the dairy after, see if Mr Brodie wants a hand with the heifer. She's due soon.'

Slightly dazed, Moira Jean took the basket. 'I . . . I'm not the only young person in Brudonnock.'

Mrs MacGregor laughed and started walking to her cottage. Moira Jean traipsed after her, feet skittering on the loose grey rocks that were scattered across Brudonnock's main street. 'You're a shameless flatterer, Moira Jean! But that'll not get you out of hard work. You're to pull your weight if you're staying here. Not to worry, I'll keep you busy. It'll not be for long – just until Duncan and Martha are wed and settled back with us. I daresay they'll be happy enough together, but I don't see why they had to run off to Glasgow like that—'

Moira Jean nearly dropped the basket. 'Duncan's married? To a— to Martha?'

'Oh aye, Mrs McLeod had the news just yesterday,' Mrs MacGregor said, calling over her shoulder as she picked her way downhill. 'Do you not remember?'

'I . . . married? *Duncan*?'

'You're as bad as Mrs Iverach,' said Mrs MacGregor, as the two of them stopped outside her cottage door. 'Mind you pay attention, next time. You can put that by the fireplace. On you go, now.'

Moira Jean left Mrs MacGregor's cottage in a daze. Duncan and Martha couldn't be married. They'd never once showed any interest in each other. Duncan had been far more preoccupied with Edgar Fitzherbert and his soft hands. And the news certainly hadn't been delivered yesterday. They hadn't been married yesterday, they hadn't been in Glasgow – they had been *here*. She had seen them. They had all seen them.

Moira Jean traipsed up to the dairy and back, her thoughts in turmoil. When she handed over the milk Mrs Iverach peered at her from underneath the frills on her mutch; she pressed a stone with a hole in it into Moira Jean's hand with the words 'for hidden things'. Mrs Iverach remembered her friends; no one else did. But everyone said Mrs Iverach's age was getting the best of her, and Moira Jean wasn't sure if her memory could be trusted. Who should she believe? And why were the two of them the only ones who remembered that her friends had been here the day before?

She went home and picked at some oatcakes and cheese for her supper. She darned her stockings by the firelight, her hands moving with her mind elsewhere. Where *were* they? Why didn't anyone remember that they had been here? But *had* they been here? If everyone else thought they were gone, perhaps *she* was the one who was mistaken.

Outside, the sun was beginning to set. It would be a slow, lazy sunset, with a good two hours or more before true darkness took hold. Plenty of time to go back to that spot in the woods and see if she really had been there, or if she'd just imagined the evening in the woods with her friends. Perhaps she was more hungover than she thought.

A man with antlers where his eyes should be—

Moira Jean shook the image away. Brushing the crumbs off her skirt, she wound her shawl tightly around her shoulders, pinning it in place with Angus's old medal as she always did. She held the medal, briefly, in the absence of holding a hand. Then she took a paraffin lamp, lit it, and set off for the forest.

The trees were never far from Brudonnock. They grew on the other side of the Aberdeen road, and every year they crept a little closer to the wide dirt track. When the wind blew the air smelled like pine and juniper, leaves rustling like gossiping women.

Moira Jean had known the woods her whole life. She had gathered bracken and dead fir roots from among the trees, to use in mattresses or as kindling. Further into the woods was a pretty but useless cottage beside a loch; the house belonged to Drewitts, and had hosted luncheons and parties and other events to which Moira Jean had been required to carry hampers of food and drink. Angus had taken her into the woods too, when he was training to be a gamekeeper—

Moira Jean clenched her jaw. This was no time to lose her head.

Now, they did not seem so familiar. Scots pines loomed over her head, her feet already swallowed by their long, pointed shadows. Here and there she caught a shock of white: birch trees, pale as ghosts. Bracken and furze and juniper clustered closer to the ground, crowding against the path that led deeper between the trees. The sun had just dipped below the distant peak of Ben Macdui, and the sky blazed crimson and purple above her, painting the firs in red-tinged gloom and lending a copper glow to the silver birches. The back of her neck prickled. Her paraffin lamp suddenly felt like a child's toy against the creeping darkness.

She set her shoulders, and walked into the forest.

She traced the path they'd taken the night before, the lantern held out in front of her. She picked her way down deer trails, furze snatching at the hem of her skirt. Bracken brushed against her waist. Tufts of heather not yet in bloom pressed against her ankles, each one the colour of old blood. The silvery bark of rowan trees seemed to hover in the darkness like spectres. A hare darted out in front of her and she flinched, almost dropping the lantern; all she had seen was a shape in the dark, and only the flash of its tail had let her know that it *was* a hare at all.

The forest rustled. Something was moving.

She pushed on, pine needles springy underneath her feet. Something slithered through the leaves and Moira Jean stopped, listening hard for the hiss of an angry adder. The sounds of the forest crowded around her – rustling leaves, distant wings, the gentle crunch of a juniper twig underneath an inhuman foot. She smelled the spice of the juniper twig breaking, and the sounds still came, but no matter how high she raised her lantern, she saw nothing in the circle of watery light.

She kept walking, clutching her shawl a little tighter. Angus's medal was cold against her palm.

The pines began to thin. Excitement surging through her, Moira Jean stepped into a clearing. A small, bare hillock sat in the centre. She'd found it.

She *had* been here the night before. There was a small circle of charred ground ringed by stones – the remnants of their fire. She examined the ashes and recognized what had once been an oatcake; she'd burned enough of them to know them on sight. Straightening up, she cast the lantern-light higher and saw footprints in the dirt. They were scuffed and frantic, but they were human, and there were six sets of tracks.

Only one set led out of the clearing.

They *had* been here. Relief flooded through her. She'd been mad to ever doubt herself. One of Callum's whisky bottles lay half-smashed against the foot of a vast Scots pine. Trampled into the dirt was a red ribbon, which she was sure had been in Martha's hair. And lying on the floor was Duncan's crutch, forgotten by the base of a silver birch.

Fear slid into Moira Jean like a knife. Duncan wouldn't leave his crutch behind. He *couldn't*. He could barely go two steps without it.

A man with antlers where his eyes should be—

Moira Jean raised the lantern as high as she could, her hand shaking. The light fluttered over the ground, crushed twigs and stray pine needles casting a carpet of shadows across the clearing that twitched with every tremor of her hand. It looked as if something under the ground was breathing, some vast thing that she crawled over the surface of like a fly . . .

Moira Jean steadied the lantern and forced herself to look for more tracks. There were none. There were only the human footprints of herself and her friends, the scuffed spot where she had fallen over, and something white out of the corner of her eye.

She froze. Something buried deep in her bones was screaming at her not to look up. She should turn and walk away, and not raise her eyes until she was home and the door was locked behind her. If she turned and ran, she might be able to make it back safely – if she was quick, if she was sure . . .

But her friends *had* been here, and now they were gone.

She straightened.

There was no way that the figure standing in the haze of light could be human. Humans were messy, imperfect creatures, aching and sweating and withering. This man – but man was not the right word, she thought – was utterly flawless. He was tall, with a sheet of white hair longer than her own, and he radiated out the kind of delicate beauty that made her instantly aware of the dirt lodged under her fingernails and the sunburn on the back of her neck. He was dressed in something long and white that seemed to glow, it looked so clean; Moira Jean was sure that she would get it dirty just by looking at it. He seemed wreathed in mist, and try as she might, she couldn't see him any more clearly than if she'd caught a glimpse of him out of the corner of her eye. It was hard to read the expression on his face, because a headache started buzzing in her brain when she tried to concentrate on his features. She squinted. A dull whining in her ears; she caught the impression of iridescent eyes and snakelike pupils, colours shifting like oil on water. But then the noise became too much to bear, and she had to look away. For a moment, she wondered if he was an angel, feeling stupid even as she thought it. But there was no mistaking the disdain that radiated off him, and she knew in her bones that there was nothing divine about him.

Terror burst through her like a firework. She had no idea what she was looking at. The figure in front of her was human-shaped, but it was far from human.

'So,' he said, and she flinched. She hadn't expected him to speak, or for his voice to sound low and quiet and so close to human. 'You have returned.'

Moira Jean realized her mouth was hanging open. She closed it.

The figure extended a graceful hand. 'Join the dance.'

A distant pipe wound through the air. The sound tugged at her, stronger than a hand around her waist. Moira Jean's hand tightened on the handle of the paraffin lantern, and the pull faded.

She glanced up at the figure's eyes – what colour *were* they? They kept shifting, bleeding together – and tried her best to smile. It seemed like a bad idea to offend him. She was so alone. 'That's a generous offer, but I've not come to dance. I'm searching for my friends.'

The shadows around the edges of the clearing seemed thicker. Moira Jean raised her lantern; the light cast unnatural shapes across the trees. She ground her feet into the dirt, ready to run.

'Perhaps you saw them. We came here the night before, to—'

'Tell me,' said the figure, 'why did you not join the dance?'

The man with antlers where his eyes should be. The owl with the long, long beak. The woman with ivy trailing from her mouth. Moira Jean remembered the dancers of the night before, and felt as if the ground had given way under her feet.

Then she knew. They had taken her friends.

The figure was looking at her. The more she tried to focus on his face, the harder it became, and a headache began to build behind her eyes. He was so perfect that it left her breathless, but she could not have said why. It was as if something slipped over her eyes when she looked at him, leaving only the barest suggestion of features visible, and the knowledge of his beauty was simply dropped into her head. Moira Jean closed her eyes, the blood rushing in her ears. Her heart beat so fast it felt like rattling. Nothing was putting things in her head. Nothing was reaching out an insubstantial hand, long, long fingers curling towards her, and rearranging her thoughts as they pleased . . .

Her eyes snapped open.

The figure stood before her, one hand still outstretched. His iridescent eyes were still fixed on her, the pupils vast and dark. Terror flashed through her, but she couldn't look away. Hands trembling, Moira Jean did her best to squash the fear back down. This was no time to lose her head. She tried to meet those strange eyes.

'I did join the dance,' said Moira Jean, 'but then . . . but then it was time to return home.' She cleared her throat. 'It's time for the others to return home, too.'

The figure tilted his lovely head. 'The mortals shall be returned should I tire of them. They trespassed upon the entrance to my halls; they must pay the price.'

'Entrance? I don't see an . . . it's just a forest.'

The figure's face twisted. His beauty slipped. The shadows of two enormous antlers flashed across the trees.

'It is *my* forest,' the figure hissed, his fingers curling into a fist, 'and you have trespassed here. I shall overlook that your people have forgotten to honour me. What care I for the tributes of mortals? But you feasted from my woods and danced to my pipes when I did not call you, desecrating the rites of Beltane. I will not stand for such disrespect.'

The clearing exploded into sound: rustling, clicking, chittering. None of the noises were human but still, it sounded like laughter. Moira Jean whirled around, holding her lantern high. She saw nothing beyond the ring of trees, not even the rest of the forest behind them. She was trapped. If she wanted to find her way back home, she would need the figure to reveal the path.

'None of us meant disrespect,' she soothed, 'not if we'd known this place was yours. We would never have dreamed of . . . of insulting someone so beautiful and powerful, if we'd only known you were here. It was only our ignorance that led us to slight you.'

Moira Jean was sweating. It was without a doubt the most transparent piece of flattery she had ever deployed. Every word rang false. She could only hope the figure found her as inscrutable as she did him.

'You are ignorant,' the figure agreed. 'Had you but known, you would have guarded your name more closely, Moira Jean.'

Dread plummeted through her like a stone.

'But ignorance must still be punished.'

'But—'

'You and your friends have wronged me,' he said, his voice like something stalking through the trees. Shadows curled around the hem of his robe, reaching for her. 'I was here before you were born, and I shall be here after you die, and I shall have the respect that is my due.' He stepped forward, the click of a cloven foot ringing in Moira Jean's ears. Fear swelled around her. 'You come here, with the stink of the new century all over you and iron in your soul, and act like this is your place. You will learn the price of forgetting the old ways. I am lord of the Land Under the Hill and I shall take what the children of men have denied me. I shall have my tribute.'

The figure stretched out a hand. The skin of the fingers hardened, withered, changed colour, until Moira Jean realized that she was staring at an eagle's talon, long, thin bone reaching right for her eyes.

'Wait!' she blurted.

The talon froze, inches from her eyes.

Moira Jean leaned as far back as she dared. The curved claws gleamed at her. 'Of course you must be respected,' she said, her voice trembling, 'but . . . but plucking out my eyes'll not bring back what you've lost. I can make amends.'

All she could see were those curved claws, black and sharp. Every detail was viciously clear. Sweat trickled down her back. 'You would become my servant?' the figure said.

Moira Jean licked her lips. 'Not that, exactly, but . . . we'll strike a bargain. I'll bring you something to make up for the food we took, and the . . . the desecrating that we did. And in return, you'll give me back my friends.'

The taloned fingers stretched out. Moira Jean jerked back. The figure caught her by the chin and forced her to look up at him, his clawed fingers scratching the soft place beneath her jaw. She stared into his face, fear fluttering through her thoughts, a headache pounding in her skull as his beautiful features swam in and out of focus.

'You will bring me what I ask for? You will bring me my tribute?'

Moira Jean swallowed, and felt his claws break her skin. 'If you'll return my friends.'

'I accept the terms of your bargain,' the figure said, 'on one condition.'

'What is it?'

'I have no desire to wait upon a mortal. My time is precious, and I do not care to waste it upon you. So, my condition is this: if you have not completed your task by Beltane, you shall forfeit all claim to the others.'

'I . . . I suppose. What's a—'

He ignored her. 'This, my servant, is my first command,' the figure said. 'Bring me a piece of a new-born.'

There was a burst of light. Something shifted, and there was a sound a little like tearing cloth, except Moira Jean could feel it in her marrow. Squinting against the light, she raised a hand to shield her eyes. When she opened them again, the figure had vanished.

A piece of a new-born.

The words loomed over all of Moira Jean's thoughts. Every twig snapping under her feet sounded like breaking bones; every sound from the woods was a baby's cry. The lantern creaked in her hand, sweat dripping down the handle. When she stumbled out of the forest the sky looked like purple velvet, and darkness pooled out from the foot of the pines. She shuddered. The shadows had followed her home.

She crept back to her little cottage – the last thing she needed now was for someone to hear her running – and bolted the door behind her. She lit every candle she could find and prodded the fire back into life, holding shaking hands out to the flames.

A piece of a new-born . . .

She put her head in her hands. They came away bloody; the talons had cut into her neck.

Part of her could not quite believe that it was real. The hazy figure in the woods seemed like something out of a dream.

Perhaps she would wake up tomorrow morning, horrifically hungover, with her friends beside her, laughing when she told them how she'd panicked. But there was blood on her fingers. That, at least, was real – and if the blood was real then so must be the being who had put it there and that didn't make any sense, the whole concept of that thing in the woods didn't make any sense. How had he been able to change his shape? And what the hell was a Beltane?

She slapped herself across the face. She had to focus.

The first task that the figure in the woods had set her, she could not do. She could never hurt a child. It was bad enough that she and her friends had been caught up in this mess, but to bring a baby into it too? That would be unforgiveable. Besides, there were no children in Brudonnock. Jim was the youngest person in the village and he was fourteen. Everyone else had moved away when they married, onto brighter and better things. She was going to do the same, before—

Moira Jean slapped herself again, harder this time. She had to focus. If she didn't fulfil her part of the bargain, the being in the forest would not release her friends. She got to her feet and started pacing the length of the cottage, chewing on her thumbnail. She crossed the room in six long strides, her skirt brushing up against the dresser as she turned.

First things first: she needed to work out what the hell she'd done. The figure in the woods was not human, and she'd just made a deal with him. Dredging up half-remembered stories, she wracked her brain for answers. Not human. Was he a ghost? She wasn't sure. He was pale and had a kind of glow about him – that sounded pretty ghostly no matter which way she looked at it – but surely ghosts couldn't change their shapes and grasp the living by the chin. She supposed he might have been one of the Fae, but she wasn't sure. She had a vague idea that fairies were supposed to be tiny, giggling little things that could shelter under mushrooms and use acorns for hats. She couldn't think of anything further from the things she'd seen in the woods.

Moira Jean ran a hand through her hair. Pins clattered to the floor as it came loose. She snatched them up, swearing. The cheap wire had bent out of shape when it hit the floor; she twisted it back into place. Her hands were shaking. She needed answers. She needed a weapon – something, anything that she could use. She needed someone with her who wouldn't insist that her friends hadn't really been taken, who would hold her hand, who would tell her that it was going to be all right . . .

Her hand found Angus's medal.

Moira Jean perched on the edge of her box bed and unpinned the medal from her shawl. Every time she looked at it, she felt herself wilting. It was a Victory Medal cast in bronze, attached to a rainbow ribbon. Scuffed and worn, the ribbon already fraying from all the times she'd run it through her fingers, it looked exactly like all the other Victory Medals she'd seen. It shouldn't have been able to make her feel better. It was just a piece of metal; the only thing special about it was that it had belonged to Angus. But when she reached for it, the weight against her palm grounded her, as comforting and familiar as the hand that would never reach for hers again.

She curled her fingers around the medal, a lump swelling in her throat. It never should have belonged to her.

Moira Jean dug her fingernails into the heel of her hand, the medal cutting into her palm. Anger bubbled beneath the sadness. The medal *did* belong to her, and there was no point wishing it didn't because that wouldn't change anything. She still didn't know what she was dealing with; her friends were still stuck in – well, they were stuck, wherever they were – and she still had to find a way to fix it.

She *would* get her friends back. If only she had a way to—

She stopped, hand straying to her pocket, and drew out the stone with the hole in it. 'For hidden things', Mrs Iverach had said . . .

Fingers trembling, Moira Jean raised the stone to her eye and peered through the hole. Nothing happened. Her little cottage looked just as it always did. But Mrs Iverach had to have given it to her for a reason, and she was the only other person in Brudonnock who knew that Moira Jean's friends were missing.

Moira Jean stood up. She had to have answers.

'Mrs Iverach? Mrs Iverach!'

Moira Jean drummed on Mrs Iverach's door, calling through the keyhole. She couldn't stop looking over her shoulder. Huddling into her shawl, the darkness pressing all around her, she was certain that at any moment, a clawed hand would swipe across her back. A stiff breeze sent clouds spiralling across the stars, shadows roiling up from the forest. Moira Jean started back, heart hammering. It was nothing. Only shadows.

She rapped on the door again and glanced over her shoulder. On the other side of the Aberdeen road, the forest was an amorphous tangle of rustling shadows. There was a creak. Something moved, swooping towards her like a pointing hand. She flinched, before she realized it was only a branch caught in the wind.

The door opened. Moira Jean yelped; she'd been leaning against it and hadn't noticed. Mrs Iverach blinked up at her, in her shift and nightcap.

'Moira Jean? What is it?' Fear flashed across the old lady's face. 'We're not being turned out?'

'Mrs Iverach! I need to—'

Mrs Iverach gripped her arm. Her rheumy eyes were desperate. 'I'll not leave, Moira Jean. I *can't*, not again. It'll kill me . . .'

'What? No, it's not that. Can . . . can I come in?'

Mrs Iverach peered around Moira Jean to look at the village beyond. 'You're sure it's not the landlords?'

'I'm sure. Can we talk about it inside?'

Mrs Iverach gave her a long look, then stepped aside. Moira Jean darted into the cottage, all but slamming the door behind her. It was much like the cottage Moira Jean shared with her mother: small, sparse, and far too clean to be called shabby. But as she looked around, she began to see the differences. A saucer of milk set by the fireside. A long plank of rowan was propped beside the door, ready to bar it. The horrible straw doll drooped against the front window, its blank face unsettlingly wide. And there was iron everywhere: placed along the mantelpiece, lined up along the windowsill, ringed around Mrs Iverach's box bed.

Mrs Iverach shut the door and lit a pine-resin candle. The match flickered; her hands were shaking. 'So if there's no one here to turn us out, why are you calling at this time of night?'

'Mrs Iverach, you saw the others yesterday.'

The old lady folded her arms. 'Did Nellie MacGregor send you?'

'I saw them too.'

'Of course, you did! We all did – all of Brudonnock was up in the north field!'

Moira Jean wrung the edge of her shawl in her hands. 'Aye. Everyone saw, but it's only you and I who remember. And that's . . . that's because of something that happened in the woods.'

Mrs Iverach held up a hand. 'Wheesht!'

Moira Jean fell silent at once. Mrs Iverach hobbled over to the door, picked up the enormous piece of rowan and slotted the bar across the door. She peered at the iron along the windowsill and mantelpiece, occasionally adjusting the nails to close up gaps in the line. Then, she took a deep breath and sat down in a rickety wooden chair.

'Tell me what happened,' she said, her voice quiet.

'I don't even know if it's real,' Moira Jean whispered, staring at the candle flame. 'We went into the woods for a drink and a dance and . . . and it was all fine, I swear. We weren't doing anything wrong – messing around a wee bit, maybe, but . . . but then . . . these *things* started coming out of the woods.' She gripped handfuls of her skirt to stop her hands from shaking. In the darkness, and with the wind whistling through the gap under the door, every rustle from outside sounded like something shambling towards the cottage. 'They were . . . they were like animals and plants and people but all rolled together in a way that came out wrong. And the others couldn't see their real faces, but I could, and when I tried to get away, they had all vanished.'

Mrs Iverach passed a hand over her face. 'God in Heaven,' she muttered.

'There's more,' Moira Jean continued. 'Since then, no one but you and I know that they're missing – everyone else thinks

that it's normal for them to be gone. So . . . so I went back
into the woods to see what I could find out and there was
this . . . person. A being? God, I don't even know!' She paused,
cringing at her own words. She sounded like she was raving.
'He . . . he said he'd taken my friends and if I brought him
what he asked for I could have them back but I've got to do
it by Beltane because we desecrated the rites and I don't even
know what a Beltane *is*, Mrs Iverach, I've got no damn idea
who that man is or what I've done and I don't know what to
do and . . . and . . .'

Her memories of the night before had torn the world she'd
known into shreds, and listening to herself gabble through a
terrified explanation was worse, because even as she was saying
it, it sounded like something no one would ever believe. She
got to her feet and started pacing, half-ready to spring out of
the door.

'This man in the woods,' Mrs Iverach said, staring into her
hands, 'tell me about him.'

A manic laugh burst out of Moira Jean. Mrs Iverach got
up and handed her a cup of water, her face grave. 'I'm not
even sure if he is a man! It's hard to tell. I can't see his face,
ever, even when I'm looking right at it. But . . . but, somehow,
I know he's beautiful, without knowing why. And his body,
his hand – his hand turned into a *kind of claw*, I *saw it* – and
he said something about iron? Oh, God.'

Moira Jean sank to the floor. Hearing herself say it all out
loud made everything worse. Fear had its hooks in her. Those
gleaming talons, coming right for her eyes; the squirming
shadows around the edges of the clearing; the suspicion that
the figure in the woods had dropped the idea that he was
beautiful into her mind without her knowing.

'Lord deliver us and save us,' Mrs Iverach whispered.

'I'm not mad,' Moira Jean pleaded. 'I saw it, I swear.'

Mrs Iverach pressed a hand to her mouth. She closed her eyes, and in the dim light from the candle, Moira Jean could see her fingers shaking, the shadows jumping across her lined face. She took a deep breath, took her hand away, and fixed Moira Jean with a glare like a steel bolt.

'No, Moira Jean. You're not mad.'

'I . . . you believe me?'

'You're *stupid*.'

'What?'

Mrs Iverach let out a long stream of furious Gaelic, gesticulating wildly. Moira Jean didn't understand a word, and she suspected it might be better that way. Mrs Iverach's hands were shaking, and all the colour had drained from her face.

Eventually, she stopped. She was still glaring at Moira Jean, and breathing hard. 'I need you to know I'm swearing at you,' she said. 'I know you don't understand me, but by *God*, Moira Jean, you need to know what a damn mess you've made of things.'

'I . . . do you know what's happening?'

'Aye, for my sins.' She snorted. 'For God's sake, get off the floor. You're a grown lass, so stand up and face your fate like one.'

Moira Jean got up from the floor. Embarrassment took the edge off her fear.

'Those things you saw in the woods were . . . were the Fair Folk.'

'Do you mean the Fa—'

Mrs Iverach pointed a gnarled finger at her. 'Not in my house, Moira Jean! I'll not have them brought here!'

Moira Jean's mouth fell open. 'Can that happen?'

Mrs Iverach threw up her hands. 'Did your mother teach you nothing? Aye, it can happen. Mind how you call them. Speak kindly of them, and they'll look kindly on you. Speak ill of them, and you'll wish you'd never opened your mouth.'

Blushing, Moira Jean closed her mouth.

'Christ alive,' Mrs Iverach muttered, 'Alma should've taught you this. Guard your name closely, and if you find out theirs, you'll take back some of your power. They can't stand the touch of iron. They can make you see things that aren't there. You can keep them sweet with milk, or cream. Some of them can change shape – Lord above, has no one told you *Tam Lin*? – but all of them are bound by their word, though they'll twist it every which way they can. When a deal is struck, they must uphold their end of the bargain, but you can't trust a word that comes out of their mouths. And don't you set one foot in their realm. Time moves strangely there, if the tales are true; a night in their halls could be a century here.'

Moira Jean ran a hand through her hair. A little of her panic was starting to subside. 'All right. Iron. And – and what're the rites of Beltane?'

For a moment, a faraway look crossed Mrs Iverach's face. 'Oh, there're all sorts. Fires, mostly. You'd drive your cattle between them, or leap over them, or break a cake over the flames. It was . . .' She gave herself a little shake. 'It was how things used to be. Why d'you ask?'

Moira Jean remembered the pieces of oatcake she'd thrown over the fire, and how she'd lunged over the embers to catch Jim before he fell, and a sense of dread settled on her anew. 'I . . . I was hoping you'd tell me what Beltane was.'

Mrs Iverach pinched the bridge of her nose and swore in Gaelic again. 'May Day.'

Panic flashed through her. That was six weeks away. 'It's *March*!' she wailed.

Mrs Iverach slapped her hand on the table. 'Aye, it is March! You've less than two months to fish your friends out of the other side and standing there wailing about it is doing no one any good. So shift yourself, Moira Jean, because you've work to do.'

Moira Jean left Mrs Iverach's cottage with her thoughts in a whirl. She stumbled back home, huddling into her shawl against the wind. The wind caught the door as she opened it, yanking it back, and she couldn't shake the feeling that something was trying to get in. Slamming the door shut, she went to the fire, adding another brick of peat to the flames she'd banked. She tried to sleep, but couldn't; her mind was too full.

The Fae were real.

Lying in her box bed was torture. She gave up on sleep some point before dawn and stoked up the fire and set some water on to boil for porridge. She wasn't hungry, but if she didn't do something nice and normal she was going to drop to the floor and scream. She measured out spoonfuls of oats, the spoon clinking against the bowl as her hands shook. The Fae were real. They were *real*, and as she'd gone about her days cooking and cleaning and sowing and harvesting they'd been real, for all this time, and she had never known. How long had they been there? Had they been watching her?

She threw the oats into the water and ran her hands through her hair. Contrary to what Mrs Iverach thought, she had been told some of the old stories as a child. They all had. She just hadn't paid attention, because usually she and Angus had been told them together when someone was minding Brudonnock's children, and even before she'd realized how she felt he'd been something of a distraction. Her eyes began to drift towards the roof of her box bed, where she'd shoved the chest out of sight.

She caught herself and pinched the flesh of her arm. She had to focus.

As her breakfast bubbled in the pot, she tried to remember if she'd been told anything else and came up blank. But that was fine, she told herself, as the panic began to well up again. Mrs Iverach had given her more than enough to go on. The figure in the woods already knew her name, but if she could find out his, she'd be laughing. And he would be bound by his word, so she'd have to watch what he said and see if she could use it. And he and his kind hated iron, so now she knew a way to keep herself safe.

Her hand found the medal again. She was sure it was what had shaken her out of the stupor of the dance. Grief closed her throat. Angus was still keeping her safe, even now, even after he—

She pressed the heels of her hands into her eyes. This was no time for tears. Mrs Iverach was right; she had work to do.

She'd keep the medal on her – it had always been too precious to take off, even before she knew it would keep her safe. She had the stone with the hole in it; her friends were hidden things, and maybe it could help. Malcolm had already taken the horseshoe from her door; she'd find another and hammer it up there herself. As for the bargain she'd struck, she'd—

An idea dawned. A smile spread across Moira Jean's face. The Fae were bound by their word to keep to the letter of a bargain. Well, she could be too. She could be every bit as twisty as some bastard in a bedsheet.

Moira Jean sprinted back up the hill again, veering off about halfway and heading in the direction of Drewitts' vast barns. Approaching, she heard the sounds of a cow in distress. Hope flickered. She hadn't missed it.

She rolled up her sleeves and pushed open the door, trying to look calm and in control. There was the cow, lowing and straining, and there was Mr Brodie, who was in charge of the dairy, already red-faced and sweating. He'd lost a couple of fingers in the war, and was struggling to grip the cow's halter as it turned its flank towards him.

'Mrs MacGregor said you were after a hand?' she asked.

He nodded. 'Help me get her into the head gate. And mind yourself, Moira Jean. I'd never hear the end of it from your mother if you were kicked.'

Moira Jean edged around the cow, careful to keep out of range of its hooves, and snatched up the rope halter. Together, she and Mr Brodie fastened it into the head gate, and Mr Brodie went around the other side to stroke the cow's nose and murmur to her until the animal had stopped rolling her eyes.

'She'll need help,' Mr Brodie whispered. 'Calving rope's over there. You're not still . . . worse for wear, are you?'

Moira Jean put her hands on her hips, indignant. 'Michael Brodie, I am nineteen. That was *not* enough whisky to lay me out for two days.'

'Get the rope, then. Jesus, but you're as bad as Hamish.'

Moira Jean fetched the calving rope and after a strenuous and messy half hour, the calf was born. As Mr Brodie stroked the heifer's nose and started to let her out of the head gate, Moira Jean pulled out her pocketknife and sliced a lock of wet hair from the calf's forehead, wrapping it up in her hand-kerchief. Then she and Mr Brodie crept out of the pen, giving

68

the mother and baby a wide berth, and Moira Jean was sent home with a fresh cheese for her trouble.

She tried not to look at all the fields that she and her friends had ploughed on her way back home. How long would they be gone for? It was six weeks until May Day – until Beltane – six weeks over planting season, no less. Almost half the village had disappeared overnight; who would work the dairy, cut the peat, sow the harvest? Moira Jean would help, of course – these were her neighbours, she wasn't about to let them go hungry – but if she helped her neighbours plant their gardens and churn their butter in the quiet months, there'd be no chance of setting off along the Aberdeen road to see what she could find for herself. She couldn't leave Brudonnock until her friends were returned – she'd be stuck, mired in hard work just as she'd always been. There would be lean months ahead. Her siblings sent money home, but Moira Jean knew the pinching, empty feeling of a long, wet spring. How hungry would Brudonnock be, when she finally brought her friends home?

Moira Jean gave herself a shake. She had fulfilled her part of the bargain, the Fae had to give back at least one of her friends now. And when they'd returned, they could help her bring back the others. It wouldn't be long before all her friends came home. She wouldn't be left alone.

She was washing her hands in the trough outside her house when her mother returned, walking stiffly through the village. Moira Jean waved, flicking suds into her own ear. 'How's Mrs Macanroy?'

Her mother kept back. 'Well enough. Moira Jean, I'm away to Drewitts for a few days.'

'You are? Why?'

Her mother was clutching her doctor's bag with both hands, her knuckles white on the handle. 'There's 'flu in Stronach.'

The world seemed to shrink down to a point. Fear seized Moira Jean in its claws, grief knocked the breath from her lungs. She clutched the water trough. *No. Not again.* She couldn't get such news a second time.

At least this time, she was where she needed to be.

'Come inside, sit down. You'd best get into bed. Oh, *Hell*! I'll do you some porridge if you—'

'Don't blaspheme!' said her mother, a smile wobbling on her face. 'I feel fine, hen. It's only for a few days, to make certain I've not picked anything up. I'll not pass anything along to you.'

'But . . . but who's going to look after you?'

Moira Jean's mother threw up her hands, the contents of her doctor's bag clanking together. 'For pity's sake, Moira Jean! I'm not at death's door. Mrs McGillycuddy's agreed to put me in a spare room and feed me for a few days. It'll be a week at the outside. I'll be fine, love.'

Tears burned in Moira Jean's eyes. 'I'll visit every day.'

'You'll do no such thing. I'll not have you spreading anything around the village. But . . . but Mrs McGillycuddy will let you know how I am. I don't want you to fret. Go on and get me some clean things, there's a lamb.'

Moira Jean darted into the house and seized handfuls of her mother's clothes, cramming them into a bag along with a Bible, an old tin whistle, and a little wooden duck that her father had carved when he was still alive. She put the bag down in front of her mother, careful not to get too close, and squeezed her hands to stop them from shaking.

'I'll be back before you know it,' her mother said, trying for a smile. 'Try and keep yourself busy, won't you? Look in on Mr Selkirk, and Mrs Iverach, and keep an eye on those chickens. And don't lose your temper with Mrs MacGregor, or I'll never hear the end of it. You . . . you be good now, Moira Jean.'

Her mother picked up the bag and started climbing the hill towards Drewitts. Limping slightly after her long walk, she looked small, frail, the bag far too heavy for her. Moira Jean's eyes were brimming with tears. At the top of the hill, her mother turned and waved, then picked her way around to the servants' entrance. Moira Jean picked up the soap and started washing her hands again, scrubbing until the skin across her knuckles began to bleed.

The rest of the day was lost.

It wasn't as if Moira Jean didn't have anything to do. Her shoes needed mending. The rubbish needed to be sorted into what could be sold and what could be burned or composted. They'd need more peat soon; the village store in the old schoolroom was running low, and when it was warm enough everyone in Brudonnock would need to traipse up to the peat bog to cut, stack and dry it. But though there was plenty of work she could not remember doing it. Her eyes kept turning towards Drewitts, looking for the little attic bedroom where Mrs McGillycuddy had put her mother, or to the vacant spot on the mantelpiece where the little wooden duck usually sat. It had been the last thing her father made before he died.

But then the sun went down. Pine needles rustled in the wind, sounding just enough like whispers to make Moira Jean look up from her sewing. She'd almost forgotten her bargain.

She wrapped her shawl around her and pinned it in place

with Angus's medal. Paraffin splashed across the floor as she refilled the lamp; her hands were shaking. She scrabbled in her pockets for the stone with a hole in it and her handkerchief. She needed it in her hand.

She headed for the forest.

Now that she knew what waited between the trees, the forest seemed to be teeming. Every split on the bark of a silver birch seemed like an eye that had just cracked open. When she ducked to avoid the branch of a pine, the needles felt like fingernails running through her hair. The wind howled and whispered and tugged at her clothes, and she was never sure how much of the noise and the fury was really just the air.

She stopped just before she reached the clearing. She took a deep breath, holding the bronze disc of Angus's medal for a moment. She wasn't sure if it would keep her from harm, or if it would just allow her to keep her wits about her. Either way, the cold touch of metal cleared something for her, forcing her fears back into line.

'Well,' she whispered, 'on we go.'

She went into the clearing.

At first, it seemed empty. The pale lamplight glimmered off broken glass, Duncan's forgotten crutch casting a long shadow across the ground. Her hand strayed to the stone, curious. But then she set down the lantern in the middle of the clearing, and when she straightened up, the figure in white was standing in front of the hillock. He stared down at her, pale and beautiful as the moon and just as remote. Behind the haze across his face, she caught the suggestion of sharp cheekbones, and – she froze – two pairs of eyes. Then she blinked, and the second pair was gone.

'So,' he drawled, 'you have returned.'

Moira Jean fumbled in her pocket for her handkerchief. Almost as soon as she drew it out, she regretted it; it was crumpled and stained and reeked of birthing fluid. She could not imagine handing something so disgusting to something so beautiful.

The figure gestured to the ground at its feet. 'Present your offering.'

'First, I'd like to know who I'm offering *to*,' she said, fighting to keep her tone light. If Mrs Iverach was right, she needed to get the being's name.

'You are offering to me,' said the figure, 'your master.'

Surprising herself, Moira Jean felt a prickle of annoyance. She was nobody's servant. She tried to keep smiling. 'Now, I never promised you my service. We struck a bargain as equals. And, as your . . . your partner in trade, I want to know what I should call you.'

The figure's eyes darkened. This time, she caught a flash of horns, vicious and sharp. 'You and I are the farthest thing from equals. You could not begin to understand how far beyond your reach I am.'

If her smile became any more fixed, Moira Jean was going to have to screw it in. 'It's a simple question. You know my name, after all.'

'My name is not your concern. You are unworthy of it. If you really must, you may call me "my lord". That will suffice.'

'No. No titles.'

The wind roared. Moira Jean threw up a hand, shielding her eyes as pine needles whirled and spun around her. Her hair sprung loose, her skirts whipped up around her knees and she would have lost her shawl, if she had not clamped a hand over Angus's medal. Over her head the trees bent and creaked in the wind, but the figure in white stood motionless, a terrible anger burning in his perfect face.

'I am the Lord of the Land Under the Hill, I am The Dreamer, I am the Many-Faced Prince. You wish to know me, human? First you must know this: you are beneath me. Now. Present your gift.'

The wind died. Moira Jean gripped the handkerchief, her heart hammering.

'Here,' she said, holding it out.

The figure prowled closer, stopping a few paces away from the hillock. Close to, he was utterly perfect, but the more she tried to focus on what made him perfect the harder it became to concentrate. When she tried to stare at his cheekbones, or his jawline, it only gave her a headache. Pride rolled off him in waves, and there was a certain haughtiness in the tilt of his chin, but those were all she could actually see. The idea of his beauty had been planted in her head, and the thought made her skin crawl. Yet she could not look away.

The figure's lip curled. He drew back his spotless white robe. 'This is insufficient.'

Moira Jean tried to shake off her headache. 'You asked for a piece of a new-born. You never said it had to be a human.'

'You are correct.'

The figure pointed upward. Moira Jean tilted back her head to look. Someone was floating in the air, fifty feet above the clearing. It took her a moment to recognize the twisted leg.

Horror swooped through her. 'Don't!'

'You asked me to return your friends. You never said I had to return them safely.'

Moira Jean lunged for the figure's pointing arm. 'Don't! Please, don't do it! I'm sorry, I didn't mean—'

74

'Do you wish to take back this offering?'

'Aye! Aye, just put him down – *safely*, put him down safely!'

The figure waved a hand. Duncan vanished. Moira Jean waited, dreading the sound of the *smack* as he hit the earth. It never came. Still, she stared up at the sky, watching pine branches waver and creak over her head.

There was a voice in her ear, low and insidious. Long-fingered hands gripped her shoulders. Moira Jean flinched; the figure was behind her, and she had not heard him approach.

'There is a tithe to be paid,' the figure hissed in her ear, 'and I shall use the mortals to pay it, unless you bring me something worth more. If this is all you can offer me, I will return your friends to the sky and the earth, and watch you recover their broken bodies.'

Moira Jean stood perfectly still, her heart rattling against her ribcage. The figure's long fingers were just visible out of the corner of her eye; there were at least four sets of knuckles in his curling hands. The shadows were waiting around the edges of the clearing and now, she could see them more clearly. Enormous curved horns. Bark legs that ended in cloven feet. A skeleton hand held together by the moss growing between the bones. And eyes, eyes of every shape and colour, and all of them watching and waiting for her to fail.

'Bring me something that you have lost,' the figure hissed, 'and do not disappoint me.'

Moira Jean stumbled back home, shaking. It took her three tries to bolt the door. She staggered over to her bed, clutching the frame and breathing hard. She was still half-listening for the crash of Duncan's body hitting the ground.

She'd thought herself so clever, and it had put Duncan in danger. Duncan, who'd survived polio and the war just to get his heart broken by a swish city boy who had never deserved him anyway. She had risked his life for a clever turn of phrase.

If he died, his mother wouldn't even know it. Like everyone else in Brudonnock, Mrs McLeod believed her son was safe elsewhere. Duncan could die a few paces from his mother's front door, and the poor woman would never know. Or worse – perhaps it would only be then that the spell would break, and she would remember he was missing?

Moira Jean ground her teeth, tears brimming in her eyes. She was not going to let that happen. She had to give that Fae something that she had lost.

But how?

Moira Jean stared around the room. How could she give anyone something that she had lost? Surely the moment she found something to give them, it wouldn't be lost any more. And besides, even if she could find something, it still had to be good enough to satisfy the Fae. Panic raced through her. The being in the woods might as well have asked her to grow wings and fly.

Desperate, she ran a hand through her hair. She had to *think*. Because if she couldn't do this, she would lose Duncan; she'd lose them all, one after the other. It was too much. She couldn't do it again, not after—

She stopped. An idea slid into her thoughts like a needle.

'Oh, you *bastard*,' she hissed.

She got to her feet. A slow, sick anger was filling her up.

Moira Jean reached up to the top of the box bed and felt around until she found the little wooden chest. Even now, with fear and anger throbbing like blisters, she could not look at its contents. Not that she needed to. She knew exactly what was inside: a bundle of letters, a dried flower, an identity tag stamped with a name:

A. Dunbar.

For a moment, she paused. Memory caught her by the throat and squeezed at the sight of the flower. It was so delicate she picked it up with both hands, careful not to let it crumble. It was a sprig of white heather, and Angus had given it to her when she was fourteen. Not long after their first kiss, Angus had realized how thoroughly susceptible she was to his worst lines, and he'd taken to delivering them while leaning on things because Callum had told him girls liked that. Angus had leaned on Moira Jean's fence, overbalancing a little as she blushed and fussed with her hair, and handed over the sprig of heather with a flourish. 'It's to bring you luck,' he'd said, and when she'd asked what she needed luck for, he'd leaned in and kissed her, saying 'Would you look at that! It works!' with that charming half-smile of his that preceded a real grin.

She closed her eyes, grief lodged in her like a hook. Then she took the topmost letter off the pile and strode back outside, fury boiling in her bones.

Moira Jean marched into the woods, forgetting the lantern. Twigs snapped under her feet; she ground them into the dirt. Branches swung at her eyes; she smacked them out of the way and heard something crack. A trail of crushed leaves and splintered twigs was left in her wake. Fury and fear propelled her into the clearing.

It was empty.

'Oi!' Moira Jean yelled. 'You want to know what I've lost?'

Her voice bounced off the trees. There was a flurry of flut-

tering as something flapped away from the sound. Moira Jean
held up the letter, her eyes burning.

'Then you can come and bloody get it!'

Silence. The hairs on the back of Moira Jean's neck stood
up. There was no such thing as silence in the forest. It was a
living, teeming thing, rich with sound even when there was no
one to hear it. But now, there was nothing.

Nothing but that voice. It came like antlers snapping, like the
crash of ice breaking and falling down a distant mountainside.

'You dare summon me with such disrespect?'

Moira Jean whirled around. The clearing was encircled by
shadows again. This time, she could see their teeth – the tusks
of boars, the fangs of foxes, the long, thin teeth of rodents.

The figure in white stood just in front of the hillock. There
was a sharpness to him now, a cruel cast to his perfect mouth.
Behind him, the shadow of vast antlers was splashed across
the trees.

'Aye,' snapped Moira Jean, holding out the letter. 'I've
brought what you asked for. Now give me back my friend.'

The figure looked down his nose at the letter. 'This is not
something you have lost. This is paper.'

'Read it!' Moira Jean yelled, her voice cracking. 'You want to
know what I've bloody lost? It's all here, pal. Take it. Take it!'

The figure lifted his gaze from the worn, crumpled pages.
He looked at her for a long time, watching her like a cat with
a mouse. 'You read it,' he said, his voice sly. 'I have no use
for such things.'

Moira Jean felt as if she'd been slapped. 'I . . . I can't.'

'Do as I command, or I shall not accept this gift.'

'Fine. Fine! But I want your word that you'll return my
friend safe and well or so help me, I'll make you regret it.'

'You shall have it.' The figure gestured to the letter.

Moira Jean drew it closer. She had not read the letter for many months, but she did not need to. She knew it by heart. She knew the feel of the cheap paper between her fingers, she knew the blurred characters on the typed letterhead, above all, she knew the rushed, messy handwriting, still such a state after all those years in school. But even though she could have read it with her eyes closed, opening the letter still sliced through her like a knife.

There was a lump in her throat already. She glared up at the figure in white, her jaw clenched, her eyes already full of tears. He was staring at her, already leaning in close, listening.

'This had better be worth it,' she muttered.

She took a deep breath.

'Dear Moira Jean,' she began, 'Well, still no news on when I'll be home again, even though it's all over. They say the ship'll be ready soon but I'll not lie to you, I've been thinking of walking home for days now. Calais is nice, but it'd be a damn sight nicer if it had you in it. Still, I suppose that gives you more time to fix your wedding clothes. You'll want to be ready at a moment's notice, because the second I get back to Brudonnock we're both away to the kirk, we've waited long enough. Unless, of course, you've thrown me over for one of those Canadian Forestry lads you mentioned. If that's so, I'll fight him, of course, but make sure you tell him what a vicious bastard I am so he's got time to sweat before I get back. Don't tell your mother I said that. Give Da my love and tell him I'll write soon. I'm writing to him myself, but you know what he's like. Your loving Angus.'

Tears were streaming down Moira Jean's face. Her voice had cracked halfway through reading, but she hadn't heard it. Staring at Angus's handwriting, reading his words aloud, she'd heard his voice, seen his gap-toothed smile, and it had gutted her.

It was the last letter she'd ever received from him. When the war had ended, she'd thought herself so lucky. She'd flung her arms around her mother, written to all her siblings, and sung through every chore. Angus had survived; he would be coming home. They would be married. They'd leave Brudonnock, hurl themselves into the loudest, most exciting place they could find, and build something vibrant and wonderful. First, Edinburgh. Then, they weren't sure where they'd go, or what they'd do. Drinking, dancing, maybe travelling; they'd find a way to afford it. Whatever life threw at them, they would face it laughing, and clutching each other's hands. Together, they could make anything work.

But he was still out there. Though the war had ended, the Spanish 'flu had not, and while he was waiting to board a ship to Scotland, Angus had died, along with thousands of other young men who'd been milling around the docks of Calais.

They'd buried his body in a mass grave. All Angus's father had received was a box of his effects, and the Victory Medal which Angus received for surviving the war. Angus's father had given the whole box to Moira Jean, and then gone to a remote bothy in the mountains and shot himself.

That had been three months ago.

'You want to know what I've lost?' muttered Moira Jean, her voice thick with tears. 'Everything.'

The figure in white was staring at her. He craned his neck forward, stretching unnaturally far. Moira Jean could still not quite focus on his face, but she knew that his eyes were flitting between the tears on her cheeks, the tightness in her jaw, and the paper in her hand. He reached out, his elegant hands hesitating just over her own.

'Take it,' she said, and she hated the pleading note in her voice. 'If you'll not take that, I've nothing worth giving.'

The figure took the letter, holding it between his thumb and forefinger. He peered at it. 'It is such a little thing,' he said, his voice suffused with wonder.

Moira Jean shook her head. It felt so wrong seeing the letter she treasured in the figure's pale hands.

'I will accept your gift,' the figure said. 'Your friend shall be returned to you safe and well, as we agreed. You may bargain for another tomorrow. Now go.'

The figure waved a hand and the ring of shadows parted behind her. Moira Jean limped out of the clearing, feeling as if something had been wrung out of her. When she got home, and saw the wooden chest still open on the floor, she climbed into bed and hid under the covers, staring at the underside of her quilt until her eyes burned.

Moira Jean awoke the next morning feeling lesser. Some part of herself had been handed over with that letter. She eased herself out of bed, her eyes still puffy, her curly hair tangled. She washed her face and changed her clothes, hoping it would make her feel like a new person, but when she had put on a clean shirt and twisted up her hair, the same grief was still pressing on her shoulders, like a familiar hand.

She sighed.

A shout came from the other side of the door. Then, running feet. More shouting. Moira Jean started upright. *Duncan*. She'd almost forgotten.

She burst out of the cottage door like a startled grouse. She was not the only one in the street. Her neighbours clustered together looking worried. Fiona's mother was standing on Mr Galbraith's doorstep, the pair of them talking in low voices. Moira Jean sidled up to them.

'Good morning, Mrs MacGregor, Mr Galbraith,' she said. 'What's—'

Mrs MacGregor seized her arm. 'Moira Jean! You've not seen Duncan, have you?'

The first ripples of panic began to spread through Moira Jean. 'Duncan? No, I . . . I thought . . .'

'He's gone!' Mrs MacGregor hissed. 'Just vanished, in the night! Poor Effie's out of her mind for worrying. You're sure you've not seen him?'

Moira Jean shook her head. 'I don't understand. He should *be* here!'

Mrs MacGregor threw up her hands. 'I *know*, Moira Jean. That's why we're out here. Fetch Mrs Iverach out of bed; Effie will want to speak to her.'

Moira Jean headed up the hill to Mrs Iverach's house, the back of her neck prickling. The truth itched at her. Fiona was missing too, but her mother didn't even know it. And, Moira Jean thought with a stab of fury, what about the bargain she'd made the night before? Duncan was supposed to have been returned safely to her. Had she opened all those wounds for nothing?

Moira Jean knocked on Mrs Iverach's door. She answered, fully dressed, her mouth set into a firm line.

'Did you do it?' she hissed.

'I think so. They know Duncan's gone, now. But no one can find him anywhere.'

Mrs Iverach patted her on the shoulder. 'We'll find him. Try the hagstone, and think on what was said. *Precisely* what was said. The . . . the Fair Folk,' she said, mouthing the name, 'are bound by their word.'

Moira Jean nodded, and went to check on Mrs McLeod. The older lady was inconsolable, her back hunched with weeping, grey head low over her kitchen table. She seized Moira Jean's hand, pleading for news of her son, and dissolved into tears again when Moira Jean said she hadn't seen him.

She left Duncan's cottage chewing on her thumbnail. Discreetly, she fished the stone with a hole in it – the hagstone – out of her pocket and held it up to her eye. Nothing, except a few strange looks. Malcolm and Mr Selkirk were standing outside the smithy, fetching lanterns and coils of rope and rifles as they prepared to search the forest. Moira Jean wanted to scream at them that Duncan was not the only one missing. Mr Selkirk was Callum and Jim's father; Malcolm was Fiona's older brother. And yet neither of them knew how badly they'd been robbed. They were sleeping, and Moira Jean was the only one awake.

Moira Jean drifted towards the trees, dazed. How could this have happened? Mrs Iverach said the Fae were bound by their word; Duncan *had* to have been returned. The figure in white had promised to return Duncan *safe and well*, and yet he was nowhere to be seen –

Moira Jean stopped.

'. . . no,' she said. 'No, he wouldn't.'

She was staring straight down the centre of Brudonnock. The new well was only a few yards from her. She crept towards it, her heart beating very fast. Her hands clutched at the stone as she peered over the rim, dreading what she might see floating in the deep, dark water.

There was nothing.

Moira Jean straightened up. Malcolm and Mr Selkirk were staring at her. She gave them an awkward smile, shaping her words clearly so that Malcolm wouldn't lose them in the shouting. 'Just a thought.'

She shuffled away from the well, feeling very embarrassed. It had been stupid to check down the well. Returning Duncan to the bottom of the well wouldn't have met the terms of their bargain. He wouldn't have been safe, in all that water.

But the old well had run dry.

Trying not to run, Moira Jean headed back up the hill. She passed the kirk and went a little further up, until she saw a patch of overgrown grass that hid the cover of the old well. Heart shuddering, Moira Jean knelt down and put her ear to the wooden cover.

From a long, long way below, something echoed up to her.

Moira Jean sprang up, tearing back down towards the smithy. She skidded to a halt just as the men were crossing the Aberdeen road, shotguns slung across their backs. They turned and stared as she ransacked the forge. Hammers and tongs clattered as she threw them aside. At last, she found a crowbar.

She sprinted back up the hill. She tripped over her own feet and stumbled, collapsing in a heap by the old well. It didn't matter. She jumped up again, wedged the end of the crowbar underneath the well cover, and heaved.

The old wood sprung free at once. She staggered back. Moira Jean fell to her knees, peering into the darkness. Many feet below, there was a shape huddled on the floor.

'Duncan!' she yelled. 'Duncan, can you hear me?'

The shape shifted. There was a groan. Behind Moira Jean, Mrs McLeod was screaming: 'What is it? Have you found him?'

More footsteps. Moira Jean turned and saw Malcolm running up the hill, closely followed by Mr Selkirk. Malcolm's broad, sunburned face went slack when he saw the uncovered well.

'How . . . but it was covered. He couldn't have . . .'

Moira Jean shoved the crowbar at him. 'Never mind. How much rope've you got there?'

'Enough, but . . .'

Mrs McLeod came running up to them. 'Is he down there? Oh God, my poor wee boy . . .'

Moira Jean put a gentle hand on Mrs McLeod's shoulder. 'Will you fetch me a light, Mrs McLeod? I'm going to bring him up.'

Mrs McLeod collapsed, sobbing. Malcolm tried to step in front of the well. 'No, Moira Jean. I'll not let you go down there. It's too dangerous, I'll go.'

Moira Jean gave him a grin and snatched up the end of the rope. 'You'd never get those broad shoulders down there, Malcolm. This is women's work.'

'No! Moira Jean, you'll—'

Moira Jean poked him in the chest. 'Oh, and I'll let *you* go down there while I hold the rope up here? He's *my* friend. I found him. Now hold this and hold your tongue.'

She passed him the other end of the rope. He took it, staring at her with his mouth half-open as she hiked up her skirts so they wouldn't tangle around her legs. Mrs MacGregor tutted, loudly, at the sight. A crowd had gathered now, whispering amongst themselves as Moira Jean tied the rope securely around her waist.

'He's down there,' she said, jerking her head towards the old well. 'Someone pass me a light, I'm going to bring him up.'

'But how did he—'

Mrs Iverach stumped up to join them, slightly out of breath. 'Ah, you know how lads are. Get themselves into all sorts of trouble. Now, are we fishing him out, or not?'

Mr Selkirk handed Moira Jean a lantern. Carefully, she tied it to the rope already around her waist. Her pulse was thumping in her ears.

'Right,' she said, standing on the edge of the well. 'If you drop me, Malcolm MacGregor, you'll have my mother to answer to.'

Malcolm planted his feet. Behind him, Mr Selkirk took up the rope, grinding his feet into the dirt. So did Mrs McLeod, and Mrs MacGregor, and Mr Galbraith, after carefully laying aside his walking stick. Only Mrs Iverach did not join them, her gnarled hands too stiff and swollen to hold the rope securely. She nodded at Moira Jean. 'On you go, Moira Jean,' she said. 'You've work to do.'

Moira Jean sat on the edge of the well, her legs dangling into darkness. She took a deep breath. As slowly as she dared, she pushed herself away from the edge. Hovering just below the rim of the well, she stared into the depths, trying not to think about fraying ropes and long, long drops.

'You all right there, Moira Jean?' asked Malcolm, his voice already strained.

'Just you concentrate on that rope,' she snapped. 'I'm heading down now.'

Slowly, she began to walk her way down the wall.

The rope cut into her waist as she descended. A circle of light swung beneath her, the handle of the lantern creaking with every step. Her shadow lurched on the wall. She kept her eyes up, focusing on the disc of daylight shrinking above her head. She placed each foot slowly, carefully, and tried not to wonder how sturdy the walls of old wells would be when no one had maintained them for decades.

Damp, cold air settled on her like a shroud. She must be close now. Malcolm's voice called down to her, but she couldn't quite make out the words over the echoes. She ignored them. Breathing deeply and refusing to look over her shoulder, she kept walking.

At last, she came to the bottom.

Duncan was lying on the floor of the well amongst a scattering of debris, curled up like a child. Moira Jean dropped to her knees beside him, relief and fear churning through her.

'Duncan? Duncan, it's me. I've come to bring you home.'

He opened his eyes. His face was pale and stricken.

'I've seen The Dreamer, Moira Jean.'

She remembered the figure in white, and all the names he had given her. At least that one didn't have a title attached. 'The Dreamer?' she prompted.

'He was so beautiful,' Duncan whispered, 'so, so beautiful.'

'I know.' She helped him into a sitting position. 'Come on. We'd best be off.'

Duncan shook his head. 'Let me sleep.'

Moira Jean straightened up and untied the rope from around her waist. 'You'll sleep in your own bed, then,' she said, as she fastened it around Duncan's midriff, 'not at the bottom of a well.'

'Let me sleep, Moira Jean. I want to dream again.'

'Did I bloody stutter?' snapped Moira Jean. 'I've no time for this nonsense, Duncan McLeod. Your ma's worried sick. Stop mucking about and get up there. Go on.'

She double-checked the knot and tugged sharply on the rope, twice. She dragged Duncan to his feet and soon, Duncan was being hauled back up towards daylight. As she watched him ascend, she remembered him floating in the sky above the forest, and shivered.

Angus's medal was cold in her palm, but still, she held it. When she stared at the daylight so far above her, and heard Duncan's mother sobbing as he was hauled over the edge of the well, she needed something to hold.

PART TWO

Part Two

The rumour was that Duncan's leg would have to come off. According to Mrs MacGregor, several bones in his foot, already weakened by polio, were broken. Moira Jean wasn't sure if this was true, and with her mother stuck at Drewitts, she had no way of knowing. Before he was found in the well, Duncan had been able to walk with the help of his crutch, but if the bones healed badly, he might not be able to put any weight on his foot at all. There was no doctor in the village – only Moira Jean's mother, and Malcolm, who'd pull teeth and set a break if she was busy. Now, he was trying to explain himself to a distraught Mrs McLeod.

'There's all sorts of wee bones in a foot, Effie, and with the polio and all I—'

'So you'll do nothing for him? You'll just let my boy suffer?'

'No, but—'

Moira Jean did her best to shut the voices out. She was in the McLeods' cottage to visit Duncan, but he had sunk into a deep sleep and did not seem likely to wake any time soon. He was layered in blankets, his face pale, his bad leg propped up on the small crate that contained Mrs McLeod's sewing machine. In the shadow of Duncan's box bed, she could see the shape of his twisted foot. It was purple with bruises, but

91

she had no idea if anything was broken. Guilt prickled through her. She should've found him sooner.

Moira Jean brushed Duncan's hair out of his eyes and left the cottage, ducking around Mrs McLeod so she wouldn't ask her how Moira Jean had known where to find her son. The sun shone overhead but still, she shivered. The chill at the bottom of the well seemed to have settled in her bones.

Moira Jean drifted back to her cottage, anxiety scrabbling at the edges of her thoughts. The Fae that called himself The Dreamer had promised that Duncan would be returned safe and well, but why wouldn't he wake up? Something was wrong. She could feel it. Panic grabbed her by the heart and squeezed as she climbed the hill. Would all her friends come back like that? Would they wake at all? She had to find out.

But when Moira Jean got back to her cottage, it was to find Mrs McGillycuddy with a list of instructions from her mother. The lazy-beds needed digging, the hem of her skirt was frayed and wanted fixing, their food stores needed a thorough examination after the winter. She was to look in on Mrs Iverach and Mr Selkirk and see if they needed anything, and tell her mother what they asked for. And tomorrow, if it was dry, the whole village would need to start sowing the harvest up at Drewitts, and that would mean several long days sweating in the fields. As the housekeeper walked away, Moira Jean clamped down on the urge to yell that she had more important things to do. She *had* to get her friends back. Frustration bubbled up inside her. But if she didn't prepare the garden and plant the harvest, she and her mother would starve. This, at least, was something that she could fix without a sacrifice.

She did her best. Moira Jean dragged out the shovel and began work on the lazy-beds, digging several raised beds in their back garden for the crops they wouldn't have to sell, sweating and swearing all the while. When she was done she dunked her head in the water trough and let her wet hair drip down her back. She fed the chickens, examined the food stores, and tried her best not to think about Duncan when she sat down to her mending.

Where, exactly, had he been?

Duncan still hadn't woken up. He'd only been gone for two days. All that time, he'd been with The Dreamer. What had he done to him?

Moira Jean set aside her frayed skirt and ran her hands through her hair. There was so much she didn't understand. More than ever, she wanted her mother, but she knew that there was no point in telling her anything. Like everyone else in Brudonnock, her mother couldn't remember that Moira Jean's friends had been taken at all. She'd go and speak to Mrs Iverach as soon as she had a moment, but it wouldn't be the same.

And then, there was Angus's letter.

She felt its absence like a missing tooth. In the moments between finishing one task and starting the next, she had been hard-pressed to keep from reaching up for the chest above her bed. She snatched her hand back every time. There was no point in keeping Angus's letters. It was torture to read them; she shouldn't do it. But knowing that one of them was not there dragged her thoughts towards them like metal to a magnet.

It should've been easier, now she'd given one of them away. She should've parcelled up the whole box and handed it over, and then she might've been free. But the memories weighed her down, like stones in her pockets. It had been three months since Angus died, and nearly two years since she'd seen him in person, but she could still picture him so clearly – scruffy, confident, a dare in his eyes whenever he looked at her. It was always the right corner of his mouth that moved first when he smiled. When she'd first noticed it she'd been eleven, and she'd never been able to stop seeing it after that.

She gave in. With shaking hands, she took down the chest and opened it.

She couldn't look at the sprig of heather. She set the identity tags aside – those had never felt his, though he'd had them for two years – and picked up the letters instead. Every week he'd been at the front, he'd written to her. The letters were messy, blotchy and spattered with something that was either tea or mud, but she'd never once minded. After he'd asked her for the news, Angus had told her how awful the food tasted, how wet his socks always were, how he'd adopted a trench rat and named it Bastard because it kept trying to bite him. They'd planned their future together in these letters; she in broad, messy strokes, he providing some of the detail. When she'd told him she wanted to live somewhere lively, he'd suggested Edinburgh, or Glasgow, or even taking posts on an ocean liner so they wouldn't have to pick what cities they got to see. When he had space on the edges of the paper, he'd fill up the margins with doodles – of Bastard, of the men in his company, of the food he wanted to eat, several of his commanding officer that were all labelled 'Idiot' – but mostly, they were drawings of her. Angus had been very generous with her curves – the real Moira Jean was lean and strong, whereas the drawings had the kind of corseted lushness that made her feel a little flustered – but she could see the time he'd taken in every line. He had her smile, the lines around her eyes when she laughed, the set of her jaw, and every curl in the tangled mass of her hair had been inked with care. When she looked at them, she saw how he'd held the memory of her face all the two years they'd been apart. The letters were the best and the worst things she owned.

There was a knock at the door. Moira Jean crammed everything back into the box and shoved the chest back in place, patting her cheeks to make sure they were dry. 'Come in!' she called, hating the roughness in her voice.

Malcolm ducked through the door, holding his cloth cap in both hands. His broad face was pale, nervous. 'Afternoon, Moira Jean. Have you seen your ma?'

Moira Jean angled her chair into the light; Malcolm always found lip-reading in the dark more difficult. 'No, she's still at Drewitts.'

Malcolm's face fell. He tugged at his blond beard. 'And she didn't tell you . . .'

Moira Jean shook her head.

His green eyes were fixed on her, troubled. They looked just like Fiona's; Moira Jean bent over her sewing.

'It's just . . .' He hesitated. 'It's just that you . . .'

'Just what?' she snapped.

'How'd you know where Duncan was?' he asked, eventually.

Moira Jean's stomach lurched. She'd been waiting for someone to ask. 'I heard a noise.'

He chewed on his bottom lip, watching her. 'Only we'd been around the whole village twice over before you came along, and none of us heard anything.'

She shot him a shaky grin. 'Must've been luck,' she said.

Malcolm brushed this aside. 'But d'you not find it a wee bit strange? How'd Duncan get down there without a single one of us knowing, and with the lid nailed back in place?'

Her fingers were slippery with sweat. She laid aside the sewing before she jabbed herself with the needle, signing as she spoke. 'What're you suggesting?'

'I've no clue,' he said, tugging on his sandy beard. 'What d'you make of it?'

Moira Jean stared into her hands. They were callused and covered in freckles, much like the rest of her. She could tell Malcolm the truth, but she had no idea if he'd believe her. He'd forgotten Duncan was ever missing – his own sister had disappeared, and he still hadn't realized.

'It almost sounds like something out of a fairy story,' she said, her voice very quiet.

Malcolm snorted. 'Aye, sure. Wee bastards in green put him down there, I've no doubt.'

Moira Jean flinched, waiting for the retribution. Mrs Iverach's words rang in her ears: *speak ill of them, and you'll wish you'd never opened your mouth*. Nothing happened. She changed tactic. 'How's Fiona? Have you heard from her?'

'Well enough,' said Malcolm.

'Where is she these days?' Moira Jean asked, watching his eyes.

Malcolm frowned. 'You don't remember? She's in Aviemore. Working at one of the hotels.'

Curious, she leaned forward. The story had changed. 'Your mother said she was down in Edinburgh.'

'I . . . I don't remember.'

Moira Jean leaned forward, hope blossoming like a flower. 'You don't? When did you last see her?'

'I . . . She's there for the tourists . . .'

'It's March,' Moira Jean snapped, 'you know it's not the season! So where is she?'

Malcolm's face was growing pale. 'She . . . she's in Aviemore . . .'

Moira Jean threw up her hands, signing frantically as she spoke. 'You know she's not! There's no tourists in Aviemore – nobody's got any money after the war, and there's the 'flu besides! Why would she be there? You can walk to Aviemore in an afternoon from here. Have you not been to see her?'

'Edinburgh, then . . .'

Moira Jean jumped up. Desperation fizzed in her veins. 'Fine. Fine! Edinburgh, is it? Where in Edinburgh? Which hotel? Has she not written to you, or your ma? She'd tell you where she was working; you know how your ma worries for her prospects! Think, Malcolm! You know she isn't there!'

Malcolm was clutching his head. 'I . . . I don't . . .'

She seized his hands and tore them away, forcing him to look at her. 'You know something's not right,' she insisted, 'I know you do.' She scrabbled in her pocket for the hagstone and held it up to his eye; maybe it would help him see. 'Here.'

He didn't take it. For a moment, Malcolm blinked at her, his green eyes full of panic. Then, the fear vanished. He smiled. He calmly took his hands away and reached into his jacket pocket, pulling out a piece of paper.

He handed it over. 'I tell a lie, she has written to me. You can read it, if you like.'

Hesitant, Moira Jean took the paper.

Dear Moira Jean, she read, *Well, still no news on when I'll be home again, even though it's all over . . .*

97

She dropped the letter as though she'd been stung. Fear slashed through her. Her breath came sharp and fast.

Malcolm picked up the paper as though nothing had happened. 'I'd best be away now,' he said, his voice calm, tucking the paper back into his jacket. Despite Moira Jean's fear, when it slid out of sight, she felt a wrench. He glanced at the hagstone, still in Moira Jean's hand. 'What's the rock for?'

Moira Jean shook her head, not trusting herself to speak. Malcolm gave her a strange look, then bid her goodbye and left, closing the door carefully behind him. For a long time Moira Jean stayed exactly where she was, staring at the closed door and trying to wrestle her panicked thoughts back into line.

She couldn't.

Not now she knew The Dreamer was watching her.

After the sun went down, Moira Jean sat in her cottage and waited for silence. She'd mended her skirt, she'd had her supper, the fire had been banked with damp peat. Flinching at every sound, she wracked her brains, trying to guess what The Dreamer might ask for next.

But when silence settled over the cottages, her hands began to shake. There was no more time. She pinned the medal to her shawl, gathered up her lantern and headed for the forest. With every step, the urge to bolt back grew stronger. What was she doing? The Dreamer knew she had tried to break his spell. He'd scratch out her eyes, or pluck out her tongue, or . . . God only knew what he'd do to her now. How was she supposed to make it through the next six weeks, knowing her every move was being watched? She stopped, lingering on the Aberdeen road. She could go. Slip off into the night, to some place so crowded with iron that The Dreamer couldn't follow her. There were still so many things she wanted to see, even though she hadn't thought she'd be seeing them alone. But if she did go, she'd be abandoning her friends. To what, she had no idea, but she did not like the sound of the tithe The Dreamer had mentioned at all. She couldn't let them pay for her mistake.

Once more, she pushed her way through bracken and ducked under branches. She followed the winding path, pine needles springy underneath her feet, the occasional splash of moonlight stark on a silver birch tree. She made her way to the clearing, set the lantern down, and stared at the hillock, waiting for The Dreamer to appear.

It happened as slowly as sunset.

First came the rustling. At first, she thought it was the wind, running its fingers through the pine needles, but then she heard the subtle click and chitter of things that were neither human nor animal. The shadows between the trees began to darken. When they shifted closer to the moonlight, Moira Jean caught flashes of strange things: eyes lidded with lichen, a hand with leaves sprouting from the knuckles, tusks that grew long, long past inhuman chins. Then, the silence came, and she knew The Dreamer was coming.

For a split second, she felt something shift beneath her feet. She stumbled sideways, taking her eyes off the hillock for just a second, and then he was there, shining down on her in all his terrible glory. Unnaturally tall, with too-broad shoulders and a too-narrow waist, she had to crane her neck to look into his opalescent eyes. The haze still lingered across his features; irritated, she longed to brush it aside.

'I see you have not learned humility,' The Dreamer said. 'You are my servant. You should kneel when you greet me.'

Moira Jean plastered on a smile. She couldn't make him angry. 'Let's not have that argument again. You've been enjoying yourself with my gift, I noticed.'

The Dreamer drifted a little closer. 'It is *fascinating*. But it does not work.'

'Excuse me?'

The Dreamer waved a hand in an elegant circle; Angus's letter appeared in mid-air, hovering just above his fingertips. 'It does not work,' he repeated. 'You wept. The others did not. Why?'

Moira Jean groped for an excuse. 'You asked for something *I* had lost. Why should they weep?'

The Dreamer reached out a slender hand and turned her face from side to side. Moira Jean froze. Her focus slipped away when she tried to look at the muscles in his hand, but his touch felt like feathers, unexpectedly gentle. 'You are not weeping now.'

Moira Jean backed away. 'It doesn't work like that. It's a letter, you have to read it. Anyway, why should you mind a few tears? You've seen them before.'

'I do not *have* to do anything,' The Dreamer drawled, 'such things are beneath me.'

'You've got to read letters to—' Moira Jean broke off. An idea struck her. 'You can't read, can you?'

'It is beneath me,' The Dreamer repeated, flicking a dismissive hand.

Moira Jean's temper flared. She folded her arms. 'D'you mean to say that I could've told you absolutely *anything*, and you would've been none the wiser?'

The Dreamer levelled a long, long finger at her. His voice was like the hiss of falling snow, a sense of sharpness crawling into his face. 'Have a care how you speak to me, girl. I indulge your insolence because you brought me something that amused me. Do not forget that your friends are still in my halls.'

'About that,' Moira Jean said, fear creeping back into her thoughts. 'What . . . what exactly are you doing to them?'

Through the haze, The Dreamer was smirking. 'Whatever I please.'

'And what is that?'

The Dreamer waved a careless hand. 'You need not concern yourself with it. They have joined the dance; that is all you need to know.'

Moira Jean thought of Duncan's bruised foot, and went cold. 'Do they ever get to stop?'

The Dreamer smiled. The haze shifted, and she saw a sharp chin, a full mouth. But then his teeth slid into focus. For a moment they were clustered together, small and sharp and in too many rows; then they shifted, and two large tusks protruded from his mouth. For a moment, she heard the pipes and the drums, the music thrumming in a way that made her whole body resonate. But this time, she could hear something beneath the music: a wild, unhinged peal of laughter that sounded more like screaming. Fear slid into her thoughts like a knife.

'All right, all right!' said Moira Jean, raising her hands, 'there's no need for any of that. I was only asking a question.'

'You ask a great many questions,' The Dreamer replied, dismissive. The tusks, she was relieved to see, had flickered out of sight.

Moira Jean fumbled for another transparent piece of flattery. 'Well . . . well, I've met no one like you before. You're fascinating. I'd like to know more about you.'

'Of course, you do,' he said, boredom seeping back into his voice. 'Your life is a tedious, small affair.'

Moira Jean remembered all the plans she'd made, how close she'd been to leaving Brudonnock behind. The urge to placate him vanished, instantly. She put her hands on her hips. 'How'd *you* know? You don't have the first idea what my life is like.'

'I should not care to know. I have more important matters to concern myself with than the petty squabbles of mortals.'

'Aye, sure you do,' said Moira Jean, folding her arms. 'And that's why you swapped one of my friends for one of my letters, is it? Because the affairs of mortals aren't interesting to you?'

'*One* of your letters?' The Dreamer asked, eyes glittering.

Panic flashed through her. She'd said too much. She tried to cover it with a snort. 'Not that it matters to you, of course. Reading is beneath you, as you said.'

The Dreamer tilted his head, considering her. 'And all mortals perform this skill?'

'Oh, aye. Everyone knows how to read. I learned when I was seven.'

The Dreamer stared at her. 'You learned when you were a child?'

'We all did. It's like learning how to walk.'

He stared at the letter again. It rotated in the air above his hand, and as the paper turned, Moira Jean's throat tightened at the sight of Angus's familiar handwriting.

'Very well,' The Dreamer said. 'You shall teach me.'

'And you'll give me back one of my friends?'

He gave her a wicked smile. 'I have already granted you one favour tonight, Moira Jean,' he said, his voice low and insidious. 'You asked me to excuse you, and I have done so.'

'Hold on, now—'

'Do not deny it. The words came from your own lips.' He glanced at her mouth, raising an eyebrow, and Moira Jean blushed. 'I do not think you know how lucky you are that I have excused your blatant disrespect – and your little display with the smith earlier. By rights, you should be punished. I have not plucked out your tongue, you may consider that a sign of great favour.'

Her stomach lurched. Moira Jean folded her arms to hide her shaking hands. She'd thought – hoped – he might have forgotten. Still, a few reading lessons were a small price to pay, compared to having her tongue ripped out. 'Well, isn't that just fantastic,' she muttered.

'It is,' The Dreamer agreed. 'I shall return another of your friends in exchange for an appropriate gift, but until then, you may begin your teaching.' He held out the letter.

'I'll not teach you from that,' she said, quickly. 'You want a real book. And – look, are you sure you want this? It's a lot of work.'

'I am your better, and I shall not be bested by human children,' The Dreamer said. 'Teach me your secrets.'

Moira Jean sighed. Her heart was beating very fast. 'I don't suppose I've any choice in the matter?'

'You have a great deal of choice, Moira Jean,' said The Dreamer, his voice silky. The letter vanished with a flick of his wrist; he saw her watching it, and smirked. 'Return here and begin your teaching, or pay for your insolence in some other manner. An eye would suffice.'

Around the clearing, the creatures chittered. Her mouth went dry. 'Reading it is, then.'

How long had The Dreamer been watching her?

The thought swarmed around her head like a cloud of midges. He'd seen her try and wake up Malcolm; what else had he seen? He'd said he had more important things to worry about than the lives of mortals – but that was not, she realized, the same thing as saying that he wasn't interested, or that he wasn't watching.

She shivered.

'You all right there, Moira Jean?' Mr Galbraith asked. The two of them were in one of the barns up at Drewitts, up to their elbows in sacks of oat seeds. The sowing would begin soon, and they needed to make sure the seeds they had stored were fit for planting.

She started, flicking seeds across the floor. 'Aye, thank you.'

'Only you came over fair strange just now,' he said.

'I was only thinking,' she replied, attempting a smile.

'Not worried about our Duncan, are you? He'll pull through. He woke up this morning, and—'

Moira Jean yanked her hands out of the seeds and glared at Mr Galbraith. 'And you didn't *tell* me?'

Mr Galbraith stared at her. 'I didn't think to . . . you're not sweet on him, are you? He'd be a fine match for you.'

'No! I only fished him out of a *well*, Mr Galbraith, I think that gives me a right to know what—'

'Christ alive,' Mr Galbraith muttered. 'Help me finish this, and then you can away to see him. We've work to do, you've no time to go tearing off all over Brudonnock.'

Smarting, Moira Jean turned back to the seeds, working through the bag in moody handfuls. She was bursting to go and talk to Duncan; he had to remember something of The Dreamer. It was ridiculous that she had to make sure none of the seeds had rotted when the fate of half the village was at risk – and, she thought, glaring at the sacks lined up in front of her, it was ridiculous that Mr Galbraith thought she was sweet on Duncan. Just yesterday, everyone had been convinced that he had run off to Glasgow to marry Martha. Moira Jean knew that she shouldn't be annoyed about that, but the inconsistency of the stories the Fae had spun was really starting to grate on her. And that was saying nothing of Angus. Did they really think she would forget him so quickly?

The moment she was done, she flung herself out the door and sprinted down the hill to the McLeods' cottage. Clutching a stitch in her side, she hammered on the door until Mrs McLeod answered it.

'Mr Galbraith said—' Moira Jean gasped, still out of breath.

Mrs McLeod gave her a watery smile. 'Aye, he's awake. Have some water before you come in, Moira Jean. You're a wee bit flushed.'

Moira Jean gulped down the cup of water and went into the cottage. The door to Duncan's box bed was open; Moira Jean ran straight to him, footsteps ringing across the stone floor. He was propped up on pillows and swathed in blankets, his face pale, but he smiled when he saw her. 'Moira Jean! What're you doing here?'

Moira Jean dragged a chair to his bedside and sat down. 'I'm here to see you, of course,' she said. 'Are you well?'

Duncan beckoned her closer. 'I have had some laudanum, Moira Jean,' he slurred, 'and I like it a lot.'

She let out a shaky laugh. Duncan was safe, he was himself, and he was stretching out the sound every time he said the letter 'L'. 'So I see. You scared us half to death down that well, you know.'

'Did I?' He reached for her. It seemed like he was trying to pat her hand, but he ended up slapping her knee instead. 'Don't you be worrying about me. I'm very tough. I was in the war, have I said?'

'Aye, Duncan, you've said.'

'Because I was,' he insisted. 'It's how my foot got all mashed about.' He wriggled his arms out from under the blankets and gestured at the bandages. 'I didn't do this down the well. It was in the—'

'In the war, aye.' She hesitated. 'Duncan,' Moira Jean began, 'how exactly did you get down there?'

He shrugged, bunching up the pillows. 'No idea. Last thing I remember is going into the woods. And . . . dancing. Then you and your lantern and your rope. I didn't like coming back up, Moira Jean. All that swinging.'

'Dancing? You remember the dance?'

Duncan screwed up his eyes. 'Aye, parts of it. God, it was such a dance. And there was . . . there was a man.'

Moira Jean lowered her voice. 'What did he look like?'

'I . . . I don't know. Beautiful. But . . . I don't know how.'

A sense of urgency was filling her up. 'Did you see the others? Were they dancing too?'

Duncan yawned. 'Others? What others?'

'The rest of us!' she hissed. 'You know – Callum, Jim, Martha, Fiona! Did you see them, Duncan?'

'Moira Jean?' Mrs McLeod asked, and Moira Jean jumped. She'd forgotten that Mrs McLeod was there. 'Why're you asking about that? You know where they are. Callum and Jim are up in the hospital, Martha's off in Glasgow with her new fellow, and Fiona's in Edinburgh.'

'She's not,' said Duncan, his eyes fluttering shut. 'She's here.'

Moira Jean gasped. 'Duncan, what do you—'

'Fiona? Fiona!'

There was shouting coming from outside. Duncan fell asleep. Moira Jean and Mrs McLeod exchanged a look. Both of them went to the door of the cottage, nerves mounting in Moira Jean's chest.

Mrs MacGregor was running down the slope of the village. She skidded to a halt, laughing, and threw her arms around a figure that had just stepped off the Aberdeen road. The figure was laughing too, and smiling, and it was only when Moira Jean saw the glint of sunlight on golden hair that she registered who it was.

Fiona had returned.

Fiona had returned, and it was all that Moira Jean could think about.

She could hear her laughing from inside the MacGregors' cottage. It sounded like her laugh had always done: a peal of giggles that became more breathless the harder she laughed. Moira Jean had tried to see her, but when she'd knocked on the door Mrs MacGregor had refused to let her in.

'For pity's sake, Moira Jean,' she'd snapped, 'will you not give us a moment to ourselves?'

She'd gone to Mrs Iverach's cottage instead, desperate for answers. The old lady had ushered her inside, and refused to let her speak until the door was barred with rowan and iron was lined up along every windowsill. Moira Jean fidgeted by the fireplace; she could feel the straw doll looking at her.

'You're making progress,' Mrs Iverach said, when the last nail had been placed against the glass. 'Young Fiona looks well.'

'That wasn't me!' Moira Jean burst out, 'I didn't do anything! She just showed up, I didn't have to bargain anything away this time. How could she – did she escape? Is that possible?'

'Wheesht!' Mrs Iverach hissed, waving at her to keep her voice down. 'Nellie MacGregor hears everything that's said in Brudonnock. You're sure you did nothing?'

Moira Jean let out a mirthless laugh. 'If anything, I've made things worse. I'm giving reading lessons to The Drea—'

'*Not in my house!*' Mrs Iverach spat, jabbing a finger at her. Her eyes were wild. 'I've been driven out of too many homes; I'll not lose another. Don't you call them here, Moira Jean, or you'll get no more from me!'

'All right, all right! I'm sorry.' Moira Jean hesitated. 'You . . . you don't mean you've met the Fair Folk before?'

'No. But I've seen their work, elsewhere. Your friends aren't the first to be taken.'

Moira Jean's stomach lurched. 'And that's how you lost your home?'

Mrs Iverach's jaw was tight. 'No. That was the landlords.'

Too late, Moira Jean remembered. She fell silent, shame coiled around her like a snake. Mrs Iverach's gnarled hands had curled into fists, and she was breathing hard. In her carelessness, Moira Jean had all but stuck her fingers into an open wound.

After a long pause, Mrs Iverach spoke again, her voice a little thick. 'Reading lessons?'

'Aye. It's a long story.'

She explained what had happened in the woods, embarrassment curdling in the pit of her stomach. Mrs Iverach pinched the bridge of her nose as she listened. 'God Almighty. I know you've a talent for trouble, Moira Jean, but this is . . .'

'*I* didn't know he'd—'

'Clearly,' Mrs Iverach snapped. 'But we've more important things to talk about. You're sure you've done nothing to set young Fiona free?'

Moira Jean nodded, still smarting. Mrs Iverach rubbed her chin, lost in thought.

'She could've escaped on her own,' the old lady mused, 'the old tales say it can be done. She could've made her own bargain. But the price she'd have paid, when the Fair Folk already have you dancing to their tune . . .' she sighed. 'It'll be high.'

Moira Jean shivered. The shadows suddenly seemed longer. She caught herself listening for Fiona's laugh again, desperate to see if she was all right.

Mrs Iverach leaned forward, lowering her voice. 'Talk to her,' she muttered, 'see what you can learn. She'll have given up something to get back here, but mind you be canny about it. She might not even know what was taken from her.'

The next few days were lost to the sowing.

At dawn every morning, Moira Jean trudged out to the fields with the rest of the villagers of Brudonnock. She craned her neck, trying to catch a glimpse of Fiona, but her blonde head was not there, and she had no time to slope back to the village and visit her once the sowing started. Hitching up the harrow and the massive seed drill to their shoulders, the villagers trudged up and down the ploughed fields, sowing oats and barley and planting potatoes and turnips while the larks sang overhead. With every step, she wished she was somewhere else. Her friends were missing; she shouldn't have to toil in the fields when she was the only one who could get them back. But she was the youngest, strongest person in Brudonnock, and without her, they would flounder. By the end of each day, Moira Jean's shoulders were screaming. Her back was purple with bruises.

Fiona had not joined them.

The first day, Mrs MacGregor had told them her daughter was resting. The second day, she'd said the same thing, but with a set to her jaw that Moira Jean did not like. She thought of Duncan, sleeping for a day after The Dreamer had returned him. Worry swarmed her thoughts. Was Fiona sleeping too?

By the time the sun set, Moira Jean ached all over. As they traipsed back down from the fields, Moira Jean caught up to Mrs MacGregor, but she brushed her aside, telling her that Fiona had a long journey and needed to recover. Moira Jean wanted to ignore her and barge right into the MacGregors' cottage, but she had no time. All the crops they'd sown belonged to Drewitts; the villagers would get a share for their winter stores, but most of the harvest would be sold off or sent south. Moira Jean needed to plant her own crops, or she and her mother would have nothing to eat. Her evenings were spent spreading compost across the garden, shoving seed potatoes into the lazy-beds, and trying not to pitch over face-first into the vegetable patch as she planted turnips, carrots and oats. She couldn't face playing The Dreamer's games when she was so tired.

It would have been easier if she'd had help. But she was alone. Her mother was still at Drewitts, her brothers and sisters had all moved away, her father dead. There was only her, and the mountain of work she needed to do to make sure that, come the summer, she would have something to eat. As much as she would've liked to have laid down on the grass and slept, she could not. She wasn't about to let her own mother starve.

It had been easier when Angus was alive. When he was *here*, and not stuck in the mud of northern France. He'd taken every opportunity to slope off and find her, ever since they were little. She could be elbow-deep in muck or crouched half-inside the henhouse and Angus would still sidle up to the fence, smiling that half-smile of his, and say 'Need a hand, Moira Jean?'

She could almost hear him. If she closed her eyes she'd see him, her last memory of him clear and cold as ice. Curls cut short by the recruiters, harvest tan not quite faded, he'd clutched her hands at the train station and promised he'd be back for her soon. He'd been smiling, but she'd felt the tremor in his fingers.

Moira Jean sat back on her haunches and wiped her eyes with the back of one filthy hand. The sun had set, painting Brudonnock in all the blues of the gloaming. Flies hung in the air. The village was quiet; everyone was too tired to stay awake for long. For a long moment, she stared in the direction of Angus's cottage, even though she knew that no one was coming.

He'd promised he'd come back.

She gave herself a shake. She fed the chickens, washed her hands, and went inside to make her supper.

On the third day of sowing, Fiona came to the north field.

Moira Jean's clothes were spattered with soil. She ached all over. A fine mist of rain hung in the air, making her fingers cold and the seed drill slippery to the touch. She was red-faced, sweating, and cursing Mr Brodie for not letting them have a cow to pull the seed drill. Surely *one* of them could be spared . . .

'Fiona! Fiona, what are you doing out of doors?'

Moira Jean nearly dropped the seed drill, her tiredness forgotten. She craned her neck to look, and relief washed over her. Fiona was walking along the edge of the north field, swathed in scarves, carrying a large pail. The rest of the villagers crowded around her, ignoring Mrs MacGregor's admonitions as they clamoured for a drink. Moira Jean hauled the seed drill up to the end of the field as quickly as she could – there was no sense leaving a job half-done – and then scurried over to Fiona before anyone could tell her that her turn wasn't finished.

Guilt blossomed in Moira Jean as she drew closer. She hadn't been to see The Dreamer for the past three days; she was exhausted, and afraid of being tricked into another fruitless bargain. But close to, Fiona looked more or less herself. She was perhaps a little paler than she had been – her eyes bright, her cheeks flushed. She was clearly feeling the chill; she had a heavy tartan shawl over her head and shoulders and clutched the iron handle of the bucket in a pair of thick leather gloves. Still, she smiled when she saw Moira

Jean. Hope sparked into life. It was five weeks to Beltane, now, and Moira Jean needed all the help she could get.

'You're a sight for sore eyes!' Fiona said, as she held out a cup to Moira Jean. 'I've not seen you since . . .'

She trailed off. Moira Jean's curiosity bloomed. What did Fiona remember? 'Aye,' she said, taking the cup and dunking it into the bucket, 'how long has it been now?'

Fiona's smile faltered. 'A fair while,' she said, recovering. Moira Jean watched her as she spoke, her eyes darting from Fiona's mouth, to her hands, to her feet. Fiona seemed just as she always had. There was no clue to what she had exchanged for her freedom. Dread uncurled in Moira Jean like billowing smoke.

'And how was . . . remind me where you were, again?' Moira Jean asked.

There. Fiona had kept her smile in place, but her hands tightened on the handle of the bucket. Moira Jean saw the smallest flash of panic in Fiona's green eyes as she glanced at her mother.

'Help me take this back to the dairy, Moira Jean,' Fiona said, loudly.

She thrust the bucket at Moira Jean and left the field, hugging her elbows. Moira Jean struggled after her, the damp soil clinging to her legs. Fiona was waiting for her just out of sight of the field, the smile gone from her face. Huddled into her shawl, she looked as if she could splinter at the slightest touch, like glass that already had a fracture.

'Can you keep a secret?' she whispered.

'Of course,' said Moira Jean, dipping the cup into the bucket, 'but have something to drink first. You look—'

Fiona snatched the cup out of Moira Jean's grasp and gulped

down the milk. She held it out for another; Moira Jean refilled it and Fiona drained the cup again. She shook off the glove, wiping her mouth with the back of her hand, licking drops of milk off her fingers. Fiona shook the cup at Moira Jean and knocked it back, gulping down the milk and holding out the cup for another refill. Moira Jean filled the cup again, and again, and again, until the bucket was empty. She looked away, her eyes burning. Had the Fae fed Fiona, in the five days she'd been away?

Fiona handed the cup back. She pulled on the glove again, her face flushed. 'Sorry, I – sorry. I'm fair starved, Moira Jean.'

'That's all right. What did you want to tell me?'

Fiona's eyes flicked to the north field and back. 'She doesn't like me talking about it.'

'About . . .'

'I don't know where I was.' Fiona's voice was cracked. She huddled into her shawl, clutching it against herself like a blanket. 'One moment I was here at the ploughing, then I was walking back along the Aberdeen road. There's nothing in between. I don't know where I was, or how long I've been away, or—'

'Wait a moment,' Moira Jean said, leaning forward. 'There's really—'

The bucket swung at Fiona's legs as Moira Jean moved. Fiona jumped back to avoid it, her face white. 'I – I – forget I said anything. Don't tell Ma.'

She started for the path back down to Brudonnock. Moira Jean made a grab for her arm. 'Fiona, wait!'

'Forget I said anything,' she repeated, shaking herself free. 'I don't . . . there's flashes of . . . I don't even know. I just – I'm away home.'

114

She left, huddling into herself. Moira Jean watched her go, still holding the bucket. Fiona's retreating back looked small, and scared, and alone.

They finished the last day of sowing when the sun was still high, and Mr Brodie brought them a pail of fresh milk from the dairy when they were done. Moira Jean could have drunk down the whole bucket, she was so hungry. But then she thought of Fiona, and stopped. She hadn't been able to talk to her since yesterday, though she'd glimpsed her pale face at the window of her cottage as she went back to the field that morning. Fiona had waved, a little nervously, but had refused to come out.

As soon as they'd cleared the equipment, Moira Jean would visit her. She helped Mr Brodie collect the cups and take them back to the dairy when they were done. A wind was beginning to gather, clouds tumbling across the sky. Moira Jean limped into the barns, her legs aching, her arms full and her hair a tangled mess of brown curls.

She deposited the cups onto an upturned crate and started wrestling her hair back into place while Mr Brodie went to wash out the pail. The calf she'd helped deliver was curled up in the corner of the birthing pen, sleeping in the straw. Its mother was nowhere to be seen.

'She'll not go near him,' came a voice.

Moira Jean started. Leaning on the fence of the birthing pen was a grey-skinned woman with a serene, heart-shaped face. Just over three feet tall, hair the colour of corn cascaded down her back, reaching almost to the floor. She wore a green earasaid draped over her shoulders, and even though she was only a few feet away, Moira Jean could not quite tell what the woman's dress was made of. Something prickled at the back of her neck. Moira Jean glanced down. Her stomach lurched. The woman did not have feet. She had hooves.

Moira Jean turned back to the calf, trying to seem calm. 'Is that so?'

'It is. She knows the calf has been marked. He is ours, now.'

'The Dreamer wouldn't take my gift,' said Moira Jean, doing her best to keep her voice mild. 'Not sure I'd call that marked.'

'A gift is a gift, whether or not it is accepted.'

Moira Jean sighed. The Dreamer hadn't even taken the poor thing, and she had still managed to hurt it. She straightened up. 'Well,' she said, going to fetch the bucket, 'I suppose that's one more thing I'm to fix.'

The woman put out a restraining hand. Her touch was as cool as stone. 'It is not your concern. It is mine.' She gazed at the small and lonely creature with something like a mother's love. 'I shall care for him,' the woman said.

Moira Jean's suspicion blossomed. What did she want with the calf? 'That's kind of you,' she said, wary.

The woman tilted her head. She was lovely, although Moira Jean supposed that she shouldn't have been surprised. The Fae seemed to have no interest in looking ordinary. Why would they be anything but beautiful?

'What is *kind*?' asked the woman.

Moira Jean sighed. 'You're not going to make this easy for me, are you?' she muttered.

The barn door opened and Mr Brodie came back in. He saw Moira Jean leaning on the fence of the birthing pen, and did not appear to notice the woman leaning beside her.

He nodded to the calf. 'His mother's taken against him, poor wee sod,' Mr Brodie said. 'He's muddling along all right, though. Have another cup of milk, Moira Jean. You look about to drop.'

Moira Jean staggered away from the fence – now that she'd stopped moving, she ached all over – and took the cup he offered. Behind her, the woman slid through the gaps in the fence, her body like water, and settled beside the calf. It laid its head in her lap, its large, dark eyes staring straight at Moira Jean.

Everything else forgotten, Moira Jean sprinted back down to the village and hammered on Mrs Iverach's door, ignoring the stares of her neighbours. The old lady opened it, took one look at Moira Jean, and hauled her inside.

'Into the chair while I—'

But Moira Jean was already slotting the rowan bar across the door. 'I'll help.'

The two of them worked quickly, yanking the curtains closed and lining up iron along the entrances to the little cottage. The nails slipped and rolled in Moira Jean's calloused, sweating hands, and every time they moved panic needled at her thoughts. If she dropped one, and it was lost, the lines barring the entrances to the Fae would be broken. The Fae could hear them, or slither up to the windows and peer inside, or skitter down the chimney and crane their too-long necks out from the fireplace, or slide their insidious fingers through the gap under the door . . .

Mrs Iverach set the last nail in place. 'I've a book for you and your reading lessons. It's on the table. Now, sit yourself down and have a wee bite to eat before you tell me what's wrong.'

She glared pointedly at the chair until Moira Jean took a seat, and handed her a bowl of boiled potatoes and a tiny sliver of butter. Moira Jean hadn't thought she'd be able to eat after meeting the Fae in the barn, but the moment the hot bowl was in her hands, instinct took over. The potatoes were gone in a matter of seconds. She sneaked a look at the book as she ate: *Tam Lin and Other Tales*. She remembered the name, and brightened; perhaps it would be useful to her.

Mrs Iverach blinked at her. 'You wee gannet,' she said, taking the bowl back. 'Still, at least the Fair Folk left you your appetite. All right, what's wrong?'

'There's one of them up in the dairy,' Moira Jean whispered. 'Just . . . just *there*.'

Mrs Iverach almost dropped the bowl. '*What*? What was it doing?'

'Nothing! Just fussing after the wee calf.'

'Let me . . . ah,' Mrs Iverach mused, setting the bowl aside. 'A bonny lass with grey skin and hooves, was it?'

Moira Jean started. 'Did you see her too?'

The old lady shook her head. 'I mind the old stories. That, Moira Jean, was—' She broke off, and mouthed the next words she spoke so they would not be heard. '— a glaistig.' Mrs Iverach glanced at the windows, then resumed talking. 'She watches over the cattle. She'll do no harm to you, if you do no harm to her. Set out a saucer for her, if you're worried,' she said, nodding towards the little dish of milk outside her own front door.

A little of the tension ebbed out of Moira Jean. 'So . . . so there's more than one kind?'

'Oh, aye,' Mrs Iverach replied. 'You know about—' Again, she mouthed the word rather than speak it aloud. '— brownies?'

Moira Jean nodded. They were house spirits, but she couldn't remember much more than that. Evidently it showed on her face, because Mrs Iverach continued.

'They'll keep your house if you'll set out a saucer of milk for them, but if you cross them, they'll smash and spill everything you own. The gift of clothes will send them on their way.'

Moira Jean dragged her chair forward, eager to learn more. 'Do you know of many others?'

Mrs Iverach rubbed her eyes. 'The names are all a wee bit jumbled. There's more kinds of Fair Folk than there are leaves on the trees. If one of them shows itself to you, you'll see them all.' She trailed off, lost in thought. 'You'll not be travelling soon, will you?'

'No idea. Why?'

'Keep an eye out for dogs,' Mrs Iverach said in a whisper. 'Green, or black, bigger than any you ever saw. Might be something wrong with their eyes. They're –' She mouthed the name again. '– the *cù sith*. They come for travellers. If they bark three times and you've not found shelter, you'll drop dead.'

Moira Jean shivered. The wind rattled the windows; she flinched. Suddenly the walk back to her own cottage seemed very long.

Mrs Iverach was still looking thoughtful. 'Only other one you want to know about is the kelpie,' she said, mouthing the name again. 'Don't hang about by the water. And if you see a horse or a man by the water's edge, just you away home quick as you can. It'll have you under the surface before you can blink.'

'They're not in wells, are they?' asked Moira Jean, unease trickling through her.

'No. Rivers and lochs, mostly.'

Moira Jean sagged with relief. There was a loch deeper in

the woods, but she hardly ever needed to go there. 'All right. Anything else?'

The old lady shook her head. 'Nothing clear. It . . . it was a long time ago I learnt of such things, Moira Jean, and it wasn't always prudent to tell the old tales. I mind what I can.'

'Mrs Iverach,' Moira Jean began, 'I never asked, but . . . how do you know all this?'

Mrs Iverach sighed, passing a withered hand over her face. 'I've lived a long life, Moira Jean. I've walked more paths than you'll ever know. There are . . . strange things, on the road. Some you can trust, and some you can't. Learn the difference, and learn it fast.'

Moira Jean's mother was out of quarantine at last.

She was waiting on the doorstep when Moira Jean got back home, and threw her arms around her daughter the moment she saw her. The top of her head clocked Moira Jean's chin. Moira Jean was bustled back inside to a litany of 'You've not been eating enough, hen, you know you're to keep your strength up for the sowing,' and spent the evening resisting the urge to straighten things while her mother boiled potatoes and cut slices of brawn.

But then the sky grew dark. Her dread gathered like storm clouds. She could not put it off any longer. The Dreamer was waiting in the woods.

She got into bed when the dishes were cleared away, telling her mother that she was too cold to undress. Then she waited. When her mother's breathing had become deep and slow, Moira Jean got up, snatched up the lantern, and slipped into the forest.

In Brudonnock, the nights were always alive. Bats skittered through the sky. Deer picked their way through the trees. She'd learned long ago to ignore the shrieking of foxes in the night. But as Moira Jean crept down the familiar path, the night did not just feel alive. It felt expectant.

She came into the clearing, and watched for The Dreamer's arrival. Rustling, chittering, darkness and shadows; then the shift of something under her feet. She kept her balance, this time, and saw him step into the mortal world.

It was not that the hillock cracked open, and The Dreamer stepped out of it. It was something just in front of it, some place in the air where the world grew thin. There was a haze like rising heat, a light, and then something that she couldn't quite focus on was pulled aside to make way for The Dreamer. He glided into the clearing while she was still trying to make sense of what she'd seen.

'I was beginning to think you would never show your face. In future,' he said, 'you shall inform me when you are not coming to seek my favour. I do not wait upon mortals.'

The words were out of her mouth before she could stop them. 'You know, it almost sounds like you missed me.' Her stomach swooped when she realized what she'd said. Disrespect would cost her an eye, or a tongue – or worse, the life of one of her friends. She softened it with a hasty smile, shifted the tension out of her stance. 'The feeling's mutual, of course,' she added, tilting her chin at him.

The Dreamer studied her for a moment, his eyes slightly narrowed. The shock of it hit Moira Jean like a slap. She could *see* his eyes. They held every colour she'd ever seen, swirling together like oil on water. The haze still clung to the rest of his features, like a veil she couldn't quite lift away.

For a moment she stared, mesmerised. Then, she realized he was smirking. 'Concentrate, Moira Jean,' he drawled. 'Begin your lesson.'

Moira Jean fished the book out of her bodice, face burning. She fetched a stick and started scratching letters in the dirt, feeling extremely stupid. She sounded them out to The Dreamer and handed him the stick so that he could copy them; he did not take it, but waved his hand and fresh letters appeared etched into the ground, far neater than Moira Jean had written them. He took to the sounds just as quickly, and soon Moira Jean was opening the book, her heart beating very fast.

She held the book open to the story of Tam Lin. 'You might know this one.'

The Dreamer drew closer. 'How is such a thing possible?'

'You're in it. Or your people are,' Moira Jean said, proffering the book with trembling hands. 'Look, I'll go over the words and read them aloud; you watch where I'm pointing so you can see what's what.'

'Your bargain is acceptable,' he said, stalking close enough to look over her shoulder. 'Begin.'

Moira Jean cleared her throat and began to read, pointing at each word as she did so. 'Once upon a time,' she began, 'there was a fair maiden named Janet. She grew up beside the forest of Carterhaugh, and was warned never to go there, for it was the home of many fey creatures.' There was an outburst of chittering from the trees around the clearing, and The Dreamer's head twisted too far around to stare at her. 'One such creature,' Moira Jean continued, her mouth very dry, 'was Tam Lin, who was lovelier than a sunrise and would steal the heart of any maiden who strayed into the woods, if they did not leave him a gift.'

The Dreamer settled back, mollified. Moira Jean thought she saw a flash of scales creeping up his neck, fading away as he turned his head back to look at the book.

She took a deep breath, willing the page not to flutter as she turned it. 'One night, Janet lost her way and was soon among the trees. Tam Lin appeared and demanded his due, and, having nothing to give, fair Janet parted with the most precious gift a young and unmarried maiden could offer – oh.'

Moira Jean stopped, blushing. She could *feel* him looking at her. He was going to ask her what it meant, she knew it, and then she'd have to explain and just the thought of saying it out loud while he smirked at her was making her want to catch fire to save herself the embarrassment.

The Dreamer's eyes gleamed. He laid a slow hand on the back of Moira Jean's neck, playing with curls of her hair too fine to be caught up into her bun. 'And what gift was that?' he asked.

Moira Jean shivered, clearing her throat. 'No idea. Shall I . . .'

He ran his hand across the back of her neck, lingering on one shoulder as he prowled behind her like a wolf. 'Go on.'

'As the months went by, Janet came to know that soon, she would be a mother, and set out in search of the father. Among the trees of Carterhaugh, she found Tam Lin, and asked him to return home with her to raise his child. But alas, he could not, for he revealed he was but a mortal man, bound by a curse to serve the Queen of the—'

The clearing erupted into inhuman shrieks. The Dreamer's hand on her shoulder tightened, his long, fine fingers suddenly ending in the sharp, curved talons of an owl. '*Enough*,' he hissed.

Fear lurched through her. The Dreamer's talons scraped across her skin, her thin cotton shirt starting to tear. 'Sh-should I stop?'

From behind her, The Dreamer muttered, 'You do not speak that name. You are not worthy of it.'

'. . . right. I'll . . . I'll just . . .' she cleared her throat and resumed reading, trying not to feel the scrape of claws breaking her skin. 'Bound by a curse to serve . . . someone,' she said, 'and unless Janet could set him free, he would be taken as part of the fairy tithe, and lost to her forever.'

The claws dug into her shoulder again, uncomfortably close to the base of her neck. His other hand curled around her throat, tilting her head up as she tried not to breathe too deep into those curved talons. He leaned down to whisper in her ear, his measured, even tone doing nothing to calm her racing heart. 'Careful, Moira Jean. You are safe if you are ignorant. Do not stray too close to that which you do not understand.'

Moira Jean stared out across the clearing. The ring of shadows had grown, spilling up into the trees and rushing across the forest floor, barely three feet away from the hem of her skirts. The Dreamer had mentioned the tithe before, and a dangerous curiosity sparked up at the word. Moira Jean needed to know what that meant, but now, with her pulse twitching underneath the point of a talon, was not the time to ask.

Pushing back her fear as much as she could, she cleared her throat. 'I'll never finish the story if you keep on like this,' she said, fighting to keep the tremor from her voice.

The clawed hands withdrew. Moira Jean gasped with relief, her shoulders heaving.

'S-so. Um . . . all right, here we are.' She gave herself a little shake, willing herself not to think about claws at her throat. 'But all was not lost for fair Janet. The next night, Tam Lin would ride in a procession for . . . for someone,' said Moira Jean, glossing over the words 'Queen of the Fairies' before The Dreamer noticed, 'and if she could but pull him down from his white horse and hold him tight, he would be saved. In her arms, the fairy magic would change him from a man to a bear, from a bear to a snake, from a snake to a living coal, and if she would only keep her grip until she could plunge him into the water, he would return to the shape of a man and be hers forever.'

Moira Jean hesitated. She looked up at The Dreamer. 'That's true, isn't it?' she asked. 'You really can change your appearance.'

At once, the haze lifted. Moira Jean saw the profile of a man, and despite herself, her breath caught. The Dreamer's face was strong, angular, with cheekbones so sharp she wanted to reach out and touch them. Despite his sheet of white hair, his brows and eyelashes were shadow-black, his lips full and pink. He still hadn't got the eyes right – colours swirled together, shifting so fast it hurt to look – but at last, he looked human. But then, he turned to face her. As his head moved, his features darkened, swirled, rippled. His eyes vanished into dark pits half the size of his face, his nose fused with his top lip and sharpened to a long, cruel point, his hair rippled into sheets of long, dark feathers. Fear grabbed Moira Jean by the throat. The words shrivelled up on her tongue. She was staring into the face of a monstrous, misshapen owl.

Moira Jean swallowed. Her mouth was very dry. The Dreamer's beak gleamed, sharp as a knife. 'You know,' she said, her voice faltering, 'you're far more handsome as a man.'

He turned back to the book, the feathers melting away. 'Continue,' he ordered.

'Right. Right, of course,' she stammered, trying not to think about the pits where The Dreamer's eyes had been.

'The fateful night came, and Janet hid herself away in Carterhaugh. She saw Tam Lin riding proud on his white steed in the procession and pulled him off his horse, clinging to him tightly. Under her hands, he changed into a bear, a snake, and countless other forms. Each one, Janet clung to, no matter the size or shape, until at last he was the shape of a burning coal. Though it burned her, Janet held tight until she reached the well and dropped him into the water, and at last the spell was broken. Released from his curse, Tam Lin returned to the shape of a man, and followed Janet home to be wed.'

Moira Jean wanted to throw up. The places on her shoulder where The Dreamer's claws had broken the skin were smarting. She passed a shaking hand over her face. The Dreamer, meanwhile, was peering at the book. 'And that is the end of the tale? None tried to take back the mortal Janet had stolen?'

'Aye,' said Moira Jean, resisting the urge to rub her neck.

'He was released, then,' The Dreamer said, wounded pride dripping from every word. 'The entertaining ones are always kept for Her amusement. No doubt that was why the challenges were set for this Janet. A spectacle was all the two of them were good for.'

Moira Jean bit back a small smirk. 'She *won* him back.'

The Dreamer made a noise of disgust. 'She had iron in her soul,' he spat, 'as do you. Only one so riddled with iron would dare such disrespect.'

She looked up. The Dreamer's face was still mercifully human. 'You don't like iron, do you?'

'You know the answer to that question,' The Dreamer said. He waved a disdainful hand towards the medal on her shawl. 'You are already using it against me.'

'I'd never dream of it,' Moira Jean lied.

'Then cast that thing aside and submit to me as my servant,' The Dreamer ordered. 'If you wish to prove your loyalty, you shall do as I command.'

Moira Jean felt a spark of irritation. Before it began to burn, she remembered The Dreamer's wrath, the scratch of talons on her skin. She plastered on the most charming smile she could muster. 'Ah, you don't want *me* as a servant. I'm sure you deserve far better.'

'You are correct. And yet you must serve me, for there is no one else.'

'There's my *friends*,' Moira Jean spat.

The Dreamer waved a dismissive hand. 'They are for my amusement. *You* are a servant. Be content with this honour.'

Moira Jean reached for her pride; she needed something to stave off the fear. She snapped the book shut. 'Oh, aye, that'll keep me warm at night,' she muttered, with more bravado than she felt. She held the book out. 'Look, I've shown you how to start. Take this, and practise all you like. You picked it up quicker than I did, you'll be fine.'

The Dreamer accepted the book, turning it over in his long, elegant hands. He turned it again, and it was gone. 'No doubt I shall master it soon enough,' he said, sounding almost bored. 'You may continue to bring me books, as a sign of your contrition, but I have no need of further teaching. You are not released from our bargain, but I shall allow you to make another.'

'Well, aren't you generous.'

'I am. And, you shall take this.'

One of the long, black owl feathers sprang up from the ground and leapt into his hand. It bulged, twisted, colour

127

rippling along its length until he was holding a perfect red rose. Moira Jean stared at it – it had been part of him, just moments before. The colours seemed startlingly deep and bright against his pale, insubstantial fingers, the thorns wickedly sharp. Despite her fear, she found herself reaching for it. It was the first fresh flower she had seen all year, so beautiful she wanted to hold it to her cheek.

'Take this,' The Dreamer repeated, holding the flower up between them. 'I shall use it to summon you. You will come when I call, Moira Jean. You are my servant. Remember your place.'

Duncan's leg would not be amputated.

Moira Jean's mother visited him the next morning, her doctor's bag in hand. She'd determined there was only a minor break, checked for fevers, and pronounced him out of danger. She'd bound up his foot as best she could, elevated it, and went round to the smithy to berate Malcolm for leaving it so long before he did anything.

She was still angry with him when she returned. 'That Malcolm MacGregor,' she muttered, as Moira Jean put a bowl of porridge in front of her. 'To leave poor Duncan like that just because he didn't want to look at it! All he needs is to rest it.'

'Did you tell Mrs McLeod?' Moira Jean asked.

'Oh, aye. She's round there now, giving Malcolm a piece of her mind. It's not a bad break – it'd be no trouble at all if it weren't for the polio. But that's another week Duncan'll need to stay in bed now. And Mrs Iverach has been round, telling her to hide it in case the family finds out and turns them both out of their cottage. She's out of her mind for worrying.'

Moira Jean went cold. 'D'you think they'd do it?'

'I don't know, hen. It's happened before – but not for a long time,' her mother said, catching sight of Moira Jean's expression. 'A lot's changed since Mrs Iverach was young. They'll be all right.'

Moira Jean scarfed down her porridge and went to see Duncan. She took the rose with her, tucking it into her hair because it stuck out of her pockets and she feared to break it. She had no idea what she was supposed to do with it, or how it would allow The Dreamer to call her, but she didn't want to risk finding out what would happen if she ignored his summons.

Duncan was lying in his bed, still very pale. In the shadows at the other end of the box bed, Moira Jean could just make out his bound foot, propped on the old sewing machine crate. But he raised his head when she came in, wincing, his shoulders shaking with the effort.

'Moira Jean?'

She pulled up a chair and sat beside his bed, trying to smile. 'How're you feeling?'

Duncan groaned. 'Awful. My feet hurt like you'd not believe.'

'Both of them?'

'Aye. The other one's a wee bit bruised.'

'D'you want something for it?' Moira Jean asked, looking around for where Mrs McLeod kept the laudanum.

He gritted his teeth. 'Your ma said I've to wait a few more hours.'

'Ah. You know Fiona's back?' she said, hoping a change of subject would take Duncan's mind off the pain.

'Aye, Ma told me. Where was she?'

'No clue,' she said, watching his face very carefully. 'D'you know?'

Duncan frowned. His eyes came a little unfocused, but

whether that was from the pain or the effects of the Fae's curse, Moira Jean could not say. 'No,' he mused, 'no, I . . . south, wasn't it? Somewhere in the Borders?'

'Did she not say, when she came to see you?'

'Oh, she's not been yet,' said Duncan. 'Malcolm was round earlier to take the horseshoe off the door, though.'

Moira Jean was taken aback. 'She's not been by once?'

'At least, not that I know of. I might've slept through it. I know you've all been at the sowing, and Ma said she's not been well since she came back, so . . .'

He trailed off. His expression was carefully unperturbed, all the worry painstakingly smoothed off his face. Moira Jean knew that look well; Duncan had worn it after Edgar Fitzherbert had sent back his last letter, unopened.

'D'you want me to speak to her?' Moira Jean asked. 'I was going to visit her after my shift in the dairy, it's no trouble.'

'No, no. I'm not much company, anyway. I've not been sleeping well. Bad dreams. I suppose it's the laudanum.'

Moira Jean thought of The Dreamer, and fought back a shiver. 'What kind of dreams?'

'Dancing, mostly. Sometimes there's a black horse, or a river flowing right the way through the village. Oh, sometimes you're there, with an angel standing over you.'

She thought of Angus. Her heart twisted. 'You . . . you don't mean . . .'

The colour drained out of Duncan's face. 'No, it's not . . . he's not . . . ah, I'm sorry, Moira Jean. I didn't think.'

'It's all right,' she mumbled.

'They're just dreams,' Duncan said in a rush, 'and not even good ones. That angel's got hair like a lass and teeth like you've never seen before. It doesn't mean anything.'

A chill crept into Moira Jean's thoughts. Suddenly she could feel the rose in her hair, and all the thorns along its stem. Duncan was not seeing an angel.

Had she been inside when the heavens opened, Moira Jean never would have seen the hound.

She was on top of the hill, just beside the dairy, her hands cramping from a morning of endless milking. Already, the distant peak of Ben Macdui was lost in purple-grey clouds. She could smell the change in the air; it must already be raining on the other side of the mountain. She hurried down the hill. Brudonnock wasn't that far off. If she was lucky, she'd be able to make it back home before she was caught in the downpour . . .

That was when it began to rain.

Rain crashed over her in a wave. There was no point running for cover; this far from the forest, there was none to be had. Moira Jean stopped halfway down the hill, swore listlessly at the clouds, and kept going. She snatched the rose out of her hair, ramming it down her shirt before it could get lost. Within seconds her hair was dripping, her feet were soaked and the water was starting to seep through her shawl. Mud slithered under her feet. Soon, she told herself, she'd be in front of a roaring fire, the smell of peat smoke warming her from the inside . . .

She turned.

There was a shape, high up on the hilltop. It stood on four legs, watching her, but through the haze of rain she could not quite tell what it was. It was vast and hairy, and seemed untroubled by the water. It let out an enormous bark, echoing all around the hillside, and Moira Jean relaxed.

She held out a hand and whistled. 'Come on! Come here, there's a good lad.'

The dog didn't move. It kept watching her.

'I'm not waiting out in the rain for you to make up your mind.'

The dog kept staring.

'Ah, suit yourself,' she said, and turned for home again. She trudged through the rain, shivering, concentrating on not slipping on wet grass or tangling her feet in damp heather encroaching on the path. When she finally made it to Brudonnock, she was soaked through. She squelched through the front door, wringing out her wet hair.

'Moira Jean!' her mother scolded. 'You're tracking mud all over my floors. Take your shoes off, you wee heathen.'

Moira Jean took off her shoes and dripped over to the fire, shivering. She took off the rest of her clothes and spread them on the clothes horse, trapping herself behind screens of wet and steaming wool. The Dreamer's rose was not even damp. It lay on the stone hearth, glistening blood-red.

'There's a dog up on the hill,' Moira Jean said, pulling the pins out of her damp curls. 'Nobody's lost one, have they?'

'I've not heard anything. Did you get a look?'

'No. Loud bastard, though.'

'Moira Jean!'

She held up a hand from behind her clothes fort. 'I'm sorry, I'm sorry! He *was* loud, though. You must've heard him.'

Her mother brandished a duster at her. 'The only thing I've heard, Moira Jean, is foul language from you. I'll not hear it again.'

The rain hissed against the thatch. Moira Jean frowned. 'You really didn't hear him?' She struggled out from behind the arrangement of drying clothes, almost tripping on her way to the window. She pointed at a black mark on the hillside, a smear of shadow under the woodpigeon-grey sky. 'Look, you can almost see him from here.'

Her mother flapped a shawl at her. 'Come away from the window, for heaven's sake! You're in your linen. Anyone could see you . . .'

'It'll just get wet. Ma, look out the window. He's up there.'

Her mother bustled her away from the glass. When Moira Jean had been buffeted back behind the clothes horse, she turned to look. 'I can't see him. He must've gone for shelter.'

The dog was still clearly visible on the hilltop. 'What're you talking about? He's right there.'

Her mother looked again. 'I can't see anything.'

'But . . .' Moira Jean's eyes fell on the rose. A sudden chill stole through her. She remembered Mrs Iverach's warning about the *cù sìth* and shivered. Meeting the glaistig had been strange enough, and she was only a kind of cattle guardian. The world outside the window suddenly seemed vast and threatening, and though her mother was standing beside her, she felt so alone.

Then, an idea struck her. She walked over to her still-damp skirt and fished out the hagstone. She held it up to her eye, trying for a playful smile, though her palms were prickling with sweat. 'Look through this.'

Her mother snorted. 'I thought you'd grown out of such nonsense.'

'It's only a wee bit of fun,' Moira Jean said, fighting to keep the strain out of her voice. 'We're neither of us heading out in this.'

'Fine.' Her mother held out her hand, and Moira Jean scrabbled the stone into it. She held it up to her face, peering through the hole in the middle. 'Happy?'

Desperate hope was writhing through Moira Jean's thoughts. 'You're to look out the window with it, Ma.'

Her mother sighed, and turned to the hillside. There was silence. Moira Jean gasped, pressing her hands to her mouth. Had it—

'Would you look at that. Nothing but rain.'

Moira Jean whirled around before her mother saw her face. Her disappointment could have choked her. She checked under her eyes; no tears yet, but she could feel them prickling.

Her mother came closer. 'You all right there, hen?'

'Just a wee bit of smoke in my eyes, Ma,' she said. She turned back around, smiling. Anxiety rippled across her mother's face.

'Mrs Iverach didn't give you this, did she?'

'Aye, she did.'

Her mother handed back the hagstone. Over her shoulder, the dog was still visible on the hillside, lurking under the shadow of darkening clouds. How could she not have seen it?

'It's good of you to spend time with her, love, but . . .' her mother sighed. 'She's had a hard life, and copes with it in strange ways. You've no need to follow her example.'

Moira Jean shook her head. 'It was only the smoke. I'll be fine.'

'I'll be the judge of that, thank you,' her mother replied. She examined Moira Jean critically. 'And I'm cutting your hair.'

Moira Jean laughed, relieved for the change of subject. 'Are you now?'

'Aye. You're shaggy as anything. Into the chair with you.'

Moira Jean rolled her eyes, dragged a wooden chair over to the window and sat in it. Her mother stood behind her and started brushing out her hair. The slow, even strokes were more familiar than a lullaby. Moira Jean closed her eyes.

134

A memory stirred. Angus, laughing. They were lying in the grass, the sun low in the sky. He'd propped himself up on one elbow to look at her, and his dark eyes were shining. He'd persuaded her to take her hair down and now, his hands were buried in it. 'There's just so much of it,' he'd said, smiling, 'how'd you cram it all into that wee bun?'

Her mother stopped brushing. Moira Jean's eyes were squeezed shut. 'Take it off,' she said, through clenched teeth.

'What was that?'

Moira Jean cleared her throat. 'Cut it all off, Ma. I . . . I don't want it.'

There was a *chink* as her mother laid the scissors down. 'Where's this come from?'

'I just . . . I just want something different.'

'I'll not do it when you're upset,' said her mother, her voice careful.

'I'm not upset,' Moira Jean insisted.

'You're just like your father,' her mother muttered. Moira Jean felt a twinge of lonely pride. Her mother laid a hand on her shoulder. 'But d'you really just want a haircut, love, or do you want something else?'

'Like what?'

'Well, I know you and Angus always talked about leaving Brudonnock, and—'

Moira Jean stood up. She snatched up her stays and pulled them on, then her shirt, then her petticoats and stockings. Her fingers trembled. She didn't want to leave Brudonnock. She wanted to *have left* Brudonnock, with Angus by her side, her friends safe in their homes, and no knowledge of the things that lurked in the woods. She shook her head. How could she even think of leaving now? What right did she have to leave her neighbours to struggle, when she was the reason their children could not help them?

'Put another brick on the fire, would you, Ma?' she said, her voice too loud. 'It's cold.'

'Moira Jean . . .'

She pulled on her skirt, shoved her feet into newly-mended boots. Her shawl was draped across the clothes horse; she yanked it towards her, sending the clothes horse flying. Her mother was standing in the middle of the room, staring at her, but Moira Jean didn't dare meet her eyes. She would crack open if she tried.

She wrapped the shawl around her and scrabbled for the medal. 'I need the—'

'Here.' Her mother held out a hand, the medal lying in her palm. Moira Jean reached for it and her mother's hands closed over hers. 'This isn't what you need, hen.'

Her throat felt clogged. The gold of her mother's wedding ring glinted up at her. Moira Jean tore her hand away. Panic, anger, grief – she wasn't sure what she felt, only that she had to escape it.

She backed towards the door. 'I . . . I left something on the . . .'

'Moira Jean—'

'I'll be back soon.'

She left before her mother could stop her. Pulling her shawl up to cover her head, Moira Jean ran through the rain. She had no idea where to go. Memories of Angus pressed in on every side. The cottages they'd played in, shrieking and laughing with the other village children. The fences he'd leant against, trying to seem nonchalant and failing because they'd both been barely more than children when they'd caught each other's eye. The peat bog, which he'd fallen into once trying to win a race. The kirk, where they should've been married. The kirkyard, where he should've been buried. The Aberdeen road, which they should have walked hand in hand, Brudonnock shrinking into the distance. There was nowhere she could go where he would not follow. How long would she have to walk the same paths they'd trod, when they'd been so certain of their future together? She hated walking in that other girl's footsteps. She'd had everything, and now it was gone.

She burst through the rotting door of one of the abandoned cottages. Rain dripped through mouldering thatch, splashing on the bare stone floor. It was deserted, damp, and stank of old birds' nests. Despite it all, she felt a stab of relief. At least this place was different to how she remembered it, changed as she was.

Moira Jean took a deep, steadying breath. She was fine. She would be fine. All she needed was a few moments to put herself together, and then she'd be herself again. Everything would be fine, if she could only get a moment's peace . . .

She buried her hands in her pockets and closed her eyes, huddling against the cold.

Something stroked her fingers.

Moira Jean swore and yanked her hands out of her pockets. A bright shape slipped to the ground. She watched it fall, her heart beating so fast it felt like it was rattling.

The Dreamer's rose. It fell gracefully to the floor, and then, it spun.

He was calling her.

* * *

Moira Jean did not want to go and see The Dreamer. Not when sadness lay thick in her throat and Angus bubbled up to the surface of her thoughts. The Dreamer had seen far too much of her grief already, and the fascination lacing his words whenever he spoke about it made Moira Jean feel as though someone was looking over her shoulder.

But Beltane was drawing near. It was almost April: she had just over a month to get her other three friends back. As much as she did not want to see The Dreamer, she could not afford to stay away long.

So she went up to Drewitts to steal a book.

Getting into the house wasn't hard. She simply stuck her head through the back door and asked Mrs McGillycuddy if she needed a hand with anything. After insisting that Moira Jean take off her muddy boots in the kitchen, Mrs McGillycuddy handed her a pile of dust sheets and told her to cover up the furniture in the dining room. As she shook out the sheets over the vast, polished dining table, a familiar worry wormed its way into Moira Jean's head. If the Fitzherberts did not come back, what would keep the villagers of Brudonnock in their homes?

When she was finished, she crept into the library. It was still afternoon, but it was so dark it felt like midnight. All the windows had been shuttered for months and it was starting to smell damp. Skirting around the bulk of an armchair, Moira Jean squinted at the bookshelves in the light from the open door. The shelves had been covered up here, too, bookcases swathed in sheets so white it looked like they'd been buried in snowdrifts. She sidled up to one and lifted up the edge, reaching behind the cotton for the first book she could grab.

'Moira Jean?'

'*Christ!*'

Moira Jean flinched so hard her wrist smacked into the shelf. She flailed, nearly ripping the sheet off the bookcase as she tugged her arm free, dropping the book she'd only just picked up. Fiona was standing in the doorway, looking puzzled.

'You gave me such a start!' Moira Jean laughed, trying not to look guilty.

'What are you doing?'

'Checking for damp,' Moira Jean lied. 'You can smell it all the way out in the corridor.'

Fiona sniffed, and wrinkled her nose. 'So that's what that is.'

Moira Jean picked up the book she'd dropped and set it on the table, trying to look nonchalant. 'Aye. How are you, anyway? I've not seen you since the day before yesterday.'

'Oh, you know,' said Fiona, glancing over her shoulder.

'Duncan said he'd not seen you lately, either.'

'Did he?' Fiona shuffled into the room, still peering nervously down the corridor. Moira Jean dropped her shawl on top of the book while she wasn't looking. Fiona wouldn't tell anyone if Moira Jean stole something – she'd always been able to keep a secret – but it would weigh on her nevertheless.

Angus's medal clinked against the wood and Fiona flinched. She closed the door behind her, plunging the room into darkness. Moira Jean squinted as Fiona's footsteps grew closer, her heart beating very fast.

'Moira Jean,' Fiona whispered, 'I think there's something wrong with me.'

'Why?'

Fiona drew closer. All Moira Jean could see was the vague shape of her, but she felt Fiona's cool, strong fingers close over hers in the dark. Her mouth went very dry.

'There's . . . gaps in my memory,' Fiona whispered. 'I don't understand how, or why. Everybody says I've been away, but I remember the ploughing, and I remember walking back into the village, but everything else . . .'

Moira Jean squeezed her hand, trying not to think about how well their hands fit together when Fiona was so upset. 'There's nothing wrong with you.'

'There *must* be,' Fiona insisted. 'Why else can't I remember where I've been?'

'Well, d'you remember anything, or is it all just nothing?'

Fiona sighed. 'Nothing that makes any sense. Dancing. The woods. A tune that I could feel, just here.'

'I can't see where you're pointing. It's too dark.'

'Oh.' Fiona laid a hand over Moira Jean's heart. 'Here,' she said, and Moira Jean felt heat rising through her like a sunrise.

She cleared her throat, grateful it was too dark to see a blush. 'Dancing?' she croaked.

'Aye. And . . . and someone in white. I've not felt right since.'

Moira Jean stilled. The Dreamer. 'How d'you mean?'

Another sigh. 'Just . . . it's hard to say. I've no appetite. My dreams are strange. Nothing's quite as good as it used to be. It's . . . it's almost as if something's missing.'

Moira Jean felt a twinge of fear. What, exactly, had Fiona given The Dreamer in exchange for her freedom? What could she have parted with that left her so listless, so cold?

'Oh, Moira Jean,' said Fiona, and started to cry. 'I don't know what's wrong with me.'

'Hey, now,' Moira Jean soothed, putting her arms around her, 'it'll be all right.'

Fiona sniffled into Moira Jean's chest, while Moira Jean stroked her soft, blonde hair. In Moira Jean's arms, she seemed unbearably delicate. It seemed impossible that anyone would want to take anything from her.

Eventually they broke apart, Fiona still snuffling. Moira Jean picked up her shawl and the book underneath it, feeling slightly bereft. The two of them crept towards the door and stole out into the corridor, the book bundled up in Moira Jean's shawl.

Fiona dabbed at her eyes. 'Don't tell Ma. You know how she frets. Can you tell I've been . . .'

'No,' said Moira Jean, 'you're all right. Listen, why don't we see how Duncan is? It'll take your mind off things.'

'Not now,' Fiona said. 'I'd only cry.' She sighed, looping her arm through Moira Jean's. They headed back down to the kitchen, Moira Jean quietly envying Fiona's composure. It didn't look as if she'd been crying at all.

When Moira Jean arrived back at home, her mother was very careful with her. The conversation they'd had hung over their heads like clouds threatening rain.

'Just you sit yourself down there, hen,' her mother said, buffeting Moira Jean towards the edge of her box bed. 'I'll get the tea on.'

'Ma, I can help—'

'No, no! No need. I'll manage.'

Moira Jean stuffed the stolen book under her blankets as her mother boiled potatoes and turnips. She watched her mother work, those gentle hands marked with a thousand tiny burns and cuts that had long since scarred over. When their food was ready, her mother watched Moira Jean eat, a flash of anxiety crossing her face whenever Moira Jean set down her spoon.

'I think I'll get an early night,' Moira Jean said, when she'd finished. 'D'you mind if I . . .'

'No, no! That's a good idea. Rest is what you need.'

Moira Jean climbed into bed, pulling the blankets up to her chin and closing the door of her box bed. She listened to her mother washing the pots and bowls, guilt rippling through her. Eventually her mother climbed into her own bed, closing the door behind her. Moira Jean waited until the sound of her mother's breathing slowed, then climbed out of her own bed. Slipping her feet into her boots, Moira Jean crept out of the door and into the forest.

Leaves dripped water onto Moira Jean's head. Damp pine needles clung to the soles of her boots. The rich smell of earth rose all around her. Above her head, bats fluttered between the trees, sending raindrops cascading down as they brushed past swaying branches. With her shawl pulled up to keep the rain off her hair, Moira Jean heard them far more than she saw them, vanishing in a flurry of wings out of the corner of her eye.

The clearing was painted in shades of grey, wet leaves glistening like oil. The moment she set foot inside, shadows rippled around the circle of trees. Chittering and clicking echoed on every side, and The Dreamer appeared before her. His face was still partially obscured by the haze that clung to him, and she felt a stab of annoyance. He'd shown her his face already, why was he hiding it now? But even through the veil, she could tell that the rain left no mark on him. His long, white robe was just as perfect as ever, although she couldn't quite tell how it was stitched together.

'This is an improvement,' he said. 'You *are* capable of showing the proper respect.'

Water dripped onto Moira Jean's nose. Her clothes were already damp again, and she prayed the dye on the cover of the book wouldn't bleed onto her shirt. She fished out the book, trying not to look The Dreamer in the eye, and handed it to him. It vanished the moment he accepted it. 'Did you call me all the way out here in the rain just to see if it would work?' she said.

'For loyalty to be proven, it must first be tested.'

Her temper flared. 'I better have bloody passed,' she muttered. 'So did you want me for anything, or can I go?'

The Dreamer tilted his beautiful head. She caught a glimpse of his strong brows as he frowned at her, confused. 'What work could be more important than this? You have been granted a rare gift, Moira Jean. Be grateful.'

'Aye, well,' she grumbled, huddling deeper into her shawl, water dripping from her nose, 'it's hard to be grateful in the rain.'

'Is that your concern?'

The Dreamer waved a hand. There was a flurry of unnatural shrieks. Shadows bubbled and rippled out towards her. The darkness reared up like a wave, ready to crash over her. Moira Jean shrank back, waiting for it to hit—

Nothing happened.

A rippling canopy of shadow was suspended over her head. Every so often, it twitched. She could not see the trees or the stars above, but nor could she feel the rain. Dread settled into the pit of her stomach. This was no kindness.

'I suppose you'll want something for this,' she said. 'Not that I asked for it, mind.'

The Dreamer smiled. It slid across his face like a knife.

'You do not use my proper titles,' he mused. 'Why is this?'

143

Bloody titles, Moira Jean thought, trying not to let it show on her face. 'Well, you've got so many to choose from,' said Moira Jean, trying to sound charming. 'I picked the one I liked best. Why . . . why do they call you The Dreamer?'

His eyes were fixed on her. Colours flashed through them, roiling together like the shine of oil on water. She thought of Duncan and Fiona and the strange dreams they had complained of, and wondered what terrible and wondrous things they saw when they closed their eyes. 'They call me many things,' he said, 'for I have many dominions. Recognize them.'

'Exc—' Moira Jean clapped her hands over her mouth before she could complete the phrase *excuse me*. There was a flash of teeth in The Dreamer's grin, and the haze across his features parted. Not teeth, Moira Jean realized. Spines.

'You are learning,' he murmured. 'Good. I have no use for a stupid servant.'

Moira Jean took a deep breath, struggling to keep a lid on her temper and her fear. The needle-like teeth vanished behind full, human lips, and once she could not see the spines it was hard to remember that they had ever been there. 'What did you mean by that?'

The Dreamer stalked closer. 'In exchange for the shelter I have provided you, you shall thank me. You shall say "Thank you, my lord", and you will know your place.'

Moira Jean tried to tell herself that recognizing his titles would mean nothing. Words were words, and nothing more. But The Dreamer was standing over her, a cruel smile on his lips, hunger radiating off him in waves. The suggestion of sharp cheekbones was somewhere behind the haze obscuring his features; as much as she feared him, she wished she could see his face clearly one more time. The longer she looked at him, the more she wanted to reach out and brush the haze aside.

But even though looking at him was like trying to see through morning mist, she could tell how much he craved to hear the words from her. He was bending over her, standing like a gnarled old tree, his elegant hands all but grasping at her dress. He didn't just want to hear her grovel for the sake of his pride. He needed it.

She could use that.

'I know my place well enough,' said Moira Jean. 'And I know that it's worth more than shelter from the rain. If you want me to thank you and call you "my lord" – and it's just going to be the once, mind – then you'll give me back another of my friends.'

The Dreamer laughed, careless and dismissive. 'Do not flatter yourself, Moira Jean. Your obeisance is not worth a mortal life.'

Disappointment slashed through her. There was just over a month until Beltane, she couldn't afford another empty bargain. Moira Jean thought fast. 'Fine. Then you'll owe me a favour.'

He went still. There was an explosion of chittering over Moira Jean's head. She did not look up. She kept her gaze fixed on The Dreamer's ever-shifting eyes.

'I have already given you more than shelter,' The Dreamer said, as though he was weighing the price of each word. 'I have given you a companion.'

Moira Jean glared at him. 'She made a bargain of her own. You had nothing to do with it. And whatever you took from her, I'll find a way to give it back. She's not . . . she's not the same.'

The Dreamer smiled like he was unsheathing a knife. 'Mortals rarely are, after seeing my realm. Are you not happy,

Moira Jean? Is seeing the face of your friend not worth far more than a favour?'

'No. Not when she's like this.'

The smile vanished. 'What favour?' he asked, his voice cold.

'That's not for you to decide.'

The Dreamer considered her. He was close enough that she could have reached out and placed a hand on his chest. His long, white robe made him look like a wraith fresh from the tomb. Moira Jean was sure that if she tried, her fingers would pass right through him.

'I accept,' he said. 'But when I have granted your request, that shall be the end of this particular bargain. Your friends are part of another; remember that.'

Moira Jean started. She hadn't thought The Dreamer would take her up on her offer. Fear flickered through her. Was she giving up more than she knew? What should she ask for in return?

The Dreamer came even closer. His white robe was brighter than moonlight. His hunger was infectious; it was gnawing at her. Slowly, he reached out, pulling the shawl away from her face. It slid over her hair, the damp air suddenly tangling itself in her curls.

'Now,' he said, his voice low and cruel, 'say it.'

Moira Jean's face was burning. The Dreamer's beauty was like a weapon; it made her into something that could be cut down to size. Her tongue seemed heavy in her mouth. But then, her fury ignited, crackling through her veins like fire through dry bracken. She'd show him *exactly* what it meant for him to lord his titles over her.

She licked her lips. He watched the movement of her tongue like a cat.

Moira Jean took a deep, steadying breath. She'd make him pay. But first, she had to get it over with.

'Thank you, my lord,' she said, through gritted teeth.

The Dreamer's smile widened. His eyes glittered. The creatures over her head shrieked and howled. Moira Jean flinched; she'd forgotten she'd had an audience. The thought alone made her want to crawl into the earth and hide.

The Dreamer ran a long-fingered hand through her hair. His palm was cold, the touch of his fingers more like stray leaves than flesh. 'You have done well. Ask for your reward, my servant.'

Moira Jean clenched her fists. 'I want your solemn oath that you'll never, ever cause me harm. No more talk about . . . about ripping out eyeballs, or tongues, or anything like that. I want you to swear by all that you hold dear, that I will be safe from you.'

The Dreamer's hand curled into a fist, gripping a chunk of her hair. It did not hurt, but it was starting to pull. 'A high price.'

She glared up at him, her cheeks still hot. 'You and I made a bargain as equals. Of course the price is high.'

His lip curled. 'As you wish.' He leaned forward, whispered in her ear. 'I should have made you *kneel*.'

Moira Jean's hand shot out. Before she could stop herself she slapped him, right across the face. It felt like hitting dead meat, and when the blow landed, his features blurred.

The Dreamer's eyes vanished. At once his face was thrown into sharp relief, and she wished she had not seen it. It snapped into focus, suddenly long as a deer skull. His mouth fell open and kept on falling. Horns sprouted from the crown of his head. The fist still buried in her hair seemed to have twice as many fingers, and while it still did not hurt, his hand suddenly felt like a spider crouched on her scalp.

147

His voice groaned like rocks tumbling down the mountain-side. '*You dare to strike me?*'

Terror flooded through her. But her pride still burned, smouldering under the fear. And while she could feel the pulling at the roots of her hair, it did not actually hurt. She ground her heels into the dirt, forcing herself to look into his empty eye sockets. 'For a bargain to be proven, it must first be tested,' she said, fighting to keep the tremor out of her voice. 'You said yourself that you have no use for a stupid servant.'

The Dreamer stared at her, his empty eye sockets fixed on hers.

Then, he began to laugh. The delight in it shocked her; it was almost human, although there was a scrape to it that seemed to drag the sound across her spine. He drew his hand away – Moira Jean caught a glimpse of a few too many long, long fingers – running it down the length of her hair. The creatures over Moira Jean's head joined in, shrieking and clicking and chittering until the noise grew so loud, she had to press her hands over her ears. As he laughed, his monstrous face faded away, the horns retracted, and soon, he was beautiful again.

'I am glad, Moira Jean, that it was you I spared from the dance,' he said, his eyes glittering. 'You are a rare prize indeed.'

Moira Jean left the clearing. The Dreamer was still laughing.

When Moira Jean came back home, the cottage was still and dark. Moira Jean shut the door behind her as quietly as she could, slipped off her boots, and—

'Moira Jean? What are you doing up?'

Moira Jean flinched. The door to her mother's bed had swung open. A match hissed in the darkness; her mother peered at her with sleepy eyes.

'Nothing, Ma,' she said, trying to look calm and unruffled. 'I thought I heard a noise. There's no one there.'

She gave her mother a kiss and got back into bed, forcing herself to move slowly and calmly. While her mother got up to peer out of the window, Moira Jean stared up at the wooden roof of her box bed, thinking of The Dreamer. At last, she was safe from him. But at what cost? What had she taught him, by agreeing to his bargain? What else could she get, if she made another like it? She rolled over in bed, pulling the covers up to her chin. It felt as if she had stepped off a precipice, and she was frozen in the moment right before she found out if she would fall or fly.

The next morning, her mother insisted they check the house and garden, to see if they could find what had made the mystery noise the night before. Moira Jean had protested, blushing, but her mother was adamant. 'It's not like you to wake up in the night, hen,' she said. It was a still morning, swathed in a thick mist that made it impossible to see much. They peered at the cottage walls, roof and garden for almost fifteen minutes, embarrassment and guilt casting a pall over everything Moira Jean looked at. She wished she hadn't had to lie to her mother.

Eventually she managed to get away by saying she was needed up at the dairy. She knocked on the MacGregors' door as she passed; Mrs MacGregor shooed her away, saying Fiona was sleeping. Worried, Moira Jean climbed up towards the barns on the other side of Drewitts. A light was on in one of the attic windows of the big house, glimmering through the mist; Mrs McGillycuddy had guests. Perhaps there was work to be had. Hope sparked into life. It would be months until harvest came and they had something they could sell.

She trudged up the slope, the damp air clinging to her hair, and stopped.

Standing directly in front of her, half-hidden in the fog, was the enormous hound. It was the size of a cow, covered in shaggy hair the colour of seaweed. Something was dripping from its vast muzzle. Its eyes glimmered like pools of mercury.

With a jolt of fear, she recognized it. This was the dog she'd seen on the hillside, that only she had been able to see. It padded closer, scenting the air. Moira Jean kept absolutely still, all the bones in her legs turned to jelly.

She was sure The Dreamer had sent it.

It prowled around her, stopping to sniff her shoes, her hair. Its breath smelled like a peat bog. As it stalked behind her, she heard something that might have been a growl, or might have just been distant thunder. She forced herself not to bolt. If The Dreamer really had sent it, then it couldn't harm her, after the bargain she'd forced him to make. She swallowed. She had nothing to worry about.

The *cù sìth* came around to face her again, its vast bulk blocking the path up to Drewitts. It stared into her eyes, its nostrils twitching as it lowered its enormous head to snuffle at her hand. The motion was oddly familiar. Despite its powerful jaws – easily longer than one of Moira Jean's thighs – she wanted to place a hand between its ears and scratch. Would its fur be soft, or would it feel like digging her fingers into grass? She didn't dare move her hand and find out. Not with those jaws. It turned and stalked away, slipping between the cottages as though it was a creature half its size. Moira Jean watched it go, the blood rushing in her ears.

'Moira Jean?'

She jumped and staggered back, swearing, almost losing her balance. Mrs McGillycuddy was standing right in front of her, frowning, clutching her shawl about her. In the mist, Moira Jean hadn't seen her approach.

'Moira Jean, if your mother knew you were using such language . . .'

Moira Jean let out a breathless laugh, her heart pounding. 'Sorry, Mrs McGillycuddy. I was away with the . . . I wasn't concentrating.'

Mrs McGillycuddy was still frowning. 'Didn't you see me? I was waving to you. You had such a look on your face when you stopped, I thought you must've heard the news.'

'No, I . . . heard what?'

The housekeeper peered over Moira Jean's shoulder. 'Did your mother not tell you? Young Duncan's staying up at the house for a few days. He's . . . he's not well.'

Panic flashed through Moira Jean like lightning. 'Is it his leg?'

'No. We're not sure, but . . . it could be the 'flu.'

There was a cold spot in the centre of Moira Jean's chest, as if her heart had been replaced with something clammy. It spread like damp, staining every part of her that it touched. Suddenly The Dreamer and all the things he'd sent after her ceased to matter.

'Is he . . .'

'Your mother thinks it could just be a chill. We'll have to see. Are you well yourself, Moira Jean?'

Moira Jean waved a hand. 'Never mind me! Does Duncan need anything? Anything you want brought up, Mrs McGillycuddy, you just say the word.'

Mrs McGillycuddy was frowning at her. 'Only you do look

a wee bit pale, you know, and you came over fair strange just now . . .'

'Bad night,' Moira Jean snapped. 'Don't mind me. Look, what do you need, exactly? I'll fetch it for you.'

'Why don't we give it a few days,' said Mrs McGillycuddy, taking a careful step back, 'just so we can make sure you're not coming down with anything. I'll let your mother know if I want you.'

The housekeeper retreated back towards Drewitts, casting nervous looks over her shoulder. Moira Jean started for home, chewing on her thumbnail as she went. Her mother would need things for Duncan; Moira Jean could help. Fear stained all her thoughts. Duncan had seemed so vulnerable when she'd seen him last. The unfairness of it all stuck in her throat. Duncan shouldn't *have* to fight off the 'flu, when he already had a broken foot, a broken heart, and the lingering effects of polio to contend with.

Her mother wasn't in the garden, so Moira Jean pushed open the cottage door. Her mother was not there, but the cottage was not empty. Fiona was standing in the middle of the floor, peering up at the place where the ceiling met the back wall.

'Fiona?'

She squeaked and whirled around. 'Moira Jean! I—'

'What are you doing here? Your mother said you were asleep.'

'I've been looking for you. I'd have waited outside, but, well,' she said, gesturing to the mist pressed up against the windows.

Moira Jean relaxed a little. 'Ah. You've heard about Duncan, then?'

Uncertainty flickered across Fiona's face. 'Duncan?'

'Aye. I ran into Mrs McGillycuddy just now, he's up at Drewitts with the 'flu.'

Fiona took a sharp step back. 'The 'flu?'

Moira Jean frowned. 'Did you not know? I thought that was why you were looking for me.'

Fiona ran a distracted hand through her hair. 'I'd better tell Ma.'

She fled the cottage without another word. Moira Jean watched her vanish into the morning mist, wondering what Fiona could have wanted to talk to her about. Had she remembered something at last? She gave herself a little shake. She'd have to figure it out later.

She shut the door. As she went to hold her hands out to the fire, she realized she was standing just where Fiona had been. She looked up, curious to see what had caught her eye, but there was nothing. Only the top of the box beds, and, not quite out of sight, the box of Angus's letters.

After treating Duncan, Moira Jean's mother was panicking. She was convinced that Moira Jean looked both flushed and pale, and kept asking her if she felt a chill, or if she needed to stop work and go to bed. But Moira Jean would not do it. A day spent in bed was a day's worth of work lost – a day her mother would have to make up. The chicken coop needed cleaning, the dresser door needed to be rehung, the thatch was slipping, and that was saying nothing of the milking. If Moira Jean did not fix these things, her mother would have to – and she was wanted up at Drewitts. A tearful Mrs McLeod had knocked on their door, begging her to check on Duncan, and Moira Jean's mother had no choice but to go.

Moira Jean listened to the two women leaving through the door. On the other side she could hear Mrs McLeod crying. 'Alma, I don't know what to do . . .'

'There now, Effie. Dry your eyes. Duncan won't want to see you upset.'

There was a lump in Moira Jean's throat. She stared at the wood of the door, her hands curled into fists, until it went away. Then she went to feed the chickens.

Ignoring the rain, she shooed the chickens into their outdoor pen and mucked out the coop. She borrowed a screwdriver from Mr Galbraith next door and fixed the dresser, and in exchange dug him a new latrine pit. Then, because she was filthy, she put some water on to boil for laundry, checked the thatch while the water was still bubbling – it was thinning, and she was sure she'd seen a mouse scurrying out of sight – and spent the rest of the day sweating over the steaming laundry tub, bashing the stains out of bedsheets and blouses in the laundry copper. It would have been so much easier if Angus were here. Work had never seemed quite so hard with him, nor the future quite so frightening. Without him, all she could think of was the sheer scale of everything before her, vast and insurmountable.

Whatever she tried, guilt and fear still writhed in her head. What was The Dreamer doing to her friends? What would she be bringing them back to, if there was 'flu in Brudonnock again? Could she bring them back at all, with May creeping closer? She'd need to bring back one a week if she was going to have them all safely home by Beltane, and the moment she worked that out she wanted to throw up. The thought of parcelling up another piece of herself to hand over to The Dreamer stuck in her mind like a nail. What was she prepared to part with? What would be left of her when their bargain was done?

She'd scrubbed and swept and sewn and shovelled and still, her thoughts would not switch off. She'd climbed onto her own roof and stared blankly at the forest; she'd smacked the washing dolly against the side of the tub until she left a dent. Nothing worked.

Steam pressed against the windows. She could feel the hot, wet air clinging to her skin. She'd stripped down to her shift hours before and still she was sweating. The rose The Dreamer had given her lay on her bed, glistening like fresh blood on her pillow. She'd had it for days, and it showed no signs of fading.

As she watched, it began to roll across her pillow.

She sighed. 'Of course,' she muttered, glaring at the flower. Even though Beltane was approaching, she didn't want him to think he'd whistle and she'd come running. She shut it in the box bed, seething. 'You can wait until I've had a wash, you bastard.'

By the time she left the house the long sunset had already begun. The heat of the laundry still clung to her, her skin prickling when she stepped out into the cold. Her neighbours nodded to her, and she nodded back, trying to keep her mounting nerves from showing on her face. Would any of them try and stop her?

Moira Jean kept walking. The rose was twitching in her hair, thorns snagging on her curls and scratching the back of her head. She crossed the Aberdeen road and slipped between the trees. No one tried to hold her back. The thought made her wilt. Soon she was lost in white birch and pines black after days of rain, and when she looked over her shoulder, she could not even catch a glimpse of Brudonnock through the leaves. Would any of them notice if she didn't come home?

The sun blazed red over the clearing. Peat smoke had caught in her clothes as they'd dried; as the crimson light oozed across the ground, the whole forest seemed to be burning. Moira Jean closed her eyes and took a deep, steadying breath. The rose in her hair went still. When she opened her eyes again, she knew The Dreamer would be standing before her.

She opened her eyes. The Dreamer was there, smiling.

The haze was gone. Moira Jean couldn't help but stare. He was tall, angular, with a feral sharpness to his cheekbones and jawline and an imperious cast to his full mouth. His hair fell in a white sheet, in sharp contrast to his black brows and thick, dark eyelashes. There was a sense of agelessness about him, his skin pale and flawless. Moira Jean squinted. *Too* flawless. There were no lines on his face at all, not even when he smiled, and the more she tried to look for veins or pores in his skin the more her focus began to slide away. And still, she had no idea what colour his eyes were. He was, of course, achingly beautiful. Now that looking at him no longer gave her a headache, she could appreciate it.

'Moira Jean,' The Dreamer said.

'Dreamer,' she nodded. 'You've changed your . . . you've changed.'

'A token of my appreciation,' he said, his eyes glittering. 'You amused me greatly, when last we met.'

She blushed. This was hardly the reaction she expected The Dreamer to have, after she had slapped him. 'I'll amuse you again if you're not careful,' she muttered, folding her arms.

The Dreamer stepped closer, his ever-shifting eyes fixed on hers. 'I know you will,' he said, his voice low. 'I ought to thank you, Moira Jean. You have reminded me just how entertaining mortal servants can be.'

'Now, I wouldn't know anything about servants,' she said, giving him her most disarming smile. 'You've a strange idea of entertainment, though. Is that what you do in the Land Under the Hill? Set each other tasks?'

The Dreamer's smile widened. For a second, his teeth were in short, sharp rows, glittering like beads. Then she blinked, and they were perfect again. He held out an elegant hand. 'Perhaps you would like to see for yourself. Your friends are poor company. I will allow you to take their place.'

'You're caring for them well, I hope,' she said, trying to keep her tone light.

'They are joyful, for they are part of the dance.'

A chill swept over her. 'They're still dancing? But . . . but it's been days! Weeks! Have they stopped? Have they slept, or eaten?'

The Dreamer waved a careless hand. 'The details of such things are beneath me. My servants attend to them, as they attended to all the other mortals who stumbled into my realm. They are happy. Be content with this.'

Her temper flared. '*Content?*' she snapped. 'How could I be content? Their families don't even know they're missing!'

'Of course. Search parties are so tiresome. Better that they think their children are safe and well, and far away.'

'You can't just . . . you can't just wipe them out of people's heads!'

The Dreamer's face grew sly. 'Out of every head but yours, Moira Jean. You cannot make them remember, but it is so much *fun* watching you try.'

Moira Jean took a deep breath and forced herself to focus. She hadn't come to argue with The Dreamer, even though he was making it so easy for her. She had come for her friends. 'Why did you call me?'

The Dreamer raised a hand. Moira Jean tried not to look at it too closely: it was hand-shaped, but seemed oddly boneless, and all the details of knuckles and veins and tendons had been smoothed away. He rotated his wrist, and the slim volume of poetry she'd stolen for him appeared in his hand. 'I do not understand the purpose of this,' he said. 'Explain.'

'You're after another lesson, then?'

'I have read it. Its purpose is not clear.'

Moira Jean took the book from him and flipped to the frontispiece. Her heart sank. It was a book of love poetry, cheaply made, with an inscription on the flyleaf that was too smudged to read, apart from a large capital C. How on earth was she going to explain this to The Dreamer?

She grinned at him and tried to sound charming. 'It's poetry. It doesn't need to make sense. Just to rhyme.'

'And that is its purpose? To sound pleasing?'

'Aye, but . . . look, it's not all that simple. It's supposed to sound nice, sure, but it's supposed to make you feel things, and think kindly on people who're sweet on you – all sorts.'

The Dreamer frowned. He waved a hand and the book sprung open in Moira Jean's grip, the pages flipping to Sonnet 130. *My mistress's eyes are nothing like the sun*, Moira Jean read, before The Dreamer began to protest. 'And this? Why should—'

Moira Jean closed the book. 'Why don't I just swap this one for another?'

'No.' The book vanished. 'You shall bring me another, but this I shall keep. I do not care to be misled.'

She ran a hand through her hair. 'Right. Well, charming as you are, Dreamer, I didn't come here for poetry. I came here for my friends.'

The Dreamer considered her for a moment. 'I will return

another of your friends,' he said. 'In exchange, you will give me a secret – one that you will never speak aloud.'

She stared at him. 'But . . . but how can I give you a secret if I can't say it? D'you want me to write it down, or . . .'

He shook his head. 'You asked why they call me The Dreamer. I will show you, if you accept the terms of my bargain.'

'All right. But you're to return them safely, mind.'

'As you wish. And now, my secret.'

'What do I . . .'

The Dreamer raised his hands. He placed one either side of her head, hovering a few inches from her hair. A strange light began to spill out of his mouth, moving like smoke, and his eyes were suddenly filled with something bright and burning.

Panic slashed through her. 'Wait—'

The Dreamer's voice deepened. His words shuddered in her bones.

'*Close your eyes.*'

Moira Jean was alone in her cottage with her head in her hands. She was hunched over the wooden table, a fistful of brown curls in each hand. Snowflakes sizzled as they fell into the fire. Outside the window, the blizzard was a whirling mass of white, turned blue in the darkness.

Why did it have to be him?

Grief had broken her open and scraped something out of her. Her throat was closed, her eyes were squeezed tight shut. If she cried, no one would hear her – the wind was too loud – but she could not do it. There was nothing there. It had all been wrung out of her.

She could not remember the past few weeks. Since she had the news, everything came in flashes: the telegram, the medal, the gunshot from far up on the hillside. Now it was December, and a month of her life had been stolen from her. The world had withered around her, and she had withered with it.

Her mother was gone. Moira Jean couldn't remember why. She'd left the day before, but then the storm had set in. She would not be back until the blizzard had burned itself out. It had been easier, when she was here. She would get Moira Jean out of bed, put meals in front of her, keep her busy. But now Moira Jean was alone, and empty.

Someone in the village was singing.

Moira Jean raised her head. The song was faint, and the wind stole the words away. But she could hear the joy in it, the life, the laughter in the singer's voice. It was the song of someone who'd come home.

Moira Jean sprang to her feet. Fury crackled in her veins. She threw open the door, her hands slipping on the latch. A foot of snow collapsed into the doorway, spilling across her boots. She didn't care. She had to get away.

She waded out into the snow, the wind whipping through her hair. Snowflakes billowed up to meet her. The song was louder. She wanted to tear up the sheet music, smash the pipes, slap the singer. Her hands were shaking, she wanted it so badly. Instead, she turned away, boiling with a rage she could barely understand.

Her skirts were drenched and freezing. She didn't care. Her feet went numb as she climbed up the hillside. She didn't care. Snowflakes blinded her, choked her, buried her. She didn't care. She had to get away from the music. She kept climbing.

Soon, she had no idea where she was. The snow was falling so thick and fast that she could not see. She knew that she was going uphill – she could feel it in her thighs – and that was enough. She had to go somewhere. She had to get away from the song, from the staring, from the whispers, from the memories. But she couldn't. There was always something in her way. Tonight, it was the storm. Tomorrow, it would be the 'flu, still churning through the Highlands like a threshing machine. After that, it would be money. There was always something.

The ground levelled off beneath her feet. The wind tugged at her hair, her curls streaming around her. Her skin was dripping in melted snow. She couldn't hear the music any more.

It wasn't enough.

It would never be enough. Her future had been cut off at the knees and the knowledge throbbed like an open wound. She was supposed to be married, making a new life for herself in a new home. She'd grown up believing they were all things that should be hers.

She'd been lied to.

And Angus—

Moira Jean slapped herself across the face. She barely felt it. She couldn't think about Angus because when she did, a pit opened up and she tumbled down into it. He wasn't going to smile at her any more, he wasn't going to take her hand, he wasn't going to find an excuse to lean on the fence and flirt with her when they both knew there was work to be done. He was dead. He was dead and there was nothing she could do. She would have reached into Hell and tugged him out by his collar; she would have snatched at his ankle and pulled him out of Heaven. But the ground was solid and the sky was empty, just like her.

Why did it have to be him? There were thousands, millions of men who'd been at the front. They'd come home. Why hadn't he? Why had Callum come home, or Duncan, when Angus was rotting in the ground? Why had they been spared? They weren't any better than him. He'd had a life waiting to be lived. He'd deserved to come home. Why couldn't it have been one of them who'd died instead of him?

Moira Jean fell to her knees. Disgust enveloped her. She pressed a hand over her mouth. Those were her friends. She'd grown up with them. She'd seen what the war had done to them: Callum, who'd lost an eye; poor, poor Duncan, who'd lied about his age three years ago and been invalided out six months later. They all deserved to come home.

But so had Angus. Angus had deserved it too, and he hadn't come back, no matter how much she wished someone else had died in his place he would never come back, and she didn't understand why the others were safe with their families and he was dead, he was dead, he was dead . . .

The snow crusted her heavy woollen skirt. It turned her shawl white as a shroud. It was the cruellest thing she had ever seen.

She turned her head up to the heavens and screamed, and screamed, and screamed.

Moira Jean opened her eyes.

The first thing she saw was The Dreamer. One last glowing coil of smoke lingered at the corner of his mouth. His lips were slightly parted. His eyes, no longer full of that strange light, were darting all around her face.

She put up a hand. Her cheeks were wet. For a moment, she didn't understand, and then something broke. Suddenly she was sobbing, her shoulders shaking, both hands pressed over her mouth. Grief and self-loathing crashed over her and she sank to the ground, ready to drown. How could she have done it? How could she have wished her friends away, even for an instant?

Moira Jean laid her head against her knees and cried. The Dreamer settled down beside her, peering at her like a curious bird.

'Who was he?' The Dreamer asked.

She wiped her eyes on the edge of her shawl. 'You know who he was,' she said, thickly. 'You've got the letter.'

'That is not the same.'

Moira Jean tried not to look at the medal pinning her shawl together. 'He . . . he was kind. Funny. Quicker than anyone I've ever known. His da used to say he was so sharp he'd cut himself . . .'

She trailed off. The memories pressed in on her like a crowd. Angus, aged nine, throwing things at her from across the schoolroom. Angus, aged twelve, blushing and stammering and tripping over his own feet when she smiled at him. Angus, aged sixteen, holding her hand and glancing over his shoulder as the two of them, laughing, sloped off to the old hunting lodge, or remote bothies on the hillside, or behind convenient trees. In his work shirt with the sleeves rolled up, tanned and smiling; in the tartan the Fitzherberts insisted the villagers wore when they visited, pulling faces at her as the family passed by; in his uniform at Aviemore station, when he'd leaned out of the train window and kissed her, in front of everyone. He'd been a firework of a boy, blazing brightly and gone too soon. She wanted to cradle each memory close, but every single one of them would burn her.

'Well,' she mumbled, 'there's no use crying about it now.'

The Dreamer frowned. 'Then why do you weep?'

She stared at him. 'Are you serious?'

'Yes. Why?'

Moira Jean ran a hand through her hair, unsure where to begin. 'I . . . look. Love doesn't just go away because they're . . . they're not here any more. You can't see it, but it's as real as anything you can see and touch – more real, maybe. It changes everything.'

The Dreamer considered her, his head tilted to one side. 'Everything?' he asked.

'That's what it feels like,' she sighed. 'But why d'you want to know? Surely you're not interested in what mortals get up to in their own time.'

The Dreamer smiled, his eyes glittering. Very gently, he wiped away a tear. 'Mortals are ordinary. But you, my servant, are entertaining.'

'*Entertaining*?' Moira Jean snapped. 'Is that what you call this?'

'Of course.'

Moira Jean scrambled to her feet, her fists clenched. 'I've had enough of this. Just you give me one of my friends back, d'you hear? And don't go sticking them down a well this time. That was uncalled for.'

The Dreamer stood up, a faint smile on his lips. 'You were disrespectful. You had to be taught a lesson.'

'Oh, aye? And what're you teaching me now? How not to have a good time?'

'That your tears go as quickly as they come.'

The Dreamer's face shimmered. He shrank. Darkness rippled through his hair. His figure swelled and curved, colour swooped across his robe and suddenly, Moira Jean was looking at her own face.

There was the curly brown hair, the mass of freckles, the hazel eyes. The Dreamer smiled at her, and her cheek dimpled as she grinned, just as Moira Jean's always did. Even her clothes were the same – but not quite the same, Moira Jean realized. Angus's medal was missing, and she couldn't quite focus on the texture of her woollen skirt and shawl.

She looked more closely. The Dreamer had not got her quite right. Moira Jean's hair was the kind of brown she'd only ever seen on mushrooms; The Dreamer's shone like polished wood. Her curls fell in perfect ringlets, which had never happened to Moira Jean even once. Moira Jean's freckles were a blotchy mass which covered her entire body; The Dreamer's were a delicate dusting across the bridge of her nose. Her cheeks were fuller, her neck was longer, and – Moira Jean went scarlet when she noticed – she had curves Moira Jean had only ever dreamed of.

Moira Jean burst out laughing. Even when The Dreamer was wearing Moira Jean's own face, she still had to be prettier than her.

'There,' The Dreamer said, in a voice just like Moira Jean's, 'you have learned your lesson.'

Moira Jean tried to hold back a smile. 'You've made some improvements, I see.'

The Dreamer gave her a slow, lazy grin. 'Do you like them?'

Moira Jean was blushing. She tried not to look at the swoop of The Dreamer's waist. Either this was something she was never going to stop thinking about, or it was something which she would never, ever, think about again. Ever. 'I'd hardly recognize myself.'

The Dreamer lifted a hand and examined it, with more grace than Moira Jean ever had. She glanced at Moira Jean out of the corner of her eye. 'Strange. I do not find I know you better. Why is it, Moira Jean, that you continue to surprise me?'

It was very hard to keep looking at The Dreamer, when she wore Moira Jean's face so much better than her. 'Perhaps I have something you don't.'

'Perhaps you do.' The Dreamer came closer, moving like a dancer. Moira Jean's mouth went dry. On the surface, The Dreamer's eyes were hazel, but something underneath them was starting to shift. 'One moment you weep, the next you laugh. I see so many things in your eyes. Does it hurt, to feel them all at once?'

Moira Jean looked away. 'Sometimes.'

The Dreamer made a dismissive noise. 'You may go. But remember, Moira Jean, that I did not leave you weeping. I could have.'

She gave herself a little shake. 'I'm not leaving without my friend.'

'They will be returned to you. You have my word.'

'But where? How?'

The Dreamer gave her a sly smile. 'I will not tell you. Watching you search is my favourite part of the game.'

Moira Jean jabbed a finger at The Dreamer. 'This isn't a game!'

The Dreamer's eyes glittered. The colours were starting to bleed out from behind the hazel. Moira Jean could not look away from her iridescent eyes. She reached out and tucked a lock of hair behind Moira Jean's ear, running her fingers along the curve of Moira Jean's jaw. She shivered.

'Of course it is a game, Moira Jean.'

* * *

166

Moira Jean sat up and waited for Brudonnock to realize another of its children was missing. Her mother, who came in well after dark, thought that she'd been waiting up for her. She pulled off the old scarf she'd wrapped around her nose and mouth, threw it in the laundry basket, and kissed the top of Moira Jean's head.

'Get some sleep, hen,' she said. 'Go on, now.'

'How's Duncan?'

Her mother didn't answer.

Moira Jean undressed and got into bed so her mother wouldn't get suspicious. She buried herself in blankets, her mind reeling. Who would be returned? How? Had The Dreamer dropped any hints? She tried to think back. It did not work. Her mind kept drifting towards the memory she'd shared, shame staining all her thoughts. Something seemed to have been flattened out of her. Colours seemed quieter, the shadows seemed deeper. The only thing that seemed sharp was the memory of The Dreamer, wearing her own face and making it beautiful. How was she going to do this two more times, and all before the beginning of May?

She only knew she had slept when she started awake the next morning. Rain spattered against the window, but that was not what had woken her. Brudonnock was full of shouting.

Moira Jean propped herself up on one elbow and pushed open the door of her box bed. 'Ma?'

'Shift yourself, Moira Jean,' her mother said, shoving her feet into her boots. 'We're all needed.'

Moira Jean knew what her mother would say. Still, she asked, dread seeping into the pit of her stomach. 'What's happened?'

'Callum's gone. Up you get, now. You're to help look for him. Poor Mr Selkirk. And with Jim still so poorly and all . . .'

'Jim's back?' Moira Jean asked, wrestling her hair back into its bun.

'You know he's in no fit state to travel,' her mother snapped, 'Callum told us himself.'

Moira Jean stumbled out of bed, her heart beginning to pound. 'When, Ma? When did he tell us?'

'Get *dressed*, Moira Jean! We've no time for this.'

Her mother stormed out of the cottage. Moira Jean threw on her clothes and followed her, tugging her shawl over her head to keep off the rain.

Once again, the village was full of her neighbours, clustered around doorsteps and looking over their shoulders. The wind howled down the hill, driving the rain into Moira Jean's face. It stung. She splashed over to Mr Galbraith, who was talking with Fiona, Mrs MacGregor and her mother under the thatched eaves.

'. . . bringing the sheep in last night,' said Mr Galbraith, 'and never said a word about going away.'

'There's not a lass involved?' asked Mrs MacGregor.

'Fiona?'

Fiona blinked at them all, looking confused. Mrs MacGregor snorted. 'My Fiona's not a lass who'd dally with the likes of Callum Selkirk, thank you.'

Her mother snorted. 'Get away with you! You're not suggesting it's my Moira Jean.'

They all looked at her.

'Oh, come *on*, Ma!' she protested. 'This isn't the time. We need to find him.'

Mrs MacGregor nodded. 'I'll go along the Aberdeen road. He can't have got far.'

'No,' Moira Jean snapped. 'He's here, I'm sure of it. Have the wells been checked?'

'The wells?' asked Fiona, her eyes wide. 'You don't think someone could have pushed him in, do you?'

Mrs MacGregor frowned at her. 'What makes you so sure?'

Moira Jean clutched at Angus's medal. Her frustration was beginning to boil over. 'Have they been *checked*, Nellie?'

'Moira Jean! Apologize to Mrs MacGregor this—'

Moira Jean rounded on her heel and marched off. A slow, sick feeling was billowing up inside her. She hurried towards the well – first the new, then the old – and saw nothing but darkness glimmering back at her. She ran between abandoned houses, wrenching open rotting doors and calling Callum's name. She sprinted up to the barns at Drewitts, where she saw the glaistig, her head laid against the flank of the abandoned calf, her corn-yellow hair spilling into the straw.

'Have you seen—'

The glaistig shook her lovely head. 'I cannot interfere. It is not my place.'

Moira Jean groaned in frustration. She whirled around and saw Mr Brodie, staring at her and clutching two empty pails. 'Are you well, Moira Jean?' he asked, his eyes flickering to the calf and back.

'Fine. Look, have you seen Callum? He's missing.'

'Missing?'

She pushed past him. Her hands were beginning to shake. After the warmth of the barn, the rain pricked at her skin like knives. She dug the heels of her hands into her eyes, trying to remember every word that The Dreamer had said to her.

You had to be taught a lesson . . .

Mr Brodie followed her out of the barn and laid a hand on her shoulder. 'We'll find him. Did Mr Selkirk send you up here to—'

She cut him off. 'D'you know who's got the key to the old schoolroom?'

'The old schoolroom? Why would you . . . '

Moira Jean sprinted back down the hill, feet skidding in the mud. She slid to a halt in front of the old schoolroom. It was a long, squat building which had once been very clean. Now, lichen was growing on the doorstep and the windows were dark. It had not been used as a school since Jim had turned ten, and had done duty as a storeroom these past four years.

It was locked.

Mr Brodie came stumbling down from the barns, his face very red. From the other side came Moira Jean's mother and a small group of villagers, including Mr Selkirk, whose face had gone white.

'Who's got the key to the schoolroom?' Moira Jean asked.

Her mother glared at her. 'Now, really! Why would Callum have gone in there?'

Moira Jean ran a hand through her hair, scrabbling for an excuse. 'We . . . we've looked everywhere else. We ought to check, at least.'

'You and I will be having *words*, Moira Jean,' her mother snapped, pointing a finger at her. 'Now would you stop wasting our time and make yourself useful?'

Mrs Iverach shoved her way to the front of the group. 'Alma, she *is* making herself useful. She found Duncan. Mind you listen to her.'

Fiona, clinging to her mother's arm, spoke up. 'How . . . how *did* you find Duncan, Moira Jean?'

Silence crashed over them. Rain spattered against Moira Jean's cheek. Suddenly they were all looking at her, curious, expectant. Panic bubbled up in Moira Jean like a fountain. They *had* to listen to her. How else would they get Callum out?

Mr Selkirk barged through to the front of the crowd. 'Moira Jean's right. We should check. Who's got the key?'

Moira Jean fidgeted as her neighbours dithered and patted their pockets. She remembered Duncan, lying in a cold heap at the bottom of the old well, and wanted to scream.

She caught Mr Selkirk's eye. 'D'you have a crowbar?'

Mr Selkirk's eyes were red. He was unshaven, hatless, his shirt half-undone. 'Malcolm!' he yelled, striding off towards the smithy. 'Get your crowbar, lad.'

Moira Jean peered in through the dark windows of the schoolroom as Malcolm fetched his crowbar, unable to stand still with all those eyes on the back of her neck. She paced around the long, low building as he strained at the lock, listening for something coming from the other side of the thick stone walls. Squealing metal, frantic swearing, and then, at last, a crunch. Moira Jean ran back around to the door of the schoolroom to see it swinging open.

She followed Mr Selkirk inside.

All the desks were pushed up against the walls to make way for the peat in the middle of the room. There were only a few hundred bricks now; more would need to be cut and dried, but the store was low enough to make a path to the back of the room. On the far wall was a blackboard grey with dust and an old map, curling away from its pins. Next to that was a large, dark cupboard, which had once held slates, pencils and books. Dim, dirty light filtered through grimy windows. The smell of old peat tangled in Moira Jean's hair.

'Callum?' Mr Selkirk called. His voice was trembling.

Moira Jean picked her way around the peat. She peered under the desks. At last she came to the back of the room, and the cupboard looming ahead of her.

Callum could not be inside. Desks and chairs were piled in front of the cupboard. Nobody had opened it since the schoolroom had been closed, she was sure. But as much as she told herself that it made no sense to open the cupboard doors, that surely Callum could not be there, she could not stop herself from reaching out a trembling hand.

'Moira Jean,' Mr Selkirk said, his voice breaking, 'he's not here . . .'

She ignored him. She dragged desks and chairs away from the cupboard, their legs scraping across the floor.

Her mother came into the schoolroom behind her. 'What are you doing? Dougal, I'm so sorry, I don't know what's come over her . . .'

Moira Jean ignored them both. She shoved the last desk away from the cupboard. Certainty settled over her like frost. The doorknob rattled in her hand.

She opened the door.

Callum collapsed out of the cupboard, barely breathing. Moira Jean caught him before he hit the floor, swearing under his weight. There were deep purple lines in his skin – bruises, she realized, from where the shelves had stayed pressed into his skin for hours. The soles of his boots were worn paper-thin.

Mr Selkirk rushed forward and took the weight of his son. 'Oh Christ!' he sobbed. 'Oh thank Christ! Callum, Callum, it's me . . .'

He slung one of Callum's arms around his shoulders, but Callum's legs wouldn't take his own weight. Moira Jean rushed forward and took the other and together, they helped him out of the schoolroom. Moira Jean did not have to look to know she was being watched; she could feel it, prickling across her skin. Only Mrs Iverach was not looking at her; she was staring at Fiona, a thoughtful expression on her face. The crowd went quiet as they carried Callum out, and as they started the long walk back to the Selkirks' cottage, Moira Jean heard the whispers scurrying around her.

PART THREE

PART THREE

There was a steady stream of visitors to Moira Jean's cottage. Mr Selkirk, with a case of his whisky by way of thanks. Mrs McLeod, begging Moira Jean's mother to go and visit Duncan; Mr Galbraith, to complain about their chickens; Mrs MacGregor, who didn't even bother to find an excuse.

They'd all come for a look at Moira Jean.

She tried to tell herself that she shouldn't be surprised. Brudonnock was a small village; she'd known since she was a child that leaving was the only way to make sure her neighbours wouldn't be watching her. But this time was different. First Duncan, now Callum: two boys had gone missing, and she'd found them both. No one knew how they'd come to be stuck in the first place. Boyish high spirits were one thing; cramming yourself into a cupboard so tightly that you left bruises on your own arms was another.

She could feel the villagers looking at her. Mrs Iverach was the only exception; she greeted Moira Jean every time she saw her, loud and smiling as though nothing was wrong. Somehow, that made things worse. Every time Moira Jean left the house whispers blew in on the wind and the rain. Every time she raised her head, she caught someone quickly looking away. Every time she went to draw water from the well, a silence descended as she lowered the bucket, as though everyone were holding their breath and waiting to see what she would pull out of the deep, dark water. In the kirk that morning, while Mr Galbraith read out the book of Job, Mrs MacGregor turned in her seat to look at Moira Jean. Moira Jean had tried to smile, but Mrs MacGregor had simply stared at her, her expression wary, assessing, until her daughter had tugged on her arm and she'd looked away.

Hours later, Moira Jean was still trying to forget it. She trudged through the rain to visit Mr Selkirk, arms aching from her shift in the dairy. Doors creaked open as she passed. Faces appeared at windows. Malcolm stopped hammering as she passed the smithy. She waved, but he didn't say anything. He just watched her go, his face a mass of deep, worried lines.

She knocked on Mr Selkirk's door. It was yanked open at once. There was a frantic light in Mr Selkirk's eyes.

'Moira Jean! Come in, come in. Where's your mother?'

'She's up at Drewitts,' said Moira Jean, hurrying in out of the rain. Mr Selkirk's house was just like everyone else's: small, built to the same pattern, and with two box beds against the back wall. Suddenly, she felt stifled. No matter which house she went into, she would still be placing herself into the same tiny box.

Callum was lying in one of the beds, loaded with blankets. A photograph of him in his uniform hung on the wall next to it. Stern-faced for the camera, and still with both his eyes, Moira Jean could not look at the picture.

'D'you know when she'll be back?' Mr Selkirk asked, ushering her over to the fire.

'She'll not be up there all day, if that's what you're thinking. Can I help? Ma sent me round to see if you needed anything, I can make myself useful while I'm here.'

Mr Selkirk glanced at Callum. 'Did she teach you anything?'

Moira Jean draped her shawl over the back of a chair. A creeping, noxious fear was starting to crawl up her spine. 'What's wrong with him?'

'Take a look.'

Moira Jean went over to Callum's bed. He was too big for it; his legs were scrunched against the foot of the bed. But his legs, like the rest of him, were swathed in blankets and scarves and old jackets, and in the slice of light from the open door of the box bed all she could see of him was his face. It was pale, drawn. Sweat stuck his dark hair to his forehead. His eyepatch had been removed, and at the sight of the jagged scar covering his empty eye socket, she felt strangely embarrassed. She remembered the night in the woods, dancing with the thing that had stolen Callum's face and smoothed away his scars, and shuddered.

'How're his bruises?' she asked.

'That's the other thing,' said Mr Selkirk. He leant over the box bed and rolled Callum onto his side, so that his back was to the pair of them. Very gently, he pulled the blankets and scarves away from Callum's feet, and Moira Jean gasped.

They were black with bruises. Several large blisters, dark and oozing, were spotted across his heels and the balls of his feet. Moira Jean's stomach dropped when she realized what she was seeing. In all the time he had been away, Callum had not stopped dancing once.

'His boots were nearly worn through,' Mr Selkirk said. 'How'd he end up like this?'

Moira Jean covered Callum's feet with the blanket. For a moment she seemed to hear the melody of the dance, felt it tugging at her. She sprang back, dropping the blanket.

Mr Selkirk stared down at his son. 'Is he all right?'

Moira Jean blushed. She laid a hand on Callum's forehead, trying to look as though she knew what she was doing. 'I think so. But he's not woken up once?'

Mr Selkirk shook his head, stroking his son's hair.

Moira Jean looked away. 'I'm sure he just needs rest. He'll be right as rain in a few days. Duncan was the same, after . . .'

'You don't think it's the 'flu?' Mr Selkirk asked, his head snapping up. 'Jim's still laid up with it, the poor wee lad. I can't pay for another doctor, Moira Jean.'

'I . . . I'm sure it's not that,' she mumbled. 'Where could he have got it? Look, why don't I fetch Ma? She'll know better than I do.'

Mr Selkirk passed a hand over his face. 'Aye, I suppose you're right there. Duncan was sure to catch something after sitting in the damp, but Callum . . .' He trailed off. 'How did he end up in that cupboard, Moira Jean?'

Moira Jean thought of The Dreamer. She set her jaw. 'I wish I knew.'

'Only . . . only people are saying . . .'

Her hands curled into fists. 'What are they saying, Mr Selkirk?'

Mr Selkirk looked down at his son. He fussed with the layers of blankets as he spoke.

'It's not that I'm not grateful to you for finding him, Moira Jean,' he said, slowly, 'Lord knows how long we'd have been searching if you'd not thought to check the schoolroom. But . . . something doesn't sit right. How'd you know that was where he was going to be?'

Moira Jean hugged herself, digging her fingers into her arms. A slow-burning panic was filling her up. She remembered Malcolm pulling Angus's letter out of his pocket, convinced it was written by his own sister, and tried not to shudder.

'I didn't know he *was* going to be in there,' she said, when excuses failed her. 'It was just a feeling.'

Mr Selkirk stared at her. 'A feeling? You had a *feeling* that someone had crammed my boy into a cupboard?'

'No!' she snapped. A flush crawled into her cheeks. 'It wasn't like – it was just a coincidence. I didn't know he was going to be there at all!'

Mr Selkirk sighed. He fussed with Callum's blankets again, and Moira Jean knew he was doing it so that he would not have to look at her.

'Something's not right, Moira Jean,' he said. 'I know it.'

The words were out before she could stop herself. 'Of *course* something's not right!' she snapped. 'You know no one could have put Callum in the cupboard, just like you know no one could have put Duncan down the well! *Think*, for Christ's sake! Something else is going on here, you know it is! You—'

She stopped. Mr Selkirk's eyes had glazed over. There was no point in saying any more. The Dreamer would make sure Mr Selkirk did not hear it. Moira Jean snatched up her shawl and stormed out into the rain, fear and anger sizzling under her skin.

The moment she left Mr Selkirk's cottage, the rose in her hair started moving again. Thorns scratched the back of her head, snagging in her curls. No one noticed. People's eyes seemed to slide off the rose when they looked at it. Or perhaps, she thought, it was her they couldn't bear to look at.

Moira Jean ignored it. She stalked back to her cottage and threw the rose on her bed. After seeing what the Fae had done to Callum, she couldn't bear to have it touching her. Never mind the fact that it was April now, and the month had dawned in a blaze of panic – she needed some time to pull herself together.

There was a knock at the door. Startled, Moira Jean slammed the door of her box bed. Cramming her hair back into place, she opened the door and saw Mrs McGillycuddy waiting on the step, looking as though she'd rather be anywhere else.

'Mrs McGillycuddy! Can I help you?'

'Could I step indoors for a moment, Moira Jean?'

'Of course!' Moira Jean held the door open and the house-keeper stepped inside, clutching her shawl close about her. Her eyes roved all across the room, fixing on the closed door of Moira Jean's bed.

'There's something a wee bit delicate I wanted to talk to you about,' she began, pushing her glasses a little higher up the bridge of her nose. 'I've noticed that there's something missing from the library at Drewitts.'

Moira Jean flushed, instantly. She hadn't thought Mrs McGillycuddy would find out, and certainly not so quickly. She pulled herself together. 'What're you saying?'

Mrs McGillycuddy was blushing too. 'I know there's not much to do up here, especially for a spirited lass like yourself. But you can't just take things from Drewitts, Moira Jean. If it got back to the Fitzherberts it'd have to come out of some-one's pay. Just you hand the book back, and I'll not say a word to your mother.'

'I don't have it. Not that I took it in the first place, mind,' Moira Jean lied. 'I can prove it.' She strode over to the box bed and flung it open. For a moment, she wondered if the Fae would spirit the book back out of spite, but there was only the rose, glistening like a smear of blood on her pillow. She went to the dresser next and opened every door, letting Mrs McGillycuddy see inside. She hesitated, and took down the box of Angus's effects too. Angling the box so she couldn't see its contents, she held it out to Mrs McGillycuddy and started to lift the lid.

Mrs McGillycuddy reached out and gently closed the chest. 'I've seen enough,' she said. 'I . . . I'm sorry, Moira Jean. I'm sure Fiona only meant—'

Moira Jean clutched the box of Angus's effects to her stomach. 'Fiona? Did . . . did she say . . . '

'Nothing like that!' Mrs McGillycuddy said in a rush, flapping her hands nervously. 'She just mentioned she'd met you coming out of the library and said perhaps you'd help. I'm sure she'd never imply . . . I must've misunderstood. I've work to do now, so . . . '

She fled. Moira Jean watched the door swing shut behind her, cradling the box of Angus's old things.

Fiona had never once tattled on her friends. None of them had. It was a code they'd all grown up with, beaten into them by years of shoving and hair-pulling if ever somebody broke it. But it wasn't just a question of Fiona running and telling her mother, and getting Moira Jean in trouble. No, Fiona had accused Moira Jean of stealing to the housekeeper of Drewitts, knowing that if the news ever got back to the family, Moira Jean and her mother could be evicted.

Moira Jean was clutching the chest so hard that the shape of the hinges pressed themselves into her hands. Very carefully, she set it back on top of the box bed. Then she slipped out of the cottage and went to see Mrs Iverach.

One look at Moira Jean's face and the old lady hauled her inside. Neither of them spoke as they barred the door with rowan and lined up iron along the doorstep, the windowsills, the fireplace. Only when it was done did Mrs Iverach push Moira Jean into a chair and say, 'What's happened?'

'It's Fiona,' Moira Jean whispered. 'She's accused me of stealing from Drewitts.'

Mrs Iverach's eyes widened. 'God in Heaven. Have the family heard? D'you need a place to go? Mind you listen to me, Moira Jean. When you and your mother take to the road, you'll need—'

'The family haven't heard,' Moira Jean said, and Mrs Iverach sagged with relief. 'Mrs McGillycuddy believed me. She'll not tell them.'

'Good.' Mrs Iverach gave her a small smile. She laid a hand on Moira Jean's shoulder. 'I'd be sorry to see you go, hen.'

'I don't understand,' said Moira Jean, her voice suddenly thick. She buried her hands in her hair, hunched over the table so she didn't have to look at Mrs Iverach. 'Why would Fiona say something like this? She knows what'd happen if the family ever found out. D'you . . . d'you think this is what was taken from her? She's not been right since she got back from . . .'

Both of them glanced in the direction of the forest.

'How's she been different, since she came back?' asked Mrs Iverach, slowly.

'She says she doesn't remember—'

Mrs Iverach waved a hand. 'But how's she acted?'

Moira Jean thought for a moment. 'I found her in my house the other day. She seemed a wee bit nervous. And she's not been to see Duncan. Or Callum, as far as I know. But

I've not seen all that much of her. She's not been working when I have.'

'She's not been working at all,' Mrs Iverach muttered. 'I asked her to help dig my garden and she's not lifted a finger. And you know she always used to—'

The old lady stopped. All the colour drained from her face. Alarmed, Moira Jean sprang out of her seat, snatching at Mrs Iverach's arm. 'Here,' she said, guiding her into a chair. 'I'll fetch you some water. And don't worry about your garden. I'll do that, it's the least I could—'

Mrs Iverach ignored her. She grabbed Moira Jean's wrist. 'Is there a horseshoe over your door?' she rasped.

Moira Jean shook her head. 'Malcolm had it off months ago.'

'And you've not seen her in the forge?'

'Not since she . . .' Dread seized Moira Jean by the throat. 'She's not . . .'

Mrs Iverach passed a shaking hand over her eyes. 'There's another kind of Fair Folk I'd not told you about,' she muttered. 'I'd only heard they took bairns, I'd not thought you'd—'

She hobbled over to the window and yanked the curtains shut. She turned to face Moira Jean. Even in the dim cottage, Moira Jean could see the fear scrawled across the old lady's face.

'*Changeling*,' she mouthed.

Moira Jean felt as if she could break apart. Even she had heard those stories. The Fae stole children and left replacements in their wake: spiteful, sickly things that never flourished. But in the stories she'd heard, the Fae had only ever taken children. Not adults. Not Fiona, who she'd spoken to and comforted and worried about for weeks without realizing that she—

Something at the back of her mind was howling. She put a hand to her mouth; her fingers fluttered against her lips like birds.

'No,' she rasped. 'No, that can't . . .'

'We'll prove it,' said Mrs Iverach. 'Get that bar off the door, and mind you don't disturb the iron.' Mrs Iverach gave Moira Jean's hand a quick squeeze. 'Be brave, now.'

Moira Jean stumbled over to the door and heaved the rowan bar away. Her hands slipped on the wood, slippery with sweat. It couldn't be right. Surely it couldn't be right.

Mrs Iverach came up beside her and opened the door. Mr Galbraith was passing, and in a voice that was impressively normal, Mrs Iverach asked him to send Fiona round to help Moira Jean lift something. He nodded, walked off, and moments later Fiona was walking up the path, smiling blithely at them both. It was so familiar, so warm, that Moira Jean's doubts began to fade. This *was* Fiona. No one else could smile like that.

'Ah, there you are,' said Mrs Iverach, with something like her usual briskness. 'Give us a hand, Fiona. My table wants moved and Moira Jean can't lift it by herself.'

'Of course,' Fiona said, taking a step forward, 'I'll just—'

Her eyes fell on the iron. She froze.

'What's the matter?' Mrs Iverach asked, her voice quiet.

Fiona looked up. Her smile was still in place, and just as lovely as ever. But her eyes were suddenly hard.

'Nothing's the matter,' Fiona said. Her smile widened, teeth gleaming. A scream was building in the back of Moira Jean's throat. She clapped her hands over her mouth.

Fiona turned and walked away. On the doorstep, Moira Jean trembled. Fear froze her. Her hand was still pressed tight over her mouth. She did not trust herself to take it away.

Changelings, like all of the Fae, could not stand the presence of iron.

Fiona had been replaced.

It took Moira Jean a long time to calm down.

If she'd been braver, she would have marched straight into the forest and demanded to know why The Dreamer had sent back an imitation of one of her friends. She wanted to. She wanted to be fearless, bold, righteous. But she wasn't. All the trees towered over the village and she could not stop flinching at every twitching shadow. She had to be in her own home, with her own things about her, to check that they were still really hers.

She helped Mrs Iverach into bed before she left. The old lady was shaking so badly that it seemed the best thing to do. Small and bundled up in blankets, she looked completely defenceless. Moira Jean heated a cup of milk for her and poured a nip of whisky in it, splashing it everywhere, but Mrs Iverach didn't notice.

'I could stay,' Moira Jean said. 'Make sure she keeps away from you.'

'Bless you, love, but it's not me she's after,' Mrs Iverach said. 'Just you get that horseshoe back up on your door. What your mother was thinking letting Malcolm get his hands on it, I've no idea.'

Moira Jean went back home, drawing her shawl over her head and hunching against the rain. She scuttled back to her cottage and slammed the door, leaning against it until her heart stopped pounding. Alone, and with no one to hide it for, her terror felt deep and dark enough to drown in. There was a *thing* walking around Brudonnock, wearing Fiona's clothes, sleeping in Fiona's bed, eating Fiona's food, and Moira Jean hadn't known it. What else was she missing? Had anyone else been replaced?

Moira Jean clutched Angus's medal like a talisman. Slowly, her fear began to recede, just as it had done when she'd held his hand.

It was strange, after everything she'd just found out, that she could miss him so much. Part of her felt guilty that she was missing him, when by rights, she ought to be missing Fiona – the real Fiona, not the thing wearing her face that had crawled out from the Land Under the Hill. But even though Angus had been so bad at planning that they hadn't even decided where they'd live after they married, it was him she wanted. She'd turned to him for comfort so many times that even now, four months after his death, she couldn't stop turning.

The rose on her bed was moving, dragging itself across her pillow. Moira Jean glared at it. Its petals were perfect, each one a rich and vibrant red that seemed to be lit from within, almost like a dying fire. The stem was long and graceful, the leaves were a lush green. Even the thorns were evenly shaped, each one exactly the same distance from the next.

She snatched it up and crushed the rose in her fist. It crumpled under her fingers, but when she opened her hand again, it was still flawless.

Anger sparked into life. The Dreamer wouldn't even let her break something. She threw the rose aside, seething. First, she'd make him wait – and calm down, and come up with some kind of plan, and work out what she was dealing with out of his sight. And then, when her head was clear, she'd go into the woods and find something she could snap.

* * *

There was, as always, work to be done – and when she was busy, she could pretend that nothing was wrong. She had her shift in the dairy, churning butter until her hands started cramping. The chickens needed feeding and their eggs needed collecting. The fence needed mending, and she spent an hour stringing wire around wet posts. Their dwindling stack of peat had to be fetched from the old schoolroom. She could feel her neighbours watching her when she went inside. Glancing over her shoulder, she opened the cupboard doors, just to check. The shelves were close up against the doors, the old slates and boxes of chalk still in place. If she tried to climb in, she wouldn't even be able to get the doors closed.

Her mother came back from Drewitts, gobbled down a handful of oatcakes, and left straight after to look at Callum. Moira Jean didn't stop her. She couldn't decide if she wanted to, and before she'd made up her mind her mother had left. Moira Jean was left standing in the middle of an empty cottage, watching the door swing shut, and suddenly there seemed no point in putting off The Dreamer any longer. Not when there was less than a month to Beltane, and three of her friends were still trapped in the Land Under the Hill.

It was dark by the time Moira Jean swallowed her pride and her fury and went back into the woods.

She snatched up her shawl, crossing the Aberdeen road quietly. It had stopped raining, but the night was damp. Water hung in the air, clinging to her clothes. Moira Jean tried not to look back at the MacGregors' cottage as she passed between the trees. There had been a light in one of their windows, and she knew with a certainty built into her marrow that if she looked back, the false Fiona would be watching her.

Mud splashed onto the hem of her skirts. Fat drops of water

spattered against her cheek. A deer froze six feet away from her, its eyes gleaming in the light of her lantern. Then, it bolted, tearing away from her and vanishing between the trees. Moira Jean was half-tempted to run with it.

All too soon, she came to the clearing. The moment she set foot inside, The Dreamer appeared. Robed in white, and with his pale hair falling in a perfect sheet, he was snow, glass, porcelain. Unmarred, whereas Moira Jean had dirt and pine needles clinging to her boots. Once, just once, she wished she could look at him and not notice her own flaws.

'I had thought,' said The Dreamer, his voice clipped, 'that you had learned not to keep me waiting.'

She folded her arms. 'I didn't want to see you.'

The Dreamer's eyes narrowed. 'Such disrespect is—'

'Don't talk to me about disrespect!' Moira Jean snapped. 'After what you did? A wee bit of disrespect is long overdue, pal. Maybe *you'll* finally learn that I am not your servant, and you've no right to . . . to replace my friends with . . . '

The Dreamer's smile glittered. 'Changelings,' he said. 'Simple creatures, but charming, in their own way. When you come to know her, you will see she is a far more entertaining companion than your friend.'

'*Entertaining?*' Moira Jean spat. 'So that's why you did it, is it?'

'Why I did it is not your concern. I do not consult with mortals.'

Moira Jean poked The Dreamer in the chest. It felt like prodding teak. She tried not to look at her own hand; it looked as if she'd touched him before she actually felt it. 'It *is* my concern.'

His fingers locked around her wrist like a shackle. 'Remove your hand,' The Dreamer hissed.

'Or what?' said Moira Jean, with a grin. 'You can't hurt me. Remember?'

Something coiled around her legs. Moira Jean shrieked and tried to back away, but she couldn't move. Long strands of ivy had burst from the ground and wrapped themselves around her ankles, climbing up towards her knees. Her stomach lurched.

The Dreamer was smiling again, his ever-shifting eyes lit with amusement. He still had her by the wrist, his thumb pressed against her stuttering pulse. 'It is just as it was on the night we first met. How sentimental I have become, since I met you.'

Moira Jean snorted. 'I'll show you sentimental, all right.' She pulled her hand away with a flourish. Out of his grasp, her wrist felt cold. 'There. I've removed my hand as you asked, and in return you can get this bloody ivy off me.'

The Dreamer waved a hand and the ivy vanished. 'You see? You are capable of learning.'

She brushed off her skirts with shaking hands. 'And what exactly was I supposed to be learning when you replaced one of my friends?'

'Nothing. I did not replace them for your benefit.'

'Clearly!'

The Dreamer's eyes rippled. As Moira Jean stared, thousands of tiny lenses blossomed across their dark surface, like the eyes of an enormous fly. 'You said I knew nothing of your life. Now, I do. I will not have you keeping secrets from me, Moira Jean.'

'They're *my*—' she stopped. A memory surfaced with a lurch: Fiona – the false Fiona – in Moira Jean's home, staring at the box of Angus's effects. 'Did you send her after my letters?'

191

'Tell me about them.'

'You – no! You don't have the right to go through my things, or to send anything else to do it for you. Those are *mine*. And you've no right to cause trouble for me either. I'll not be turned out of my home because of *her*.'

'Changelings are impetuous creatures,' The Dreamer said, drifting closer. His arm slid around her shoulders like a snake, his voice almost comforting. 'They are cruel when the fancy takes them. I gave her no such orders, and I shall not have you sent away. She shall be punished, when she returns to the Land Under the Hill.'

Moira Jean folded her arms and looked away. 'Aye, sure you didn't,' she muttered.

The Dreamer took hold of her chin in long, cold fingers and lifted it, so that she had no choice but to look him in the eye. 'Now, Moira Jean,' he murmured, 'why would I do anything to upset my favourite toy?'

She flushed. He grinned. All Moira Jean's embarrassment was burned away in a flare of irritation. He thought he'd *won*.

She matched his grin with a smirk of her own. 'Try some lines I've not heard before.'

The Dreamer let go, his fingers brushing against her neck as he took away his hand. 'So demanding,' he said, his voice mild.

A giddy bravado was filling her up. The sensible part of her was screaming that she needed to be respectful and keep his favour. But Moira Jean had spent all day sensibly cleaning and fixing things, and that hadn't made her forget the horror of knowing something else was walking around in her friend's skin. She no longer had the patience to hold herself back.

She shrugged off his arm, facing him head-on. 'I know what I want. And that, Dreamer, is to know why you called me here. Your changeling has insulted me. Unless you're going to make amends, I'm away home.'

'*You* have insulted me,' The Dreamer countered. 'The changeling is a necessary measure. She will be removed when you have proven that you can be trusted.'

She snorted. 'You're in no position to tell me about trust, pal.'

'But I cannot trust you. You bring iron into my home, you hide your secrets from me, you persist in trying to awaken the others. The sooner you stop, the happier you will be. You must learn to trust in my power. The villagers will not awaken without my command. No matter what you try, they will not know the truth unless I reveal it.'

Moira Jean tilted her chin at him and smirked. 'If I can't awaken the others, then what does it matter if I try?'

'You cannot.'

She laid a hand on Angus's medal. His eyes followed the movement of her hand like a cat watching a mouse. 'I woke myself up, didn't I?'

'By chance, not by skill.'

'You sure about that? Or was it only chance that let me win back two of my friends, and stopped you from laying a finger on me?'

The clearing was utterly silent. The quiet pressed against her ears, heavy and dull. Between the trees, the formless mass of shadows that made up The Dreamer's court was still, expectant. It was only because she could not see beyond the edge of the clearing that Moira Jean knew they were there at all. Pride blazed beneath her fear. She'd left them speechless.

'I am not beneath you,' she said, staring into The Dreamer's

193

flawless face. 'I've matched you three times now, and I'll do so again. So you've two choices. Either you can make amends to me, and we'll continue as equals, or you can keep on under-estimating me, and I'll show you exactly what else I'm capable of. Which is it?'

The Dreamer looked at her for a long time. She held his gaze, even though it made her head hurt. His face could have been carved from ivory, marble, alabaster, or a thousand other cold and lovely things without a beating heart. The longer she looked at him, the more profane she felt. Shame wormed its way into the back of her mind. How could she have made such demands of something so perfect?

'Perhaps you are more worthy of my notice than the rest of your kind,' The Dreamer said at last, his voice thoughtful. 'You have proven yourself far more entertaining than the others I took, over the years. But if we are to continue as equals, you too must amend for the insults you have given. Then we may begin anew.'

Moira Jean considered. 'What are you suggesting? Do we both just apologize on the count of three, or what?'

'An act of trust,' said The Dreamer. 'You will demonstrate your faith in me, and I shall show you that you are worthy of my protection.'

'Such as?'

'Spend the night with me.'

Moira Jean froze. All her clothes were suddenly too hot, and too tight.

'Right. Let's just get one thing straight,' she said, her cheeks burning. 'I'm not cheap. If you want to sleep with me, you'll give me back all of my friends, you'll fix Duncan and Callum, and there'll be no more of this nonsense where you put people in cupboards and down wells and . . . just none of that, all right?'

A devastating smile spread across The Dreamer's face. 'What a proposition,' he purred, and Moira Jean's mouth went dry. 'But tempting as it is, I must decline. If I accepted, I should never see you again, and I have grown to enjoy your company.'

Moira Jean felt a stab of disappointment. Never seeing The Dreamer again was sounding better and better. Although she doubted that she would actually be able to sleep beside him, considering she was so embarrassed she wanted to crawl under the roots of the nearest tree and stay there, possibly forever. Not that it would be so bad, a voice in the back of her mind whispered.

She gave herself a little shake. 'Have you, now?'

'Of course. You are . . . new.'

'Well, isn't that the choicest compliment I've ever heard,' Moira Jean muttered, folding her arms.

The Dreamer accepted this with a gracious nod. 'The terms of our bargain are these,' he said. 'You shall spend the rest of this night with me. You shall sleep in my presence, as a mark of your trust in me. In return I shall watch over you, to prove that I value your safety and comfort. When you awake, we shall truly be equals.'

Moira Jean considered the offer, wracking her brains for old bedtime stories and everything Mrs Iverach had told her. 'I've heard stories of those who sleep in your realm,' she mused. 'They think it's just a night, but when they wake up, they've missed years of their lives. I'll not have any of that. If it's to be a night, it'll be *one* night. And I'll not do it here, nor in the Land Under the Hill. If you value my comfort so much, you'll find me a bed.'

The Dreamer's eyes flashed. 'Will you invite me into your home?' he said, failing to hide the eagerness in his voice.

'No,' said Moira Jean, immediately. The thought of The Dreamer running disdainful fingers over all her things made her skin crawl. 'I know somewhere better. Follow me.'

She turned on her heel and marched off into the woods, her face still burning. The shadows around the edges of the clearing parted, and she knew The Dreamer was following her. She ducked around birch and pine and pushed through wet bracken until the trees began to thin again. A small house perched on the edge of a loch came into view. The windows were shuttered and one or two tiles had dropped off the roof, but otherwise, it could have been painted on a box of chocolates.

The Fitzherberts called it The Cottage, even though it was three times the size of Moira Jean's home. It had stone walls, painted shutters and a garden full of overgrown flowers, but no peat store leaning up against the back wall, no vegetables in the garden, and no water trough outside. In short, it was pretty and useless, much like the pretty and useless Fitzherbert daughter it had been built for. When she'd been a child, she'd demanded a house of her own to play in, and so that was what she had received. She'd held tea parties there, and all the villagers in Brudonnock had to trek through the woods to deliver firewood, food, water and wine to the useless little house – and, when the Fitzherbert girl had got a little older, pretend they hadn't seen the equally useless young men stumbling through the woods with bottles of champagne.

Moira Jean had met the Fitzherbert girl once. She'd laughed at Moira Jean's freckles when she'd worked up at Drewitts.

Moira Jean felt no guilt whatsoever when she pulled out one of her hairpins and picked the lock.

She held the door open for The Dreamer. 'Come in. Make yourself at home.'

Dust bloomed up to meet them as they went inside. Sneezing, Moira Jean saw a wide, high-ceilinged room with all the windows shuttered. Heavy velvet curtains drooped at the glass. The walls were clustered with paintings, too dark to see their subjects. A vast fireplace dominated one wall, and a selection of squashy-looking armchairs sat forgotten in front of it. A gramophone sat in the corner, gathering dust.

It was strange to see The Dreamer constrained by four walls. He seemed so much a part of the forest that Moira Jean half-expected the floorboards to start sprouting beneath his feet. Among the trees, he was ethereal, graceful, balletic. With a roof over his head, it became clear that the body he'd made for himself was far too tall, the proportions not quite right. She could not imagine him sitting on one of the dusty chairs, or holding his hands out towards the ornate fireplace. This was not his domain.

But despite how out of place he looked, he still managed to suck the beauty out of everything around him and claim it for his own. The room seemed to wither under his gaze. She saw the bald patches in the velvet curtains, noticed the scratches on the legs of the mahogany chairs, saw how the paintings on the walls had faded. With a shudder, Moira Jean wondered if he did the same to her.

'This is how you live?' The Dreamer asked, peering into a cabinet full of crystal glasses.

Moira Jean started building a fire in the grate. 'It's how some of us live,' she muttered.

The Dreamer flicked the horn of the gramophone. 'But you do not.'

'No.' She finished stacking up the logs – peat was too smoky for the Fitzherberts – and found some matches on the mantlepiece. The fire caught easily; the wood had been stacked out of the rain for years.

She did not hear The Dreamer's footsteps but suddenly, his voice was a good deal closer. His long-fingered hands alighted on her shoulders like birds. 'Would you like to?'

She looked over her shoulder and raised her eyebrows at him. 'Are you after another bargain?'

'This is not finery,' said The Dreamer dismissively. 'I could offer you far better. In days gone by, men sought me out for the sake of what I could give them – but they have not done so for many years.' He glanced in the direction of the gramophone, disbelief writ large on his face. 'Is *this* what they have chosen, instead of my gifts?'

'Among other things.' She straightened up. A vast chaise longue stood against one wall; that would do for her bed. Moira Jean dragged it over to the fire and brushed as much of the dust away as she could, sneezing. She climbed onto it, feeling very stupid as she settled back against the cushions, and couldn't stop herself from wondering if the Fitzherberts sat about like this all the time.

The Dreamer stood behind her head, looking down at her. His long, white hair fell across his face. If she reached out, she could have touched it.

'What would you choose, Moira Jean?'

Angus. The thought cracked across her mind like the lash of a whip. There was nothing she would not have given to have the past four months rewritten. Angus would have come home, they would have been married, they would have built lives that were vibrant and marvellous and filled with joy. They would have taken positions on an ocean liner and, by now, be laughing together on the deck of a sleek ship, while the stars glittered around them. But she knew that it was not possible. The Dreamer could not change the past, and if he tried to give her a false Angus, as he had done with Fiona, it would break her.

Tears prickled at the corners of her eyes. She rolled over, staring into the flames. 'Nothing that you can give me,' she said.

'I can give you many things,' The Dreamer murmured. Gently, he laid a hand on her head. 'You have only to ask.'

She shook her head. 'Not this. Never this.'

Moira Jean was fourteen and laughing and a flower was in her hair. She'd stolen it. It was made of silk, and she'd decided to snatch it off one of the Fitzherberts' daughters' dresses when they'd dropped their laundry at her feet. She ran, giggling, into the woods, and Angus followed, glancing back over his shoulder.

'Moira Jean! Wait . . .'

She turned and Moira Jean was eight years old, now, and kneeling by her father's bedside while her weeping brothers and sisters clustered around her. Even then, she'd wished she hadn't understood why her mother's face had grown so pale, or why the villagers kept knocking on their door, asking if they needed anything. Angus was hesitating in the doorway, his eyes round, his dark hair sticking up at the back in the way it always did when he wouldn't let his mother brush it.

'Moira Jean? Are you . . .'

199

She turned again and they were seventeen and Angus was blind drunk, staggering back towards his father's house with an arm around her shoulders. He'd just enlisted, even though she'd asked him not to, and he'd made up a song to try and cheer her up. 'Moira Jean, your eyes are green,' he sang, 'you are the queen of Aberdeen. You've never been to Aberdeen, but if you did, you'd be the queen.'

He stumbled. She snatched him back before he fell. 'They're hazel. Who knew you were such a bloody poet,' she grunted, struggling to keep him upright.

'Ah, it's because I love you, Moira Jean. Besides, hazel doesn't—'

She stopped. He turned, and suddenly she was looking into the face of a man who was suddenly and instantly sober . . .

There was a hand on her shoulder. Angus's hand, tanned and scarred and strong. She turned and saw him standing on the platform of Aviemore station, dressed in his uniform. He opened his mouth to say something, but then there was another hand on her shoulder, and another Angus was waiting when she turned – twelve years old and tongue-tied for the first time in his life. Angus at ten, the gap between his two front teeth already wide; Angus at five, toddling over to apologize immediately after pushing her into a puddle; Angus at fifteen, staring after the military recruiters with naked interest on his face. He smiled, he frowned, he laughed, he cried, and he waited for her in every single gap between the trees. They pressed in, each knot in the bark a staring eye. Soon the branches were clawing at her. Thorns tangled around her ankles. She reached for Angus – any Angus – but his fingers were always, always, just out of reach . . .

* * *

Moira Jean started awake. Her heart was pounding. The first thing she saw was The Dreamer, his pale face luminous in the dark. For a moment, he did not seem to see her. But then, he smiled, and for once it seemed genuine.

'And now,' he said, 'we are equals.'

The fire had gone out, but the smell of woodsmoke still lingered. She sat up, her head still fuzzy. Trees full of eyes and ten thousand versions of Angus's face crowded all her thoughts. 'Did you . . . '

'You promised to trust me, Moira Jean.'

'Always out for what you can get,' she mumbled, softening the words with a smile. 'I'm only curious. Those dreams weren't . . . they weren't you, were they?'

The Dreamer nodded. His eyelashes cast long, dark shadows across his face. 'Perhaps I should have warned you. Mortals named me The Dreamer for many reasons. This is only one.'

Moira Jean threw up her hands. 'Aye, perhaps you should've! You didn't see them, did you?'

'I did. That was part of our bargain. There is a tithe to be paid, and things that would crawl inside your head to find something to pay it. I kept them off.'

Fear prickled at the back of her neck. 'You mentioned a tithe before. Is that . . . '

'I shall not speak of it.' He took her hand, his face grave. 'You should not think of it, for your own safety. You may think me cruel, Moira Jean, but there are far crueller things than I.'

Moira Jean shivered and put her shawl back on. The Dreamer watched her shake out the cloth and wrap it around herself, like a cat waiting to pounce.

'That boy,' he said, after a long silence, 'he is the one who fell, is he not?'

201

Moira Jean nodded.

The Dreamer raised his eyebrows. 'Well.'

'Well what?' Moira Jean demanded.

'You could have chosen anyone. Why him?'

She folded her arms. 'And what's *that* supposed to mean?'

'He was just like every other mortal,' The Dreamer said. 'What made him worth the choosing?'

Moira Jean hugged herself, pulling the shawl a little closer. The memories of Angus had seemed so vivid that with every blink, she was sure she'd open her eyes and see his face again. She wanted to cradle them to her, but they were already starting to slip away. One day they would be gone altogether, but until then, she'd hold the memory of his quick laugh and his easy smile as closely as she could.

'You'd have seen it, if you'd ever met him,' she mumbled.

'Would I?' The Dreamer smirked, brushing a stray curl away from her face. 'It seems to me there is only one mortal worth the choosing.'

The fire had gone out long ago, but a dim grey light was oozing around the edge of the shutters. The sun would be rising soon. Guilt twisted through her when she noticed. Her mother would be worried sick.

'Well,' she said, getting to her feet, 'this has been . . . something. I'm away home. Ma will be worried.'

The Dreamer snapped his fingers. Something skittered out of the shadows. Moira Jean started back with a yelp. Two blurs of brown hair no higher than her ankle scuttled out of the darkness and hurled themselves at the legs of the chaise longue, dragging it back into place. They melted into the shadows, and though she stared at the darkened corners of the room, she could not see them again.

'I will not keep you here, if you wish to leave,' said The Dreamer. 'But before you go, tell me this. Does this house always stand empty?'

'Aye, should do. Why d'you ask?'

'Good.' The Dreamer glided closer to the mantlepiece, peering at an ornate clock. 'I have no wish to be disturbed.'

He said nothing more, and after a few moments Moira Jean left, shaking her head. She was still a little muzzy, and in the half-light before the sunrise, she had to concentrate to find the path back through the woods. Mulch squelched under her boots. Her feet slipped in the shadows. She snatched at a birch to keep herself from falling and yanked her hand back at once. She kept expecting the knots in its bark to blink at her.

By the time she drew close to Brudonnock the sky was turning blue in the east. Voices echoed down the hillside. Lights bobbed around the village. For a moment she wondered why everyone was up so early, but then she saw her mother, and guilt swallowed her whole.

'Oh *no*,' she muttered.

She stepped out of the woods. At once, someone shrieked, 'She's here! I've found her!'

Moira Jean's mother came running over. Her face was white.

'So help me *God*, Moira Jean Kinross! Where have you *been*?'

'D'you have any *idea* how worried I've been?'

Moira Jean sat at the table, staring at the old, worn wood. Her mother was pacing up and down the cottage, her footsteps ringing on the stone floor. Outside, dove-grey clouds were gathering, but it was not yet raining, so there was nothing to stop all of Moira Jean's neighbours from slowing their pace and listening as they passed her cottage.

'I'm sorry, Ma . . . '

Her mother whirled around, pointing an accusing finger at her. 'Sorry isn't good enough! What're you playing at, wandering off into the woods at night? No note, nothing left with the neighbours – for Christ's sake, Moira Jean, I thought you'd done yourself a mischief!'

Moira Jean fidgeted in her chair. 'I didn't mean to scare you,' she mumbled, shame filling her up like smoke. 'I only wanted a walk.'

'A *walk*?' Her mother stopped pacing. She stared at Moira Jean, her mouth slightly open. 'You kept the whole village up all night because you wanted a bloody *walk*?'

Her temper flared. 'It's not like I can go anywhere else!'

'Don't you *dare* take that tone with me!' her mother shouted. 'I've not had a wink of sleep, I've been worried out of my mind – I'll have none of your lip, not tonight!'

Moira Jean resisted the urge to point out that it was morning.

'For Christ's sake,' her mother muttered. 'A walk. A bloody *walk*. Even your brothers wouldn't try such nonsense! Tell me the truth, Moira Jean. Where were you?'

She could feel the rose in her hair. It wasn't moving, but the thorns scratched at her head nevertheless. There was no point in trying to tell her mother the truth. The Dreamer had shown her that, time and again. Suddenly Moira Jean felt as if she'd folded in on herself and become something small and stupid.

She sighed. 'I . . . I just needed to get out of the village for a wee while,' she said. 'With Duncan and Callum disappearing like that, and everyone here's been . . . '

'Been what?' said her mother, sharply.

204

'Have you not seen it?' Moira Jean asked. 'They're . . . they're always staring at me, or whispering, or . . .' Moira Jean sighed again and stared at her freckled hands. 'They don't trust me, Ma.'

Her mother went quiet. 'No,' she said, eventually. 'No, I'd not seen that.'

'I really did want a walk,' Moira Jean said. 'But I lost myself in the woods and I didn't want to keep going after it got dark, I thought it'd make things worse. I found my way to The Cottage and stayed there.'

The lies prickled on Moira Jean's tongue, all the sharper for not truly being lies. She was sick of being stared at, sick of being talked about, sick of chasing after The Dreamer's endless whims. If she could have left Brudonnock, she would. There were bright and vibrant things in the world outside the village, and she wanted to find them. But it was so much harder to strike out with no familiar hand in hers, and there always seemed to be something holding her back. The Dreamer, the 'flu, her lack of money – not to mention that she had no idea where she'd go. With a slow, creeping dread that opened up in her stomach like a pit, she wondered how long her life was going to be like this. Would she ever get a chance to set the road beneath her feet, and take the freedom she'd once thought could be hers? Could she take her future into her own hands by Beltane, or would she have withered on the vine before her chance came, forever marked by failure?

Sighing, her mother pulled out the other chair and sat down. 'You did right to stay put,' she said, rubbing her eyes. 'God knows where you could've got to, wandering off in the dark. But you're not forgiven, mind. After Duncan and Callum . . . you've no idea how worried I was, love.'

Moira Jean took her mother's hand. 'I *am* sorry.'

'I know. And I . . . I'm sorry too. I didn't know you'd been having a hard time. I've been up at Drewitts almost every day.'

Fear prickled at the edges of Moira Jean's thoughts. 'Is Duncan not getting any better?'

'Both of them're up there now. Callum woke up, but he's delirious if I ever saw. All sorts of nonsense coming out of that boy's mouth. But don't fret. It'll pass.'

'It will?'

'Well. We'll see.'

'Could I not come along with you and help? I could . . . I could roll bandages, or something.'

Her mother laughed. 'You don't need bandages for the 'flu, pet. Help with the laundry, if you like, but I'll not have you up at Drewitts. Not while they're so ill.'

'Teach me what you know,' Moira Jean pleaded. 'I want to help. And maybe when this is all over, I'll train myself up as a nurse, or—'

'No.'

Moira Jean stopped, taken aback. Her mother's pale, drawn face was set, her mouth in a hard line. There was a glint in her eye that was harder than granite. Disappointment settled on Moira Jean like snow. 'Why? I thought . . .'

'Never you mind about that,' said her mother. 'I'll not have you putting yourself in harm's way. I'll manage on my own well enough.'

Before she left for Drewitts, Moira Jean's mother laid down the law. She insisted that Moira Jean pick up and deliver the laundry from the house while wearing a pair of thick leather gloves and a scarf wrapped around her mouth and nose. Moira Jean was to keep the scarf on until everything was in the water, and to wash her hands every time she touched something, and to make sure she put all the gear on before she climbed up the hill to Drewitts.

Moira Jean tried. But twenty steps up the hill her hands and face were slippery with sweat, so she gave up and took them off. There'd been a sharp burst of hail that morning, and the cold air sliced through her.

'Moira Jean!'

She turned. Mrs Iverach was struggling up the hill; Moira Jean went down to meet her at once. The old lady was leaning heavily on her cane, already flushed. 'What is it?' Moira Jean asked. 'What's wrong?'

Wheezing, Mrs Iverach slapped a piece of iron into her hand. She squinted up at Moira Jean, her lips pressed tight together. Nothing happened.

Then, she sagged, and Moira Jean jolted forward, ready to catch her. 'Oh, thank the Lord,' Mrs Iverach muttered. 'I thought you'd been taken.'

Guilt lurched through her. 'Oh. No, no. I'm sorry.'

'But you're well?' the old lady asked. 'You've not had to . . .'

'I'm fine, I promise.' Lowering her voice to a murmur, Moira Jean explained where she'd been the night before. Mrs Iverach's eyebrows shot up as she spoke.

'Just you be canny about this,' she whispered, when Moira Jean had finished. 'You've his attention, now. That's not a good thing. Not in any tale I heard.'

'I'll be careful. But you've no need to worry about me now. I'm away to Drewitts, I'm helping Ma with the laundry.'

Mrs Iverach looked alarmed. 'Is that safe?'

'Oh, aye. I'll be fine.' Moira Jean looked down at Mrs Iverach's wrinkled face, and a new fear wormed its way in. 'I might not visit quite so often, though. Just to be safe.'

Mrs Iverach blinked, very rapidly. She patted Moira Jean on the arm. 'Do what you think is best, hen.'

Guilt blazed through her. 'I'll still dig your garden. Any outdoor work you want done . . .'

'You're a good lass.' She gave Moira Jean a watery smile, and Moira Jean was flooded with guilt and shame. 'On you go, now.'

Moira Jean resumed her climb, picked up the laundry and staggered back home laden with packages and buckets. No one offered to help her. They watched her pass, and sometimes they nodded, but no one wanted to touch Duncan and Callum's things before they had been boiled to within an inch of their lives.

Moira Jean did not mind. She'd thought she would. She'd thought she'd spend days at a time roiling with fear, like a pot about to boil over. But laundry for two 'flu patients was still just laundry, as hot and tiresome as it had been before they'd got sick. It was only sometimes that the truth of it loomed above her like a vast wave about to crash over her head – they were so sick they'd been taken from their families, Angus had *died* of the 'flu and she was handling their things, what was she *thinking* – and then she had to go outside and scrub her hands in the water trough until they bled. Most of the time she was too busy to think, and fear only revealed itself when her hands stilled. The butcher had heard about Duncan and Callum and had said he wouldn't be bringing any more meat to Brudonnock until the 'flu had burnt itself out. A group of Travellers – the Galbraiths, according to Mrs MacGregor – had been turned away from Stronach by men with borrowed rifles and suspicious, darting eyes. One by one, all her siblings had written to their mother to say they wouldn't be home for Easter, and written to Moira Jean to ask if their mother was being careful, if she was feeling well, if they needed anything. Then, everything else shrank down to nothing. In those moments there was only the fear, vast and immutable, and she wondered if she'd lived in it so long that she'd become used to its shadow.

She tried her best to scrub it out.

Moira Jean went back and forth to the well every day, heaving buckets of water and boiling them one by one. The cottage was full of bedsheets and shirts soaking in buckets of soda and lye, ready to be washed the next day while Moira Jean went up to the dairy for her shift. Her hands, already worn, were cracked and bleeding before she hauled herself out of bed, throbbing from the caustic chemicals and hot water. Her cottage was full of steam, fogging up all the windows, damp heat sticking to her skin and making her curls wilder than ever. And when she wasn't doing laundry, she was making soap, swearing when lye got into the cuts on the back of her hands, and biting back a constant howl of frustration.

She had help.

It arrived three days after she'd come back from the woods. Early that morning, Moira Jean had been to the peat store in the schoolroom, and then to the well, and she was already tired enough to drop, even though she still had milking left to do. At least she'd get to sit down for that. She built up the fire and set the water on to boil, and as the room grew hotter she stripped down to her shift and stays, sweat scratching in the roots of her hair. She was reaching for her knife and a chunk of laundry soap – it dissolved so much easier when she shaved off tiny pieces and dropped them into the water – when she stopped.

There was twice as much soap as there'd been the day before.

Moira Jean lifted a hank of damp hair out of her eyes and stared. She hadn't made any more. She would've remembered; it was another long, hot task that involved hours of standing over a pot full of boiling fats. She shook her head, sure that it was only the haze of steam playing tricks on her eyes – and saw a full stack of peat, dried and neatly lined up in a basket by the door.

Moira Jean sighed. The Fae had been at work, she was sure. This was the last thing she needed. She pinned her hair up again, fished Angus's medal out of the clothes she'd just discarded, and fixed it to the front of her shift.

'All right,' she said, with her hands on her hips. 'Out you come.'

Through the steam, the creature looked like a matted hank of brown hair that scuttled along the floor, but as it drew closer she could see arms, legs, a face with bright black eyes. It stopped inches from her foot, and she saw a tiny, squat creature that seemed uncertain if it preferred four legs or two, and so ugly that it was almost endearing. It raised its broad, crumpled-looking face, staring up at her with a calculating look in its bright eyes.

'I suppose The Dreamer sent you,' she said.

The creature nodded.

'Why?'

'My lord sends his compliments,' the creature said in a voice like cracking twigs. Moira Jean flinched. She hadn't expected it to speak. 'He has sent you a servant to command as you wish, as he does with his own.'

'A servant?' said Moira Jean, turning to the tubs of bedsheets soaking in lye. 'Well. Doesn't that make me grand.'

The creature dipped a tiny hand into the tub and yanked the corner of a wet bedsheet out of the water. It scuttled up the wall, snatched a bar of soap in its teeth, and began to scrub the damp cotton with its tiny, hairy hands. It moved so fast its hands were a blur, lathering the soap onto as much of the sheet as it could press against the side of the tub. For a moment Moira Jean considered stopping the little thing, but she soon thought better of it. It was quite nice to have someone else scrubbing for a change, even if the someone else in question looked like a clump of hair with eyes.

She picked up another sheet and scrubbed that one herself. 'You're a brownie, then,' she said, as she worked in the soap.

'Aye,' the creature said. 'I'm yours to command. My lord has ordered it.'

Moira Jean thought back to what Mrs Iverach had told her. All she came up with was that brownies should not be given clothes, and she looked down at the laundry with alarm. 'This doesn't count, does it?' she asked.

'It's no gift. You may free me if you wish,' the brownie added, 'it makes no matter to me. The Land Under the Hill is waiting for me, and will always be waiting until I return.'

Moira Jean wrung out the sheet. 'I'll free you if you like. You've only to ask.'

The brownie blinked up at her. 'Then I shall ask, when I've stories enough to tell my children.'

'Stories of what?'

'Of you, lady.'

Moira Jean dropped the wet sheet on the floor. 'I . . . me?'

The brownie scrambled up onto the edge of the tub as she heaved the sheet into the boiling pan. It watched her as she poked everything under the water with the laundry dolly. 'Did you not wonder why we'd all come out for a look at you? The court is all a-flutter. They're all after a mortal of their own, since my lord declared you his equal. Will you bear his children?'

She dropped the laundry dolly in the boiling water, flushing. 'Absolutely not,' she snapped.

There was a knock at the door. Moira Jean glared at the brownie and answered it, only to come face to face with Mr Galbraith.

'Your bloody chickens, Moira Jean – oh my word.' He saw that she was in her shift and stays, her arms and legs bare, and closed his eyes at once. A flush was crawling up his neck.

'I'm sorry!' Moira Jean said, slamming the door and stumbling into her skirt. She threw on her shawl like a toga and opened the door again. 'I'm so sorry, Mr Galbraith, I was doing the laundry and I wasn't expecting—'

Mr Galbraith still had his eyes closed. 'No, no, you . . . you take your time. Those chickens of yours, though . . .'

She shoved her bare feet into her boots. 'I'll bring them in. Is the onions they're after?'

'Aye, same as always.'

'Right. I'll just . . . just sort things out and I'll be along in a minute. You go on ahead.'

Mr Galbraith left, stumping back to his cottage with his ears bright red. Moira Jean groaned and turned back to the brownie. 'Keep an eye on things here,' she hissed, stumbling properly back into her clothes. 'Don't let anything boil over.'

She shut the door. When she turned, the false Fiona was staring at her, her glittering smile wide. Moira Jean's hand

212

leapt to the medal, the blood rushing in her ears. The false
Fiona's face was identical to the real thing, except for her
expression. The real Fiona had never had such schemes in
her eyes.

'Why, Moira Jean,' she said, her voice low and smooth,
'what on Earth are you doing? Answering the door half-dressed,
talking to yourself . . . you are well, aren't you?'

Moira Jean's temper flared. She took a step forward, glaring.
'Where's Fiona?'

The changeling's smile widened. 'But *I'm* Fiona, Moira Jean.
You know, you look a wee bit flushed. Are you feeling—'

'Don't you dare,' Moira Jean snarled, as she made to leave.
'I know what you are, and you've no power over me.'

'Well,' said the changeling, her pupils suddenly narrow and
snakelike, 'let's put that to the test, shall we?'

The brownie was as good as its word. While Moira Jean had
chased the hens off Mr Galbraith's onion patch it had boiled
the bedsheets and wrung them out. Her cottage was wreathed
in steam by the time she got back, but the sheets were rinsed
and wrung out again, and the brownie was lathering soap
onto Duncan and Callum's shirts and drawers.

It seemed happy enough in its work, so she let the brownie
get on with it. She piled the wet sheets into a basket. It was
a clear day, but windy, the first new nests swaying in the trees.
If she hung the sheets up in Drewitts' back garden then Mrs
McGillycuddy could bring them in without needing to put on
her mask. Besides, if she went up there she could try yelling
and waving at the servants' rooms, and seeing if Duncan or
Callum was well enough to lean out of the window and shout
back down to her.

213

She set off, the basket banging into her hip with every step. The wind tangled her curls into one brown snarl and soon, she was shivering after the heat of the laundry. Ignoring the stares, she stumped up the slope and started hanging up the sheets in the servants' garden, swearing every time the wind tried to snatch them away from her. There was no sign of Duncan and Callum at the windows, but off on the hillside, she could see the dark shape of the *cù sìth*, staring down at the village. Moira Jean tried not to think about what that might mean.

She hurried into the dairy and spent an hour churning butter, and slipped into the cowshed the moment she was done, her arms sore. The little calf was still in its pen, wobbling on legs it had not yet grown into. It lowed at her when she came in, banging its head against the fence. Something clanged as it moved.

'Poor wee thing,' she said, 'what's gotten into you?'

She moved closer. The calf was lashing its tail from side to side, moaning. It knocked its head into the fence post again – but no, she realized. It wasn't headbutting the fence. It was scraping its head and neck against the wooden post, and something was jangling as it moved. Moira Jean peered between the fence posts. The calf was wearing a thick leather collar with an iron buckle and a heavy bell suspended from an iron ring.

'So that's it,' she said. Reaching over the pen, she grabbed the calf by the collar. It struggled, tossing its head and bucking as she fumbled with the buckle. The bell jangled, the calf rolled its eyes, and suddenly the strap came free. It bolted away from her, lowing, and huddled at the far end of the pen.

Moira Jean stared down at the collar. The iron gleamed in her hand.

Suddenly, the glaistig was beside her. Her grey face seemed paler than usual, her thin frame swaying. She laid a hand on Moira Jean's arm. 'Lady, I—'

Alarmed, Moira Jean dropped the collar. She put an arm around the glaistig – she really was tiny, barely coming up past Moira Jean's elbow – and lead her to the edge of the cowshed. She made the glaistig sit on an old milking stool and fetched her a cup of milk. 'Get that down you. You look about to keel over.'

The glaistig drank. She sighed. She kept her eyes closed, breathing heavily, and Moira Jean made sure there was no iron near her. Panic was starting to churn through her thoughts. She had no idea what she'd do if the glaistig passed out – she couldn't exactly run and fetch her mother.

Moira Jean poured the glaistig another cup of milk instead and made her drink it, and then another. After the third, the richness of the glaistig's grey skin had returned, and she opened her eyes again.

'What will you ask for in return, lady?' she said.

Moira Jean stared at the glaistig's pretty face, taken aback. 'Lady?'

'If you are equal to the lord of the Land Under the Hill, then you are a lady,' said the glaistig, getting to her feet and crossing to the wooden fence. The calf trotted over to her and bumped her grey fingers with its muzzle.

Moira Jean scratched behind the calf's ears. 'Does he make you call him that?' she asked.

'It is his due,' the glaistig replied, 'as it is yours. Many things are due to you now. You have removed the iron from my charge, and now both of us are in your debt. Name your price.'

'My price? Don't be daft. He was upset, anyone would've done the same.' Moira Jean glanced at the glaistig's delicate features, her pretty, pointed chin. She was so small that if Moira Jean put an arm around her, the glaistig would have to tilt her head all the way back to look Moira Jean in the eye. 'And . . . lady? Really? You're far more of a lady than I am,' said Moira Jean. 'You're so much more . . .'

She trailed off. The glaistig laid her slender, stone-grey fingers on Moira Jean's arm. 'You are generous, my lady. And kind.'

'Ah, less of that,' said Moira Jean, flushing. Not for the first time, she wished that the Fae were not so attractive.

The door to the cowshed creaked open. Moira Jean froze mid-scratch, tamping down a sudden spike of panic. Mr Brodie was standing in the doorway, a yoke bearing four buckets balanced on his shoulders. She smiled, trying not to look guilty. There was no reason to panic, she told herself. Mr Brodie couldn't see the glaistig. To him, it would look as though Moira Jean had come to fuss over the calf, and nothing else.

'Did I hear talking in here just now, Moira Jean?' he said, looking around.

'Only me,' she said, trying for a breezy, carefree tone and missing wildly. 'Just wanted to see how the poor wee thing fared. His collar was giving him grief, so I took it off.'

Mr Brodie set the yoke and buckets down with a groan. 'He's taken to you. He'll not let me near him. He's a funny wee thing, just stands about and stares half the time. Help me get these buckets off the chains while you're here.'

Mr Brodie lifted the yoke out of the way while Moira Jean unclipped the chains from the handles of each bucket. 'You've not seen anything of the boys, have you?'

216

'Mrs McGillycuddy tells me they're no better, but no worse, either.'

'You couldn't get me in there, could you? Just for a visit?'

Mr Brodie pointed at her with his mangled hand. 'Oh, no. I'll not help you get past your own mother. She'd have my guts for garters.'

Moira Jean grinned. 'Only if she found out. I'll go around you if I have to, you know.'

'I *do* know. I was up all night last time you tried to "go around" your mother's orders. We all were.'

Shame settled on Moira Jean like snow. 'Sorry.'

'Aye, well, just don't do it again. A man needs his sleep,' Mr Brodie said, pouring the buckets into a milk churn. 'Best you get back to work, tire yourself out. You'll not have the energy to wander off in the middle of the night, then.'

Moira Jean left the cowshed with her whole face burning. The glaistig had been standing right next to her the whole time, stroking the calf's soft muzzle with her grey hands. She hadn't looked at Moira Jean, but the glaistig had been listening.

Moira Jean stumped back down the hill, irritation carrying her forward. What did it matter what the glaistig thought of her? It made no difference what stories she brought back to the Land Under the Hill. The Dreamer was quite capable of embarrassing her without them.

About halfway down the hill, something made her stop and look back.

Mr Brodie was standing in the door of the cowshed, talking with a woman who'd pulled her shawl over her head to keep off the wind. They were both turned towards her, watching her go. Mr Brodie noticed she'd seen them and raised a hand.

Moira Jean did the same, and froze as the woman lowered her shawl and waved back.

It was the false Fiona, her blonde hair shining. Even from this distance, Moira Jean could see her smile. Panic fluttered in her chest like a caged bird. Moira Jean told herself that she should be sensible. The changeling had no power over her. She'd be safe. Surely, she'd be safe.

Mr Brodie disappeared back inside the cowshed. The false Fiona followed, but not before she looked at Moira Jean and winked.

Mud and bog water plastered Moira Jean's legs, all the way up to the knee. She stopped to wipe her forehead for a moment, breathing hard, and her feet sank deeper into the mud. A dragonfly skipped low over the ground; she watched it go, an emerald glimmer above the rich, black earth.

It was her least favourite time of the year: peat-cutting.

The whole village had traipsed up to the peat bog, weak April sunlight slithering out from behind the clouds. Or rather, what was left of the village. Duncan and Callum were still up at Drewitts, Mrs McGillycuddy was looking after them with Moira Jean's mother, and Mrs Iverach was too old for the hard, slow work of rolling back the turf on top of the peat bog. The false Fiona was not there, either. Mrs MacGregor was telling everyone that her daughter was in bed with a terrible chill, and watching to see who rolled their eyes.

Moira Jean would have given anything to have been somewhere else. She could have stolen into the library, or asked Mrs Iverach for what else she knew about the Fae. She could have been doing something that would actually help get her friends back, instead of standing hip-deep in a bog, watching powerless as spring unfurled itself and Beltane drew closer. But it was this, or go without fires for a year. She still had some time. If she was quick, she could get back before the rest of the villagers and see what Mrs Iverach might tell her through her window. If she pushed herself, she'd have time.

She spurred herself on. They sliced into the grass, the dark earth squelching, carving out long, straight rows of earth so rich it almost looked purple. Underneath, the stripes of last year's cutting could be seen. Moira Jean caught herself trying to remember where, exactly, she'd plunged her *tushkar* into the earth the year before and pulled up a long brick of peat. This time last year, everything had seemed so much simpler. Before The Dreamer, before the 'flu, before Angus . . .

She gave herself a little shake. Something caught her eye in the distance: the *cù sith* again, prowling around the ruined croft. She shivered. If she dug deep enough, would she find the tracks of the old villagers in the mud? Would any of them have known the *cù sith*, and kept away? Could any of them have helped her?

There was no sense in wondering. She had no time for it, when Beltane was drawing close. Nerves roiled through her. She had three weeks left: three weeks to claw back three of her friends from the Land Under the Hill. Every green shoot, every blossoming flower, every new-laid egg were bright and bitter reminders. Time was running out.

When the turf had been rolled back, they shouldered their tools and went back home. The peat would need to dry before they could cut it, and dry once again before they could take it home to be burned. Moira Jean slithered down the hill with the hem of her skirts still tucked into her waistband; her legs were so plastered with mud that it seemed stupid to take it down. The *cù sìth* stalked behind the old croft as she passed, and did not come out again. Evidently, The Dreamer had told it not to bother her.

When she was home, she hauled up a bucket of water from the well and washed her filthy legs. Then it was up to the dairy for another turn at the butter churn, and back home again with two pails of milk: one for Moira Jean and her mother, and one for Mrs Iverach. She trudged back down the hill – no sign of the dog, she noticed – and knocked on Mrs Iverach's door.

There was no answer.

Moira Jean went home and took her pail of milk inside. The brownie stared at it from the moment she came in, its eyes massive. It barely seemed to hear her, when she said hello. She put out a saucer for it by the hearth and took the other pail back to Mrs Iverach's cottage. Her garden was speckled with green seedlings; at the sight of them, Moira Jean felt a jolt of panic.

Still, no answer.

Moira Jean pushed open the door. 'Mrs Iverach?' she called. 'I've brought your milk.'

She peered inside. The cottage looked as it always did: neat and clean and strangely sparse. There was no sign of the old lady. Moira Jean set the milk down by the dresser, starting to worry. Where could she have gone?

At the forge, Malcolm told her that Mrs Iverach was looking for her; she'd said she would stop by her cottage. Moira Jean hurried back home, but Mrs Iverach was not there. The cottage was empty, apart from the brownie. It was lying on the floor, eyes closed and belly swollen, the saucer of milk licked completely clean. Moira Jean felt a little twist of panic as she tidied away the saucer. Mrs Iverach was so careful about keeping the Fae out of her home. What would she say, when she saw that Moira Jean had been given one of them as a servant?

Moira Jean put another brick of peat on the fire. She fetched a pail of water from the well and set it onto boil, watching it bubble as the stack of laundry beside her threatened to fall. She put the clothes in to soak as the sun slowly drifted below the horizon, staining the blue sky red, and still, Mrs Iverach did not come.

Moira Jean bit her lip. Her clothes needed to soak anyway; there had been a lot of mud stuck to them. There was no harm in sticking her head out of the door to see if Mrs Iverach was home again, and had simply forgotten to visit. She was nearly ninety, after all. She was allowed to forget things.

She opened her door, stepped outside – and saw Malcolm and Mr Selkirk, walking down the hillside from the old croft. Between them, they carried something long and white. An awful sense of certainty swelled in Moira Jean, eclipsing all her thoughts.

Mrs Iverach was dead.

There was no minister in Brudonnock, nor in Stronach. The villages were too small. If Mrs Iverach was to have a proper funeral, they would have to write to the Elders of the Kirk up in Inverness, and see if anyone could be spared – if any of the villagers could be persuaded to take the letter, if they were not turned back when they reached the city, if the minister did not refuse to come at all.

They gathered in the kirk to discuss it, every face drawn. It was a plain, simple building with a pew reserved for the Fitzherberts that, out of habit, nobody ever sat in. The false Fiona was quiet, her head resting on Mrs MacGregor's shoulder. Mrs McLeod refused to leave Duncan, Mr Selkirk was torn between his sons, Mr Galbraith was too old for the journey, Mrs MacGregor wouldn't leave her daughter. There was no question of Moira Jean's mother being sent: she was needed up at Drewitts, and she wielded this like a cudgel.

'Send Moira Jean,' Mrs MacGregor said. 'It'll keep her from running off into the woods in the middle of the night . . .'

Moira Jean felt a stab of panic. Inverness was a day's travel away, and it was nearly the middle of April. With three weeks until Beltane, she couldn't afford to travel to Inverness for a few days.

'If Moira Jean goes, I go,' her mother said, 'and you can find someone else to look after the boys.'

They all fell silent. Mrs MacGregor's mouth set into a thin line. Moira Jean's mother was the closest thing to a doctor the village had. She wouldn't dare send her away.

'We can't just leave her,' someone said. 'It could be months before we get someone down . . .'

A lump came into Moira Jean's throat. *Months.* Blinking very fast, she left the kirk, and went back to her cottage. She came back with the shovel and an old crate, chose a spot clear of the other graves, and began to dig.

It was hard work. The wind tugged at her hair, making her eyes water. Her shovel plunged into the earth, again and again, every green shoot reminding her of how little time she had left. The slow, steady rhythm of it should've quieted her thoughts. It didn't.

Mrs Iverach didn't have any family – or if she did, she never spoke about them. Moira Jean had the impression that she'd been moved along too many times to put down roots. But as she lifted spadeful after spadeful of the damp, dark earth, she realized she had no idea if that was true. The old lady had grown up speaking Gaelic, was terrified of eviction, and at some point in her life had come into contact with the Fae. Moira Jean would never find out anything else. Half the people she'd known and the places she'd been were gone with her, and Moira Jean would have no way of ever honouring those memories.

She realized she was crying. She wiped her eyes on her sleeve and kept digging, sniffing loudly. When she was done, she propped the crate against the foot of the grave and climbed out of it, then went back into the kirk.

The villagers were still talking. They turned at the sight of her, and her mother's eyes widened. 'Moira Jean? What have you been doing?'

'We can't just leave her,' Moira Jean rasped, her voice thick. 'There . . . there's a spot for her outside.'

'Oh, love,' her mother murmured, her eyes filling with tears.

They all filed out, carrying Mrs Iverach's body between them. As she passed, Moira Jean heard the false Fiona hissing to Mrs MacGregor: 'What's she thinking? We can't put her in the ground without a minister, it's not right . . .'

Moira Jean ignored her. She wouldn't make a scene. Not at Mrs Iverach's graveside, at any rate. She owed her that much.

Mrs Iverach's body was lowered into the grave. The villagers watched. Without the lull of the funeral service, nobody knew what to say. Instead, Moira Jean listened to the wind rustling through the trees, the flutter of crossbills,

223

and the distant lowing of cattle from the dairy. Freshly cut grass, pine, and the richness of the earth tangled around her, and as she closed her eyes, she hoped that Mrs Iverach would not mind.

She turned to Mr Galbraith. 'Will you read something?'

The old man looked taken aback, his eyes glistening. 'I'll not do the rites, Moira Jean. It wouldn't be decent of me, not being a minister.'

'I know, but . . . she should have something.'

He sighed. 'Aye. She should.'

Mr Galbraith stumped into the kirk and came back out with the Bible. He opened it, and began to read from Job. Moira Jean let the words wash over her, hearing none of them, and held her mother's hand.

When it was over, everyone but Moira Jean went to Mrs Iverach's cottage. She had food in her larder that would spoil, and there was no sense letting it rot with months until harvest. Moira Jean stayed behind to fill in the grave. Malcolm had offered to help, but she shook her head. After all Mrs Iverach had done for her, she needed to give something back.

The last shovelful of earth fell just as the sun was starting to set. Sore, her mind blank at last, Moira Jean shouldered the shovel, picked up the crate and went back home. She collapsed into a chair, completely numb, and her mother held her close and stroked her hair. The brownie peered at her from the depths of her box bed, its black eyes glittering. When Moira Jean went to bed it crouched on her pillow, staring directly into her face with its head cocked to one side. Gently, she scooped it up and put it outside the box bed. The brownie seemed sweet, in its own way, but that night she couldn't stand to be studied.

In the morning, she hauled herself out of bed and went to Mrs Iverach's cottage. She fed her chickens, collected the eggs they'd laid and, before she could stop herself, went inside to put them in the pantry so the old lady wouldn't have to bend down. Her hand was on the cupboard door before she realized what she was doing. She supposed they were her eggs now. Maybe even her chickens, if no one else wanted them.

As she turned to go, something caught her eye. Or rather, a lack of something.

All the iron nails that Mrs Iverach had used to bar the Fae from her home were gone.

It was evening before Moira Jean saw her mother again, and she collapsed into bed the moment she got through the door. Her hands dripped soapy water all over the floor as she crossed the room. She was wan, haggard, and even as Moira Jean took off her mother's shoes for her and hung up her shawl, her eyes began to droop. Duncan and Callum were no better, she said. They had drifted in and out of sleep, unable to stay awake long enough to eat, and Callum had been raving. She'd spent the day trying to spoon broth into their slack mouths, and trying to lower their temperatures as best as she could. There were two long lines across her cheeks, where the mask she'd been wearing all day had cut into her.

The moment she saw her, Moira Jean bit back the questions that had been running through her head all day. Though she'd been at the milking for hours, and then the laundry, she hadn't been able to stop wondering how Mrs Iverach died. Was it the 'flu? Her heart? Or something tangled up with the *cù sith* she'd seen on the hillside? Surely it couldn't be that; the *cù sith* only came for travellers, and she would have heard it barking. But this was no time to ask her mother, not when she could barely keep her eyes open.

Moira Jean cajoled her mother into sitting up and put a bowl of mashed turnips into her hands. She had to keep nudging her awake to make sure she finished it. When it was done, her mother collapsed onto her bed, not bothering to undress.

'If it gets any worse, I'll stay at Drewitts,' she said, 'I don't want to bring anything back to you, hen.'

Panic twitched like a nervous spider. 'D'you think it will?'

Her mother yawned. 'Hard to say. I don't understand it. You'd think I'd have caught it by now. You'd think one way or another, the boys would—'

She broke off when she saw the look on Moira Jean's face. 'You'll be all right on your own if I do have to stay up there, won't you?'

'Sure, I will. D'you mind if I sit up, Ma? I know you're tired, but I've some things I ought to be getting on with . . .'

Her mother smiled, snuggling under her blankets. 'I don't mind. You're a good lass, Moira Jean.'

She closed her eyes. Within moments, her mother was asleep. Moira Jean watched her as she worked her way through a pile of darning. There were so many lines on her face. She shut the door of her mother's box bed, guilt scrabbling at her thoughts. How many of those lines had Moira Jean put there?

The brownie scuttled out from under a chair, eyeing the pile of clothes with suspicion. There were a few scrapings of mashed turnip still in the pot, so she put them on a plate for the little creature.

'I'd ask you to clean that,' she said, nodding to the pot, 'but I know iron's no good for you and your kind.'

'I'm bound to obey your commands, lady,' the brownie said.
'I know,' she replied. 'That's why I'm not asking.'

It watched her for a moment, then set about the mashed turnips. They were burned, and wanted salt, but it seemed to enjoy them all the same.

Soon, the rose in her hair began twitching again. Moira Jean sighed. She'd thought her newfound peace might last a little longer. But for all his talk of being equals, The Dreamer was just as demanding as he'd ever been.

The brownie scuttled to the door, giving her darning pile a wide berth. 'He may not summon you, lady,' it said. 'If you're tired, I will be your messenger, and tell my lord you cannot come.'

Moira Jean stood up. Her bed looked soft and inviting. But then she thought of her mother, and all the new strands of grey in her hair. Beltane was a little over three weeks away, and panic spiked through her at the realization. She couldn't afford to stop now. Moira Jean's carelessness had put her friends in danger. She had to try to make it right.

'That's kind, but no. Stay here instead, and watch over my mother while I'm away.'

The brownie pressed a tiny, hairy hand over its heart. 'No harm shall befall her. This I swear.'

It looked at her, and suddenly Moira Jean realized she was expected to say something.

'Good lad,' she managed. 'There's a bowl of cream in this for you.'

The brownie's eyes shone. It bowed low and opened the door for her, its tiny hands hauling back the wood with ease. Moira Jean huddled through the night, pulling her shawl over her face. She slipped into the library at Drewitts, the sound of the back door opening lost to the wind and the rain. Hopefully the changeling wouldn't sell her out this time. With another stolen book crammed inside her shirt, she crept past darkened houses and into the woods.

The wind lashed at her, her skirts snapping at her legs. It was a relief to get into the shelter of the trees, even though her trepidation mounted with every step. By the time she reached the clearing a fine layer of wet pine needles had stuck themselves to her calves. She clutched her shawl around her, shivering, and waited.

The court came first. They rustled, they clicked, they chittered. But this time, they did not hide themselves under their veil of darkness. They stood in ordinary shadows on a thousand different kinds of feet – hooves, gnarled roots, formless smoke. Hands the colour of moss, of soil, of ripe berries all reached out, holding vast lumps of gold in too many fingers. Some of them had tried to be human, and smiled with mouths that looked as though they'd been tacked onto their faces. Some of them had tried to be grand, and hung fresh white furs over their bark-like skin, or stuck spirals of iridescent beetle wings into bodies that looked like formless wood mulch. Moira Jean tried not to look at them. If she did, she would scream.

Then, the haze appeared. The ground shifted. A headache built behind her eyes, but Moira Jean forced herself to watch the place where the world split open.

The Dreamer stepped into the mortal world.

He had changed again. His hair was still bright and perfect white, his skin was still flawless, he still moved with a grace more fluid than oil. But he was not quite so tall, nor so thin. His arms and hands had more substance to them – she could actually see his knuckles, instead of her focus sliding off the backs of his hands like a drop of water rolling off a leaf. She no longer had the sense that he was gliding towards her on casters when he came closer.

He'd shaped himself more like a man.

He smiled when he saw her. 'Moira Jean.'

'Dreamer.' She steeled herself. 'I've something I want to ask you.'

'And what is that?'

Moira Jean licked her lips, wondering where she should begin. The Dreamer watched the movement of her tongue like a cat. Blushing, Moira Jean tried not to think about it.

'There's – there *was* an old lady in Brudonnock. She was my friend. She . . . she passed, suddenly, right after I saw your dog on the hillside. That wasn't . . . you didn't . . .'

She trailed off, suddenly nervous. The Dreamer's smile never faltered.

'Do you think so little of me, Moira Jean?' he asked. 'We are equals. Why should I want to upset you?'

An unexpected sense of relief dawned on her. 'Well. I had to ask, you understand.'

The Dreamer took her hand. His touch was cold, and when he ran his thumb across her knuckles, it felt like a leaf dancing over her skin. 'Of course, you did. Mortals die all the time, and your kind insist on asking about it.' He looked around, smirking. 'I see my court have been tempting you.'

The wind howled. Moira Jean shivered and clutched her shawl closer. 'I hear I'm popular, now.'

'Of course. Your charm has won them over, and now they all want mortals of their own.'

She raised her eyebrows at him. 'I thought we were equals.'

The Dreamer took a step closer, pulling her towards him. He still hadn't got his eyes right; they no longer shifted, but she couldn't quite pin down what colour she thought they were. 'Of course we are equals,' he said, his voice low, 'but that does not make you any less *mine*.'

Moira Jean shivered. She told herself it was the wind. The Dreamer saw and snapped his fingers. It sounded like stones clicking together. The wind died at once, but Moira Jean couldn't stop staring at his hand. She'd actually seen the muscles moving under his skin. He'd been paying attention. She blushed, yanking her hand out of his grip.

'I suppose you'll want something for that,' she said, lowering her shawl and shaking out her hair.

'I want many things from you, Moira Jean, but that you may consider a token of my favour.' His eyes flicked down to the medal pinned to her shawl.

She snorted. 'Aye, sure. Speaking of wanting things,' she said, fishing the book out from her shirt, 'I've brought you another book. You might find this one a wee bit easier.'

She'd tried to choose something he might understand – or at least, something that wouldn't require the concept of human emotion to be explained to him in order for him to enjoy it. A large book covered in red cloth, *The Treasury of Knowledge* took some wriggling to get past her collar, but she hoped it would be worth it. It was essentially a children's encyclopaedia, but it would tell The Dreamer a great deal more about the world than she ever could.

'Get stuck into that,' she said. 'Take your mind off my famous charm.'

The Dreamer gave her a smile that went all the way through her. 'Are you really going to make me say it?'

The words were out of her mouth before she could stop them. 'Depends. What'll you ask for in return?'

The Dreamer ran his fingers through her hair. 'Anything I want.'

His hand was icy, his fingertips too sharp to be human. The sensation jolted her back to the present. What was she doing? She'd come here for one of her friends, not to moon over the thing that had taken them in the first place.

She stepped back, her face burning. 'Did you call me here to flirt, or are you after another bargain?'

The Dreamer sighed, but his eyes glittered. 'Always so brusque. Anyone would think you did not enjoy my company.'

'Imagine that,' muttered Moira Jean.

'I could hardly bear it,' said The Dreamer, a smirk lingering at the corner of his mouth. 'But since you ask, that is why I have called you here. Now that we are equals, our bargain must be renewed.'

'I'll not have you changing the terms,' Moira Jean snapped, planting her hands on her hips.

'Nor would I want to,' he said, his voice calm. 'But you must agree that gifts between equals are quite different between those a servant presents to her master.'

'And what d'you mean by that?'

The court around them had gone quiet. 'A master does not expect to receive worthy gifts from his servants. Equals, however, have a right to expect such things. Whatever you give me, Moira Jean, must be far more worthy of me than the things you gave before.'

'Worthy!' she spat. Her heart was starting to race, but whether it was anger or fear, she could not say. 'And what *exactly* is worthy of you, may I ask?'

The Dreamer was suddenly close again. His eyes were gleaming. 'I want something *real*,' he breathed, all his calm vanished. 'Something you cherish. Something that matters.'

Her mouth went dry. She felt as if she was reaching into the dark, waiting to see what her hand would brush up against in the shadows. 'Like what?' she whispered.

'I want,' said The Dreamer, 'your first kiss.'

Moira Jean burst out laughing. She clapped a hand over her mouth, but she couldn't stop giggling. It was all so childish. 'It's a wee bit late for that,' she said, trying to keep the amusement out of her voice. 'For most of the other firsts as well, while we're on the subject. You've not been getting your hopes up, have you?'

To her surprise, The Dreamer was still smiling. It unnerved her. She'd thought laughing in his face would have put him off. 'Do you imagine that you shock me? Of course you have had your first kiss. I would expect nothing less, from a girl as rare as you. But you do not understand me. I want the memory of your first kiss.'

Fear trickled through her thoughts like icy water. 'You . . . you want to mess about with my memories? You want to make me like all those people in Brudonnock, who don't even know what they lost?'

'Moira Jean,' The Dreamer soothed, reaching for her hand again, 'I would never want you to be like all the other mortals. Then you would not be entertaining.'

She yanked it back. 'Is that supposed to make me feel better?'

'It is the truth. How you feel about it does not depend on me.'

Moira Jean let out a long, long sigh. She turned away, clutching her elbows to stop her hands from shaking.

The Dreamer laid his long-fingered hands on her shoulders. He bent down and whispered in her ear, his silky hair falling across her chest. 'I offer this deal for your own sake, Moira Jean. Do you think I have not seen your grief? You carry it proudly, but I can see how it weighs on you. Let me do this for you. It will be easier, if you lay your burden down.'

Her throat suddenly felt tight. 'Easier?'

'Far easier,' The Dreamer murmured. One of his thumbs stroked the spot where her shoulder met her neck. 'Such memories will only hurt you. Give them to me, and I shall keep you safe from them. I would not see you shed any more tears for the sake of that boy.'

Angus's medal was cold in the palm of her hand. When she took it away, she knew the winged figure of Victory would be pressed into her skin. She kept holding it. She didn't want to forget Angus. She wasn't sure if she could, no matter what she bargained away. He was a part of her. They'd grown up together, their lives so intertwined that half the village had known they'd fallen in love before they did. If she forgot Angus, she'd forget her own childhood. No. She didn't want to forget him.

But she was so, so tired. She was tired of walking past his abandoned cottage and feeling her throat close over. She was tired of the cold core of her, which only ever eased when she cried. She was tired of knowing that grief had marked her out as one of its own, like a smear of ash across her forehead. With a start, she realized her cheeks were wet, and shame flooded through her, hot and sharp. She was tired of that, too. Angus had gone to war, she ought to have made her peace with his death the moment he went. She'd known there was a chance; she should have been prepared. But she hadn't. She'd spent two years pushing away the thought that he might not come back, and when he hadn't come home, it hadn't hurt any less.

And she was so, so tired of it.

The Dreamer wiped away her tears. His fingers felt like the touch of a feather; still not quite right. 'Let me do this for you,' he whispered. 'You do not need to weep.'

'It's not that easy,' she mumbled, her voice thick.

'Why?'

'We grew up together. I hardly know when our first kiss was. And . . . there were a fair few of them.' Moira Jean scrubbed at her eyes. 'But this isn't going to work. I don't want to forget Angus.'

The Dreamer stroked her hair. 'Nor shall you, if you do not want to. It would only be in part – and mortals are far from perfect. You may find there are parts you do not wish to remember.'

'What d'you mean?'

'Only that you shall still remember most of him. And of course, it need not be permanent. If you want your memories back, you may bargain for them. You know you may ask me anything. We are equals, after all.'

She started, and looked into The Dreamer's perfect face. 'You'd . . . you'd really give them back?'

He smiled. 'For a price, of course.'

Moira Jean stared into her own hands. She'd been right. The figure on the medal had pressed itself into her flesh. Her temper rose at the sight of winged Victory, glorious in her triumph. She wished she'd never seen it.

'All right,' she said. 'You can have the memory of my first kiss, and all the ones that came after, if you'll give back another of my friends. Will . . . will I know what I've given away?'

'Only that they were memories,' said The Dreamer. 'I do

not want you to feel another loss. Remember this, when you ask for their return.'

Moira Jean squared her shoulders and faced The Dreamer head-on. 'All right, then,' she said again. 'I'm ready.'

She expected The Dreamer to smile. She expected to feel a flash of regret, or fear, when the light started coiling out of his mouth like smoke and his eyes began to burn. But he did not smile, and all she felt was relief. She could parcel up her memories of Angus until their edges had dulled. It was finally going to get easier.

The Dreamer reached out a hand and caressed her cheek, his bright and burning eyes fixed on hers.

He wiped away a tear. '*Close your eyes.*'

Moira Jean was four years old and everything was unfair. She sat on the doorstep of her house, her chubby legs sticking out in front of her, while her mother yelled at Hamish for pushing her over. Her knees were scraped and they hurt more than anything else in the world, and she was sure she was going to cry herself inside out.

Angus came trotting over, his dark hair sticking up at the back, chewing on the side of his finger. He plopped down next to her on the step and gave her a kiss on the cheek. ''S better now,' he said. 'Don't cry . . .'

Moira Jean was thirteen years old and everything was still unfair. She lay on the hillside with Angus, waving her arms wildly as she complained. It was unfair that Hamish was still taller than her, it was unfair that her mother wouldn't let her sleep in or try any whisky, it was unfair that the Fitzherberts lived in their fine house and she had to clean it. It was also unfair that Fiona had turned out so blonde and pretty and

Moira Jean didn't quite know what to do about that, but she didn't say this out loud. There were some things she couldn't say out loud, even in front of Angus.

'D'you know what else is unfair?' Angus gabbled, when she stopped to draw breath.

'What?'

He kissed her, sharp and quick, right on the mouth. Moira Jean stared at him, shocked, and he blushed to the roots of his hair.

'How's that unfair?' she said, after a long silence.

'I don't know,' he muttered. 'I just needed something to say before I did it . . .'

Moira Jean was sixteen and her mother did not know that she and Angus had been together since breakfast. They'd slipped off into a bothy on the hillside, far away enough that they would not be missed until they eventually stumbled back into the village several hours later, full of unconvincing excuses. They lay on the floor, tangled in each other's arms, and Moira Jean felt as if she was made of sunlight, she was so happy.

'I love you, you know,' she said, stroking Angus's chest.

'Ah, well, you would say that,' he said, with a grin. She poked him right underneath the ribs and, laughing, he leaned down and—

—and then there was nothing.

Moira Jean opened her eyes.

Even after she'd bartered her memories away, she was not sure what she was expecting to feel. She was still upright, her clothes were all still on, she was still in the clearing. The Dreamer was still standing in front of her, one hand still cupping her cheek. Her thoughts still made sense – at least, she thought they did. She still felt like herself – or rather, the version of herself that had taken The Dreamer's deal. She had not truly felt like herself for a long time. Since Angus's death she had faded, and she was not sure if her brightness would ever come back.

The Dreamer blinked. The last of the light left his eyes. Glowing smoke still lingered around the corners of his mouth like the remnants of a last cigarette. He did not take his hand away from her face, and it felt as smooth and cold as porcelain.

'My poor Moira Jean,' he murmured.

She jerked back, knocking his hand away. 'Don't . . . don't.'

The Dreamer's face was gentle, like a statue of a saint. 'It will soon be easier. You will thank me yet.'

'I'll be the judge of that,' Moira Jean sniffed, wiping her eyes. 'Now give me back one of my friends.'

'It shall be done by the time you awake tomorrow morning,' The Dreamer promised.

'And where are you going to leave them this time?'

The Dreamer smiled. 'Surely you will not deprive me of all my pleasures. It is such a treat to watch you searching.'

She saw the glint in his eyes, and did not rise to the bait. 'At least give me a hint.'

'And what will you give me in return?'

She groaned. 'Not this again!'

'If you tire of our bargain,' said The Dreamer, 'we may make another. Yourself, in place of your friends. You will like the Land Under the Hill, Moira Jean. Flowers bloom all the year long in my realm, and I would cast each one of them at your feet.'

'What I wouldn't give for a straight answer,' she muttered. 'All right, then. I'll find them on my own.'

'I am sure you shall. But if you cannot, remember my offer. There will always be a place for you in my halls.'

She found something a little like a smile. 'Aye, as one of the hunting trophies, I've no doubt.'

The Dreamer's smile vanished, his face suddenly serious. 'You know I would never hurt you.'

'Because I've forbidden it,' she returned. 'I'm away home. Your . . . your court'll not try and stop me?'

'No,' The Dreamer said. 'They know that I have claimed you. I have taught them not to risk my wrath.'

His eyes glittered as he spoke. Moira Jean remembered all the shapes he'd taken before and had to fight back a shudder. She left the clearing resisting the urge to look back over her shoulder.

Her mother was still asleep when she came home. Moira Jean slipped back inside and bolted the door as quietly as she could, taking off her shoes with trembling hands.

The brownie scuttled out from under the kitchen table and Moira Jean flinched. It bowed, pointing at her mother's bed. 'I did as you asked, lady. She is safe.'

'So I see. Well done. I'll away to the dairy tomorrow morning, see what I can find for you.'

'You'll not forget?'

She shook her head. 'I promise.' She unpinned her shawl, then hesitated. 'Could you turn around?'

The brownie obeyed. As she changed into her nightdress, she tried not to think about how it would always obey, no matter what she asked of it. It had offered to clean the iron

238

pot, even though that would burn it. Could the little creature say no at all?

'Do I look different to you?' she asked, when she'd got into bed.

'You asked me to turn around, lady,' said the brownie, sounding worried.

'You're all right. Just while I was changing. Well?'

The brownie scuttled up the frame of her bed and perched on the edge of the door, inches away from the tip of her nose. 'You look . . . tired. Sad.'

She tried to smile. 'Same as ever, then.'

'No,' said the brownie, 'not quite the same.'

She slept, eventually. Her dreams were full of holes. By the time she woke up the sun was only just rising and her mother was already gone, a hastily scribbled note explaining she was back at Drewitts again left on the table. Moira Jean felt the brownie's impatient eyes on her, and as soon as she was dressed, went up to the dairy to wheedle some cream out of Mr Brodie.

'For my mother's sake,' did the trick, and Moira Jean carried the pint of cream back to her cottage, feeling lopsided now she was not taking anything back for Mrs Iverach. Tears pricked at the corners of her eyes as she set a saucer of it by the fire for the brownie. She made sure that her boots were securely laced, that her hair was not going to escape, that she was dressed in her warmest clothes. Then she sat at the table and waited.

Sure enough, before long the shouting started. Then came the knocking on doors, and hinges creaking as people left their breakfasts behind. Then the dull scrape of metal as spades were pulled away from walls, and rifles taken down from their hooks.

Moira Jean opened the door. Mr Galbraith stood on the other side, his face white, his hand raised as if to knock. Her neighbours clustered behind him in groups, trying to pretend they weren't peering into the cottage.

'Is it Martha?' she asked.

Mr Galbraith's mouth fell open. 'How . . . how did you . . .'

Moira Jean shut the door. 'Ah, for Christ's sake! It's written all over your face. Where've you looked so far?'

'Everywhere,' he gabbled, wringing his hands. 'I don't understand, it's not like my Martha to take off like this . . .'

'When did you see her last?' she asked, watching his face closely. The Dreamer always gave her something to go on.

'Last night. She said she was going back to work in one of the Edinburgh hotels and I said she wasn't going anywhere until the 'flu was over with and . . . oh God, Moira Jean, what if that's the last thing I said to my poor wee Martha?'

He burst into tears. Moira Jean patted him on the shoulder and tried to think.

They started at the southern end of the village, close to the smithy and the Aberdeen road. Moira Jean peered into other people's houses, opened chicken coops, hauled away ploughs and harrows from the walls they leaned against to see what lay behind. She checked the old well, the new well, the schoolroom, while the villagers whispered to see her set foot in the places where their children had been found. There was no sign of her in Mrs Iverach's cottage. Moira Jean did not linger there; seeing the old lady's chair set slightly apart from the table, as if she'd only just got up, made something inside Moira Jean wilt. She even checked Angus's old cottage, hesitating with her hand on the latch while she tried to work past the lump in her throat. It was empty.

She glared at everyone as she came back outside. The false Fiona stood with Malcolm and Mrs MacGregor, her brow furrowed in exaggerated concern. 'The poor wee thing,' she hissed, in a whisper that carried on the wind. 'You know she's not been the same since . . .'

Moira Jean stormed off, grinding her teeth. The last thing she needed was a changeling meddling in her business. She'd searched the whole village, and still no sign of Martha. Panic was starting to scratch at her every thought. Martha had to be *somewhere*. The Dreamer had promised to return her, and return her safely. He'd *promised*.

She stood in the middle of the street, the eyes of all her neighbours fixed on her. They held shovels and rifles and coils of rope. Her stomach turned over at the sight of them. They were to help bring up Martha. They weren't for her. She shook the thought away, ignoring the itch on the back of her neck. The Dreamer always gave a hint. She just had to think, and then she'd have it . . .

Mr Selkirk had his hand on Mr Galbraith's shoulder. 'We'll try up at Drewitts,' he was saying. 'Perhaps she's only visiting the boys. Mrs McGillycuddy won't mind . . .'

An idea dawned. Moira Jean remembered The Dreamer's words from the night before. *Flowers bloom all the year long in my realm . . .*

She set off towards Drewitts.

'Moira Jean! Where're you—'

'You try the house, I'll try the gardens!' she called over her shoulder.

She sprinted up the hillside, her neighbours surging after her. She threw herself over a low hedge and hurtled across the manicured lawns, heart pounding. She scrambled over another hedge and landed on a path, gravel spraying against her ankles. Apple trees swayed overhead, buds of white blossom only just beginning to show among the green. No flowers here; it was still too cold. She still had time. But the greenhouse shone at the other end of the path, and she could see the colours glowing behind the glass from here.

She ran towards it. Gravel splashed up her legs as she skidded to a halt in front of the glass door. It was locked. She peered through the glass. The panes were covered in a faint haze of green, but she thought she could see something on the other side.

She whirled around, panting. Her neighbours were ringed around her, waiting to see what she would do. The false Fiona was there too, the corner of her mouth twitching as she tried to keep looking worried.

'Right,' Moira Jean demanded, 'who's got the key?'

The false Fiona stepped forward. 'You're not thinking straight, Moira Jean,' she said, in tones that would soothe a spooked horse. 'How could Martha have got in there? It's locked. Look.'

Fury boiled in her guts. 'Don't make me ask again!' she snapped. 'She's in there, I know she is!'

The false Fiona gasped. She put a hand to her mouth and whispered, '*How* do you know, Moira Jean?'

'Oh, for Christ's sake!'

Moira Jean barged through the crowd. Anger and fear churned through her. She clenched her fists to stop them from shaking. Mr Cameron, the head gardener at Drewitts, was peering out at her from the windows of his shed. She ran over and hammered on the door.

'Mr Cameron!' she yelled. 'I need the keys to the greenhouse!'

'I'll not let you in, Moira Jean!' he called back. 'There's 'flu up at—'

'I *know* there is!' Moira Jean howled. 'Chuck them through the window if you'll not let me in, but give me the bloody keys!'

The keys jangled on the other side of the glass. 'I'll be speaking to your mother about this,' said Mr Cameron, as he cracked open the window and tossed her his keys.

She caught them. 'Aye, you and everyone else,' she snapped, and ran back to the greenhouse.

Her neighbours were still clustered around the door. The false Fiona's eyes were wide, and she was clutching Mrs MacGregor's arm like a child hiding behind their mother's skirts. Moira Jean ignored them and tried key after key in the lock, keys slipping through her sweaty fingers.

Click.

The lock gave way. Moira Jean's mouth went dry. Blood was rushing in her ears. Not sure whether she wanted to swear or pray, she pulled open the door.

She stepped into a lush, prickling heat, heavy with the scent of lilies. Red and yellow tulips crowded together in vast pots. Pink and purple sweet peas brushed against her skirt as she passed down the narrow aisles. Swags of jasmine hung from the glass ceiling, curling languorously up one wall. And everywhere she looked were clutches of lilies – creamy white, pale orange, blushing pink – choking her with their heavy, funereal smell.

Moira Jean crept down one aisle, picking her way past overgrown beds and stacks of terracotta pots. She could hear the muttering from over her shoulder. The false Fiona's voice came loudest of them all: 'D'you think we ought to fetch her ma?'

243

She rounded a corner at the very back of the greenhouse, and gasped.

Martha was lying in a bed of flowers. Lilies clustered at her head and feet. Low-hanging jasmine curled itself around one of her arms. Pollen gilded the lenses of her glasses. Blowsy peonies pressed up against her legs, and her dark hair was tangled around a brilliant purple iris. Moira Jean could only stare. It felt like her legs had been kicked out from underneath her. Martha was breathing, but she was laid out like a corpse.

Moira Jean cleared her throat. 'She . . . she's here.'

Mr Galbraith came rushing in, catching his walking stick on a discarded trowel. 'Martha? Oh God, is she . . . '

Moira Jean shook her head. 'No. Look, she's breathing.'

'Martha?' said Mr Galbraith, kneeling beside his daughter and patting her cheek. 'Martha, love, wake up . . .'

Moira Jean knelt beside him. She almost didn't want to disturb Martha, sleeping so peacefully among her flowers. It seemed cruel to drag her from her soft and scented bed, into an ordinary and uncaring world. But then Martha's eyelids fluttered, and relief crashed over Moira Jean like a wave.

'Let's get her out of here,' she said, hauling Martha into a sitting position. 'She'll want fresh air.'

Mr Galbraith nodded, his mouth pressed into a thin, tight line. Martha whimpered in her sleep. Moira Jean shifted Martha's legs away from the bed of peonies, and saw her feet. Her stomach lurched. Only the uppers remained of Martha's boots, still neatly laced. The soles were worn clean through, a few scraps of tattered leather still clinging in place. Underneath, her feet were a bloody mess.

'Good God,' Mr Galbraith spluttered. 'How did she . . .'

'Let's just get her out of here,' Moira Jean repeated, tearing her eyes away.

The two of them dragged Martha off the floor, her head lolling onto her chest, as the muttering outside the greenhouse grew louder. Mr Galbraith's face was bright red, his hand white-knuckled on the handle of his cane. Sweat pooled in all the lines on his face.

'I'll take her,' said Moira Jean. 'Would you clear a path? I'd hate to trip on a trowel.'

'She's my daughter!' Mr Galbraith snarled, 'you get your hands—'

He stopped. Shame crawled into his eyes. But it was too late. The words rang in Moira Jean's ears. Mr Galbraith had been her next-door neighbour since the war. Before that, he and his family had passed through on their wagons every summer, and each year he'd told her how much taller she'd gotten. He'd watched her grow up, she'd played with his children – just the other day, she'd borrowed his tools and dug him a new latrine pit in exchange. But though he'd known her all her life, he was afraid of her. All the times she'd helped him didn't matter. He did not want her near his daughter.

'Moira Jean,' he began, 'I—'

She set her jaw. Her eyes were burning. 'It's fine.'

Tucking Martha's glasses into a pocket so they wouldn't fall, Moira Jean dragged one of Martha's arms around her neck, then hoisted her up, bracing Martha's weight across her shoulders, careful not to touch her bloody feet. Mr Galbraith hurried back outside, kicking trowels and flower-pots out of her way. Moira Jean followed them, her back already starting to ache. More than anything, she wanted to stay in the greenhouse until everyone else had left. She could hear them all, praying, whispering, swearing and muttering, and that was bad enough. She dreaded the moment that she'd actually see them. All her desperate determination had fled, along with her excuses. What was she going to tell them? Was there any point trying to make up excuses at all? They'd all seen her bolt across the lawns, heading straight for the greenhouse. They'd think *she* was the one who'd put Martha in there . . .

Moira Jean staggered through the greenhouse door. Martha's head lolled against one of her shoulders, her arms dangling loose. Silence crashed over them. Moira Jean couldn't look up. Her neighbours were all staring at her, she could feel it, but the thought of meeting their eyes made something curdle inside her. It wasn't her fault. She'd done nothing wrong. Couldn't they see that?

Mr Selkirk stepped forward. 'Give her to me, Moira Jean. I'll get her to your mother.'

Relief swept through her. Moira Jean handed Martha over, gasping when the weight was finally lifted from her shoulders. She looked up, mouth open to speak, and stopped when she saw the look on Mr Selkirk's face. His mouth was set, his eyes were wide, and she had no idea if he was afraid for Martha or afraid of Moira Jean.

The moment Martha was secure in Mr Selkirk's arms he was off, carrying her up towards Drewitts. Mr Galbraith stumped after him, trying to keep up and talk to Martha at the same time. Mrs McLeod ran ahead, waving her handkerchief at Moira Jean's mother, who was rushing down from Drewitts to meet them. But the MacGregor family was still standing outside the greenhouse, all of them staring at her, along with Mr Brodie and Mr Cameron, who was giving the crowd a wide berth. Their faces were pale, their eyes wide, and as she closed the greenhouse door Malcolm shifted his weight, putting himself between Moira Jean and the thing he thought was his sister.

Moira Jean went back into the greenhouse and fished out the keys from underneath a planter. She set them down on an upturned plant pot, very carefully. Her stomach swooped. Then she turned and marched back home with her head held high, feeling the stares on the back of her neck.

PART FOUR

PART FOUR

The brownie was dozing by the fire, its saucer of cream empty, and Moira Jean was the only one who could see it. The *cù sìth* was up on the hillside, staring down at her cottage, and Moira Jean was the only one who could see that, too. When she'd come back from Drewitts she'd heard weeping echoing around the houses, and had to stop herself looking to see where it was coming from when she noticed her neighbours staring at her.

It had been three days since Martha had been found in the greenhouse – three days for all Moira Jean's frustration to come bubbling to the surface. Mr Cameron had disinfected his keys and asked Malcolm to install a bolt on the greenhouse door, after wiping everything down with iodine. Moira Jean's mother had come home and given her the requisite talking-to, but her voice had faltered halfway through. Her eyes kept flicking to the distant shape of Drewitts, where Martha was sleeping. She still hadn't woken up. The rest of Moira Jean's neighbours closed their doors when she went past. Each time, it felt like a slap. She'd done nothing wrong. Couldn't they see that? She'd found their children, not harmed them, and yet door after door was closed in her face.

But other things could open them fine.

In the three days since Martha had been returned, the village had been overrun. The *cù sith* stalked through the street, growling at passers-by. Brownies peered from the doors of abandoned houses, their tiny, hairy hands full of old feathers or the bodies of dead mice. When the rain lashed against the window, Moira Jean saw a bent-backed old woman hobbling past, gusts of wind tumbling around her like excited puppies. On clear days, when she turned her eyes to Ben Macdui, Moira Jean could have sworn she saw a vague, dark shape moving up the mountainside. But her neighbours saw nothing. Their eyes glazed over the vast dog; they blamed the wind on doors that brownies closed. Moira Jean knew better. Brudonnock was alive with unseen things, and she could see them all.

It was starting to become a problem.

Her mother opened the door, windswept and drenched. 'That fence has come down,' she said, dropping her wet boots in front of the fire. The brownie scuttled out of her way. 'I put the planks near the coop for you, but you're to fix it tomorrow, Moira Jean.'

'I will, if this has blown over,' she said. 'Did you see anyone coming back?'

Her mother snorted, stripping off her wet things. 'See who? Anyone with any sense is in bed – as *you* should be. I told you not to wait up for me.'

Moira Jean passed her a bowl of porridge. 'Aye, you did say that.'

'You've not seen anyone out in this weather, have you?' her mother asked, sprinkling salt on the porridge.

She *had* seen someone: the old woman, hobbling along the road with the wind in her wake. The old woman had stood outside Moira Jean's house, peering in through the window, her gaunt face wreathed in shadows. Moira Jean had flinched when she saw her staring, and the brownie had scrabbled its way up to her shoulder.

'It's the *cailleach*,' the brownie squeaked. 'Don't let her in.'

'Is she dangerous?' Moira Jean had asked, unable to look away from those hollow eyes.

'Storms are always dangerous,' said the brownie, 'and she brings them with her. She'll blow the place apart without meaning to. Give her a cup of milk and let her be on her way.'

Moira Jean did as the brownie said. She opened the window, wind and rain splashing through at once, and handed over the cup. The cailleach took it, drained it, and handed it back. It was so cold that Moira Jean nearly dropped it. Frost had webbed its way around the handle, and the rim that had touched the cailleach's mouth was coated in frozen milk. Moira Jean had put the cup by the fire almost a quarter of an hour ago, and it still hadn't melted.

To her mother, she said, 'No, no one's been by.'

'Why'd you open the window, then?'

Moira Jean froze in a flash of panic. Her mind was racing. The brownie peered out from its new hiding place – underneath Moira Jean's pillow – and she tried not to look at it. It didn't work. Her mother noticed, and looked over her shoulder to catch a glimpse of what she'd seen.

'I . . . was looking for you,' Moira Jean lied. 'It was coming down something fierce, and I thought . . .'

'Was that what you were doing?' her mother said, as she took another spoonful of porridge. 'Because if I didn't know better, Moira Jean, I'd say you were . . .'

'I was what?'

Her mother fixed her with a look that pinned her to her seat. She put down her dinner and went to the window, examining the sill with a critical eye. Moira Jean kicked the discarded cup behind her mother's boots when her back was turned. It clattered, and Moira Jean winced.

Her mother whirled around. 'And what was that?'

Moira Jean snatched up the brownie's discarded saucer. 'Just dropped this!' she said, trying to be cheerful. 'No harm done, though. Sorry, Ma. You know how clumsy I am.'

Her mother stalked back to the table and started eating again. 'I also know when you're lying, Moira Jean. Don't you forget that.'

Moira Jean hated going to the well now.

She couldn't avoid it. They needed water. But every time she walked through the street the doors would close, faces appeared at every window, and the false Fiona would insinuate herself into the crowd. She would pantomime fear, clutching at the arm of whoever was nearest and making a noise like a lamb stuck in a fence.

Moira Jean ground her teeth and tried not to say anything. It was *so* hard. She longed to be somewhere where she'd be nothing more than a face in a crowd, free to do as she pleased. The only thing that soothed her was imagining dumping her buckets of water onto the false Fiona's head, and she couldn't daydream too long. The false Fiona always noticed, and pointed it out.

She was there now, standing in the doorway to the MacGregors' home and clinging to Mrs MacGregor's arm. The two of them were whispering to each other as Moira Jean tied the first of her buckets to the rope.

'. . . still can't find the books,' the false Fiona hissed, 'and Mrs McGillycuddy said there's no one else that's been in that part of the house.'

Mrs MacGregor tutted. 'Are you sure, hen?'

There was a perfectly staged pause. 'She's my friend, I'll not hear a word against her. But . . .'

'But what?'

'Well, she's not been herself lately, has she? And all that business with poor Martha . . .'

Moira Jean's fingers had frozen halfway through tying the first knot. Anger itched at her thoughts. She let the rope slip through her fingers, her pulse drumming in her ears.

She snatched up the empty buckets and whirled around, marching up to the MacGregors' cottage. The false Fiona started back with a squeak. Moira Jean pointed at her, still holding the heavy bucket. 'D'you have something you want to say to me?' she demanded.

Mrs MacGregor pushed the false Fiona back indoors. 'I'll not have you threatening my Fiona.'

'Teach her some manners and I'll not need to!' Moira Jean snapped.

'And what's that supposed to—'

'It *means*,' Moira Jean interrupted, 'that maybe you shouldn't talk about someone when they're standing ten feet from you!'

Mrs MacGregor went scarlet. 'Moira Jean! I'll be speaking to your mother about this, you mark my words!'

'Aye, go on and speak to her, then!' Moira Jean retorted, glaring at Mrs MacGregor. 'And while you do that, I'll away and fetch some water from the loch, because unlike *you*, Mrs MacGregor, I'm actually helping Ma care for her patients instead of standing about gossiping!'

She stormed off, leaving Mrs MacGregor spluttering on her doorstep. Fury propelled her through the woods. She swung the buckets at the branches in her way, and relished the sound of them snapping. The moment she reached the loch, she dropped the buckets and screamed. Her whole body shook with anger. The loch stretched out in front of her, slate-grey and serene as a mirror. She wanted to smash it. Instead, she stood at the water's edge, fists clenched, breathing very deeply.

'*Bastard*,' she muttered.

If she'd been better behaved, she would have regretted what she'd said. Mrs MacGregor did not make idle threats. Moira Jean's mother would not stand for any lip, no matter what Mrs MacGregor had been saying to provoke it. But Moira Jean could not bring herself to care. Duncan, Callum and Martha were all up at Drewitts, in the grip of the 'flu – 'flu that her mother could catch at any moment. Jim and the real Fiona were still trapped in the Land Under the Hill. Mrs Iverach, the one person who could have helped her, was dead. Beltane was just over two weeks away, and panic burst through her every time she thought about it. And after all that, she still had to find work for the summer – if there was even any to be had. What did Mrs MacGregor's opinions matter, when Moira Jean had so many other problems looming over her?

Moira Jean sighed. She stared across the water, so still and calm, and wished she could deal with her problems one by one. But they kept coming, no matter how tired she was, and they would not stop.

And she still needed to get the water. At least that was something she could fix.

She sat down on the edge of the loch and took off her boots

and stockings, tucking the hem of her long skirts into her waistband. Her legs were bare to the knee, but the rest of her clothes would be dry. She took up a bucket and waded into the water.

Wet stones dug into her bare feet. Pond weed tangled around her ankles. The water was freezing, so cold that each step deeper into the loch felt like a slice across her calves. She bent down, dunking the bucket into the water – she wanted to be done, she wasn't going to go any deeper – and when she looked up, a naked man was in the centre of the loch.

Moira Jean shrieked and dropped the bucket. 'Christ!' she yelled, 'what are you—'

She faltered. The loch was deep; she could feel the slope of it underneath her feet. But the naked man was standing right in the middle of it, and the water was only coming up to his waist. And, she realized with a mounting sense of irritation, he was extremely handsome. Sleek black hair rippled over one shoulder, his large, dark eyes fixed on her. Even from this distance, she could appreciate the muscles glistening under his skin. He was another one of the Fae.

Moira Jean glared at him. 'That's not going to work,' she said, snatching up the bucket. 'Go on back under the water. I've work to do.'

To her astonishment, the man sank down into the loch with a sad little look. She dunked the bucket into the water, feeling smug. She'd have to try that with The Dreamer.

She sloshed back to the lakeside and fetched the other bucket, wading back into the water. She bent to fill it, and when she straightened up the naked man was gone, and the dripping head of a black horse was emerging from the loch. It was closer now.

257

'That's better,' she said, trying to sound calm. This was a kelpie; if she let it carry her away, she would be drowned. 'Mind you behave yourself. I've no quarrel with you, so you can let me alone.'

The second bucket was full now. She lugged it back to the shore and set it down, feet skittering over the pebbles as she picked her way through the water. When she turned back, the kelpie was standing inches away from her, water cascading off its vast black flanks. Pondweed was caught in its mane, and its eyes were deep and dark. She hadn't heard it move. There wasn't even a ripple in the water.

Moira Jean took a step back. Her heel scratched against damp rock. 'Come on, now,' she said, staring into its eyes. 'It's only water.'

The kelpie snorted. For a moment, she thought it was going to snap at her, but then it lowered its head and nudged her arm with its nose. Its muzzle felt cold, almost scaly, against her skin. Moira Jean understood. It was just like The Dreamer; it wanted something in return for the water she had taken.

'Here,' she said, drawing closer. Moira Jean was tall, but she still had to stretch to reach the kelpie's head. She began picking the pondweed out of its mane and flicking the plants back into the loch. It stank of stagnant water, and of the algae that coated its neck. She raked through the tangles in its hair with her fingers when she was done, and smiled to see the way its black hair gleamed.

'There,' she said, 'now you're—'

She stopped. Her hand was stuck. Something cold was oozing over her fingers. Panic fluttered in her chest. She tugged at her hand. It wouldn't budge. Clammy green algae was sliding across her skin, crawling around her wrist. Her stomach lurched.

The kelpie turned back towards the centre of the loch. Moira Jean was dragged around in a wide arc, splashing as she stumbled. Water sloshed up her skirts.

'Get off!' she yelled, yanking at her hand. The kelpie walked deeper into the lake, dragging Moira Jean with it. Water slipped over her thighs. Fear flooded through her. A few more steps, and she would drown.

Moira Jean seized Angus's medal and wrenched it free. She pressed it into the kelpie's neck. It screeched, bearing a mouth full of pointed teeth. She tore her hand away and splashed towards the shore, still clutching the medal.

A snap of teeth behind her head. She ducked. Something brushed past her shoulder. The kelpie surged up, suddenly in front of her. Moira Jean held out the medal like a talisman. The kelpie screamed, disconcertingly human, as the medal touched its nose. There was a sound like a crashing water-fall, and then the kelpie vanished. A column of dirty green water slapped back into the loch right where the kelpie had been standing.

Moira Jean stood and stared. The medal was still clutched in her outstretched hand. Her heart was hammering. The two metal buckets were still sitting on the edge of the loch. They looked so normal that she almost wanted to laugh, but she was afraid that if she did, she wouldn't be able to stop.

Her hands were shaking. Her shawl was drifting away on the water, but the thought of wading out to fetch it made her want to throw up. With clumsy fingers, she pinned Angus's medal to her shirt. Panting, she edged around the spot where the kelpie had disappeared, and picked her way towards the shore.

A hand curled around her ankle.

There was no time to scream. There was a flash of white on the bank and then she was under the water. She kicked, scrabbling for the surface. Teeth snapped at her flailing feet. Pondweed wrapped itself around her legs. Moira Jean tore the medal away from her shirt, lungs already screaming, and pressed it against whatever she could reach. She burst free. One hand broke into cold air – but then she was yanked back down again. Water flooded into her mouth. She kicked, she hit, she twisted, but still the kelpie was dragging her down and her heart was pounding and the water was pressing in on all sides and all she could think was *no no no no no* . . .

The pressure on her ankle vanished. Moira Jean shot up like a cork from a bottle, bursting out of the loch and into cold, clear air. Spluttering and retching, she hauled herself back to dry land and collapsed onto the bank, throwing up loch water on her hands and knees. She fell onto her side, her lungs aching so badly it felt like she'd been punched in the chest.

The Dreamer was standing over her.

She flinched back. He was staring out at the loch, his face sharpening, lengthening, all the colour bleeding out from his skin. She blinked, and two vast antlers had sprouted from the top of his bone-white head. She blinked again, and the antlers were gone, but three rows of eyes were staring out from The Dreamer's cheeks. Another blink, and his fingers stretched and curled like claws; another, and ivy wound itself around one arm, long strands of it rushing towards the water's edge like eager dogs. Anger rolled off him in waves. She dreaded the moment he saw her.

He stepped over her. Hooves clicked against the stones. He

glided down towards the loch, plants withering under his feet. The water rushed and bubbled as if it was boiling, and it swelled and twisted into the shape of the naked man, kneeling at the very edge of the loch.

The Dreamer extended a hand – too long, with too many spindly joints. The kelpie seized it, pressed it to his lips. Doubt slid into Moira Jean's thoughts like a needle. Then, The Dreamer flicked his wrist and suddenly his too-long, bone-coloured hand was clamped over the kelpie's face. All Moira Jean could see of the kelpie were his large, dark eyes, still with something of the animal in them. They were rolling, just like those of a frightened horse.

She tried to say something. Later, when she lay in bed staring at the ceiling, she would think about how she had tried. But when she tried to speak she only coughed up more water, spluttering and shaking.

The Dreamer's hand rippled. The kelpie's eyes went wide. It started to shudder, letting out a strange, muffled keening. Water gushed over The Dreamer's hand, rushing out of the kelpie's staring eyes. The water kept coming faster and faster, the screaming grew louder and louder, until suddenly the kelpie broke. A mass of dirty water slopped back into the loch, and The Dreamer was left standing on the shore, one hand still outstretched.

Moira Jean threw up. Loch water spattered onto the ground. She couldn't stop shaking. She felt as if she'd witnessed an execution, or an unforgiveable sin. She rolled onto her side and retched again, staring away from the loch. Away from The Dreamer.

Footsteps, coming closer. Moira Jean forced herself not to look up, her heart beating very fast. Would it be antlers, or eyes, or something worse waiting for her when she looked into The Dreamer's face? She didn't want to find out. She wanted to be somewhere warm and dry, buried in blankets, somewhere so soft and safe that she couldn't even imagine something like this happening.

The footsteps stopped. The Dreamer knelt down in front of her. Panic surged through her, but when she looked into his face, it was human. The colour had returned to his skin, his lips were full, his eyes glittered like opals. No trace of the kelpie marred his spotless white robe.

'You are safe,' he murmured, pushing a lock of wet hair behind her ear.

Moira Jean tried to speak. When the air hit her throat it spasmed and she started coughing again, water spilling out of her mouth. Fear flashed through her. Had the kelpie done something to her, when she was under the water?

The Dreamer lifted her into a sitting position, bracing her against one of his arms. His other hand – the hand that had melted the kelpie – was hovering inches from her face. 'Open your mouth,' he said. 'It will hurt less.'

Her stomach lurched. She tried to speak, but it dissolved into spluttering. She snatched at his wrist, shaking her head.

'Trust me, Moira Jean,' said The Dreamer, giving her a sad smile. 'I only want to keep you safe.'

She stared up at him. He was perfect again, so beautiful that it was hard to imagine his face had ever flickered into something monstrous. It was harder still when she saw the look in his eyes. They were gentle, almost tender, and full of concern. But moments before, he had shattered the kelpie into water, his fury so strong that it had made him lose control over his own shape. She owed him her life. What would he ask for in return?

She tried to think, but her thoughts had fled, like birds taking to the air after the first gunshot. She ached all over, her chest was burning, and she couldn't stop shaking. And The Dreamer was leaning over her, cradling her against his chest, and smiling at her as if he could make it all stop.

Moira Jean let go of The Dreamer's wrist. She nodded, heart beating very fast, and opened her mouth.

The Dreamer's hand descended. It stopped, just in front of her open mouth. His fingers curled into a fist. Then, he dragged his hand backwards. Something twinged in Moira Jean's chest. It tightened. A terrible burning rose higher up her chest, getting tighter and tighter. She tasted stagnant water. Scrabbling at The Dreamer, she tried to speak, but all that came out of her mouth was a bubbling sound. Her chest felt like it was twisting, shrinking. Her throat started to close. Fear flooded through her. She snatched at The Dreamer's hand as the water rose at the back of her throat but he was pulling it further and further away, his eyes closed. A dull whine built in her ears, tears burned across her cheeks and she could feel it again, the weight of all that water, except now it was inside her . . .

Moira Jean retched. A vast bubble of green-tinged water spilled out of her mouth, and suddenly, she was free. Air flooded back into her lungs in a rush. She gulped it down and fell back against The Dreamer's shoulder, gasping. The bubble of water was still floating in mid-air. The Dreamer opened his eyes, flicked his wrist, and the bubble burst, spattering across the ground in a million tiny droplets.

'Thank you,' she rasped.

The corner of The Dreamer's mouth twitched. 'There was a time you would have made me bargain for that.'

She tried to smile. 'We all change, don't we?'

'I do not,' The Dreamer said.

'Really?'

He ignored her. He stood up, dragging her with him. The world lurched around her and she staggered against him; it felt like smacking into a wall. With one arm still around her, he guided her inside The Cottage, the door opening by itself as they approached it.

The fire was already roaring and the chaise longue was drawn up next to it; brownies scuttled back into a corner as they passed. Moira Jean sank onto the floor in front of the fireplace, her wet hands dripping onto the grate as she reached for the heat. For the first time, she noticed the scratches on the palms of her hands, from where the rocks at the bottom of the loch had scraped across her flesh. Guilt prickled at her when she saw them. She'd be useless until they healed – a day's washing gone, maybe two. Would her mother cope, without her help?

There were more scratches on her legs and feet. They twinged as she tried to stand. She thought of the dancers, and shuddered. 'I should . . .'

The Dreamer put a hand on her shoulder and pushed her onto the chaise longue. She landed with a squelch. 'There are many things you should do,' he said. 'Leaving is not one of them.'

Moira Jean slid off the chair and knelt on the floor. 'I can't sit on that,' she said, edging closer to the fire, 'I'd leave a mark. I'll just . . . I'll just stay here.'

'Then you must change your clothes.'

'Now hold on a minute . . .'

The Dreamer snapped his fingers. There was a scuttling as brownies ran across the floor and moments later, an assortment of clothes were thrown across the back of the chaise longue.

Silk stockings, scarves, a chiffon peignoir, one leather glove, a man's knitted sleeveless jumper, and, almost as an afterthought, a bearskin rug. Moira Jean stared at the bear's glassy eyes, and wondered if The Dreamer and his kind actually knew how clothes worked, or just how they looked.

'I'll . . . I'll need a towel. Or a big sheet, if you can't find one,' she said to the brownies. They came back with one of the curtains. She took it. The Cottage had no airing cupboard and all its laundry was done up at Drewitts; this was probably the best she was going to get.

She eyed The Dreamer, suddenly nervous. 'Could you turn around?'

He blinked at her. 'Why?'

'Never mind,' she muttered, her face burning. She draped the curtain across her shoulders like a cape and wriggled out of her clothes underneath it, cold fingers fumbling with buttons that were suddenly too small. Finally, her cotton shift hit the floor with a wet slap and she huddled into the heavy velvet, shivering. The brownies scuttled up with a champagne bucket and deposited it at her feet; she wrung the water from her hair and squeezed as much as she could from her sodden things.

The Dreamer watched her, staring at the movement of her hands as she wrung out her blouse. 'Put that down,' he ordered. 'You have no need to work, while you are with me.'

'I need dry clothes,' she said, ignoring him. 'I can't away home in this.'

'You shall not go home until I am satisfied,' said The Dreamer, lifting her wet shirt out of her hands. He pulled a revolted face and threw the shirt to the brownies, who scampered out of its way. 'The velvet is an improvement.'

'The velvet is a *curtain*,' Moira Jean snapped, her pride

265

smarting. She'd made that shirt. She picked it up and draped it over the back of a chair. 'And I'll have you know that I'll away home whenever I damn well please.'

For all her bravado, she felt as wrung out as her clothes. Her legs trembled as she walked and every breath she took made her feel colder. The Dreamer pushed her back onto the chaise longue, his hand smooth and cool on her bare shoulder. It did not feel quite like a hand, but it was close. 'You shall stay here,' he commanded. 'Do not forget that I have done you a great service, which has not been repaid. If I tell you to stay, then you shall stay.'

She folded her arms. 'So that's how you want to play it, is it?'

'This is not a game, Moira Jean.'

She smirked at him, remembering the night when he'd borrowed her own face. 'Of course it's a game, Dreamer.'

His face contorted. He grabbed the back of her neck, forcing her to look up at him. He was losing focus again, his eyes glinting with all the colours of mother of pearl. 'It is not a game,' he hissed. 'You could have—'

'Take your hands off me!' she snapped. 'And don't you start with all this "it's not a game" rubbish. You were the one who set the terms. You're the one who's been leaving my friends hidden around Brudonnock when you could've just *given* them back. It's always been a game to you!'

The Dreamer's grip loosened. He did not take his hand away. It sat at the nape of her neck, half-buried in her hair. He seemed to have forgotten it was there. He was staring at her, his lips slightly parted, his face distraught, his ever-shifting eyes fixed on hers. With that expression on his face, Moira Jean was suddenly aware of her bare shoulders, her wet hair, and the feel of the velvet on her skin.

266

'It is not a game,' The Dreamer said again, his voice low.

She knocked his hand away, blushing. 'Repeating something three times doesn't make it true,' she snapped. She shivered, and slid off the chaise longue to sit directly in front of the fire. She could feel The Dreamer's eyes on the back of her neck.

After a long moment, he sat beside her. His white robe spread out around him like the petals of a flower, not a single fold in the cloth. 'Moira Jean,' he said, 'I asked you to stay because you are too weak to go home. Mortals sicken. You must be careful.'

'Oh, you're asking now, are you?' she muttered.

'I could ask you a great deal more,' he retorted. 'You owe me your life. And, as it is mine, I expect you to take care of it.'

She rounded on him. 'That's not how that—' She broke off. The Dreamer was grinning.

'I read your book,' he said. 'Are all the things in it true?'

'Aye, more or less,' she said, stretching out a hand to the fire.

The Dreamer shuffled closer. His eyes were gleaming. 'Will you show them to me?'

'Depends. What d'you want to see?'

'Everything,' he breathed. 'How did you teach yourselves to fly? Start with that. And then you may tell me where your engines take you, and whether they must all be made of iron. You must show me. I must – why are you smiling?'

Moira Jean was trying very hard not to think about the first time Jim had seen a motor car. He'd been six years old, and he'd worn the exact same expression of gleeful disbelief as The Dreamer had now. She shook her head. 'You'll have a fair wait. There's no aeroplane or steam engine tucked away in Brudonnock, I'll tell you that much.'

'Then you must find one, and bring them to me. I shall see them, Moira Jean. And you shall see them with me, and explain to me how they work.'

'Ah, you don't need me,' she said, leaning against the stone fireplace. 'You've the book to explain it to you, and you can away to Aviemore whenever you like. There's always trains running through there.'

The light in The Dreamer's eyes dimmed. 'I may not leave until Beltane. There is a tithe to be paid.'

At the mention of the tithe, a spark of fearful curiosity made her sit up a little straighter. Moira Jean winked at him, trying to seem nonchalant. 'Nothing wrong with skipping out on your rent. This . . . this tithe . . .'

'The tithe *must* be paid. But I shall keep you safe, and afterwards, you shall accompany me to Aviemore. I shall require a guide.'

'Now why would you need to keep me safe from this tithe you keep bringing up?'

The Dreamer's expression did not even flicker. 'Because I wish to go to Aviemore, and you must show me the way.'

Moira Jean gave up. She poked him with the tip of her foot. 'I'm not your retainer. Don't you forget that. I'll come and go as I please. Maybe I'll not want to away to Aviemore with you. D'you ever think of that?'

'Tell me,' he said, 'what is it that keeps you in Brudonnock when so many have left?'

Moira Jean sighed, all her playfulness gone. 'Work,' she said. 'My mother needs me. She'll not manage on her own. And my friends need me too. If I'm away too long my mother will go hungry, or the sheets won't be washed, or—'

A piece of the velvet curtain had fallen near The Dreamer;

268

he traced a pattern across it with one long finger, making the rest of it shift ever so slightly across Moira Jean's skin. 'Such ordinary things,' he mused. 'Do you like them?'

'It's not about whether I *like* them,' said Moira Jean. 'I need food, and clean clothes, and . . .'

'And everyone else needs *you* to give them these things, which are so very dull,' The Dreamer interrupted. 'You should not have ordinary things in your life, Moira Jean. They are not worthy of you.'

She rolled her eyes. 'Oh aye, I'll lounge about in champagne and caviar all day. That'll bring the rent in.'

'It would be an appropriate start. But when you have deigned to give them their trifles, what do they give you, in return?'

The words slid under her skin like a needle. Rattled, Moira Jean hugged her knees to her chest. 'It's not like that,' she said. 'It's . . . we . . .'

'So you do not like doing these things,' said The Dreamer, 'and you receive nothing in return. Why do you do them?'

'That's not how it works!' she snapped, a strange panic rising in her chest. 'You don't understand. If we only ever did anything for ourselves the whole world would tear itself to pieces. I help my mother and my friends because I love them, and because I know they'd do the same for me.'

The Dreamer's hand slid across the velvet, moving towards her ankle. 'But they weigh on you, Moira Jean. I know they do. Your cares are so heavy, and you have no one to share them with who is not already burdened down. So you carry on alone, and the further you go, the more alone you are.'

Moira Jean went still. It was as if he'd looked inside her head. All this time, she'd thought he was too alien to understand her, and yet he could cut to the core of her so easily.

'You do not deserve such toil,' he murmured, his hand sliding over her leg. 'Do you not want to be free of it? When was the last time a day stretched in front of you, completely and utterly yours? I can give you these things. I can give you anything you ask for.'

Her mouth was suddenly dry. 'I . . . you don't understand . . .'

'*You* do not understand,' The Dreamer urged. 'You do not need to work. You will not need anything, in The Land Under the Hill. You will be free of all of it. What is waiting for you, in your home? Nothing but sickness and toil. But they cannot touch you, when you are with me. Why would you want to hurry back, when that is all that waits for you?'

She shook her head, ignoring the voice in the back of her mind that was urging her to listen. 'I'll not leave my mother.'

'But she has left you,' The Dreamer countered, his hand finding hers. 'How often is she away from home, tending to other people's children? Why should you hurry back to her, when she will not be there to care for you?'

She tore her hand away. 'Don't you *dare* talk about my mother like that!'

The Dreamer seized her fingers. 'Moira Jean,' he said, 'I tell you these things because I must. You already know them to be true. And yet you keep working for those that are not there, and those that do not know how you suffer on their account. Stay here – just until your clothes are dry,' he said, as she began to protest. 'Let them see how much they miss you.'

Moira Jean wished she could have found an excuse, but none of them seemed to matter. All that was waiting in Brudonnock was a mother too busy for her, friends too sick to be out of bed, and endless, unrelenting work. There were always fields to plough and crops to sow and fences to mend and things to clean, and ten thousand more things that sprung to mind the moment she sat down. But now she was sitting beside a fire, draped in material that was warmer and softer than anything else she owned, and The Dreamer was holding her hand and looking at her in a way that no one had looked at her since—

She took her hand away. Something cold seemed to drop into the pit of her stomach. She remembered all the clothes she had wrung out over the bucket – shift, shirt, skirt and stays – and realized that none of them had hidden a hard lump of metal.

Angus's medal was gone.

Moira Jean looked everywhere. Under the chaise longue, in the woodpile, behind the curtains. She rolled back the Turkish carpet, peered inside the champagne bucket, and shook out all her clothes, flicking water across the floor while guilt scrabbled through her.

Angus's medal was nowhere to be seen.

She tried to search outside, but The Dreamer's hand clamped around her arm. 'Do not go back into the loch, Moira Jean. There are more than kelpies under the water.'

'But . . .'

'My servants will search for you,' The Dreamer said, and the brownies scuttled out of the door at his words. 'You will stay here, as you promised.'

He led her back inside, one cold arm around her bare shoulders. She thought she wouldn't be able to stay. Surely doing nothing would gnaw at her from the inside, clawing at her thoughts until she had to get up and move around. Instead, she fell asleep. Her dreams boiled and seethed with a mess of eyes: the kelpie's eyes, dark and twitchy; Angus's eyes, brown and smiling; The Dreamer's eyes, sometimes the colour of oil on water, sometimes yellow and snakelike and in three even rows, sometimes clustered together and glittering like a fly's. Guilt surged through her the moment she woke, even though she ached all over.

Her clothes were filthy and torn, but dry. She put them back on, wincing. When she was done, she turned to The Dreamer. 'Have they—'

He shook his head. 'They will not stop until they find it. In return, Moira Jean, you must promise me something.'

'What is it?' she asked, unease prickling at the edges of her thoughts.

'Do not go back into the water,' he said, taking her hands. 'That's it?'

He nodded, and she made the promise. As much as she wanted Angus's medal back, the thought of stepping into the flat, dark water one more time made her hands tremble. She turned her back on the loch, picked up the buckets and went home, feeling the smooth, grey surface of the water over her shoulder all the way back to her cottage. Guilt settled on her like snow as she walked. She knew she ought to have used her time more wisely. Beltane was two weeks away. She should have made another bargain with The Dreamer, while he was speaking softly to her by the light of the fire. But she was so tired, and the thought of parting with another piece of herself when she had come so close to drowning towered over her, like a mountain she could not climb.

The sun had nearly set by the time she was back in Brudonnock. Burnt orange clouds streaked over her head, turning red and purple as they tumbled closer to the west.

Copper light reflected off every window; it dimmed and flared as shutters closed when she passed. One door closed after another, like bolts being slammed into place by a jailer.

Her mother was waiting for her when she got home, lips pressed together in a thin line. 'Moira Jean!' she snapped, 'what's this I'm hearing about you – what's wrong?'

Her mother's eyes darted from Moira Jean's missing shawl to her torn blouse to her algae-stained skirt, and all the colour drained out of her face.

Moira Jean put the buckets down. She shut the door. Her hands fumbled with the catch. She felt numb all the way through. The Dreamer's voice was ringing in her ears: *What is it that keeps you in Brudonnock?*

Her mother laid a hand on her shoulder. 'Moira Jean?'

It was too much. Anger, she could deal with; work, she was used to. But gentle words and a hand on her shoulder seemed like the cruellest and the kindest things in the world.

'Oh, Ma,' she said, and burst into tears.

Her mother led her over to the table and made a cup of tea while Moira Jean sobbed. She couldn't stop crying for long enough to drink it. Her mother stood next to her, rubbing Moira Jean's back as she howled into her mother's embrace like a child.

'What happened, love?' her mother asked, her voice gentle.

'I lost the medal,' Moira Jean wailed, 'I lost it! It dropped in the loch and then I fell in and I didn't know it was gone until . . .'

'Slow down, hen. Start at the beginning.'

Moira Jean took a deep breath, wiping her eyes and trying to decide on her lie. She couldn't tell her mother the truth. Her eyes would glaze over the moment Moira Jean mentioned

The Dreamer, and she could not bear to see that empty expression on her own mother's face.

'All right,' she said, still sniffing. 'I went to the well for water. The MacGregors were there, saying I stole from Drewitts.'

'Love, you know you shouldn't listen to – they said *what*?'

'It doesn't matter. Mrs McGillycuddy doesn't think it's true. At least, she didn't used to. But Mrs MacGregor and I had words, and I know I shouldn't have, but I did, so don't be angry. Anyway, I didn't want to be there after that so I went to the loch instead.'

Moira Jean's mother was clenching her jaw, clearly fuming. 'I'm not angry. Well, not with you. Go on.'

Now came the part that made her shrivel. The lie, when all her mother wanted was to help her. She looked away. 'I'm not sure how it happened. The medal must've fallen into the loch, and I was scrabbling about looking for it, and I think I got caught on something? I don't know. I got stuck under the water—'

Her mother held her tighter.

'I'm all right,' Moira Jean insisted. 'I got out. I'm fine, Ma, you needn't worry. But I was soaked and I felt a wee bit shaky so I dried off in The Cottage. I'm fine.'

'Oh, Moira Jean,' her mother said, her voice trembling. 'My poor wee lamb . . .'

'I'm fine,' Moira Jean said. 'I promise, I'm fine.'

Her mother held her at arms' length, staring into her face. There were dark shadows under her eyes, and her mouth was set into a taut line. Her throat worked, and guilt spread through Moira Jean like a blight. She'd never meant to make her mother worry.

'I don't think you are fine, hen,' her mother said, very gently.

Tears burned in Moira Jean's eyes. Her throat was suddenly tight. 'I—'

There was a knock at the door. Her mother glared at it. 'So help me *God*,' she growled, 'if that's Nellie MacGregor, she and I are going to have *words*.'

The knocking came again, faster now. Her mother disentangled herself from Moira Jean and wrenched the door open. 'Just you – oh. Dougal. What're you doing here?'

Mr Selkirk was standing on the doorstep, twisting his cloth cap in his hands. 'Alma, you'd best come quick. Mrs McGillycuddy's taken ill – just dropped, right on the kitchen floor.'

'What? How long was she there for?'

Mr Selkirk shook his head. 'I don't know. Effie found her, she couldn't say. D'you think it's . . .'

Her mother passed a shaking hand over her face. 'Lord Almighty. Who's looking after the children?'

'I . . . I don't . . .'

Her mother snatched up her doctor's bag and shawl. Moira Jean felt like she was shrinking as she watched her do it.

'Ma . . .'

Her mother faltered at the door. 'I'll . . . I'll only be a few minutes, love. You'll hardly know I'm gone.' She planted a fierce kiss on Moira Jean's forehead. 'You're to get out of those clothes and straight into bed. I'll be back in under an hour to sort your supper. Don't you dare try and do it yourself; I'll know if you've been out of bed. Go on, now.'

She left. Moira Jean stared at the door long after she had closed it, trying desperately not to think about what The Dreamer had said.

* * *

Moira Jean did as her mother said. She changed her clothes and got into bed, layering herself with blankets. She cracked open the door of her box bed and stared at the cottage door until her eyes began to prickle, but the room had grown dark and her mother had still not returned.

She slept late, waking long after dawn. Moira Jean propped herself up on one elbow, looking blearily around the room. Her mother's bed hadn't been opened, let alone slept in. She was still up at Drewitts. Moira Jean got dressed and tried not to hear the words *tending to other people's children* rattling around in her head. Her eyes kept snagging on the little wooden duck her father had carved before he died. He would've known what to do. Moira Jean pinned up her hair, trying to force herself back to briskness. If her mother could not leave Drewitts, then Moira Jean would go to her.

She snatched up an old scarf and wound it around her mouth and nose, tucking the ends into the neck of her blouse so the wind wouldn't tug it out of place. Then she set off for Drewitts. No one stopped her. They just watched her go, standing on their doorsteps with folded arms. Moira Jean held her head higher. She'd brought their children back. She had nothing to be ashamed of.

There was no one waiting at Drewitts. All she saw were the perfect lawns, the shuttered windows, the carefully scrubbed front steps. The house might've been deserted. Moira Jean let herself in through the back door and saw a puddle of blood drying on the kitchen floor. Her stomach swooped. She knew it must belong to Mrs McGillycuddy – Mr Selkirk had said she'd fallen – but she wouldn't rest easy until she'd set eyes on her mother.

'Ma?'

The remnants of Mrs McGillycuddy's dinner sat on the kitchen table – the dregs of gravy and two half-eaten potatoes, now swarming with flies. Moira Jean headed up to the main hall, her footsteps echoing along wood-panelled corridors and bouncing off stone floors. The house was dark, gloomy even in full sunlight. Portraits of dour Fitzherbert ancestors stared down their painted noses. Stuffed deer heads cast strange shadows on the walls; she flinched away from those, thinking of The Dreamer and his court.

'Ma? Where are you?'

She climbed sweeping oak staircases that she was only allowed to clean. She peered into rooms that cost more than her little cottage and everything it produced. She passed enormous mirrors, spotted with age, and her reflection seemed like another blot on their silvery surface. It was hard to hold her head high, in here. Disdain seeped out of the walls like a bad smell.

At last she came to the top of the house, and the door that led to the servants' rooms. She pushed it open and, at last, heard something. Someone was whimpering, and there was a distant clinking of glass bottles.

'All right, now,' came her mother's voice, calm and assured, 'you'll be right as rain once you've had some of this.'

'Ma?'

'Jesus *Christ*!'

There was a clattering sound, followed by sharp footsteps. Then her mother wrenched open one of the doors, glaring at Moira Jean over the top of her mask.

'Moira Jean! What d'you think you're playing at, coming up here at this time of . . .'

'It's morning, Ma,' Moira Jean said, 'I've come to see if you want a hand.'

'No, it's not.' Her mother strode over to the window and threw the shutters open. Light streamed in, bright and sharp, and she stumbled back.

Moira Jean rushed forward and caught her mother by the elbow. 'Have you eaten? There'll be something I can scrounge from the kitchen.'

'Oh, love,' her mother said, her eyes suddenly full of tears. 'I'm so sorry. I never meant to stay so long – oh, Lord, I sent you to bed without your supper. Did you eat breakfast?'

'I wasn't hungry,' Moira Jean lied. Guilt shone in her mother's eyes.

'Stay here,' she said, 'I'm away to the kitchen. I'll find us something to eat. But don't you go in the rooms, hen. I'll not have you taking ill as well.'

She bustled down the servants' staircase. As she left, Moira Jean saw her wipe her eyes. A lump formed in Moira Jean's throat. She hardly ever saw her mother cry, but when she did, it was brutal. Moira Jean turned away, fighting the urge to follow her.

She was standing at the very top of the house, where the servants' bedrooms were. Once they'd belonged to house-maids, kitchen maids and laundry maids, most of them village girls who'd piled into Drewitts in time for the hunting season every year. They'd stood empty for years, dust settling on the narrow little rooms like snow. Someone – and Moira Jean was sure it was her mother – had tried to clean them, but couldn't quite reach high enough to get down all the cobwebs. It was almost a relief to see them; here was something Moira Jean could fix. She took up a duster leaning against the wall and began to clean.

She tried not to think about how four of the bedroom

doors were closed. Reaching up to the cobwebs on the ceiling, she forced herself not to listen as she passed each one. Her friends were on the other side. She wanted, more than anything, to open one of the closed doors and see if they were all right, but she didn't dare. They needed their rest. They needed her mother, who actually knew what she was doing. They didn't need Moira Jean barging in and prodding at them to see if they would still wake up. That was why she didn't open one of the doors, not because whenever she got close to a handle she remembered Angus's father, standing on her doorstep and clutching the box of Angus's effects, then falling to his knees . . .

Moira Jean jerked back, nearly dropping the feather duster. She stalked back along the corridor and threw it back into place. She was done anyway. She'd go down to the kitchen and help her mother, keep herself busy. Her mother wouldn't mind. She didn't want Moira Jean up here anyway; she'd be glad of another pair of hands . . .

'Moira Jean?'

Moira Jean froze. The voice had come from one of the four occupied rooms – the one closest to her. But the door was closed. She hadn't spoken a word since her mother left. How had any of the patients known she was still here?

'Moira Jean? Is that you?'

The voice was quiet, hoarse. It took her a moment to recognize it – Duncan's, but so faded it seemed to have shrunk. Moira Jean hesitated. Last year's winter was lost in the haze after Angus's death. But she remembered the coughing, the shadows under her neighbours' eyes, and the long line of freshly dug graves in the kirkyard. She knew what she could be risking, if she opened that door. But the 'flu patients were not ordinary patients – they had been to the Land Under the Hill. Who knew if they even had the 'flu at all?

She opened the door.

The room was small, narrow, with dust sheets hastily shoved in a corner. There was a chair, a chest of drawers, and a narrow bed, and that was it. Duncan was on the bed, heavy blankets pulled up to his chin. His face was pale, with two high spots of colour on his wasted cheeks. His eyes glittered, too glassy to focus on her for long.

She adjusted the scarf around her nose and mouth and went inside. Her skin began to itch. She shouldn't *be* here. The room was small and close. She could taste the bitter tang of the sickroom, even through the scarf over her face. It wasn't safe. Her pulse twitched in her throat. She crept closer to the bed, trying to look as though she wasn't panicking – but this was how Angus had *died*, this was how her neighbours had died, this was how thousands of people all over the world had died . . .

She tried to smile. 'Duncan,' she said, her voice wobbly, 'are you well?'

Duncan attempted to prop himself up on his elbows, shaking. 'I thought I heard your voice.'

'You've not answered my question,' she said, keeping out of arm's reach.

'I feel rotten,' Duncan groaned. 'My foot doesn't hurt any more. Just the rest of me.'

Moira Jean glanced at the foot of Duncan's bed. His bandages had been removed, although he still looked a little bruised. She sagged with relief.

'Why're you not dancing?' he asked.

Moira Jean froze. Duncan had sounded perfectly rational.

He was peering at her owlishly, head raised off his pillow a few inches. But his eyes were glassy, and there was a rasp to his breathing that she did not like.

'I'm needed downstairs,' she said, backing away.

'For the dance?' asked Duncan, nodding. He sighed, falling back on the pillows. 'I envy you, Moira Jean. I'd give anything to dance with him again. I could be anything I wanted, in that dance.'

Moira Jean scrambled out of the door and pulled it shut, her hands slippery with sweat. She wiped them on her skirt, pulse hammering. He'd seemed so normal. She edged away from the door to Duncan's sickroom, and as she did, she heard voices.

'Moira Jean?'

'Lady?'

A slow, sick curiosity was filling her up. Every instinct screamed that it was a bad idea to linger here, even as she opened the next door and stepped inside.

This was Callum's sickroom. He lay on a bed just like Duncan's, piled with blankets, his face just as pale, his eye just as glassy. His eyepatch had been placed on the chair next to his bed, and a damp flannel was stuck to his forehead.

'Moira Jean?' he rasped. 'Have you seen him?'

Moira Jean shifted the scarf a little higher, sweat prickling across her cheeks. 'D'you mean—'

'Take me with you. Ask him if he'll have me back. Please, Moira Jean. I don't want to be here any more. I feel . . . hot.'

Pity seized Moira Jean by the throat. She bustled over to the bed, blinking very fast. ''Course you're hot,' she said, removing one of his blankets, 'look at you, all bundled up. There. You'll be right as rain, soon enough.'

Callum twitched, his face twisting in pain. It looked like he'd tried to sit up, but couldn't.

'You don't really want to go back, do you?' she asked, her voice small. 'You . . . you couldn't have stayed there. Your da would've worried himself sick.'

He laughed. It came out wheezing. 'There's no sickness, in the Land Under the Hill.'

Moira Jean hesitated. The scarf around her nose and mouth seemed tighter than ever. Dense, close air pressed in on every side. Even though she and Callum were alone, and the corridor behind her was empty, she couldn't shake the feeling that she was standing in the middle of a crowd.

'What . . . what was it like?'

Callum tried to speak. He started coughing, a huge, wet cough that made the bedframe shake. Moira Jean shrank back at once, and shame spread through her like a blush. This was no way to treat a friend. Face burning, she hoisted Callum into a sitting position, patting him on the back and rearranging his pillows so that he could sit up comfortably. When she leaned him against the pillows, his head seemed oddly loose on his neck.

'Better?' she asked.

Callum ignored her. Enraptured, he stared at nothing, his whole face lit up. 'It was wonderful, Moira Jean,' he breathed, 'just wonderful. It was always summer, and there was always music, and everyone was so, so beautiful. We feasted and danced and sang and we never stopped, not even for a moment. I didn't even want to close my eyes.'

Moira Jean could see the shape of Callum's bandaged feet beneath the blankets, propped up to keep them elevated as they healed. She remembered the strange sleep he had slipped into after she'd brought him back. Callum had been gone for nearly two weeks before she'd found him; had he been dancing all that time, too giddy to sleep? She shivered.

'It was wonderful,' Callum said again, still breathless. 'No one wanted for anything. Nothing hurt. There was no work. No war. There was only dancing and feasting and singing – oh, Moira Jean. It was everything I hoped the world would be.'

Sadness settled on her like frost. She took his hand. 'Oh, Callum.'

He squeezed her fingers. They trembled against her hand. 'I could do anything there,' he whispered, '*be* anything there. And now . . . please, Moira Jean. Don't leave me here.'

Guilt writhing through her, she looked away. 'It's not that simple,' she mumbled. 'But don't talk like that. You'll do anything you please, once you're well again. Just . . . just get better, d'you hear?'

Callum sighed. All the light went out of his eye. Moira Jean helped him lie back down again, settling him on the pillow. He turned his face away. 'What's left for me, now I've been cast out of the dance?'

There was a basin of water in his room and a cake of soap; Moira Jean lunged for it, flicking lather across the floor as she washed her hands. She darted out of the room, grabbing the doorknob through the folds of her skirt so she wouldn't have to touch it. She didn't want to touch anything in that room. Her heart was hammering.

She closed the door, drawing the scarf tighter across her face the minute she was outside. It scratched at her nose and cheeks, sweat prickling across her upper lip.

'Lady?'

It was barely Martha's voice. Through the door, she could hear wracking coughs, and a desperate *whoop* as Martha gasped for air. Moira Jean's hand trembled on the doorknob. She was terrified of what she might see. But she couldn't leave Martha there. She was coughing. She needed help. And despite her fear, Moira Jean wanted answers.

Slowly, Moira Jean pushed open the door.

The smell of blood hit her at once. It was easy to see where it was coming from. Like Callum, Martha had her feet propped up to help them heal, and blood was seeping through the bandages. Underneath the cloth, the shape of them didn't look right, as if something was broken, or missing. Moira Jean clapped a hand over her mouth, fighting back the roiling in her stomach.

Martha twitched a hand in Moira Jean's direction. Her face was wasted, and covered in sweat. 'Lady,' she whispered, her voice worn down to nothing.

Moira Jean turned away. She couldn't bear to see the sheen in Martha's eyes. There was another basin of water in this room; Moira Jean poured out a cup of it to give herself an excuse to look away. How would Martha feel, if she saw the panic on Moira Jean's face? She had to get herself under control. With a deep breath, she brought the cup over to Martha, slid an arm underneath her shoulders, and raised her head so that she could drink. Every time she moved, Martha whimpered. The sweat on the back of her neck oozed through Moira Jean's sleeve.

'There, now,' Moira Jean murmured, lowering Martha back onto her bed. 'That's better.'

Martha's hand flopped against her arm. It felt strangely boneless. 'The dance,' Martha rasped. 'The dance.'

'Aye, Martha, I know. Why don't I find you something to read?'

Martha shook her head. 'The *dance*,' she insisted. Her fingers spasmed, as if she was trying to grab Moira Jean's hand. 'Take me back.'

Moira Jean fought to keep her voice level. 'Not just now. You need your rest.'

Martha laughed like rustling leaves. It sounded empty. Moira Jean backed away. Martha's eyes were manic, high spots of colour burning on her cheeks. When she laughed, she looked like a puppet, her mouth falling open too wide.

'The dance!' Martha called, as Moira Jean fled from the room. 'Take me back!'

When Moira Jean got home, someone had lined up a long row of buckets outside her cottage. Each one was full of water. She spotted them as she was washing her hands, trying to scrub off the panic she'd felt in the sickrooms of Drewitts. She took them inside and used them to soak the laundry, wincing as the handles rubbed against the scratches on her hands. She almost scratched the brownie behind his ears, but caught herself just in time. No matter how much he *looked* like an exceptionally ugly cat, he wasn't one. She put out a saucer of cream for him instead; he'd been working hard.

The next day there was a small pile of soap, which her mother almost tripped over. Then, there was Mrs McLeod, who said she'd come to borrow her mother's big bowl but left without taking it, after some careful conversation. Moira Jean waved her off, and saw Mr Selkirk in her garden, fixing the fence. 'It's no trouble,' he'd said, when she'd tried to shoo him away, 'no trouble at all. You get on and rest.' She shot the brownie a hard look as she went back inside. It hadn't been responsible for all those buckets after all.

The last straw was Malcolm, leaning a ladder against the wall of the cottage. He had climbed halfway up and was staring at the thatched roof, looking utterly perplexed. Already wobbling, he reached out and tugged at the straw, panicking when a lump of it came away in his hand. Moira Jean left the cottage at once and marched around to the ladder, waving her arms to get his attention.

'Malcolm MacGregor,' she said, 'what in God's name are you doing to our roof?'

Malcolm wobbled. She rushed forward to steady him. 'It'll be good as new when I'm through,' he said, with an unconvincing smile. 'You get on back to bed, Moira Jean. I'll be no bother.'

'Back to bed?' Moira Jean laughed. 'It's *noon*. I'm not the bloody Queen of Sheba. Get down from there before you do yourself a mischief.'

'You've been up and about all this time?' Malcolm asked, picking his way down the ladder.

'Of course, I—' she broke off. She remembered Mrs McLeod's gently phrased questions, Mr Selkirk telling her to rest, and suspicion settled on her like falling snow. She stood in the light so that Malcolm could understand her clearly. 'Why should I be in bed, Malcolm?' she asked, her voice icy.

Malcolm glanced back towards the MacGregors' cottage. 'You . . . you do remember it, don't you? You didn't hit your head, when you went . . . you know,' he mumbled, jerking his head in the direction of the distant loch.

Moira Jean folded her arms. 'Do I *look* like I hit my head?' she asked.

He blushed. 'Aye, well, you can't always tell what's wrong with a body by looking,' he said. He shot her a nervous glance.

'But Moira Jean, if there *is* something wrong, you don't have to . . . I mean, you know where to find me.'

'Excuse me?'

'Not that I'm saying it has to be me,' he said in a rush, his face scarlet. 'Just, you know, anyone, really. We'll all pitch in, if anything's a wee bit . . . difficult.'

Moira Jean took a deep, steadying breath. The shape of what Malcolm did not want to say was becoming clear, and a dull, burning anger was sitting in the pit of her stomach like embers that wouldn't die out. This was the work of the false Fiona, she was sure. 'Difficult,' she said, through gritted teeth.

'Aye, well, you've not had an easy time of it,' said Malcolm, 'what with you by yourself most days, and the others so sick. And . . . well, I know you don't like to talk about it, but now Angus is gone you've not had much in the way of . . . er . . . things to look forward to, and so I said to myself, I said, "Malcolm, you best make sure Moira Jean doesn't want for a man's help about the place", and – not that I want to replace him! No, I mean, you're a fine lass and all but . . . but . . .'

Malcolm was babbling now, his face bright red. Moira Jean watched him flounder, her temper building like a storm. 'Malcolm,' she interrupted, signing out her words with shaking hands, 'd'you know what happened the other day?'

A strange mix of relief and fear swept across his face. 'Aye, Fiona told me. Look, I know I'm no Angus, but if you just wanted a fellow to talk to . . .'

'I fell in the loch,' she said, firmly. 'Angus's medal dropped into the water, and I got stuck on something trying to find it. *That's it*. Nothing else.'

Pity scrawled itself across his face. 'Oh, Moira Jean,' he said, his voice unbearably gentle, 'it's all right. You don't have to do this. I know the truth.'

She stepped back, smacking into the water trough. A lump was swelling in her throat, and she hated it for being there. She wanted to be furious. Anger was easy; keep it hot for long enough and the urge to cry would fade. It was easier to be herself when she was angry. But this? This had always shrunk her down to nothing.

Malcolm backed away. 'I'll away home,' he said. 'I'm sorry, Moira Jean. I only wanted to help.'

Moira Jean pulled her face into a smile. 'If you want to help, send Fiona,' she said. 'She and I could use a talk.'

By the time the false Fiona knocked on the door, Moira Jean had put herself back together. Her hair was tidy, her shirt was neatly tucked into the waistband of her skirt, and her mother's old shawl was wrapped around her shoulders. There was no mirror in the cottage, but Moira Jean had made the brownie polish the bottom of a pewter mug and hold it up to the light to check her reflection. She didn't look upset, which was the important thing.

She answered the door with a bright smile. The false Fiona stood on the doorstep, an equally false smile plastered on her lovely face. Mrs MacGregor was standing not too far away, trying to look as though she wasn't keeping an eye on her.

'Hello, Moira Jean,' the false Fiona said, her green eyes glittering. 'Malcolm said you were after a wee chat?'

Moira Jean stepped outside, closing the door behind her. She wasn't letting the changeling inside her home. 'Aye. Let's go for a walk, just you and me.'

The false Fiona clapped her hands. 'A walk! Oh, what a lovely idea. Where shall we go?'

'This way,' said Moira Jean, resisting the urge to roll her eyes. She set off up the hillside, desperate to put some distance between them and all of her curious neighbours. The false Fiona took her arm, giggling, and twisted back to wave at Mrs MacGregor. Moira Jean ground her teeth.

She said nothing as they climbed the hill. She was too annoyed. The changeling clung to her arm the whole time, occasionally stopping to turn and wave at the village below. She said nothing until they'd climbed the hill, and she'd checked to make sure there was no one there. The hilltop was empty, apart from the old croft. It had been ruined for all Moira Jean's life, the stone walls overgrown with moss and grass, and you could still see the scorch marks around the doorframe where the thatch had been burned away. Ordinarily, she avoided it, but today she wanted privacy. It felt a little strange being there, as Mrs Iverach had died so close to it, but Moira Jean shook her doubts away. There was a clutch of crocuses around the door, and the sight sent a spike of panic through Moira Jean. Beltane was near. She was sure the old lady would've agreed that it was time for a more direct approach.

'Come on,' she said, ducking under the old stone lintel. Her skin began to crawl the moment she stepped inside. The walls of the old croft had stood a hundred years or more. Still, she couldn't shake the feeling that something was going to drop on her head, even though the roof had been torched almost a hundred years ago, when the old villagers had been driven out of their homes.

The false Fiona followed her inside, smiling guilelessly.

'Why, Moira Jean, what a funny wee place to have a chat! You could've just come round for tea, you know. There's no need to—'

'That's enough,' said Moira Jean.

The changeling smiled. In that moment, she stopped looking like Fiona. Her face was still the same, but something behind it had shifted, and Moira Jean was left wondering how anyone could mistake this creature for her friend.

'And I was having so much *fun*,' the changeling pouted. Even her voice was different: deeper, hoarser, in a way that made Moira Jean think of old whisky.

'Is that what you call this?' asked Moira Jean. '*Fun*?'

The changeling laughed.

'Well, aren't you just the life and soul of the bloody party,' Moira Jean snapped. 'God, d'you not have anything else to do?'

The changeling smiled. 'Nothing quite so interesting.'

Interesting. Moira Jean tried not to grind her teeth at the word; she was sick of being described as though she were on display. 'Well, you can pack that in. I've enough to be getting on with and I don't need you interfering. *Leave me alone*.'

The changeling came closer, stalking through the long grass like a tiger. 'What will you give me, Moira Jean?'

'Christ alive,' Moira Jean muttered, pinching the bridge of her nose. 'Not another bloody bargain. Let's get one thing straight. I'm not asking. You can't give me anything I want, all right? You've nothing to bargain with.'

The changeling drew closer. She moved into a patch of sunlight, and her hair blazed gold. Her eyes shone like green glass. She reached for Moira Jean's hand. 'Everyone wants *something*.'

Moira Jean jerked back, heart beating very fast. 'Look, you're no part of this. Just tell The Dreamer I'm keeping your secret. Leave me in peace.'

'I am not The Dreamer's servant,' the changeling hissed, 'and I am certainly not *yours*. I go where I please. You cannot send me back to that dull, drab, little—'

'Dull? D'you . . . d'you want to *stay* here?'

The changeling's eyes were burning. 'Why would I want to return?' she retorted, tilting her head up to look Moira Jean in the eye. 'You and your bumbling friends were the first new things I saw in a century, and I didn't even get a chance to play with them, the court were clamouring so. But here . . .' She smiled, and shook out her blonde hair. 'Here, everything is new. I can go wherever I please – *be* whoever I please. Don't concern yourself, Moira Jean. I'll be moving along when the tithe is paid at Beltane. Dear Fiona will discover a sudden passion for a sailor, or for the stage, or for whatever else takes my fancy. I intend to taste it all.'

Moira Jean hesitated. 'And the real Fiona?'

The changeling shrugged. 'She is no concern of mine. You must win her back from The Dreamer, as you did the others.'

Her temper flared. 'So you'll just trot around Scotland wearing her face while she's stuck in the Land Under the Hill?'

'Yes. She will be—'

Moira Jean snapped. She lunged forward, pinning the changeling up against the old stone wall, her forearm braced across the changeling's chest. 'That's not good enough!' Moira Jean spat. 'You go ahead and do as you please, but I want her *back*.'

'But I'm so much more *fun* than she is,' the changeling murmured, sliding her hands around Moira Jean's waist. All at once, Moira Jean was plunged back to the age of eleven, when she first started noticing how blonde and pretty Fiona was, and the old panic crashed over her. The changeling pulled her closer and suddenly their faces were inches apart, the changeling's lips were parted and what was Moira Jean supposed to *do*, she hadn't ever kissed anybody, not even Angus. The changeling knew this, of *course* she knew this, and she also knew that Moira Jean had just realized that when she'd braced her forearm against the changeling's chest, she had not been thinking about two extremely significant problems, and now she had absolutely no idea what to do with one of her hands.

Moira Jean staggered back, her face scarlet. The changeling laughed.

'Don't you . . . don't . . . that's not fair!' Moira Jean spluttered.

The changeling smirked at her. 'No. It was *fun*. Learn the difference.'

'I *hate* you.'

'Do you? Dear me.'

Moira Jean stepped back a few more paces. Even though it had no roof, the ruined house suddenly seemed airless and hot. 'Don't you *dare* do that again,' she said, still blushing. 'I'll . . . I'll have no more of your meddling. In *anything*, all right? So you can put an end to all your bloody rumours, and . . . and whatever *this* is, because I'll have no more of this nonsense.'

Stone bumped into her shoulders; she'd backed herself into a corner. The changeling sauntered towards her, hips swaying, her eyes glittering like the scales of a snake. She leaned in close, *too* close, and Moira Jean wondered how she was ever going to look the real Fiona in the face again.

'I think,' she said, running one long finger along Moira Jean's throat, 'that if you want me to stop, you're going to have to make me.'

Moira Jean's mouth went dry. The changeling's face shifted, settling back into Fiona's familiar features. She winked. Then she left, and Moira Jean could not tear her eyes from her as she walked away.

It took Moira Jean a long time to get herself back home. She'd been too embarrassed to go running after the change-ling, and half-afraid of what she might do if she did. To think she'd pinned her up against the wall and nearly *kissed* her, after everything the changeling had done! She'd thought herself more sensible than that. It seemed a good deal easier to sit on the floor of the ruined croft and stare at the moss crawling over the walls, trying to think about calm and reasonable things.

Of course, if it had been the *real* Fiona, Moira Jean told herself, she wouldn't have panicked. She wouldn't have pinned her up against the wall, either – but at that thought, she started blushing again. It was not completely true to say that there were absolutely no circumstances in which Moira Jean would have snuck off somewhere quiet with Fiona. If Moira Jean hadn't fallen in love with Angus so early, she might've tried it – although in Brudonnock, with all her neighbours watching, that secret would've been nigh-impos-sible to keep. But she wasn't going to think about that, because she was absolutely sure that if she did the changeling would know.

She slunk back home as it was beginning to get dark, praying that nobody would see her. Fae creatures peered at her as she passed, and she tried not to look them in their many eyes. She made it back home without anyone stopping her, and leant against the door the moment she'd closed it behind her.

'*Fun*,' she muttered, and swore.

She splashed some cold water on her face and forced herself to think. Confronting the changeling had gone about as badly as she could have imagined – she was *nineteen*, even if she hadn't been kissed before she should've known not to panic – but she'd still learned something. The changeling didn't want to go back to the Land Under the Hill. Why not?

Moira Jean stoked up the fire and put some water on to boil. If her hands were busy, they would not shake. The Land Under the Hill had cast a shadow over her imagination since her friends had first been taken. It sat at the edges of her thoughts like a waiting maw, ready to swallow her whole.

Something had happened to her friends there. Exactly what, she was not sure. Pale and listless, it was as if some part of them was still trapped under the earth. Was that what had happened? Without it, would they sicken, and die?

Was that why they all wanted to rejoin the dance?

But The Dreamer had said there was *no* sickness, in the Land Under the Hill. He'd never lied to her. She was not sure if he could. And the 'flu was a human sickness, as she knew all too well. She reached up for the medal and came away empty-handed, a quietness settling over her as her fingers closed on air. Her friends had fallen ill in their own homes, just like thousands of other people before them. And if Mrs McGillycuddy had picked it up, could it really be something supernatural? *She* hadn't been to the Land Under the Hill.

Moira Jean's head was spinning. Her friends had said they could do anything in the Land Under the Hill; the changeling said it had nothing new; The Dreamer said it could give her everything she'd ever wanted. Which of them should she believe? All of them, or perhaps none. She had the feeling the place could be many things all at once. Either way, she was getting a headache just thinking about it.

The water came to a boil and she started peeling turnips. The brownie peered out from the drawer underneath her bed, its bright eyes interested, and an idea struck her.

'You know,' she said, slicing off another long coil of turnip peel, 'you could have some of this, if you'll have a wee chat with me.'

The brownie scuttled up the leg of the table and cocked its head at her. 'And what would you want in return?'

'Answers.'

The brownie took a long piece of peel in its tiny, hairy hands and started nibbling on it. 'Ask your questions.'

'You're from the Land Under the Hill, aye?'

The brownie nodded, its mouth full of turnip.

'What's it like?'

The chewing slowed. 'It is many things, and none,' it said, eventually. 'For me, it is home. For the uninvited, it is teeth, and ice, and darkness. For you, lady, it will be whatever you ask. My lord will make it so.'

'And for my friends?' A horrible thought dawned on her. 'If I can't get them all back before Beltane, will they be safe?'

The brownie hesitated. 'They are happy,' it said, 'my lord likes mortals to be happy in his presence. Safe is different. If you ask him to keep them safe, he will do so.'

'For a price, I've no doubt.' Moira Jean handed the brownie another piece of turnip peel. 'And you answer to The Dreamer when you're there?'

'I answer to my lord wherever I am,' said the brownie. 'We all do. The creatures you have seen are all members of my lord's court.'

Moira Jean frowned. 'If there's a whole court waiting on him, why'd he bother taking my friends?'

'Mortals are different,' said the brownie. 'They are new. They are real. The Land Under the Hill does not make such things, and so my lord must have them. As lord, he may take what he pleases.'

'So he rules over everything on . . . the other side?'

The brownie's eyes darted around the room. It hunched its shoulders and, very quickly, shook its head.

She leaned forward at once. 'Who does?'

'We do not speak of Her,' the brownie whimpered. 'Lady, do not make me. It is not safe. She listens.'

'Will The Dreamer tell me, if I ask?'

The brownie huddled around its piece of turnip peel. 'You should not ask. To speak Her name is to summon Her, and it is a dangerous time, with the tithe yet to be paid. My lord will keep you safe from Her, for your own sake.'

Moira Jean fought the urge to look over her shoulder. The brownie was shrinking in on itself, huddling behind the piece of turnip peel. Guilt spread through her like a blush. It was cruel to keep asking about this woman when the brownie was so frightened of her, no matter how much the mention of the tithe unnerved her. 'So the Land Under the Hill is only a wee bit of . . . of the place you're from?'

'Aye,' said the brownie, relaxing and taking another bite of peel. 'There are other places, in other parts of the mortal world.'

'Have you seen them?'

The brownie shook its head. 'You must enter through the

mortal world.' He took another bite, chewing loudly. 'They are not *worth* seeing. Not when the mortal world is so fine.'

'Finer than the Land Under the Hill?' said Moira Jean, trying to sound nonchalant.

'There is no cream in the Land Under the Hill,' the brownie pondered, 'but then, there is no hunger. There is no fire – but then, there is no cold. But why do you ask these things, lady? You must tell my lord what you want the Land Under the Hill to be, and he shall make it so.'

Moira Jean gave the brownie a half-smile. 'No cream, is it? Aye, that's a hardship if ever I heard one.'

'It *is* a hardship,' the brownie agreed. 'But you will want for nothing, of course. Except cream,' it added.

'Poor wee fellow,' said Moira Jean, wondering whether it would be rude to scratch the brownie behind the ears. 'I'll see if I can't fatten you up.'

You must tell my lord what you want the Land Under the Hill to be, and he shall make it so.

The words echoed around Moira Jean's head. If she could speak a world into being, what would she say? Would mountains and rivers come pouring out of her mouth, or would it be palaces and feasts that never ended? She was not sure. All she was certain of was that it made the real world so much harder. When her mother left for Drewitts each morning – always before dawn – Moira Jean lay in bed and struck sickness from the world she would make. When she trudged to the peat bog with the rest of the villagers, slicing into the peat and hauling up long bricks of it to dry on the hillside, it was hard work that she banished. When her neighbours turned away from her Moira

Jean daydreamed about scrubbing gossip from the face of the earth. Sometimes, she thought of her friends' swollen and bloodied feet, their pale and listless faces, and shame rushed through her. Why was she even imagining such things, when the Land Under the Hill had danced them down to the bone? Spring was unfurling itself all around her, the first flowers only just starting to bloom. Beltane was close. She had to get her friends back, but the more she told herself that, the less convincing it sounded. She remembered the transported looks on their faces when they spoke of what they'd seen, and possibilities bloomed in every colour. Perhaps, if she could make it safe for them, they would be better off there. If there was no sickness in the Land Under the Hill, she could bring them there, and they would be cured. She could make a better world, and it would be vast, vibrant, and brimming with possibilities; loud and fierce and full of the sharpest kind of joy. It would be nothing like Brudonnock.

The village seemed emptier every day. Ever since she'd come back from the ruined croft with the false Fiona, Moira Jean's neighbours had all turned quiet. The gifts had stopped. Moira Jean brought silence with her like a pestilence; when she walked into a crowd the quietness descended, seeping into her neighbours one by one. When she left, the whispering started. Moira Jean did not see the false Fiona – Mrs MacGregor made a point of shuffling her back inside their cottage whenever Moira Jean passed – but she knew that this was the changeling's handiwork. She ground her teeth, and promised herself that in her world, there would be no changelings.

But promises were not enough. Her mother left for Drewitts before dawn every day, and came back too tired to do anything but eat and collapse into bed – when she came back at all. Her neighbours all avoided her. Memories stuffed her cottage to the rafters: her absent siblings' heights were marked against the doorframe, her father's last toy gathered dust on the mantel, the chest full of Angus's effects crouched on top of her box bed like a spider. Sometimes she spent whole days with no one to talk to but the brownie. There was nowhere she could run to where her ghosts would not cluster around her. There was nowhere she could run to at all. No one passed along the Aberdeen road, and there was no news from outside the village – not even any papers, because no one would deliver them. There was no leaving: Stronach had put up a road block, she'd heard, and everyone knew the 'flu was spreading through cities like a rash. All Moira Jean had was the endless pile of laundry, and one day she looked at her own hands, red and cracked and elbow deep in suds, and wondered what on earth she was doing.

She finished the load feeling as though she was floating outside her own body, watching her hands move from a long way off. Steam clung to her hair, her skin, as though she was shrouded in fog. The brownie watched her through the haze, his bright eyes fixed on her face. It was dark outside, and neither of them had noticed. Moira Jean was not sure when she had last eaten, but it scarcely seemed to matter. All she wanted was to be out of that house, and away from the endless work.

She stepped out into the night. It was later than she'd thought; her neighbours' windows were dark. But that did not matter, it meant none of them would see her. She'd stripped down to her shift to do the laundry, and the heat still clung to her. The night air felt deliciously cool on her skin. She raised her face to the sky and breathed in the smell of pine – gentle, clean, after a long day of breathing in fumes that stung the inside of her nostrils.

She needed more.

She headed for the woods. As she crossed the Aberdeen road, she hesitated. She could just leave. Just walk along the Aberdeen road until Brudonnock was far, far behind her. If she spent one more minute in her cottage she was going to scream. She felt like a spider in a jar, scrabbling as she tried to climb the sides. She needed the wind in her hair, the road under her feet. She needed to know if there was something vibrant and joyful at the other end of it. But she knew she couldn't leave. The road was blocked at Stronach, and besides, they all knew her mother there. When they saw Moira Jean, they'd only send her back. If she wanted to escape, she'd have to go somewhere else. But where *could* she go, that would be kind to a girl with no money or prospects and that was not riddled with the 'flu?

But she didn't want to escape, she thought, as she ducked underneath the bough of a pine tree and picked her way over the needles in her bare feet. How could she leave her friends behind, and set off alone and penniless into a future vast enough to drown in? No. She only wanted this to stop. She wanted to see her friends well and strong and smiling, to see her mother stop and rest a moment, to see Angus walking – no, running – back down the Aberdeen road, grinning as he saw her. They were simple things, but she could not have them. She wished she could stop want-ing them.

The moon shone through the leaves. The forest was painted silver. Birch trees glowed under its light, bracken glistened like jade, velvety shadows pooled around the heather at her bare feet. The clearing was up ahead, in a vast circle of moonlight, like a stage waiting for an actor. Moira Jean hesitated. She hadn't meant to come this way. It was not a good idea for her to see The Dreamer tonight, even though she had ten days left until Beltane – just ten days to decide how she would return her friends to the real world, if it was even worth it. If he invited her into the Land Under the Hill again, she was not sure what she would say – and God knew what she'd give up, if she made another bargain now. Besides, whatever she said, she would have to say it in front of The Dreamer's clicking, chittering court, and the thought of all of those eyes on her made her shudder. She'd come back tomorrow, and make another bargain then.

'Anyone would think that you were not eager to see me,' said The Dreamer.

Moira Jean flinched and whirled around. The Dreamer was standing behind her, close enough to see every one of his thick, dark eyelashes. She should've felt his breath on the back of her neck. But she'd felt nothing – *did* he need to breathe? She wasn't sure – and now he was so close, he must feel the heat radiating from her skin.

'God Almighty!' she snapped, heart hammering. 'D'you have to *lurk* like that?'

'These are my woods,' The Dreamer said. 'I may go where I please.'

'Aye, and that involves hanging about in corners, does it?'

The Dreamer stared at her, his head tilted to one side. He was different again. He still wore the same lovely face, but it seemed even more tangible somehow. If she reached out and stroked his cheek, it would be soft beneath her fingertips. His clothes were different, too – they finally looked like *clothes*, and not a clinging white shape that gave her a headache if she looked at it for too long. Now, it was a white robe tied at the waist that fell in graceful folds, made of something that looked soft enough to stroke. The neckline gaped halfway down his chest, and Moira Jean tried to tell herself that it was steam lingering in her clothes that made her feel so hot.

'Why have you come here?' The Dreamer asked. 'I have not called you.'

'I wanted some air,' she said, still blushing. 'That's no crime, is it?'

The Dreamer's eyes narrowed. With a shock, she noticed they were one colour: a vivid emerald green. 'That is not all you want,' he said, slowly.

She blinked at him. 'How do you know?'

The Dreamer smiled, and twirled a lock of her hair around one finger. Moira Jean was suddenly aware of her shift clinging to her skin, slightly damp after a day wreathed in steam. How must she look, flushed and blotchy and barely dressed, next to his effortless perfection?

'Because I know *you*, Moira Jean,' The Dreamer said. 'Tell me what troubles you. I can make it disappear, for a price.'

Moira Jean reached for her anger as if it were armour. She could not be defenceless in front of The Dreamer. 'I'll tell you what's bloody troubling me,' she said, forcing the venom into her voice, 'it's your damn changeling! Just you call her back, d'you hear?'

'What has she done?'

She remembered the changeling's hands around her waist, her parted lips, and took a sharp step back. 'It doesn't matter,' she gabbled. 'Just call her off, all right?'

302

The Dreamer's eyes flashed. Now, they were bluer than a summer sky. He took a step closer, a smirk tugging at the corner of his mouth. 'You are keeping things from me, Moira Jean. This is foolish. My servants are everywhere; they will tell me what they saw. You may tell me the truth now, or I will uncover it later, but I shall find it out. Tell me.'

Moira Jean squirmed. She could not imagine anything worse than telling The Dreamer what had happened with the changeling, except, perhaps, some half-concealed Fae servant telling The Dreamer and his entire court what had happened with the changeling, and then having The Dreamer lord it over her for days afterwards. At least if she told him now, there wasn't going to be an audience.

'She . . . she tried to kiss me,' Moira Jean muttered.

His face flickered, just for a moment. 'And you object to that?'

'Of *course* I object!' Moira Jean exploded. 'She spends *weeks* gossiping about me, making everyone in the bloody village think I've lost it, and *then* she thinks she can just . . . just . . .'

'You surprise me,' said The Dreamer. 'Not too long ago, you offered me your body in exchange for your friends. A kiss is worth far less.'

'I did *not*!' Moira Jean snapped, going scarlet. 'Besides, this is completely different! I've done all of that before, but I've not . . . I've never . . . and she can't wear Fiona's face and *say* such things, not when . . . look, it's a problem. All right?'

Boiling in her own embarrassment, Moira Jean could not look at him. She wanted to shrivel up into her clothes and disappear completely, or perhaps just bolt into the woods like a startled hare. But she had backed herself into the trunk of a pine, and The Dreamer was standing too close for her to get past him. Even though she was resolutely *not* looking at him, she could not ignore the blinding white of his robe, and her glance kept catching on the corner of his mouth.

He smirked. *Oh, no*, Moira Jean thought.

Then, he changed. His face softened, became delicate. His shoulders narrowed, and then his waist, and then Moira Jean had to shut her eyes because it had just become incredibly clear that she was looking at the body of a woman, and the low neckline of The Dreamer's robe was suddenly a much more serious problem.

She heard – felt – The Dreamer drawing closer. The hem of her robe brushed along the forest floor, and then, over the tops of Moira Jean's bare feet. One long, slender finger ran up the length of Moira Jean's neck, lingering on the soft place underneath her jaw, and Moira Jean couldn't stop herself from tilting her head back.

The Dreamer leaned close to her ear. When she spoke, The Dreamer's voice resonated, like a harp string that had only just been plucked.

'Why is it a problem, Moira Jean?'

Her mouth was suddenly very dry. 'It just *is*,' she mumbled.

'I asked you a question,' The Dreamer murmured. 'Answer it.'

Moira Jean opened her eyes. This was a mistake. The Dreamer was standing over her, one arm braced against the tree. It was impossible to escape her beauty. A curtain of pure white hair fell over one shoulder, her lips were full and soft, and the delicate lines of her collarbone were devastating. She was flawless.

This made everything worse.

Men, Moira Jean could deal with. She and Angus had flirted all through their teens, and become engaged after some years. She had an idea of what to do. But a pretty woman sent Moira Jean straight back to the blushing and stammering she thought she'd grown out of, and The Dreamer was beautiful, so beautiful. She did not want the truth in The Dreamer's elegant hands; she would only use it against her. There had to be something else she could say.

'I . . . I've never kissed anyone,' Moira Jean muttered.

The Dreamer stilled. Her eyes shone like gold coins. 'Is that so?'

Moira Jean looked away, hugging herself. Her face was still burning. 'Look, it's not . . . it's just *that*, all right? Everything else is fine, but this . . . I've just not done it – at least, I don't think I have.' She glanced back at The Dreamer's lovely face, thoughts suddenly stilling to a point. 'I know I gave you some memories . . .'

The Dreamer wound one long finger around a lock of Moira Jean's hair and gave it a gentle tug. 'Do you really think you would have parted with something so important?'

'That's what I thought,' said Moira Jean, not sure if she should be relieved or disappointed.

'This *is* a surprise,' The Dreamer purred. 'You are so devoted to your fallen fiancé. I was sure that he had kissed you.'

Moira Jean knocked The Dreamer's hand away. 'Don't you talk about him like that!'

'You are defending him, still?'

She hated the tears that came into her eyes. 'He's not here to defend himself!' Moira Jean hissed.

'Perhaps that is for the best,' The Dreamer sighed. 'I fear you may have been too generous in your affections. Are you quite sure he would have married you?'

'Of course he would! He loved me!'

The Dreamer raised an eyebrow. 'Then he would have kissed you.'

Moira Jean felt sick. She had been sure that Angus had loved her, sure that they would have married and started a life together. But why hadn't he kissed her, if he'd loved her so much? Her mother had warned her about the things men might do and say to get what they wanted. Had Angus been just like them, and she'd been too blind to see it?

The Dreamer caressed Moira Jean's cheek. With a shock, Moira Jean realized that the hand against her face actually felt human – warm, soft, and strong. 'My *dear* Moira Jean,' The Dreamer said, 'I tell you these things because you must hear them. I cannot bear to see you pine after a man so unworthy of you. Do not weep for him.'

The Dreamer buried a hand in Moira Jean's hair. Her face was lit with a strange kind of urgency.

'You need never weep again,' she continued. 'I can keep all your cares at bay. I can give you anything you ask for – *be* anyone you ask for. Why do you stay here, in this world of hard work and sickness and men who disappoint you? Come away with me, and leave them all behind.'

Moira Jean stared up at her, adrift. The Dreamer's eyes had changed again; they were dark and large, like a deer's. 'Are you serious?'

'Yes,' said The Dreamer, pulling Moira Jean closer. 'Think of what I can give you! You will want for nothing, in the Land Under the Hill. Nothing! I will show you such joy, such riches, such—'

'But what about my friends? My family?'

The Dreamer slipped a hand around Moira Jean's waist and held her tight. 'They do not matter,' she urged. 'You may keep them with you in the Land Under the Hill, or you may let them go. The choice is yours. I am yours to command, if you come away with me.'

Moira Jean's mind was reeling. The Dreamer's arms were wrapped around her, pressing Moira Jean's body against her own. If she had been smirking, or smiling, it would have been easier; Moira Jean would have known it for a ploy, and shaken it off. But The Dreamer's face was perfectly sincere, her eyes almost pleading.

Could she really do it? Could she really leave behind everything she knew, and go into the Land Under the Hill?

'You're . . . you're asking a lot of me,' Moira Jean managed, her mouth still dry.

The Dreamer's grip on her waist tightened. 'I am *offering* a good deal more.'

'I know,' said Moira Jean. 'I just . . . I need some time to think.'

'Then you shall have it,' The Dreamer said at once. 'You shall have anything you ask for.' The Dreamer let go, and suddenly Moira Jean felt the cold. The night air slid inside her shift, damp from the steam of the laundry, and she shivered at its touch. Moira Jean glanced down, and started back. Gnarled roots were crawling out from the hem of The Dreamer's robe, reaching for Moira Jean's feet. They had almost tangled themselves around her ankles, and Moira Jean hadn't noticed.

The Dreamer took both her hands. 'I know you do not trust me,' she said, squeezing Moira Jean's fingers, 'but I shall show you that you can. Tomorrow, another of your friends shall be returned to you.'

Something inside Moira Jean seemed to wilt. 'And what d'you want for that?'

'Nothing.'

Moira Jean's mouth fell open. 'I . . . what?'

'All I want is you,' said The Dreamer. She came closer, her

307

thighs brushing against Moira Jean's, drawn towards her like a magnet. 'Your friends do not matter to me. Why should I keep them, when you are the only mortal worth keeping? They do not deserve the luxuries I can give them. You do. This will be the first gift I give you, but it shall not be the last.'

The Dreamer's eyes were wide, desperate. There was no trace of a smile on her face, only a strange kind of eagerness. She clutched Moira Jean's hands as though they were the only real things in the world.

'You mean it?' Moira Jean asked.

The Dreamer nodded.

Moira Jean hesitated. But The Dreamer was still holding her hands, and just for a moment, Moira Jean thought she saw a familiar tinge of panic in those ever-shifting eyes. So she stood on her tiptoes and, cautiously, pressed a gentle kiss on The Dreamer's soft lips. She came away blushing, and not entirely sure if she had done the right thing. But then she saw the shock on The Dreamer's face, and laughed. A touch of pride blossomed in her chest. It felt so good to surprise her.

'That was not a part of our bargain,' said The Dreamer, still staring at her. 'You did not have to repay me for . . .'

'I'm not repaying you,' Moira Jean said, and gave her a small smile. 'It is a gift.'

She took her hands away and stepped back, before The Dreamer could get any more ideas. But The Dreamer let her go, her eyes still fixed on Moira Jean. The Dreamer raised a hand to her lips, her fingers tracing the outline of her own mouth.

'A gift,' she repeated.

'Ah, don't make a fuss,' Moira Jean said, rubbing the back of her neck. 'I'm away home now. I need a wee think. I'll . . . I'll let you know what I decide.'

She left. The Dreamer watched her go, one hand still raised to her face. With every step, Moira Jean fought the urge to turn back.

Moira Jean could not sleep. She climbed into bed and stared up at the ceiling, all her thoughts buzzing. Whenever she closed her eyes, she saw The Dreamer, beautiful and earnest and promising the world.

She wished she could say she wasn't tempted. The Dreamer had taken her friends, tested her for the sake of watching her solve puzzles. After all of that, she knew that she should not trust him. But she could feel the pull of the Land Under the Hill, and The Dreamer had promised to make it hers. An entire realm would be hers to mould into something bright and joyful. If she accepted his offer, she wouldn't need to bargain anything else away: her friends would be returned, healed, safe. Why should she deny herself a world without sickness and hard work? Didn't she have a right to lay her burdens down?

But then she thought of her mother. She was up at Drewitts, working through the night to keep the others alive. She could not bear the thought of her own mother not knowing where she'd gone. Who would keep her fed and plant her harvest, while Moira Jean feasted under the earth? Her neighbours would help out, and Moira Jean's siblings always sent money home, but it would not be the same. Someone needed to be there, to take care of her when she had no time to do it herself. Moira Jean's father had died in this house; leaving her mother alone in it would be cruel. But perhaps her mother wouldn't stay in Brudonnock at all. She'd been saving for a ticket to Canada ever since Moira Jean's father had died, planning to go and join her sister once her children were grown. Perhaps the only reason she was still here was because Moira Jean was holding her back. Of course, The Dreamer had said she could bring anyone she liked with her, if she came to the Land Under the Hill, but she was not sure if she believed that. The Dreamer had promised to care for Moira Jean, but not her family.

She gave up on sleep and dressed before dawn, drawing some water before any of her neighbours awoke. Her eyes felt fuzzy, she was so tired. She forced herself to choke down some porridge and sat slumped at the kitchen table, waiting for the sun to rise and the panic to start.

The shouting began. Moira Jean put her head in her hands, and toyed with the idea of letting whoever it was find their own child. She worked so hard, and her neighbours never thanked her for it. But as the calls grew louder, she got to her feet. As much as she wanted to spite her neighbours, she didn't want to forsake her friends. She'd let them down enough already.

She waited for the knock. It did not come. After five minutes of waiting, her head drooping and her eyes aching, she gave up and opened her own door.

A clutch of her neighbours stood opposite her cottage – a distraught Mr Selkirk, Mrs MacGregor, and the false Fiona. They stopped talking when they saw her, their mouths set into hard lines. The false Fiona clung to Mrs MacGregor's arm, cowering. Moira Jean ground her teeth. It seemed she was stuck with the changeling for a little longer.

'You've shown your face, then,' Mrs MacGregor snapped.

Moira Jean pinched the bridge of her nose. 'Where've you looked?'

Mrs MacGregor glared at her. 'And how'd you *know* we're looking for Jim?'

Mr Selkirk trudged forward, his hat in his hands. 'Moira Jean, I'll not say a word to your mother, I swear. Only let me see my boy.'

He might as well have slapped her. Mr Selkirk had watched Moira Jean grow up. He'd brought her father a bottle of whisky the day she was born. And after nineteen years of knowing her, he thought her capable of taking his son.

'I've not seen him,' she said, trying to keep her voice gentle. 'Where've you looked?'

Mrs MacGregor shook off the false Fiona and pushed Mr Selkirk aside. 'Just you stay out of my way, Moira Jean,' she said, barging past her and into the cottage.

'Hey! What're you doing?'

'I told you to stay out of my way,' said Mrs MacGregor, peering into the box beds. She pulled aside the covers, upended the laundry basket, opened the cupboards on the dresser, craned her neck to see up into the rafters.

Moira Jean grabbed her arm and tried to haul her outside. 'Get out of my house!' she snapped. 'You've no right to—'

Mrs MacGregor whirled around and slapped Moira Jean across the face. Moira Jean staggered, hitting the back of her head on the stone wall. 'I've every right!' Mrs MacGregor yelled. 'You think I don't know what you've been up to, Moira Jean? If your mother had any sense she'd turn you out, after what you've put us through—'

Moira Jean's head was throbbing. There was a ringing in her ears. Dazed, she watched Mrs MacGregor turn over her cottage, feeling as though she was observing everything from a long way off. For a moment, she couldn't understand. But then she remembered the changeling, and lurched out into the fresh air. She leaned against the cottage wall and soon, she was on the ground, not entirely sure how she had got there.

Moira Jean hauled herself into a sitting position and leaned against the wall, waiting for the crashing to stop. The world tilted around her. No one came to sit beside her, or to ask how she was. Her neighbours just stood and stared. Moira Jean felt nothing. Maybe she would, when everything had stopped swaying, but for now she was just going to try not to feel the pulse throbbing in the back of her head.

The noises stopped. Moments later, Mrs MacGregor marched out of Moira Jean's house, panting. She planted herself in front of Moira Jean, hands on her hips. 'Well?' she demanded.

'Well what?' Moira Jean mumbled.

'*Where is he?*' Mrs MacGregor snarled.

Moira Jean stared up at Mrs MacGregor. She swung from side to side like a sign in the wind, and a distant part of Moira Jean decided that she was going to stay sitting down until her mother got here. 'I told you,' she slurred, 'I've not seen him.'

The false Fiona appeared at Mrs MacGregor's elbow. Real panic was scrawled across her face. *Of course*, Moira Jean thought. The Dreamer would punish her, if Moira Jean was hurt. 'She's hit her head, Ma,' the changeling said, and knelt in front of Moira Jean. 'Moira Jean? Can you hear me?'

Moira Jean tried to push her away, but her arms felt loose. 'What d'you care? You'll just take my place. No one'll tell the difference.'

Mrs MacGregor placed a hand on the false Fiona's shoulder and hauled her back. 'Don't you lay a hand on my daughter!' she yelled at Moira Jean. She grabbed Moira Jean by her collar and dragged her upright. 'Now tell us where Jim is!'

Moira Jean tried for a grin. It felt wrong. 'So *now* you want my help, aye?'

Mr Selkirk rushed over. He laid a hand on Mrs MacGregor's arm and stared at Moira Jean. When he spoke, his voice trembled. 'Please, Moira Jean. With Callum so ill . . . I can't lose both my boys.'

'I'm sorry. I don't know where he—'

Mrs MacGregor dropped her. Moira Jean collapsed, and her stomach lurched. For a second, it felt like her vision had snapped free of its tethers. 'You *always* know,' Mrs MacGregor hissed. She stalked away, calling to the others as she went. 'Search the houses! We don't need her. He has to be *somewhere*!'

Moira Jean stayed on her hands and knees in the middle of the street, breathing very slowly and carefully. Her stomach roiled. She stared at the same patch of ground, waiting for it to settle, as her neighbours went through each other's houses, one by one. When the ground was solid again and her nausea began to ease she sat back on her haunches, trying to focus on the cold, clean air and not the shouts echoing through the village.

The brownie scampered up to her and laid a tiny hand on her knee. 'You are hurt,' it said. 'You must rest.'

'I can't,' she said. 'The others are right. I'm the only one who can find Jim.'

'Lady, that is unwise.'

She tried to smile. 'Now if I were wise, I'd not be in this mess, would I?'

The voices were close now. The brownie scuttled back inside as Mrs MacGregor's hand closed on Moira Jean's arm, dragging her to her feet. 'It has to be her!' she yelled, 'she's the one who—'

Moira Jean threw up. Mrs MacGregor let go of her at once and she staggered back. She braced herself, ready for the fall, but someone caught her, almost buckling under her weight.

The false Fiona slung one of Moira Jean's arms around her shoulders and glared at Mrs MacGregor. 'What have you *done*?' she hissed.

'Fiona? Come away from her, you don't know what she'll do—'

The changeling ignored her. She wrapped her other arm around Moira Jean's waist, staggering a little. 'Lose some weight,' she hissed.

'No,' said Moira Jean. 'Change into someone stronger.'

Mrs MacGregor was staring at the two of them, her face flushed. 'What is she saying?'

'She hit her *head*,' the false Fiona snapped. 'Never you mind what she says.'

'Clever,' Moira Jean slurred. 'Now. Where've you looked?'

The false Fiona began to walk Moira Jean back towards her cottage. 'Oh no. If you think I'm carrying you all over the village . . .'

Moira Jean dragged her heels in the dirt. 'Your *mother* wants me to look for Jim.'

'Will you shut up?' the changeling whispered. 'I am trying to help you.'

'No, you're not,' said Moira Jean, pushing the false Fiona's hand away. She stumbled, her stomach lurching again; the changeling tightened her grip before she fell.

'*Fine.*' The false Fiona turned around and started leading Moira Jean back through the village again. Their neighbours parted to let them through, all their faces white.

The changeling dragged Moira Jean past every house. They

stopped in the doorway of each one, but there was no point in looking inside. They were too small, too bare, to hide a fourteen-year-old boy. The villagers followed them, Mrs MacGregor growing quieter and more nervous with every step. They checked the wells, the schoolroom, and all the empty houses, until all of them gathered on the front lawn of Drewitts, staring up at all the shuttered windows.

Moira Jean still felt queasy. Her head was starting to feel as though it was disconnected from her body. The false Fiona did not look much better: she was red-faced and sweating from lugging around Moira Jean. Not that Moira Jean felt guilty about it. The changeling deserved a little hard work, after what she'd put Moira Jean through.

'Has anyone checked the smithy?' Moira Jean asked.

'I told you to shut up,' the false Fiona whispered. She raised her voice. 'We'll look here first, Moira Jean.'

They traipsed around to the back door and let themselves in. As one, the men removed their hats. There was no one in the kitchen. Dirty pans crowded one of the sinks, and a fine layer of dust coated the high shelves. They spread out, opening cupboards and peering into the larder, as the changeling dropped Moira Jean into a kitchen chair. Moira Jean put her head in her hands, groaning. Every clatter sent a spike of pain through her. Why did they have to make so much noise?

The false Fiona sat beside her. She leaned forward, laid a hand on Moira Jean's arm, and whispered in her ear. '*Think. What did he tell you?*'

Thinking *hurt*. Also, all her rational thoughts were eclipsed by The Dreamer, smiling and holding her the night before. Still, she tried.

They do not deserve the luxuries I can give them . . .

'Main house,' Moira Jean mumbled.

The changeling gritted her teeth and hauled Moira Jean out of her chair. She kicked open the door to the main house and dragged Moira Jean through it. The others followed. 'Well?' the changeling muttered.

'Somewhere nice.'

'You're *so* helpful.'

Staggering under Moira Jean's weight, the false Fiona opened the doors to dining rooms, drawing rooms, billiard rooms and morning rooms. All of them were empty, dust clinging to mahogany furniture and the brass fittings of lamps. She hauled her up the stairs, the pair of them stumbling over the steps, and opened the door of bedroom after bedroom. They opened wardrobes and looked under four-poster beds – Moira Jean couldn't bend down, her stomach roiled every time she tried – but still, there was no sign of Jim.

Eventually, there was only one room left. It had belonged to the Fitzherberts' daughter, and it sat at the end of the corridor, furthest from the stairs. Moira Jean had cleaned it a few times, before Mrs McGillycuddy had realized that she'd been the one who'd been knocking things over. It had a view of the forest and fine velvet curtains, and a vast fireplace with pointless and expensive ornaments on the mantlepiece above it.

Moira Jean and the changeling exchanged a look. Then, they opened the door.

It was dark inside the bedroom, but Moira Jean could still see the shape of the enormous four-poster bed, the canopy almost reaching to the ceiling. The silver embroidery on the bed-hangings glinted in the light from the open door. She shuffled further into the room, raising a hand to block out the light – and saw the shape on the bed.

It was Jim. He had been carefully posed. He was flat on his back, his eyes closed, his hands neatly folded on his chest. If he'd been holding a sword, Moira Jean thought, he could've been a sleeping knight right out of a fairy tale. But there was a pool of blood around his feet, the scraps of his boots tied around his ankles, the flesh of his heels partially worn away. All his toes were broken and bent out of shape, and bile rose at the back of Moira Jean's throat.

'There you go,' she said.

Mr Selkirk rushed into the room. He ran over to the bed, clutching Jim's shoulder. 'Jim? Jim, wake up. Wake up, son!'

The rest of the villagers followed him inside. They crowded around the bed, hauling Jim into a sitting position. Mr Galbraith took off his jacket and slid it underneath Jim's ankles. Mrs MacGregor hung back, watching Moira Jean and the false Fiona. Her eyes darted between them and Jim, her face pale.

'Come on now, Fiona,' she muttered. 'You leave her be.'

The changeling shook her head. 'She's hurt. She needs her mother.'

'That's nothing for you to worry about,' Mrs MacGregor replied. 'Come away now. She'll be fine.'

'You say one more word, Nellie MacGregor, and I'll crack you over the head.'

Moira Jean's mother was standing in the doorway. Her mouth was set into a thin line, her hands were planted on her hips, and naked fury radiated out from her like the chill emanating from a block of ice. The room went quiet.

She stalked into the bedroom. Every step rang out. The sound made Moira Jean wince. Her mother noticed, and went to her at once. She peered into Moira Jean's eyes, pressed a

317

hand to her forehead, and gently ran her fingers over the back of Moira Jean's head. They came away bloody.

Moira Jean's stomach dropped. 'Ma?'

Her mother's face was white. 'Get her into a chair,' she ordered, 'and bring me some light.'

Mrs McLeod dragged over the chair from the dressing table. Mr Galbraith struck a match. The false Fiona deposited Moira Jean in the chair – gently, with her mother glaring at her all the while – and Moira Jean bent forward to let her mother examine the back of her head, her stomach roiling.

There was absolute silence.

'Looks like a scrape,' her mother said, and the room relaxed. 'But you've a bump coming up. I want you in bed the moment we're home, Moira Jean. No arguments.'

Relief flooded through her. Moira Jean took her mother's hand, her eyes filled with tears. 'Ma, I'm sorry . . .'

'You've nothing to apologize for, hen,' said her mother, giving her a quick kiss on the forehead. Then she straightened up, her eyes flashing. '*They* do.'

The temperature of the room dropped. The only sounds were the shuffling of awkward feet, and Jim's slow breathing. Moira Jean's mother tapped her foot, once, and the sound rang through the room like a shot. Everyone flinched.

'Now,' she said, 'is anyone going to tell me what happened to my daughter?'

There was utter silence.

'Let me see,' she continued, her voice still eerily calm. 'She can't stand by herself. She's bleeding from the head. And she's found our Jim, I notice.' She walked towards Mrs MacGregor, each step slow and measured. 'D'you know what else I noticed, Nellie? There's vomit on your sleeve, and my wee lass has been slapped across the face, and you're not saying *anything*, Nellie MacGregor.'

Mrs MacGregor set her jaw. 'She took Jim. She left him here! I had to make sure—'

'Did she now? And d'you have any proof of that?'

'It's always her, she always finds them . . .'

'And you never stopped to think that maybe she finds them because my Moira Jean's sharper than the rest of you put together?'

The words came out perfectly pleasant. Moira Jean could hear the smile in her mother's voice. But the anger was pulsing off her in waves, freezing everything it touched.

'If you're of a mind to fetch the constable and make your claims to him, you can away to Stronach with my blessing,' she continued. 'But if you do, Nellie, I'll tell him the truth – that I've been on the floor above with my patients all night and I heard *nothing*, not a blessed thing. And, *Nellie*, I'll make sure to tell him how you struck my own child, gave her that bump on her head and then dragged her all around the village, even though she'd brought up her breakfast onto your sleeve and she couldn't stand upright. D'you understand me?'

Mrs MacGregor ground her teeth. Her fists were clenched.

'I *asked* if you understand me, Nellie MacGregor!'

'Aye, I heard you the first time, Alma!' Mrs MacGregor snapped.

'Good. And that's Mrs Kinross, thank you.' She turned back to Moira Jean. 'Are you feeling better for a wee sit down, hen?'

Moira Jean nodded.

'Right. Up you get. Let's away home.'

Her mother helped Moira Jean out of her chair. She watched her for a moment, looking closely at Moira Jean's eyes. Then she took Moira Jean's arm and looped it through hers, holding tight to her hand. Her fingers were trembling.

They headed for the door, very slowly. 'Just you tell me if you want to stop along the way,' her mother said. 'We'll wait as long as you need.'

'Thank you, Ma.'

'Less of that, now.' She stopped at the threshold and turned back to the silent room. 'Effie?'

Mrs McLeod flinched. 'Aye, Mrs Kinross?'

'See to the patients. I'll not be back.'

'But . . . but . . .'

There was steel in her mother's voice. 'But what, Effie? If you'd wanted me to treat your son, you should've thought to take care of my daughter. Now go on. There's everything you need upstairs.'

Mrs McLeod's eyes were full of tears. 'But . . . but what do I . . .'

'Find someone else to do it, if you're worried,' her mother said, 'or send someone along to ask me if you want advice. But I'm staying with my Moira Jean. Apparently I've no choice, seeing as the lot of you have just shown me that *you can't be trusted around my daughter*!'

She spat the last words like a venomous snake. Then, shoulders set, she led Moira Jean out of the room and back to their cottage, taking each step with the greatest care.

Mrs MacGregor had turned out all their cupboards, upending chairs and throwing clothes across the floor, and it took hours for Moira Jean's mother to set it all to rights. She wouldn't let Moira Jean help. True to her word, the moment they'd got home Moira Jean had been bundled into bed, and when she'd tried to get up and help, her mother had gently but firmly told her that she would shut Moira Jean in her box bed if she didn't lie back down.

Moira Jean slept through the next day in fits and starts. A pall of guilt hung over her – Beltane was days away, she couldn't be lying around – and her dreams were full of blossoming flowers and her friends' frightened faces. Whenever she awoke, her mother was there. Talking to Mrs McLeod at the door, receiving a stack of peat from Mr Selkirk, carefully closing the door to shout at Mrs MacGregor about the state she'd left the cottage in. The brownie was there too, peering at Moira Jean from her pillow with its big, bright eyes. She scratched it behind the ears; it let her do it, but it looked very confused.

'Will you do something for me, brownie?' she asked, when her mother finally went to bed.

'Anything, lady.'

'Ask The Dreamer what he'll take in exchange for Fiona. The real Fiona.'

The brownie scuttled away. Moira Jean drifted off to sleep; when she awoke, the brownie was crouched on her pillow again.

'Well?' she asked.

'My lord says all that he wants is you. He shall give you whatever you desire, if only you stay in the Land Under the Hill.'

Moira Jean blushed. Right now, all she wanted was for her head to stop hurting.

Her headache eased away over the next few days. Soon she was sitting up in bed, but her mother still hovered around her every time she tried to get up. Even Moira Jean walking from her bed to the chair was enough to worry her. She was always reaching for her daughter, ready to catch her if she fell.

'I'm all right, Ma,' Moira Jean said, when her mother refused to let her put the plates away.

She lifted them out of Moira Jean's hands. 'I'll be the judge of that. How's your head?'

'Better.'

'Hmm.' Her mother stepped outside for a moment, washing her hands in the water trough. When she came back in, she said 'How d'you feel about staying with Alastair for a few weeks?'

Moira Jean gripped the back of a chair. She couldn't afford to go away now. Beltane was a week away, if that. 'Alastair? Why?'

Her mother's voice was carefully casual. 'Does he need a reason to see his wee sister? It's been almost a year, Moira Jean.'

'No, but *you'd* need a reason to send me down to Fife while the 'flu's still going.' She glanced down at the table, a horrible thought dawning. 'You don't . . . you don't believe what the others are—'

'Oh, love,' her mother said, taking her hand. 'Of course I don't. But I'm worried about you staying here. Effie's asked me to come back and nurse the others – the poor woman's out of her depth, she'll only make things worse. I'd rest a lot easier if I knew there was someone about to keep an eye on you.'

An old sadness twinged as Moira Jean tried not to think of her father. It would be so much easier if he had lived. She looked away and saw the brownie perched on the bed. It was watching her intently; she tried not to make eye contact. 'I've done nothing wrong,' she said, folding her arms. 'I don't see

why I should away to St Andrews to make Mrs MacGregor
feel better.'

'It's not about that,' her mother insisted. 'There's talk, Moira
Jean, talk that I can't protect you from. You're better off away
from it. If they call in a doctor—'

'For the patients up at Drewitts? Long past time!'

'No, love. For you.'

A chill descended on Moira Jean. 'You don't mean for the
bump on my head, do you? I'm all right, Ma. I am.'

Her mother shook her head. 'No, hen. I mean an asylum
doctor.'

'But . . . but there's nothing wrong with me!'

'Well, I've noticed you've not been yourself lately, but that's
by the by,' her mother said. 'That business with the rock . . .'

Moira Jean's stomach plummeted. 'I was only messing
around, Ma . . .'

Her mother held up a hand. 'It doesn't matter if there's
anything wrong with you, Moira Jean. If you're sick, I'll care
for you, just as I've always done. No daughter of mine is
setting foot in an asylum – and if that means you've to stay
with your brother until this blows over, then I'll send you
off myself.'

Moira Jean squeezed her mother's hand. 'It'll not come to
that, Ma. I'll . . . I'll be . . .'

'Think about it,' her mother said. 'That's all I ask. It might
do you some good to get away. I know you and Angus talked
about leaving Brudonnock, after you were wed. You don't
have to stay here, just because he . . .'

She trailed off.

Moira Jean shifted. She'd been trying not to think of
Angus lately. She'd been so sure that he'd loved her, but

323

since she'd spoken to The Dreamer all her certainty had dissolved. She wouldn't be the first girl who'd been blinded by hope. Had he been using her, all the time they'd known each other? He'd *said* he was going to marry her, but she was no fool: some men would say anything, if it got them what they wanted. Except it had worked. She was a fool after all.

The thought withered everything it touched. She'd been taken in. She'd been tricked, over and over again. She'd thought herself strong and sharp and far too clever to be caught out, but now she knew the truth. She'd been caught by the oldest trick in the book, like millions of women before her.

'Ma,' she said, 'did you like him?'

Her mother gave her a small smile. 'As well as any mother likes a lad with his eye on her youngest daughter.'

'You . . . you didn't think he was after what he could get?'

'If Nellie MacGregor's been putting ideas in your head . . .'

'No, no. It's just . . . d'you really think he would've married me?'

Her mother went very still. 'Moira Jean,' she said, her voice quiet, 'did something happen?'

'No! No, I don't think so. I . . . I've just been wondering.'

Her mother skewered her with the most calculating glance she'd ever seen. 'Well,' she said, 'I can't speak for what passed between the two of you, but I'll tell you this: he asked every one of us for permission to marry you. Wrote to all your brothers and sisters even after he'd asked me. He told me he wanted to make sure.'

Moira Jean blinked back tears. 'He did?'

Her mother patted her hand. 'He knew exactly how precious you are, hen. Just you make sure you know that, too.'

Her mother kissed her on the cheek and went to add another block of peat to the fire. Moira Jean wiped her eyes, and glanced at her bed. The brownie was gone.

The peace did not last.

Moira Jean's headache had finally cleared when Mr Selkirk had come running down from Drewitts, his face white. Mrs McLeod had collapsed, shaking and sweating. The 'flu had her in its grip, and no one could wake her. He told them this while Moira Jean's mother stood in the doorway, gripping the wooden frame with white-knuckled hands.

Moira Jean laid a hand on her shoulder. 'Go on, Ma,' she said. 'I'll be fine.'

And just like that, it was as it had always been. Her mother was cramming things into her doctors' bag and making Moira Jean swear that if anything happened, she was to find her straight away. And then she was gone, pelting back up the hill towards Drewitts, leaving Moira Jean alone in the cottage and with the promise of another stack of laundry to get through. Moira Jean sank into a chair as the door closed. Nothing had really changed.

She tried. She stoked up the fire, boiled up the water, set the sheets to soak. But when she dropped the last pile of cotton under the water, she could not make herself pick it up again. She just stared at the wet sheets and the little flakes of soap bobbing in the water, her thoughts swirling like a blizzard. Why was she doing this? Why was she scrubbing and soaking and boiling and brushing when she could be in the Land Under the Hill, free to do exactly as she pleased?

'Brownie?'

The brownie scuttled out from behind an old mug. 'I am here, lady.'

'Could you get this lot going?' she asked. 'I'm away for a wee walk. I'll not be long.'

It nodded and she left the cottage, not really knowing where she was going. She couldn't go to Drewitts: her mother would worry. She couldn't go to the forest: she still wasn't ready to give The Dreamer her answer. She couldn't leave the village. So she drifted up towards the dairy. She was due for a shift anyway, and perhaps the glaistig would be there. She'd always seemed kind, for something that did not understand kindness.

Doors closed. Windows slammed shut, and she winced at the sound. Moira Jean barely noticed. What did it matter that all her neighbours were watching her? They wouldn't be watching her for much longer.

Soon, she would be gone.

The thought felt cold, final. She faltered on her way past the old schoolroom. Her own mother thought she wasn't safe in Brudonnock, but the truth was that she wasn't safe anywhere. If it wasn't her neighbours turning against her, it would be the 'flu, or some other man who'd say what she wanted to hear until she stopped giving him what he wanted. It was time to leave it all behind. If she followed The Dreamer through the tear in the fabric of the world, none of those things could touch her. Of course, she would still have to be careful. Her friends were a warning, a bitter reminder of what the Land Under the Hill could do if she forgot herself there. But The Dreamer had promised her anything she wanted; she could heal them, return them safely home, make it as if they'd never left at all. The Land Under the Hill would be whatever she wanted it to be, and she would make it a place where she would thrive.

What world would she make?

Warm, of course, but not hot. The wind would only ever be a breeze. Her clothes would always be clean, and not because she was the one washing them. Also, they'd be better than the ones she had, and so would the food, and the beds, and she wasn't ever going to have to slog through a muddy field or chase a chicken or haul someone up from the bottom of a well ever again. No more toil. No more tears. No more secrets that burned in her chest like a brand, that she was too scared to speak aloud. She would only ever be happy, and full, and wanted. Safe.

It would mean leaving her mother. Her heart wrenched a little at that. But, she told herself, if her mother knew where Moira Jean was going, she would be thrilled. What mother wouldn't want to keep her child away from anything that could harm her? Surely she would be happy, if she knew. And perhaps The Dreamer would let her see her, from time to time. He had promised her anything she asked for, after all.

The cowshed was in front of her now, and she could barely remember how she'd got there. She went inside. The little calf was still in the birthing pen, tottering on spindly legs that seemed too long for it. Moira Jean checked for iron: the collar was gone, but a horseshoe had been placed at the foot of each post on the birthing pen. She picked them up and put them on a shelf, careful to keep them far from the pen so the glaistig wouldn't be kept away.

Moira Jean stuck her hand through the fence and clicked her tongue at the calf, but it just looked at her, blinking placidly. Then the glaistig appeared beside her, and it trotted over.

'Now why doesn't he come over for me?' Moira Jean asked, trying not to feel offended.

'He knows who he is loyal to,' said the glaistig. 'We all do. Lady, I would repay you for your kindness.'

Moira Jean frowned. 'What d'you mean?'

The glaistig laid a grey-fingered hand on Moira Jean's arm. 'We must all obey the Lord of the Land Under the Hill. *All of us*, Moira Jean.'

Moira Jean rolled her eyes. 'Aye, well, I'll not be obeying anybody.'

'You do not understand,' said the glaistig. Her grip on Moira Jean's arm tightened. 'You are not one of us.'

'I don't—'

Voices came through the thin wooden door of the dairy. Moira Jean couldn't quite make out the words. She crept a little closer, listening.

'. . . seems a wee bit drastic,' said Mr Brodie. 'Are you sure that's wise, Nellie?'

''Course I'm sure,' Mrs MacGregor snapped. 'You've no children, Michael. You'd understand if you did.'

Mr Brodie ignored her. 'All I'm saying is to give it time. You know how she was last year, and with the 'flu starting up again . . .'

Silence. Moira Jean shuffled along the floor of the cowshed, praying she didn't make a sound.

'You saw how she was after Angus died,' Mr Brodie continued, and Moira Jean stopped, drenched in panic. They were talking about *her*. 'She was a wreck. I'd not be at all surprised if losing that boy put the quietness on her.'

'Quietness!' Mrs MacGregor scoffed. 'If only it were quietness. She's threatened my Fiona.'

'Has she, now?'

'Aye. She'll be after Malcolm as well, I know it,' Mrs MacGregor snapped. 'You didn't see her with that Angus. The pair of them! Always slipping away into corners . . . *what* they got up to I don't care to say, but if Alma Kinross didn't know about it, she's more of a fool than I thought. You know I caught them kissing, up in the old croft? If I'd not been there, I don't know what would've . . .'

For a moment, Moira Jean's thoughts skipped over the words. They didn't make any sense. Mrs MacGregor couldn't be right. She hadn't kissed anyone apart from The Dreamer . . .

The Dreamer. She had given him some of her memories in exchange for Martha, but which ones? She couldn't remember. Surely she would have told him what she was prepared to part with, surely she hadn't just let him plunge into her mind and take whatever he liked. She *had* to have told him. But she couldn't remember. He'd been flattering her in the clearing, and then there was a gap, and then his eyes were glowing and tears had been pouring down her face.

She thought back, hard. There had to be something. But it didn't feel right. When she reached for the memories it was as if she was reaching through mud. Her heart began to pound. What had she given him? What had she done?

She took a deep breath and forced herself to remember. Mrs MacGregor said she'd found Moira Jean and Angus kissing in the old croft. Moira Jean screwed up her eyes, willing herself to come up with something. She remembered Angus's hand in hers, climbing the hill together. She'd been a little nervous – she hadn't liked the old croft, she never had – but Angus said they didn't have time to get to a bothy, and didn't she want some privacy? Smiling, he'd pulled her through the old stone doorway, and she'd let herself be soothed – and then the memory snapped to Mrs MacGregor yelling at them both while Moira Jean was up against a wall, with Angus's arms still around her. There was nothing in between. But Mrs MacGregor had said she'd seen them kissing, and Moira Jean remembered being caught out, and why would Mrs MacGregor lie when she didn't even know Moira Jean was listening?

Moira Jean thought back further. She remembered sitting on her doorstep with a scraped knee at the age of four. Angus had toddled up to her, sat down beside her – and then there was a gap. She remembered complaining on the hillside at the age of thirteen, and Angus saying '*D'you know what else is unfair?*' and then she was saying '*How's that unfair?*' and there was nothing in between. She remembered lying tangled up with Angus on the floor of a bothy at sixteen, telling him she loved him, and he'd smiled and leaned down and then there was nothing, there was *nothing, there was nothing.*

Moira Jean's hands were shaking. Fear and anger crackled underneath her skin. She could feel them filling her up, burning everything else in their path.

The Dreamer had lied to her. He had taken the memories of all the times she had kissed Angus and stuck his fingers into the gaps they left behind, pulling and stretching and tearing until she doubted everything else she remembered. And when she'd asked him, actually *asked* him, if those were the memories she'd parted with he'd responded with a smile like silk and, she realized, an answer that was no answer at all. He'd told her she was unhappy, and told her that she deserved better – and she was unhappy, and she knew she should get more from her life than hard work and grief. But those things had not been weaknesses, until he had made them so. But he liked to see her weak, she realized. How many times had he watched her cry, or tried to frighten her, or transformed himself to see her flush and stammer over her words? They were not accidents. They were choices, and he had chosen to shrink her down again and again until she was ready to follow him into the Land Under the Hill – the place that had ruined four of her friends.

Moira Jean's hands curled into fists. She felt like she was burning, she was so angry.

How had she ever trusted him? He had taken her friends. He had taken her memories. He had watched her run around Brudonnock, frantic and afraid, because it was *amusing* for him to see her solving his damn puzzles. He had sent the changeling, who'd turned all her neighbours against her. He'd sent the cailleach, who'd made her stare, dumbfounded, at things that only she could see. He'd sent the *cù sìth*, whose call could make travellers drop down dead, when Mrs Iverach had been on the hillside and Moira Jean had been occupied with a task too loud for her to hear. He'd sent the brownie, who'd spent weeks telling her that the Land Under the Hill would be whatever she wanted it to be. And he'd sent the glaistig, who was still standing behind her.

Moira Jean turned. She felt as if something had snarled up inside her. The glaistig was standing next to the birthing pen, one hand still resting on the calf's head. She met Moira Jean's eyes, her head held high.

'We must all obey the lord of the Land Under the Hill,' she said. '*All* of us. Do you understand me, Moira Jean?'

For a moment, she did not. But then she remembered the kelpie, and how it had knelt before The Dreamer, and fury burned away the last of her fear. The Dreamer had sent that too. But of course he had, she thought, as a wave of bitterness swept through her. Thanks to the kelpie, she'd lost Angus's medal – the one thing she'd had that could ward off the Fae.

'Remember this, when you go into the Land Under the Hill,' the glaistig said. Then, she vanished.

Making herself wait until dusk took every ounce of Moira Jean's self-control. She could not be seen slipping into the forest; who knew what her neighbours would do? But she could not go home, either. She did not want to see the brownie. Had it been spying on her since the beginning? How much of her grief and her doubts had it whispered into The Dreamer's ear? So she turned away, climbing the hillside until the shape of Ben Macdui seemed larger and closer than ever. In that moment, she wished she could grind the mountain into dust.

She stayed away from the village until the sun began to set, stalking between bothies, wind tangling her hair. She clenched her fists so tightly that her hands cramped and her arms began to ache. Little by little, her fury hardened into something that she could use. There had been tears, but by the time the sun went down all that was left was a cold, sharp rage that she could wield like a sword.

The sky blazed crimson, and Moira Jean came down the mountain. She headed straight for the woods, relishing the sound of twigs snapping underneath her feet. Things slithered and rustled alongside her as she walked. She almost wanted them to come near her, to try something. Her hands had been balled into fists for hours. She ached to use them.

She stepped into the clearing.

At once, The Dreamer's court materialized around her. She ignored them. She glowered at the spot where reality tore and The Dreamer stepped into the mortal world, already smiling at her. He was in his usual shape today, tall and beautiful and utterly flawless. It was the shape he had worn when he had taken her friends, and her memories besides. *Good*, Moira Jean thought. It was the face of a thief, and at last, she recognized it.

'Moira Jean,' said The Dreamer, 'have you come to—'

'The deal's off.'

The words came out in a snarl. The court went quiet, each inhuman head suddenly still. The Dreamer froze, his perfect smile still in place. 'I . . .'

Moira Jean took a step forward. 'I *said*, the deal's off. I know what you did.'

The Dreamer's smile still hadn't flickered. 'I have done many things,' he said. 'They have been for your own sake . . .'

'No. You've been lying to me. You've twisted everything up and made me think . . . it doesn't matter. I know the truth now. I know what you've done!'

'But why would I lie to you?' The Dreamer asked, drifting closer to her, hands outstretched. 'Moira Jean, you are confused. The brownie told me you had been struck, and hit your head. Your mind is clouded . . .'

Moira Jean jabbed a finger at him. 'Don't you *dare*! I know *exactly* what you've done. I know what memories you took, I know what you said about Angus, I know you killed Mrs Iverach, I know you sent the kelpie to drown me – I know everything!'

The Dreamer froze mid-step. 'Moira Jean . . .'

'*Don't.*'

The Dreamer's face was starting to slip. His eyes were bleeding back into that old iridescence, his shape starting to blur at the edges. He was staring at her with eyes like oil on water, looking as though she had torn something out of him. If he'd been human, if he hadn't hurt her, she might have pitied him. But when she looked into his face, she felt nothing but anger.

'It's only ever been a game to you, hasn't it?' she muttered.

'No,' The Dreamer rasped.

'Liar!' she spat. 'Well, it's no game for me, pal. You—'

The Dreamer grabbed her arms and pulled her close. Something sharp scratched against her skin. His hands were no longer hands, but the taloned claws of an eagle.

'It is not a game any more,' he insisted. 'I swear it. It was, before, but now . . . Moira Jean, you are the first new thing I have seen in centuries!'

She aimed a kick at his kneecaps. Tree roots burst from the ground and coiled themselves around her legs. 'I am not a thing!'

The Dreamer ignored her. The roots climbed higher, wrapping themselves around Moira Jean's waist like loving hands. 'Do you know how long I have lain forgotten, in the Land Under the Hill?' The Dreamer asked. 'Decades. Centuries. I never cared, until I met you. I had my halls, and subjects to fill them, and nothing else mattered. But you showed me that they were all hollow. You showed me what is real and what is true. You showed me how the world had changed, how much was waiting for me to discover. Everything else is empty, next to you! You have pulled my world apart and shown me that there is nothing inside it – nothing! Do you call that a game?'

The roots were coiling themselves around Moira Jean's wrists now. She tried to tear her hands away, but The Dreamer was still clutching her arms, pinning them to her sides. Fear flashed through her, hot and sharp. 'Get off me!'

'I need you,' said The Dreamer, his voice pleading. 'I cannot go back to the Land Under the Hill without you beside me! You must understand. I never spoke a lie to you, and I never shall. I never meant to harm you! The old woman was poisoning your mind against me. *I* never harmed her – and if I had known she meant something to you, I would have told my servants to do the same. I sent the kelpie to rid you of that trinket, the only thing that was keeping us apart. Do you not see? You are far too precious to leave in the mortal world. You shall wither and die and I will not allow that, Moira Jean, I will not allow you to be taken from me! Everything I have done was only to make you come to the Land Under the Hill, where you will be safe.'

'I'll not be safe from *you*!' she spat.

The Dreamer flinched, his breath catching. His eyes were full of dismay. 'You will be safe,' he repeated, 'and happy. I will make it so. You do not understand how weak you are. I *do*, and so I am the only one who can truly protect you. I *must* keep you safe, Moira Jean. I . . . I love you.'

Moira Jean glared at him. 'No. You don't.'

The Dreamer froze. The tree roots stopped too. Moira Jean tore her hands away and gave The Dreamer a short, sharp push. He stumbled back and she scrabbled out of the roots' grip, her hands trembling.

'You don't love me,' she hissed. 'You don't even know what love *is*.'

The Dreamer reached for her hands again. 'Then show me!'

Moira Jean slapped him. His features blurred. 'I'm not here

to show you a damn thing!' she yelled. 'I'm here for my *friends*. The only reason I'm here is because you took them.'

'Then take their place!' The Dreamer waved a hand, and the split in the air opened. 'You are worth ten thousand of them. I will restore them all if you swear to—'

'No more bargains!' Moira Jean snapped. 'You've no right to ask anything more of me, after what you've done! No. You want to know what happens next, Dreamer?' She jabbed him in the chest. 'You give back Fiona and you cure my friends, or I come back here with an iron shovel and dig up your bloody hill myself! D'you understand me?'

At once, there was an explosion of chittering and clicking from the court. Moira Jean flinched. She'd forgotten that they were there, but now the ring of shadows was creeping ever closer, antlers and teeth and tusks all glimmering at her.

She forced herself to focus on The Dreamer. It was getting harder. His shape was growing fuzzy, the details slowly fading away. He was starting to flicker too. One moment antlers were sprouting from his head, then ivy was crawling up his throat, then his skin was as rough as bark. Only his eyes remained the same. They changed their shape and colour, but no matter what they looked like, they were utterly stricken.

'You owe me,' she spat. 'You've lied to me, whether you spoke the words aloud or not. You nearly had me *drowned*, for Christ's sake! You've turned everyone I know against me, you've poisoned my friends, you meddled with my mind . . . you're in no position to bargain, after everything you've done! So here's how it's going to go.' She advanced, crackling with anger. 'You're going to give me back Fiona. She'll be returned safely, and she'll be well. You'll fix whatever it is you've done to the others. And then, Dreamer, you'll never see me again.'

'No,' he whispered.

'I told you no more bargains,' she snapped. 'You don't get a choice! You say you love me?'

'Yes. Moira Jean, I—'

She leaned forward. 'Then *prove it*. Fix them. And then *go*. Because, Dreamer, no amount of love is ever going to make up for what you did.'

Moira Jean stepped back. She glared around the clearing. The ring of shadows had frozen inches away from her feet. No matter which way she looked, clicking and chittering and rustling came from a spot just behind her ear. But she was not afraid. Fury burned through her fear, leaving no room for anything else.

'I'll be back here tomorrow night with a shovel,' she said. 'If I don't see Fiona, I'll start digging. You have my word on that.'

She strode towards the ring of shadows. It buckled, and parted.

'Wait—' The Dreamer called.

Moira Jean ignored him. She left the clearing, feeling as though something was about to burst out of her. Fury coursed through her veins. For a moment she thought she saw something following her between the trees, but when she turned and glared, the shape went still. *Good*, she thought. Let them fear her. There was iron enough in the forge. Tomorrow she'd fill her pockets with it, take up the largest shovel she could find, and get her friends back. And then, at last, she'd be done with The Dreamer, once and for all.

Sunlight streamed through the window. Moira Jean had been waiting for it. She had been too angry to sleep and had spent the night pacing the cottage, fighting back the urge to kick something. The washing still sat around, soaking in buckets of cold water and soap scum. She couldn't make herself pick it up. It only made her think of the brownie, who'd been spying on her all this time, and who she hadn't seen since she realized the truth. Then her anger threatened to choke her, and she had to set it aside.

But now that it was daylight, she could act.

She headed for the forge. The sky was already a brilliant blue, and two steps out the door the wind was tangling her hair. Today would be warm and clear. Moira Jean smirked. Perfect weather for digging. The rest of her neighbours would be thinning out the turnips in Drewitts' fields today – she'd heard them laughing as they passed her cottage – and wouldn't notice if she raided the forge for scraps of iron.

Halfway down the street she stopped. There was a cart outside the forge with a man leaning against it, and Malcolm was leading a large dun horse in for shoeing. She hadn't planned for this. She hadn't thought she'd need to. The butcher hadn't passed through Brudonnock in months, let alone any other travellers.

Malcolm saw her and waved. 'Morning, Moira Jean!'

Curious, she went over. 'Morning. Didn't think you'd be busy today, Malcolm.'

'Ah, well, you know how it is. Could you give us a hand with this one? He wants a woman's touch.'

'Don't we all,' she said, automatically. Malcolm flushed. She took the bridle from him and stroked the horse's nose as Malcolm ran a hand down its leg. The horse lifted its hoof obligingly and Malcolm began to change the shoe. Moira Jean brushed the horse's soft brown mane away from its eyes and tried not to think about the kelpie.

Soon, Malcolm was finished. He led the horse back out to its owner, a small, wiry-looking man with dark hair and little round glasses. Moira Jean frowned. Surely *he* would've been the best person to calm the horse, not her.

Malcolm turned to her. 'Were you wanting something?'

'Aye,' she said, as the man fixed his horse to the cart. 'Have you any nails going spare? Our fence wants mended.'

'Oh aye, somewhere. Are you well, Moira Jean? You don't look . . .'

She tried to smile. 'Bad night's sleep. And it doesn't have to be nails, Malcolm. Any old scrap will do, if I can hammer it in.'

Malcolm turned over an empty barrel he used for water and set it down, at the end of the forge closest to the cart. 'Have a wee sit down,' he said. 'You're to be careful, after you dinged your head. I'll see what I can find.'

Moira Jean perched herself on top of the barrel and waited as Malcolm rummaged around in various buckets. A little of her anger ebbed away. Malcolm had always been kind. She turned to the stranger, who was watching her out of the corner of his eye. Clad in a dusty brown suit and bowler hat, the stranger had a thin face and deep lines around his mouth. 'What brings you to Brudonnock?' she asked.

'Just passing through,' he said, in a broad Aberdeen accent. 'Is there a well about, miss?'

''Course! I'll get you a bucket.'

She did so, and pointed the man towards the well at the centre of the village. Moira Jean was left with the horse, while Malcolm clattered about in the forge. It was standing placidly, the reins loosely tied to a post. Moira Jean relaxed a little. It was nothing like the kelpie. The kelpie had twitched and snorted and snapped at her fingers; this horse was quiet, and gentle.

The man came back with a bucket of water and a flask, wiping his mouth. 'That's better,' he said, setting the bucket in front of the horse. He held the flask out to Moira Jean. 'Will you not have a drink? If you don't mind my saying so, miss, you look a wee bit flushed.'

Heat was already blasting out from the forge. Even though she was sitting at the opposite end of the smithy, she could still feel it. She took the flask, gratefully. 'That's kind of you,' she said, and drank. It tasted a little off, but she tried not to pull any faces. She was in no position to judge if this stranger hadn't rinsed the rotgut out of his flask properly.

Malcolm glanced over his shoulder and stopped rummaging in his buckets. Moira Jean was glad of it, the sound was starting to give her a headache. She closed her eyes, massaging her forehead. But perhaps it wasn't Malcolm, she thought. She hadn't slept at all, and her eyes were starting to ache. The heat of the forge was stifling. When Malcolm had given her the iron, she'd go home and lie down, see if she couldn't catch a few hours' sleep.

She slid off the barrel, stumbling as her legs hit the ground. The man caught her arm as her knees buckled. 'Steady, now,' he said, and led her over to the back of the cart. 'Just you sit up there.'

Moira Jean shook her head. A rush of dizziness swept over her. 'No. No, I'm away home.'

The man lifted her into the back of the cart. 'Just you sit up there,' he repeated.

'No,' Moira Jean insisted, but her words felt wrong in her mouth. 'Malcolm, tell him I'm away home.'

Malcolm said nothing. He looked like he was about to cry, but his mouth was set into a thin line. A door opened. Further up the hill, Moira Jean saw Mrs MacGregor standing in her doorway, her arms folded.

Moira Jean clung to the side of the cart. She tried to push herself upright, but her hand kept slipping off the wood. 'Malcolm?'

The man lifted her legs, pitching her into the back of the cart. It had been lined with sacking, so that she wouldn't hit her head. 'Come on, Moira Jean,' the man said. 'We've a long way before us, and Dr Macready doesn't care to wait.'

There was shouting coming from somewhere in the village. Moira Jean dragged herself upright on the side of the cart and tried to focus. It was hard; everything was spinning. But the false Fiona was running down from the fields and someone was yelling 'Malcolm! Malcolm, what've you done?'

'Malcolm?' Moira Jean asked.

But Malcolm wasn't talking to her. He was talking to the false Fiona, saying that she didn't understand, that she hadn't heard what Moira Jean had said in the clearing, and then after that the man climbed up into the driver's seat, clicked his tongue and the horse trotted away. Moira Jean slumped back down onto the sacking and stared at the spinning sky. A small part of her knew she should be angry, or frightened, but she was just so tired.

Her eyes began to close. She would be angry in the morning.

The sun beat down, harsh and hot. Moira Jean squinted, and tried to shield her eyes. But when she raised her right hand, the left came with it, and her wrists began to ache.

She blinked.

Her hands were tied.

She scrambled up, her heart pounding. Her hands were tied

and she was sitting in the back of a cart and her head was reeling and she was going to be sick and where was she, *where was she* . . .

Moira Jean forced herself to think. The last thing she remembered was being put in the back of the cart as her legs gave way. Malcolm had been there, and the false Fiona, and Mrs MacGregor had watched her go from the doorway of her home, a look of grim purpose on her face. And the man had said there was someone waiting for her, a doctor . . .

Moira Jean went cold. He was taking her to the asylum.

She risked a glance over her shoulder. The man driving the cart had his back to her, whistling to himself. Amid the creaking wheels and the steady *clip* of the horse's hooves, he didn't seem to have heard her wake up. That was something she could use.

Moira Jean forced herself to take a deep breath. No one was going to take her anywhere. If she could only get back to Brudonnock, back to her mother, everything would be all right. And she'd find a drink along the way, something to flush whatever had been in that flask out of her system. Her mouth tasted like old vinegar, and her head still hurt.

She looked around.

There was nothing in the cart that she could use. The sacking had been fixed to the floor of the cart, and there was no hope of prying a nail loose. Nothing sharp or heavy, either – the man was taking her to an asylum, after all. But the cart she was sitting in was a simple hay cart, wide and flat and open to the sky. Whoever had sent for it clearly hadn't been able to afford anything more secure.

She edged a little closer to the back of the cart, peering over the side. Hope sputtered into life. They were still on the

Aberdeen road. Long past Stronach, and surely not much more than a couple of hours away from the city, but it was a road she knew. She could find her way back.

There were vast fields on either side of the road. The driver would be able to spot her, if she ran straight home. But there, running along one side of the wide dirt track, was a ditch. That would give her the cover she needed.

There was a pause in the man's whistling. Moira Jean immediately went limp, sprawled across the floor of the cart. She held her breath in the silence. Then, the man started whistling again.

Forcing herself to calm down, she made herself count to a thousand before she risked a move. She raised her head, peering over her shoulder. The man was watching the road, and didn't seem to have noticed her at all.

Her heart was pounding. She brought her wrists up to her mouth and bit down on the rope, worrying at the knot like a dog. It came loose. Relief flooded through her. She checked her ankles: nothing there. But then, he'd drugged her. He had no reason to suspect any trouble.

Moira Jean edged closer until she was right up against the foot of the cart. She curled one hand around the wooden rail, watching the driver. He didn't move. Then, as quietly as she could, she swung herself over the back of the cart. She hung there for a moment, praying that the driver would not turn around. Then – slowly, carefully – she lowered her legs, readying herself for the drop. She couldn't make a sound. If the driver heard it, and turned to look . . .

She let go. Her feet crunched on loose stones. She ducked. The cart kept moving. The iron-rimmed wheels trundled over everything, the rumbling loud enough to mask her footsteps.

Moira Jean scurried to the side of the road and scrambled into the ditch. Water seeped into her shirt. Soon, she was shivering, even as she felt the harshness of the sun on her skin. But she did not dare move. She lay in the dirty water and listened, until the sound of the wagon had faded. She did not move until the heat started easing off her skin, and the brilliance of the sky began to fade. Only when the sun began to drop into the west did Moira Jean haul herself out of the ditch, still shivering, and make her way home.

Moira Jean walked under a canopy of stars. They glittered above her like eyes. The nights were already beginning to shorten – it was nearly May, and even at midnight the sky would not be truly black until August. Without the moon to dim them they seemed as bright as a new coin, but they could not light her way. She had to trust in the sound of her own feet crunching over gravel, and not slipping and stumbling over grass and broken twigs.

Just after dusk, and just before dawn, she slipped into villages to draw water from their wells. She gulped down buckets, so fast that she thought she was going to be sick. But her mouth tasted of dust and her head still pounded, and once she started drinking she couldn't stop. No matter how much she drank, the heat of the sun never left her; she must be badly sunburned.

When it was light, she kept off the path. She ducked behind hedges and snatched a few hours' sleep, or slipped between the trees at the side of the road. It would be the best part of two days before she reached Brudonnock, if she was any judge, but the man who'd been paid to take her to the asylum had a horse and cart at his disposal. He could reach the village by noon, if he drove his horse hard enough. As long as he might be searching for her, she would keep off the road.

Again, she walked all night, sneaking into darkened villages to steal water. Hunger gnawed at her, and she stuffed great handfuls of wild spinach and raw mushrooms into her mouth, when she found them. Her legs ached from walking but still, she kept going. If she could just keep walking, she'd be back just before Beltane – not that she needed to be, now. She'd grab the first shovel she found and haul Fiona out of the earth, Beltane or not.

When she was home again, everything would be all right. Her mother would be there, and when she found out what had happened, she'd never let anyone lay a hand on Moira Jean again. Her brothers and sisters would come, and woe betide anyone who tried to cross the Kinross family then. Until then, Moira Jean would need to watch her back.

By the end of the second night her feet were blistered and throbbing, but she was almost at Stronach. She picked her way off the path and curled up against the foot of a pine tree in the woods by the side of the road – tame woods, not the vast depths of The Dreamer's forest. Shivering, her sunburn stinging, she slept. It was afternoon when she awoke and she set off, aching all over and carrying her shoes in one hand. She kept to the edge of the path, ready to dive into the woods at the first sound of a cart, but none came. At Stronach, she went back into the trees, picking her way through the branches to get past the old carts that were doubling as a road block. Soon, she had passed through. The rhythm of the walk settled into her, even though she walked on leaden feet. She knew this path like she knew herself. Soon, she would be home. Her mother would be there – she'd have been worrying all this time, if she hadn't already sent for the constable. And if The Dreamer had kept his word, Fiona would be back from the Land Under the Hill at last. If he hadn't, Moira Jean would bring her back herself. There had been real grief in his eyes, when she'd broken off their deal. Perhaps he really would give back Fiona and cure her friends, if only to get back in Moira Jean's good books.

Moira Jean traipsed around a bend in the road, shielding her eyes with one sunburned, freckly hand. Her temper raised its head. The grief in The Dreamer's eyes did not matter. Of course he was sad, she thought, she'd deprived him of his favourite pastime. He'd never once understood how much the things she was bargaining with mattered to her – or perhaps he had, and simply hadn't cared. He had tricked her, even if he'd never actually told her a lie. He had treated her life, her memories, as though they were toys. What did it matter if he'd pleaded with her and told her he loved her? The things he said were meaningless, next to the things he did.

Well, she thought, one way or another, she would have her friends back. She would have her memories back. And then her life would be her own again, and she'd go far, far away from that damn clearing in the woods.

A breeze picked up as she rounded the corner and started down the long, straight stretch to Brudonnock. Moira Jean squinted at the village, shivering. It was quiet. Disappointment prickled at her. She'd thought at least her mother would be looking for her, even if nobody else was. But, she supposed, she could be stuck at Drewitts. Moira Jean turned her gaze to the big house, casting a long shadow over the village. The servants' rooms were shuttered at the top of the house, and there wasn't any laundry in the garden. In fact, there wasn't any laundry anywhere in the village and it had been a long, hot day. And the door of the old schoolroom was propped open, and there was no heat haze coming off the smithy, and in all the time she'd been coming towards the village she'd heard nothing – no calls, no footsteps, no singing . . .

Dread touched its cold fingers to Moira Jean's heart.

Brudonnock was not quiet. It was empty.

PART FIVE

Moira Jean sat slumped against the new well, shivering as the sun seared her skin. Was it the kelpie, who had dragged itself out of the well and whispered in her ear? There had been something of that awful scream in that hollow, echoing voice. For a moment, she was frozen, waiting for a hand or teeth to drag her back down into the water. But nothing happened. Whatever was in the water dripped onto her shoulder, and then slowly pulled away, sloshing as it retreated back into the depths.

Of course, she thought. It wasn't going to hurt her. The Dreamer wanted her in the Land Under the Hill, and the creature in the water was bound to obey his orders. And it was not the only one. Things were crawling out from the doors of her neighbours' cottages, peeking out from under the eaves of thatched rooves, clawing themselves up from the ground. Some of them, she recognized. Brownies in the houses, the *cù sith* padding down the hillside. Most of them, she did not. There were tiny, rodent-like creatures that seemed to have something oozing from their skin. A green head crested with fins raised itself above the edge of a water-trough. A gnarled old man, stooped and grey-skinned, was fading into the stone wall of the MacGregors' house, while a woman carrying piles

351

of bloody linen slipped through a crack in the Galbraiths' front door. Everywhere Moira Jean looked, there was something watching her.

Brudonnock was not empty. It was overrun.

She got up, ignoring her aching feet. The creatures froze. A dozen hairy hands pointed her towards the forest. She paid them no attention. Instead, she limped home.

It was exactly as she'd left it. The washing was half-done, the door of her box bed hung half-open. Her mother's bag was gone, and despite herself, Moira Jean felt a flutter of hope – she could be up at Drewitts – but even as she thought it, she knew it was not true. There were no people in Brudonnock. It was a truth she felt in her marrow.

They had all been taken to the Land Under the Hill, and Moira Jean was going to have to get them back. But first, she had to be ready.

She drew some water from the well and drank it down in buckets. She washed, and changed her clothes, and tried to cool her blisters and the worst of her sunburn. She fed the chickens, because who knew how long they'd been left alone, and collected their eggs. She ate, her hands shaking as she scrabbled at oatcakes and boiled eggs and day-old milk. She tried to snatch a few hours' sleep, telling herself that she had to be sensible from what felt like a great distance. The Land Under the Hill would try to tempt her into staying. The fewer things it had to tempt her with, the easier it would be. But although she knew she needed food and water and sleep after two days of walking, every instinct in her was screaming to get up, to go, to get them back.

She woke up when the sun was setting. Purpose had settled on her like a frost. After one last boiled egg and a cup of milk, she grabbed the hagstone and left for the smithy, filling her pockets with iron. The chill radiating off the forge seeped through her, though the day was still warm. It had always been lit, ever since she could remember. Then, she took up a shovel leaning against the wall, and headed into the forest.

The creatures watched her. None of them came close, while she held the iron shovel in her hands. But the trees parted, the branches bending themselves back, bracken sweeping itself out of her way as if she were a queen. Strange lights glimmered between the swaying trees, lighting her path to the clearing in green and white. They moved like moths, throwing unearthly shadows across everything they touched.

She reached the clearing. There was nothing there. But then she lifted the hagstone to her eye, and through the hole she could see something had torn, just in front of the hillock. The threads of the world had parted, revealing a bright, white haze, and something was shifting behind the light. It called to her. Something like music had curled around her heart and was pulling her forwards. The dance was waiting, just for her . . .

She tightened her grip on the shovel. The pull faded, just a little. Moira Jean slipped the stone back into her pocket and edged closer, raising the shovel like a rifle. Cautiously, she eased the tip of the blade into the light. It felt like she was pushing through treacle. She craned her aching neck, trying to see around the other side of the portal. The shovel seemed to have vanished.

'All right, you bastard,' she muttered, cracking the joints in her neck. 'Let's see what you're made of.'

She stepped into the Land Under the Hill.

* * *

At first, there was nothing. There was no sound, not even her own breathing. She was shrouded in a darkness so heavy she was not sure if her eyes were even open. She tried to blink, and panic burned through her when she couldn't even feel her own body moving. 'Hello?' she tried to call. She had no idea if it worked. She heard nothing, she couldn't even feel her own mouth moving – did she even *have* a mouth now? Had it been taken? She tried to take a deep breath, to calm herself down, and felt nothing, *nothing*, she didn't even know if she was there and *oh God*, what was she going to do . . .

Her hands tightened on the shovel. The wooden handle scraped across her palms, and relief flooded through her. It was real. It was *here*, in her hands, and if her hands were here then the rest of her had to be here too.

She just needed to open her eyes.

Then, there was everything.

Light and colour and sound and feeling burst into life around her. Every song she'd ever heard shrieked in her ears, so loud it vibrated in her skull. Things howled, snarled, twittered, snapped and she had no idea where the sounds were coming from because she was surrounded, now, by bones strung together with lichen and things with furred gills and claw-footed women and colours that swayed like pondweed and trees that twisted themselves around and around and it was too much, it was all too much. She screwed her eyes shut but that was worse – she could feel them now, running twiggy hands through her hair, plucking at her clothes and her shoes with fingers that left slimy trails across her skin.

Moira Jean swung the shovel in a wide arc. The things shrieked and leapt back, the shapeless colours dissolving into fog. But as she swung, she kept spinning, or perhaps it was just that everything else was spinning around her, but suddenly everything was blurring together and she felt like she was falling but her feet were still on the ground, she was sure she was still standing, *there had to be something under her feet . . .*

She landed. Stumbling, her head whirling, Moira Jean looked up.

The colours and the shapes and the spinning were gone. At last, she could feel solid ground underneath her boots. And she was beautifully, blessedly alone. She was standing in the middle of a vast field, copper-gold wheat coming up to her waist. Above her, the sky was a luxurious blue, and something about the way the light shone through it made her think of silk. The scent of ripe apples hung in the air, so strong her mouth began to water. She scrabbled for the hagstone and held it up to her eye, peering through the hole with her heart pounding. There was nothing but a grey, formless mist, almost as if she'd gone blind.

She put the stone back in her pocket, and the field returned. Moira Jean was panting. Her chest felt tight. She swore. The word rang across the field like a bell, and the sound of it sent relief flooding through her, so strong that her knees almost buckled.

'Right,' she said, pushing her hair out of her eyes with a shaking hand. 'Right.'

She began to walk, holding the shovel like a shotgun and already aching all over. The ground stayed solid beneath her feet. Her skirts brushed against the wheat, sounding more like the soft hiss of rain than wool against stalks. Eyes darting around the field, she kept the shovel ready. A gentle breeze tugged at her hair, warm and sweet-smelling. The wheat was still, until she drew near. It only moved for her, bending and swaying out of her way to reveal a perfectly straight path beneath her feet.

She kept walking. It was warm, and her blistered feet were already starting to ache. Sweating, she kept going. Who knew what damage The Dreamer had already done, in the time it had taken for her to get back to Brudonnock? She could not stop for a moment, no matter how much she wished she could take off her boots and rest her feet on something cool and forgiving. Her friends – her *mother* – were in danger. That was the only thing that mattered.

Her footsteps rang out, suddenly hard and sharp. Moira Jean looked down, and saw polished green marble under her shoes. It stretched across the field as far as the eye could see. When she bent down to touch it, it was as smooth as ice. Exactly what she'd wanted.

Making sure she didn't let go of the shovel, Moira Jean took off her boots, stockings and shawl and tied them up in a bundle. She swung the shovel over her shoulder and set off again, her bare feet sliding across the cool stone.

It was time to test a theory.

She closed her eyes and thought about apple trees. She could smell the apples already, sweet and sharp, but now she pictured the tree in her mind's eye, laden with heavy, red fruit. And when she opened her eyes the field was gone, replaced by vast swathes of apple trees.

Moira Jean smirked. The Dreamer had been telling the truth. The Land Under the Hill *would* be whatever she wanted it to be. She was going to use it.

She closed her eyes and thought about her mother. Moira Jean held her mother's face in her mind, remembered the grey in her hair and the lines around her mouth. Then, she stepped forward. Something shifted. The sound which was not quite rain and not quite rustling had vanished. Moira Jean's hands began to shake. When she opened her eyes, would her mother be waiting for her?

She opened her eyes.

Moira Jean was standing in a forest, the green path still glistening under her feet. Her mother was nowhere to be seen. But the trees on either side of the path were curving and twisting into one familiar shape, repeated over and over, wood cracking as they moved. Branch after branch looked like reaching hands, ivy swept down the trunks like skirts, and a large, smooth bump in the wood just before the branches split was swelling on every tree, growing and stretching and turning to look at Moira Jean as she passed. Her stomach lurched. She snatched up the hagstone. Through it, she saw long, thin shadows, crowding on either side of the path like bulrushes, their elongated faces turning to watch her.

There was a *crack*. Moira Jean flinched and nearly dropped the hagstone. Bark split in clouds of splinters. Moira Jean stared in horror as the tree-women's faces, still blank, twisted around to look at her, the suggestion of noses and eyes bubbling up beneath the bark, and the lines around the mouths that were not there deepened as the tree-women's faces split into smiles dripping with sap . . .

Moira Jean bolted. She sprinted down the marble path, thinking *field field field* as hard as she could. The world lurched around her in a blur of green and gold and suddenly, she snapped back to the field again, with nothing but wheat as far as she could see.

Moira Jean collapsed, her knees slamming into the marble.

She curled herself around the shovel, gasping for breath, as horror rose at the back of her throat like vomit. Had those trees really been . . .

She slapped herself across the face. None of them had been her mother. She had the hagstone, which showed her hidden things, and there was iron in her hands. It punctured Fae illusions; she would have known at once if her mother was really there. But she couldn't stop shaking, no matter what she told herself. She wanted to crawl off the path and screw her eyes tight shut, until the memory of those tree-women had been squeezed out of her like tears. *If only that was the memory that The Dreamer had taken*, she thought, and burst out laughing. She stopped. It sounded shrill, brittle, like wire strung too thin.

Eventually she hauled herself to her feet again. It was still warm. There was still an apple-scented breeze. Quickly, she peered through the hagstone again, but the formless grey mass held no shadows. She was alone. She began to wonder how long she had stayed here for. There was no way to mark time. How long had she been here – hours, or days? If she stayed for years, would she still smell apples on the air? She shuddered.

Moira Jean considered her options. There was no way she was going to try and think herself closer to the villagers again. She didn't want to see any more faces leering out of tree bark, or carved into stone, or God knew what else. But she was back where she had started with nothing to show for it. She wasn't even sure if she was walking in the same direction as before: the green marble path was infinite under her feet, and there was nothing in the wheat field or the sky that would do for a landmark. She had to do something, otherwise she'd be stuck walking this path for eternity. Dread trickled through her. Would the rest of the villagers waste away, while she walked the marble path until her hair turned white?

Time for another test.

She closed her eyes and thought: *water*. When she opened them again, she was standing at the edge of a lake, and the green marble path led straight into the depths. She closed her eyes and thought: *snow*. When she opened them again, she was surrounded by deep, pillowy snow, sparkling in the light of a sun she could not see. She closed her eyes and thought: *mountain*. When she opened them again, she was standing on a narrow ledge, staring down into clouds that swirled with every colour she could imagine. Mouth dry, she backed up against the ledge. She needed something solid at her back.

'Right,' she said, her voice echoing down the mountainside.

Were these all different places? Were they all the same place, wearing a new skin that she'd thought up? The hagstone could not help her if there was nothing hidden. She reached into her pocket and pulled out one of her bits of scrap iron – an old nail, rusting and bent out of shape. Iron was safe from the Fae; if she guessed right, they would not be able to move it. She set it carefully down beside her right foot. Desperate to get off the little ledge, she closed her eyes and thought: *field*.

When she opened her eyes, she was back on the green marble path, wheat stretching out as far as the eye could see. The old nail next to her foot was gone. She *had* been travelling. Hope surged through her. She might not be able to find people, but places, she could manage.

And The Dreamer had said that her friends were in his halls . . .

Moira Jean put her shoes and stockings back on. She swept her hair back into its bun and tied her shawl around her waist. Squaring her shoulders, she tightened her grip on the shovel.

Then she closed her eyes and thought: *halls*.

She stepped forward.

Wind tugged at her hair. The ground shifted under her feet. Excitement surged through her – she'd found something, she knew it – and Moira Jean opened her eyes.

She was still standing on the green marble path, but it ended a few feet in front of her. It led into the wall of a vast building, which shifted as Moira Jean looked at it. When she'd first opened her eyes it had been a round drystone hall that was every shade of green, with swan feathers instead of thatch on the roof. She took a step closer and hulking walls loomed in front of her, made of something black and glittering. Another step, and they shifted into woven birch branches; another, and they were panels of coloured glass, each one swirling and shifting as though shadows were trapped in the pane.

She glared at it. 'Make up your mind,' she snapped. To her astonishment, the building stopped shifting. It settled into something that looked halfway between stone and smoked glass, so large that all she could see of it was one vast wall, stretching off into the distance in both directions. There was no door, but as she came closer, the wall split, like two curtains being pulled aside for her.

She took one step forward and then, suddenly, she was in the hall.

If she had not known she was inside, she would not have guessed it. Flowers clustered around her ankles. She could not tell precisely where the walls were; golden trees pressed in too close to see them, each one strung with lush garlands of ivy that curled high over her head. Dappled light, now green, now amber, shone down onto three long tables, each one gleaming like obsidian.

The villagers were sitting there.

They were talking, laughing, smiling. They cracked open steaming loaves of bread with their bare hands; they bit into fruit that shone like jewels, juice dribbling down their chins. Everyone Moira Jean had ever cared for was sitting at those three tables, and she'd never seen them look so happy. Duncan, Callum and Martha were sitting together, laughing with Fiona and Jim, their faces no longer pale and their feet no longer bloody. Mrs MacGregor was there, relaxed and smiling, handing over a basket of apples to Mrs McLeod, who was telling jokes to Mr Selkirk. Mrs Iverach was there, flirting with Mr Galbraith, and Moira Jean's mouth fell open at the sight. Even her brothers and sisters were there – had they come back to Brudonnock, when their mother found out Moira Jean had been sent to the asylum? – and they were all ruffling each other's hair and poking each other in the ribs, teasing each other about things that had happened when she was just a child. They saw her, and waved – and there was someone else with them too, a broad-chested man with the first flecks of grey in his beard, whose face Moira Jean could only just remember.

Her father.

She took a shuffling step forward. There was a lightness in her chest; she clutched at it, afraid of what it would make her do. This couldn't be her father. Her father had died when she was eight years old. He was buried in the kirkyard. But he looked just like she remembered, and her brothers and sisters were all chatting with him as though he'd never been away, and there were tears in his eyes as he smiled at her.

'Moira Jean! There you are!'

Her mother was at her elbow. She was smiling, there were no shadows under her eyes, the backs of her hands were not cracked and bleeding from constant washing. Moira Jean threw her arms around her, almost dropping the shovel. Her mother laughed, rubbing her back in the same way she'd done since Moira Jean was a baby.

'What's all this, now?' her mother said. 'Come and have a wee bite to eat. You look about to drop.'

Moira Jean didn't let go. She kept thinking of the trees shaped like her mother, and couldn't stop her hands from shaking. 'Let's away home,' she mumbled, her voice thick.

Her mother patted her arm. 'Not yet. You're to eat something first – and sleep,' her mother said, disentangling herself from Moira Jean's embrace and examining her at arms' length. 'You've not slept a wink, have you, love?'

'We've no time for sleep,' Moira Jean urged. 'I'm here to rescue you, Ma. All of you.'

Her mother looked bemused. 'Rescue me? From what?'

'From *this*,' said Moira Jean, waving her hand at the hall. 'It's not real, Ma.'

'Nonsense,' said her mother, looping her arm through Moira Jean's. 'And you can put that shovel down, hen. You've no need to dig for anything here. Come and sit with your father. He's missed you.'

Moira Jean had been protesting. At these words, she fell silent. She looked back towards her father. When he saw, he raised a tentative hand and waved to her.

'Ma, he's not . . . he . . .'

'Come along, now,' her mother said. She lead Moira Jean over to the table. Her brothers and sisters shouted to her, told her she'd grown even taller and frecklier since they'd seen her last, but she barely heard them. All she saw was her father. He looked just as she remembered, before he'd become so ill. They shared the same hazel eyes, the same freckles spattered across their faces. A familiar web of scars and callouses spread up his hands and forearms; there was one long scar on his right palm that she was responsible for, when he'd tried to teach her how to whittle and he'd caught the knife when it had slipped from her hands. His old woollen waistcoat was worn just below one shoulder, because when each of his children had sat in his lap, he'd supported them with his left arm and let them lean their heads against that exact spot. He'd been buried in that waistcoat. When he'd died, none of them had been able to look at it.

Her throat closed over. She stood and stared, half-afraid that if she blinked, he would disappear. Could it really be him, after all this time?

'No,' said Moira Jean. 'It's not . . . this can't be . . .'

She backed away. The shovel hung loose from one hand, dragging a path between the flowers on the floor. This couldn't be right, she told herself. Her father was dead. He couldn't be here, sitting and smiling at her and looking as though he felt guilty for every day of those eleven years he hadn't been with them. But hadn't she wanted to see him? Hadn't she watched the other children in Brudonnock being carried on their fathers' shoulders, and burned with envy? Hadn't she wished that there was someone else to stay with her mother, so that Moira Jean could set out into the world without worrying about if her peat had been cut or her garden had been dug? Hadn't she wanted him to come back?

Moira Jean fumbled for a handkerchief. The shovel slipped out of her grip.

'We should . . . we have to . . .'

Her mother glanced over Moira Jean's shoulder. 'Ah,' she said, smirking. 'No wonder you're in such a hurry. You take your time, hen. We'll still be here.'

Moira Jean turned.

Someone had followed her inside. They were hesitating a few feet away from her, one hand outstretched. Green and amber light cast strange shadows over their face. But then they stepped forward, and Moira Jean's breath stopped.

It was Angus.

Frozen, Moira Jean could only stare. It was as if he'd never left. His dark hair was still a little shorter than she liked, shaved too close by the recruiters. The harvest tan had not yet faded from his hands and face, and she knew if she peeled off the jacket of his uniform, he would be brown to the elbows. He smiled, one corner of his mouth quirking up higher than the other, and her eyes were so full of unshed tears that they ached at the sight of it. He was *here*, he'd come back at last, and he was looking at her as if he'd known – no, *felt* – exactly how much she'd missed him.

'Angus?' she whispered, her voice breaking.

His smile widened. He opened his arms. There was a desperate joy on his face when he held out his hands to her.

Moira Jean stayed where she was, tears streaming down her face. Angus was dead. He shouldn't be here – he *couldn't* be here. But he was standing right in front of her looking exactly as she remembered, when she'd waved him off to war. If she'd known what was going to happen, she would have never let him go. But he was here now, he was back at last, and—

—and his medal was gone.

Moira Jean gave herself a little shake. Angus should have his medal; he'd earned it. But where was it? Then she remembered: it was at the bottom of the loch, thanks to the kelpie that had tried to drown her. But it was Angus's medal, and if he'd come back, he should be wearing it. But he hadn't come back. He'd *died*, hundreds of miles from home and with no one to hold his hand. Moira Jean took a step back. How could he be here, looking as though he'd never left, when she knew he'd —

Moira Jean went still.

Angus had left Brudonnock more than two years ago. His hair should've grown back, his tan should've faded. He should have aged. But here he was, looking exactly as she remembered him on the day he went to war. As if he had stepped straight out of her memories.

It was not Angus. It was The Dreamer, wearing his face.

Moira Jean's hands curled into fists. Raw anger burned through her tears. She raised her head, and saw panic flashing in The Dreamer's stolen eyes.

'I liked you better when you were a lass,' she hissed.

She snatched up the shovel and swung it at his face. There was a *clang*, far louder than it should have been. The Dreamer's face rippled. Moira Jean caught a flash of a distended jaw, gleaming tusks, and an oozing eye. Then, the hall was plunged into darkness.

Moira Jean tightened her grip on the shovel. She ground her feet into the earth. Flowers withered under the soles of her boots. Suffocating darkness pressed in on every side.

'Dreamer!' she called. Her voice echoed around her. 'Give them back!'

A low rumbling, from somewhere far off. The smell of smoke and ozone. And, closer, the rush of something with many legs.

'I told you I'd come for them!' she yelled. 'Here I am!'

Something snapped behind her. She whirled around. Silence, darkness – no sign of what had made the noise.

'*Fine*,' she spat.

She pointed the blade of the shovel at the earth and brought it crashing down. There was a squeal, like rocks grinding together, and the ground shuddered under her feet.

'*WHY?*'

The voice had come rippling out of the darkness. She felt it in the juddering earth.

'You *know* why,' she yelled. 'You took them. You took them all! You had no right!'

'They took *you*!'

Long, long hands shot out of the darkness. They were all she could see. Moira Jean held tight to the shovel. The hands folded themselves over her own, papery and cold.

'Why would you come back for them?' said The Dreamer, the anguish in his voice echoing all around her. 'Why? They sent you *away*. You would have been lost to me forever – you would have forgotten me! I will not have it, Moira Jean. You will not be taken from me!'

'That's not your choice to make!' Moira Jean spat. She tried not to look at The Dreamer's hands, and the six sets of knuckles in his long, long fingers.

'You cannot leave me,' The Dreamer pleaded. 'You cannot forget me! You do not know what it is to be forgotten. If you did, you would not leave me here. I know you, Moira Jean. You could never be so cruel.'

She tried to tug her hands away. 'Try me!'

'Tell me what you need to make you stay,' The Dreamer urged. 'Tell me, and I shall make it so. I know how you miss your fallen fiancé, but say the word and you shall—'

'Don't you *dare*!'

'Something else, then!' The Dreamer cried, and snapped his too-long fingers. At once, light blazed around them. Moira Jean was standing in a glittering ballroom, her shovel planted in a marble floor. Her friends were talking and laughing and dancing, all of them dressed in gowns and suits and piled with jewellery. He snapped his fingers again and the sun blazed onto a crystalline sea, Moira Jean's shovel half-buried in sand. Now her friends were stretched out in the sun, splashing each other in the water and shrieking. He snapped his fingers once more and a vast fire blazed under the stars, her friends dancing around it and swigging from a stolen bottle. The Dreamer changed too, flickering between faces, each one more beautiful than the last. He was a man with scarlet hair, then a woman with eyes like the moon, then a person in-between who was so heart-stoppingly beautiful she could not look them in the eye. But long, long fingers were still curled around her wrist, and when she looked down, tree roots bubbled out from underneath the hem of their robe.

'Anything you want,' The Dreamer urged, his face shifting back to the one she knew. 'Anything! I will give you back everything you have lost. You will never know grief again, nor hunger, nor fear. Who else can give you these things? No one! No one could ever love you like I do. Let me show you.'

Moira Jean hesitated. She looked over The Dreamer's shoulder. Her mother was arm-in-arm with her father, laughing and leaning her head against his shoulder. But now that Moira Jean could see clearly, and there was iron in her hands again, the shape of her father was beginning to fade. Her brothers and sisters were fading too, along with Mrs Iverach. She peered through the hagstone, and fear caught in her throat. Her neighbours – her *mother* – were surrounded by elongated shadows, their reed-thin bodies towering over them. The villagers did not notice. They were stuck in their dreams, smiling and joking as the people they had lost slowly slipped out of sight. Moira Jean closed her eyes, and wished that she had never seen them at all.

'You . . . you don't even understand what you've done, do you?' she said, her voice thick.

'I have shown you my domain, I have laid it at your feet . . .' The Dreamer began.

Moira Jean's temper flared. 'You took my friends. You took my *mother*. You . . . you had *creatures* pretend to be my brothers and sisters and my dead father and . . . God! Were you just going to keep me here and lie to me forever, while you wore Angus's face? You don't love me, Dreamer. You don't know *how*.'

The ground was juddering beneath her feet. Moira Jean fought to keep her balance. The Dreamer's hands were still clutching her own, scales crawling down his wrists and across his fingers. 'I *must* love you,' he insisted. 'You have made everything else seem hollow, faded – everything but you is a shadow, Moira Jean! What is that, if not love?'

'I don't know,' Moira Jean snapped, 'and I don't care! I'm not here to help you puzzle out your feelings. I'm here for the people you stole from me – and let me tell you, Dreamer, if you loved me half as much as you say you never would've taken them!'

A tree root tried to curl itself around her ankle. Moira Jean kicked it away. Anger boiled through her, blistering everything it touched.

'And even if you do love me,' she continued, venom dripping from every word, 'that doesn't make a blind bit of difference. How'd you think I'd ever love you, after what you've done? You're selfish, you're cruel – you've taken so much from me! How'd you ever—'

The earth gave another shudder. Moira Jean stumbled, almost losing her grip on the shovel. The Dreamer put out a hand to steady her; she shrugged it off.

Moira Jean ground her teeth together. 'You can tell me that you love me all you want, Dreamer. I'll never love you. You made sure of that, when you stole from me.'

The Dreamer's face twisted. Horns curled through his long white hair. 'Everything I have done, I have done for *you*. Everything! And this is the gratitude you show me? Will you not even thank me for—'

'Thank you? *Thank* you?'

'*Yes*,' The Dreamer spat. His face was growing sharper. He grabbed her by the collar, pulling her off-balance. When he spoke, she caught glimpses of a forked tongue. 'I have let you shape my kingdom as you please. I have kept those you care for from harm, even though I have a tithe to pay and too few souls to pay it. I have laid my heart at your feet – and this shall *not* be how you repay me.'

The Dreamer leaned forward. All the colours Moira Jean had ever seen bled together in his desperate, angry eyes.

'I have done everything in my power to make you happy,' The Dreamer hissed. 'If you cannot thank me for it, I will make you.'

Panic flashed through her. She couldn't let him put her in

a dream. There'd be no escape. Thinking fast, Moira Jean wrenched the shovel out of the ground. 'D'you really want to make me happy?' she asked, her voice quiet.

The Dreamer dropped her collar. Relief dawned on his lovely face. The scales on his hands receded; his horns shrank back into his skull. He reached for her cheek. 'It is all I want, Moira Jean.'

'Then let me be happy without you.'

Moira Jean swung the shovel like a cricket bat. The Dreamer snatched at the iron blade. He screamed, his taloned hands burning, but he did not let go.

Moira Jean did.

The Dreamer raised one blistered hand, pointing at Moira Jean. Tusks sprouted from his jaw; moss crawled down his outstretched arm.

'Then be without me,' he snarled, 'and see how long you last.'

The ground lurched sideways. The villagers dropped to the ground like marionettes with the strings cut. One of The Dreamer's hands sizzled on the blade of her shovel, the smell of smoke and ozone billowing around them, his face stricken. He snapped his fingers, and the world closed in around her.

Moira Jean was trapped in darkness. Something squeezed against her chest, her back, pushing the air out of her lungs. Struggling, she tried to work an arm loose, but they were pinned to her sides. Her breath came sharp and fast. She was stuck, she couldn't get out, she was going to die crushed in darkness without even being able to raise a hand to—

She stopped. Her hands were pinned to her sides – right by her pockets. Wriggling, she scrabbled around until she found a piece of cold iron. Easing the nail out of her pocket, she pressed it into the thing wrapped around her.

It screeched. The sound rang in her ears, vibrating through her whole body. She screwed up her eyes and pushed the nail in harder. The scream grew louder, louder and then there was a burst of light, air rushing in behind it. Moira Jean scrambled out of the thing's grip, dragging the iron nail across its – flesh? shell? – as she did so, and staggered out of its reach, her ears ringing.

Gasping for breath, she looked around. She was in another forest, much like the one outside Brudonnock. There were pines and birch and larch trees all around her, a springy carpet of pine needles underneath her feet, and no sign of the green marble path. Despite herself, hope began to flicker. Had The Dreamer sent her back home?

Something curled around her ankle. Moira Jean stamped down, hard. There was a *crack*. A splintered root was wriggling beneath her boots. She jumped, disgust surging through her. Looking over her shoulder, she saw the thing she had escaped from – a vast elder tree, the trunk of it split and oozing sap. Its twisted branches were still reaching for her, roots slithering through the bracken like snakes.

Moira Jean slashed out at the nearest branch, the iron nail clutched in her hand. The branch whipped back, that same shrieking noise ringing in her ears.

'Let me be,' she snarled. 'I've more iron in my pockets, you bastard. The next nail's going right into your trunk.'

The roots retreated. Moira Jean glared at them as they went, rubbing her ribs. Fear fluttered beneath her anger. There was a strain in her chest when she breathed; had the tree broken something? She shook her head. It didn't matter. She was still upright, even though she ached all over. She could still keep moving.

She closed her eyes and thought: *halls*. Even as she did so, she knew that nothing would happen. This was The Dreamer's realm; she could not shape it unless he wanted her to. Sure enough, when she opened her eyes the forest still surrounded her.

It did not matter. Moira Jean ground her teeth and curled her hands into fists, threading one iron nail through each gap between her fingers. The path had been hidden from her. No trees bent themselves backwards to clear her way. She struggled through thorns and snagged her hair on holly but still, she kept going. She *would* find her way back to The Dreamer's halls.

Things crept alongside her.

At first, she only saw them in flashes. Antlered heads. Slithering shadows. Teeth. She ignored them, and kept her head held high. She knew The Dreamer's work when she saw it. He wanted her afraid, uncertain – it was how he'd always wanted her. But she had finished giving him what he wanted. She was strong, sure-footed, and no matter what he threw at her she would face it.

The creatures came closer. Beautiful, bloody-mouthed women reached for her with elegant hands. Wizened old men no higher than her knee grinned at her with too many teeth. Hunched and slavering bogles bounded alongside her like hunting dogs, snapping at her heels to see if they could make her run. She swiped at them with hands full of nails and they sped, gibbering, into the trees.

Her hair had come loose, snagged out of its pins by low-hanging branches and things that flew too close to her head. Something that looked stuck between the shape of a wolf and the shape of a man had lunged for her; she'd lashed out, but it had caught her shawl in its teeth and torn it. When she came across a small, dark-haired man shrouded in a cloak of leaves and moss, she held the shawl out to him, taking care to remove the iron from her palm.

'It's yours, in exchange for directions to The Dreamer's halls,' she said. 'He'll pay handsomely for something of mine.'

The shawl vanished under the little man's cloak. 'He'll make no more bargains until the tithe is paid. Go where the way is closed, and you'll find his halls.'

Suspicion curdled in the pit of Moira Jean's stomach. 'How'd you pay this tithe?' she asked.

'And what'll you trade for—'

Moira Jean cut him off. 'No more bargains, did you say? Fine by me, pal. On you go.'

The little man bowed and spun round on the spot, vanishing in a whirl of leaves. Moira Jean looked around her, considering his directions. *Go where the way is closed . . .* It made sense. The Dreamer did not want her back in his halls: therefore, the hardest path would lead her back to him. She fished out the hagstone again and peered through it and, sure enough, where there had been a dense patch of brambles there was now the faintest shimmer of green, just visible through the grey haze.

Wishing she still had her shovel, Moira Jean headed straight for the thorns. She struggled through them, her chest growing tighter with every step. As she pushed back the brambles, her thoughts snagged on the tithe. The Dreamer's words echoed in her head. *There is a tithe to pay, and I have too few souls to pay it . . .*

She stopped. Her breath caught.

Her friends were in more danger than she thought.

* * *

The iron was slipping out of Moira Jean's fists. She kept them ready, waiting for something to step out of the brambles and try her patience. But her hands were covered in sweat and starting to cramp. When she pushed aside another bramble, another nail slipped between her fingers. The forest fled from them, branches and roots scurrying away from the fallen iron.

Moira Jean had pushed her way through the tangle of thorns, swiping at branches with iron to make them draw back. The hem of her skirt was in tatters and there were long, thin scratches all across her arms. Now she stood on the edge of a vast bog, dark mud sucking at her shoes. Mist hung in the air. Lights glimmered in the distance, but she knew better than to follow them. They would lead her into the mire, where the bogwater would trickle into her lungs. But perhaps that was the way to The Dreamer's halls, she thought, a slow, sick fear seeping through her. What path could be harder than one that would drown her?

'So that's how you want to play it, is it?' she said, to no one in particular.

'Moira Jean?'

She whirled around, one foot catching the edge of the bog. A familiar voice was coming from somewhere off to her left. She edged towards the sound, creeping around the edge of the mud. Blue and green lights glimmered in the fog, casting strange shadows over the waiting mire. As she drew closer, a gnarled, twisted shape came into focus – a vast black hawthorn tree, growing out of the dark, murky water. It was easily twenty feet away from her, but through the fog she could make out a pale shape pinned to the trunk, arms raised above its head.

She caught a glimpse of blonde hair. Hope surged through her. 'Fiona? Is that . . .'

'Moira Jean!' said the figure. 'Oh, thank goodness, you've come to save me . . .'

Irritation sparked into life. She knew that voice.

'For Christ's sake!' cried Moira Jean, throwing up her hands. 'I know it's you, changeling. Pack it in!'

There was a moment's silence. Then — '*Fine.*'

Moira Jean folded her arms. 'So what're you doing here?' she called. 'Did The Dreamer send you to distract me?'

'Do you find me *distracting*, Moira Jean?' the changeling purred.

She flushed, very grateful for all the fog floating between them. 'Stop your pouting. I can't even see you. Look, I've no time for this, so if you've nothing more to say then I'll be on my way.'

She started off. 'Wait!' the changeling cried. 'Don't leave me for the tithe!'

Moira Jean hesitated. 'So that's why you're out here?'

'Yes,' the changeling hissed. 'This is my punishment. Moira Jean. If you leave me here, I will die. There isn't much time. Cut me loose, before She arrives.'

'She? Who's—'

'Just do it! Quickly!'

Not entirely sure why she was bothering, Moira Jean waded into the mud. It slipped around her ankles, seeping into her boots. 'What're you being punished for, anyway? Aside from annoying me, I mean.'

The changeling stared at her. 'That *is* what I am being punished for.'

She froze. 'What?'

'Just get me out of this thing!' the changeling snapped. 'I'll give you anything you ask for if only you'll set me free!'

Moira Jean pushed deeper into the bog. The mud oozed over her knees, sucking at her shoes with every step. She struggled closer to the tree, trying not to remember the kelpie dragging her under the surface of the loch. Anything could be lurking under the dark, still water, waiting to curl its long fingers around her ankle . . .

The changeling was waist-deep in mud. Part of the wood had grown over the changeling's wrists, pinning them above her head. She glared at Moira Jean, panic in her eyes. 'Well?'

Moira Jean uncurled one of her fists. She only had two nails left, and she still had not faced The Dreamer. Was it really wise to free the changeling, who'd brought her nothing but grief? She needed all the weapons she could get. But the changeling was twitching, flinching at every passing light and every shriek from the mist. She was terrified. No matter what she'd done, Moira Jean couldn't leave her here to die.

'Hold still,' she said, and pressed the iron nail into the tree.

It screamed. The changeling screamed. The dark wood bulged, rippled, and then tore, splitting the trunk right down the middle. The changeling dropped into the bog, mud splashing everywhere. Moira Jean caught her before she went under. Together, they limped back towards the edge of the bog, one of the changeling's arms slung around Moira Jean's neck.

When they'd finally clawed their way out of the mud, the changeling didn't take it away. 'Oh, Moira Jean,' she murmured, sliding her other arm around Moira Jean's neck, 'however can I repay—'

'Take me to The Dreamer's halls,' Moira Jean demanded.

The changeling froze. 'But . . . but Moira Jean, The Dreamer is the one who left me here. You wouldn't give me back to him, would you?'

Moira Jean softened. There was real fear in the changeling's eyes. 'Get me inside. That's all I ask. You don't need to come too.'

The changeling looked at her for a long time, green eyes narrowed. Then she said, 'You are a fool, Moira Jean. He will not give them back.'

'Then I'll just have to take them. Why d'you care? It's no business of yours.'

'No,' the changeling mused, 'it is not. But . . .'

'But what?'

The changeling shook her head. 'Never mind. Remember I tried to warn you, Moira Jean.'

She vanished. So did everything else. There was a moment when Moira Jean was surrounded by nothingness, and then, The Dreamer's halls burst into life around her.

Moira Jean stood and shook in the middle of The Dreamer's empty hall. It withered before her eyes. The flowers under her feet turned grey and papery, crackling with every step. The golden trees lost their shine, sagging under the weight of slick and rotten ivy. Even the light seemed to sicken. An unearthly glow hung over the hall, turning the skin of everyone it touched corpselike.

The smell of smoke hung in the air, but The Dreamer was nowhere to be seen.

Moira Jean ran to her mother. She was lying on her side, roses withering all around her. Moira Jean skidded to a halt in a burst of brittle thorns and dropped to her knees. She scrabbled for the hagstone – it could be a trap – but when she looked through it, there was no haze. Only her mother, lying perfectly still.

'Ma?'

Her mother did not wake up. Carefully, Moira Jean lifted her mother's head and shoulders, one hand bracing the back of her neck. Her head lolled, unsettlingly loose. Moira Jean thought of her father the last time she'd seen him – the *real* him – and remembered how limp and cold his hand had been, when she'd tried to hold it.

'Ma?' she whispered, her voice cracking. 'Wake up, Ma.'

She wasn't cold. That was what Moira Jean had to keep telling herself. Her mother was only sleeping. She could wake up yet. Moira Jean had seen the dead before – held their hands, kissed their foreheads while she said goodbye – and remembered the chill of their skin. Her mother wasn't cold. Not yet.

She patted her mother's face. She bent down and yelled in her ear. She shook her by the shoulders. Nothing happened. Moira Jean shouted herself hoarse trying to wake her mother up and dissolved into a fit of coughing. Her throat felt like knives, her eyes were burning, and she had absolutely nothing to show for it. She knew she should try and wake up one of the others. Someone else could help, if she couldn't get her mother awake. But the thought of laying her mother on the ground and turning her back on her sliced into Moira Jean and stuck there. She couldn't leave her alone.

Moira Jean huddled over her mother, clutching her close. Tears poured down her face. If only she would wake, it would be all right.

'I'm sorry, Ma,' she sobbed. 'I'm so sorry.'

'Lady?'

Moira Jean looked up, wiping her eyes.

The brownie was peering up at her from a clump of dead

roses. It crept towards her, its large eyes flicking between her and her mother.

'Can you wake them?' Moira Jean asked.

The brownie shook its head. 'They are dreaming. I did not give them their dreams, and so I cannot take them away.'

'Can you take them home?'

'I do not have that power.'

Moira Jean let out a mirthless laugh. 'So you've come to wash the sheets and light the fire while they sleep here, forever. Brilliant.'

'My lord sent me to serve you, lady,' the brownie said. 'I must heed his command.'

'Then get us back to Brudonnock!'

The brownie looked away. 'My lord wishes you to remain in his halls. I cannot disobey.'

Moira Jean scoffed. Then the brownie's words sunk in. 'Wait,' she said. 'If I stay here, can you get the others away home?'

'No. I do not have that power. But there is one who does.'

The brownie scampered to a distant wall. It made a complicated movement with its hands, something a little like lifting a latch and a little like turning a key. Then the trees parted, swinging forwards like a door, and the glaistig walked in. Her skin shone like silver in the dim light of the hall. At her back were a long line of cows, each one black as pitch or white as snow.

'I shall lead them into the mortal world,' she said. 'We must all obey the lord of the Land Under the Hill, but he has given no commands about your friends. Only you, Moira Jean.'

Moira Jean's throat closed over. 'You'd do that? For me?'

The glaistig nodded. 'For the sake of an iron collar.'

'For the sake of a bowl of cream,' the brownie added.

Hope sparked into life. Moira Jean didn't dare trust it. 'But they're such small things,' she said.

'They are small things,' said the glaistig, 'but they are real. The Land Under the Hill is full of dreams. Real things are worth more.'

Moira Jean coughed to cover the cracks in her voice. It went on longer than she would have liked. Hauling her mother up with her, she got to her feet. 'So . . . how will you . . .'

The glaistig beckoned the cows into the hall. 'My herd shall carry them into the mortal world. The brownie and I can open the way. We may take them back to your village, but only my lord can set you free. I am sorry, Moira Jean.'

'Don't be,' said Moira Jean, dragging her mother over to the nearest cow and hoisting her onto its back. 'This is more than I'd have dared hope for.'

One by one, Moira Jean lifted the sleeping villagers onto the backs of the glaistig's herd. By the time she was done she was sweating, shaking, with a dull soreness in her limbs as if she had been working for days.

'Thank you,' she rasped. 'Both of you.'

The glaistig nodded. The brownie scampered up the leg of a white cow and perched on top of its head, staring gravely at Moira Jean. 'Good fortune, lady. That is all we can wish for you now.'

Moira Jean attempted a smile. 'Likewise.'

They left. Moira Jean watched them go, her eyes fixed on her mother's prone figure. The procession wound its way through the trees in a long, silent line. She stared until her eyes started burning again, long after the last cow had vanished from sight.

She dried her eyes and followed them through the door. The

road they had taken seemed a good one, and she was in no mood to sit around and wait for The Dreamer to come back.

She made it three steps outside The Dreamer's halls before the ground beneath her feet vanished, and she went plummeting into darkness.

Moira Jean burst out of the ground, choking and spluttering. Soil was matted in her hair. She didn't understand. She'd dropped like a stone, how could that mean she'd shot out of the earth like a cork from a champagne bottle? But then she started coughing, and mud dribbled out of the corner of her mouth. It tasted of nothing.

She hauled herself out of the hole on shaking limbs.

Moira Jean was crawling over cracked earth the same colour as a tombstone. The sky was a dull, deep red. Black, glittering things whizzed over her head, tiny and gleaming, each one with a point like a needle. She tried to wave them away. When she moved, three of them stabbed themselves into the back of her hand, vanishing the moment they broke the skin. Blood oozed up from the cuts, dribbling down her fingers. Each drop landed in the dirt, and the ground quivered beneath her feet.

Fear prickled at the back of her neck. The woods and the bog had been bad enough, but at least they were familiar. She'd never seen anything like this blood-coloured sky.

Moira Jean lurched upright. Binding up her hand with a handkerchief, she tried not to panic. Of course The Dreamer would be angry. She'd set the changeling free, she'd stolen back her friends and family from his own halls. There would be consequences. Her hand found the hagstone and the last nail, snagged at the bottom of her pocket. She clutched them. It would be so easy to lose such small things.

There was another tremor under her feet. Moira Jean staggered sideways. It was as good a direction as any, so she kept going. Surely she would run into something, sooner or later. But the longer she walked, the less there seemed to be. Soon she wondered if she was even moving at all. Everything looked so similar that she had no idea if she was any closer to the horizon, and the hagstone showed her only grey.

She stopped, squinting up at the sky. There was nothing there but the vast expanse of red. Fear trickled through her thoughts. How long would she be stuck here?

A dark blur had just come into view. It moved through the red sky like starlings, curling and twisting around itself. Slowly, it grew larger, closer. Moira Jean felt a stab of dread. Dark wings stuck out at odd angles – wings, and teeth.

She bolted.

A keening, screeching roar echoed around the empty landscape. Wings flapped, hooves crashed against – against nothing, thought Moira Jean, they were in the *sky* – and claws clicked together. Moira Jean threw herself back into the hole she'd crawled out of as the mass of things bore down on her. This wasn't like the creatures she'd faced in the woods. They had taunted her, snapping at her heels and outstretched hands, but the worst she'd got were scratches. Something snagged in her hair, tearing a handful of curls out by the roots. She screamed, and the things over her head crowed in savage joy.

Talons flashed over her head. Grey dirt cascaded onto her as a thousand inhuman hands reached for her and clutched the earth instead. Moira Jean shut her eyes tight and curled into a ball, shaking. A claw caught the back of her shirt and tugged. The collar went tight around her throat, choking her.

'Moira Jean!'

Something tore. Air flooded back into her lungs. High, brittle howling came from over her head. But there was nothing scrabbling at her back, or snatching at her hair.

She looked up.

The Dreamer was kneeling in front of her, his face set, one of his arms outstretched. It had stopped being an arm just after his shoulder. The skin had become a rough greenish-brown, scored with deep vertical lines. It broadened, stretching all the way over her head and sprouting long, green leaves. Something slammed into it. The Dreamer winced. Through the leaves, Moira Jean caught a flash of a mouth that was all teeth, and then sap dripped onto Moira Jean's cheek.

She scrambled back. 'Get away from—'

The earth shifted underneath her. Moira Jean had time for a second's panic. Then she dropped through solid ground and landed, with a splash, in water.

Moira Jean spluttered up to the surface. A dark wave crashed over her head. Treading water, she looked around. The host that had been screeching in the sky was gone. So had everything else. Now, she was bobbing in dark green water, with no land in sight. The sky above her was black as pitch, and something seemed to be oozing out of it. A vast, bulbous drop of sky drooped down towards her, swelling. Then, it blinked.

Fear and disgust lurched through her. One glistening black eye was staring into the water. Moira Jean kept as still as she could. The eye was moving, glinting as it scanned the waves. She knew, in her bones, that it was looking for her. Dread curdled in the pit of her stomach as she remembered the changeling's words. *Cut me loose, before She arrives . . .*

There was a *snap* from behind her. Pain flared on her scalp. She twisted, splashing, and saw a long, dark head plunge back under the water. She put a hand to her head, and found a smarting patch of skin. Something had torn out a chunk of her hair.

Water rushed against her legs. She threw herself onto her back just as something flashed underneath her. There was a screech from underneath the water. Moira Jean pulled her arms in tight. A vast horse burst from the water beside her, right where her arm had been. It had seaweed for a mane and rows and rows of long, needle-like teeth. Moira Jean splashed out of its path. It lunged for her, strands of her hair caught in its teeth, and she threw herself under the water.

It was a mistake.

The water was teeming with squirming, squalling things. Some were horses with teeth like knives. Some were like men, but completely hairless, with one long fin rippling down the backs of their heads. Some she could only see pieces of – scales, spines, teeth and claws. They had all seen her.

She burst back out of the water. The eye was fixed on her. There was no expression in it. Moira Jean went cold. If she had seen anger there, or triumph, she would still have been frightened, but she would have known that on some level, she mattered to this thing. But there was nothing, nothing at all, and now she was terrified.

Water rushed behind her. Moira Jean turned. An enormous wave was building, stretching high into the air. Things were writhing in it, already snapping their teeth. She was directly in its path. It was too big; she'd never escape it. She took a deep breath, her lungs screaming, and plunged back under the water. The wave crashed over her, shunting her backwards. Hands and hooves and claws and teeth came smashing down towards her, swiping at her hair, her clothes, her face. Her chest throbbed, the water pushing against her mouth and nose. She needed air.

Moira Jean struggled up to the surface. Teeth snapped at her fingers. Hooves stamped at her head. She ducked, twisting out of the way – but something was wrapped around her waist, dragging her back down . . .

A hand seized her by the hair and yanked her head out of the water. Air flooded back into Moira Jean's lungs, so fast she couldn't stop coughing. Blinking salt water out of her eyes, Moira Jean stared up into the face of The Dreamer. It was white, his eyes wide and staring. His mouth was set in a thin line, two wickedly sharp tusks jutting out from his lower jaw. They'd cut into his lips, sending black blood streaming down his chin.

'Dreamer?'

There was a screech from the sky. Fear flashed across The Dreamer's face. He hauled her out of the water and threw her backwards. Suddenly Moira Jean was falling, screaming, the water nowhere to be seen as she went tumbling down . . .

Moira Jean's back slammed into grass. All the breath was knocked out of her. Salt was crusted on her skin, but she could not taste it, nor could she feel the chill of her sodden clothes. Wheezing, she hauled herself to her knees, shaking too badly to stand.

Five pillars of stone surrounded her, one a little shorter than the others. Each one was worn smooth by many years of wind and rain. Faded carvings marked each one. When she tried to look a little closer, they seemed to move.

She looked up. The vast black eye hung in a sky blue with stars. Moira Jean's stomach dropped. It was staring straight at her.

Too late, Moira Jean remembered the conversation she'd had with the brownie. It had said that The Dreamer was not the ruler of the other side. His domain was the Land Under the Hill, but he answered to a higher power. She remembered, too, how when she'd been reading *Tam Lin* in the forest, The Dreamer had refused to let her speak the name aloud.

The Queen.

Moira Jean did not move. Neither did She. The eye considered her, just as empty as it had been before. Earth trembled under her knees. The stone pillars surrounding Moira Jean twitched, the top sections of stone crooking themselves forward. They were not pillars, Moira Jean realized. They were fingers. She was kneeling in the palm of Her hand.

Every nerve in Moira Jean's body was screaming at her to run. There were wide gaps between the stone fingers. She'd make it, before they curled into a fist and crushed her. But she could not move. A dull ache was grinding into her bones, making every part of her heavy. Her limbs were cold, slow, and she could not stop shaking.

Moira Jean opened her mouth. She had no idea what she was going to say.

There was a flash of white from beyond the stone circle. The Dreamer had appeared, dropping instantly to one knee. Even from this distance, she could tell he was flawless again. He was clean, dry, his soft white hair falling over one shoulder. Anger flickered in the vast black eye. That strange smell drifted towards Moira Jean – something between ozone and smoke – and kneeling figures materialized around the stone circle. Kelpies, glaistigs, brownies – those ones, she recognized. But there were others Moira Jean hadn't even dreamed of. Trees with faces sprouting from every branch. Antlered skulls hovering at the top of vast columns of shadow. The glistening, scaled flank of a beast too large to see. She scrabbled in her pockets, but they were empty. Fear curdled in the pit of Moira Jean's stomach.

'My Queen,' said The Dreamer.

The ground rumbled. The Queen's stone fingers began to descend. Moira Jean scrambled to her feet, lunging for the gap between the stones. Something whipped around her ankles and she toppled over, slamming into the dirt. The stone fingers stopped moving. Long strands of ivy were climbing up her legs, anchoring her to the centre of the Queen's stone hand. Moira Jean felt a slash of dismay. It was just as it had been on that night in the woods, almost two months ago.

This was The Dreamer's work.

He was still kneeling on the other side of the stone fingers. Moira Jean caught a glimpse of him as the ivy dragged her back to the centre of the stone circle. He was staring at the ground, one hand pressed flat against the earth, his perfect jaw set.

'My Queen,' he said, his voice clear and strong, 'I would not have you sully your hands with this mortal. She is not worthy of the tithe.'

The eye did not move when the Queen spoke. Nor did the stone fingers. In truth, Moira Jean could not have said exactly where the voice was coming from; it could've been her own head. But surely she could never have imagined a voice so rich and lovely. It was smooth as honey and clear as spring water, and Moira Jean's tongue seemed to shrivel when she heard it. What was the point of speaking again, when her own voice was so shrill and rough by comparison?

'She has brought iron into my realm,' the voice intoned. 'She must be punished.'

'Give her to me,' The Dreamer said. 'Give her to me and she shall not trouble you again.'

Amusement and disdain dripped from the Queen's voice. 'She is a mortal, and she does not want you. Find another. There are plenty of them, and some are far less troublesome.'

'I can make her stop,' The Dreamer said.

Fear prickled at the back of Moira Jean's neck.

The Dreamer got to his feet and glided into the stone circle. Moira Jean tore at the ivy around her legs. It did not move. He came closer. All traces of the sap dripping from his arm, the blood, the tusks and the green water were gone. His long, white hair fell in a rippling sheet. His perfect features might have been sculpted from snow. His eyes gleamed silver, brighter than the moon, and she could see every one of his thick, dark eyelashes. She had never seen him more beautiful, or more terrifying.

'I have indulged her whims until now,' The Dreamer said, 'I found them novel. But at your command, my Queen, I will bring her to heel.'

The Dreamer laid a hand on Moira Jean's head, stroking her hair. His face was utterly serene. She stared up at him, horror rising at the back of her throat.

'She has not tasted the full extent of my power,' The Dreamer continued, his voice soft. He ran his long fingers down her cheek, tracing the shape of her mouth. The smell of smoke and ozone grew stronger. 'I have not yet shown her, for I enjoy the game too much. But I can make her love me. I can make her do anything I please, and thank me for the privilege of serving me. I can smooth away her wilfulness and disobedience until she is the perfect servant. She will not be troublesome then.'

Moira Jean blinked back tears. Surely he wouldn't do it. She remembered The Dreamer after he had pulled her out of the loch, insisting that it was not a game any more, and something inside her seemed to wilt. He had tricked her, just as he had tricked her about Angus. Moira Jean slumped. It shouldn't hurt. She'd known The Dreamer would say and do anything to get what he wanted. But even after all the pain he'd caused her, some part of her wanted to expect better from him, even though she knew just how foolish that was.

She wished she hadn't been right.

'Give her to me,' The Dreamer said. 'Give her to me, and I will show her that it is not a game any more.'

Hope flickered. Moira Jean looked up. The Dreamer's eyes were boring into hers.

The Queen's voice rang clear and true. 'She must be punished. This I have decreed. There is no taming this one. She has iron in her soul.'

The Dreamer's face softened. He stroked Moira Jean's cheek. 'Yes,' he murmured. 'She does.'

He shrugged his shoulders. In an instant, he shrank down to nothing, so fast he seemed to disappear. There was the sound of something hitting the earth, just before the Queen let out an ear-splitting screech. His white robe fluttered down to the ground and stopped halfway, settling on something underneath it. Moira Jean reached up, the ivy falling away from her legs, and lifted the cloth.

It was the shovel.

She snatched it up in both hands and drove it into the nearest stone finger.

The iron sliced into the rock, the stone crumbling the moment it touched metal. The Queen screamed. Her stone fingers descended. Moira Jean lurched out of the circle, heart pounding. She felt flushed with anger and sick with fear, but there was iron in her hands again, and The Dreamer had given it to her.

She was not alone.

The creatures were closing in. Kelpies gnashed their teeth. Women with bloody mouths and hands grinned at her, crimson dribbling down their chins. A man with antlers where his eyes should be stumbled towards her. Moira Jean's hands slipped on the shovel. She gripped it tighter, her mouth dry. If they caught her . . .

She raised the shovel like a battering ram and ran into the crowd. They scattered before her, diving out of the way of the iron. Hands snagged at her hair. Things lashed at her ankles. But she kept running, trampling over spindly fingers and reaching roots and something that splashed beneath her boots.

She tightened her grip on the shovel and kept running. The Queen screeched over her head. Something wailed. A long talon scratched at her shoulder. Moira Jean ignored it all. She closed her eyes and thought *halls halls halls please halls please —*

— and the shouting died.

She was back in The Dreamer's halls again. Dead flowers crunched under her feet. She collapsed, coughing, the shovel spinning out of her grip. The blood rushed in her ears. No matter how much she wheezed, she couldn't get enough air.

The Dreamer knelt beside her and helped her to her feet, fear scrawled across his face. 'I don't—' she began.

'Moira Jean, you must go.'

'Are you . . . are you sending me home?'

The Dreamer nodded.

She stared at him. 'Why? After everything you did . . .'

He smoothed her wet hair away from her face. His hands came away bloody. 'I never wanted to hurt you.'

'You *did*,' she snorted.

The Dreamer looked away. 'I do not think I knew what hurting meant, until I met you.' He gave her a small smile. 'Another thing that you have shown me.'

A distant *thud* rang through the hall. For a moment, The Dreamer's eyes glazed over. The edges of his body blurred, then snapped back into clarity. 'You must go now. You do not have long before the Queen finds you again.'

The Dreamer passed his hand in a long vertical line. Something in the air tore. A slice of the clearing in the woods shimmered in front of her, rich and dark in the starlight. On either side of the gateway, The Dreamer's halls were dead and grey.

The sight of the clearing lit Moira Jean from within. She couldn't quite bring herself to trust it. 'And . . . and this isn't a trick?'

The Dreamer shook his head. His eyes glistened, full and bright.

She watched the rip in the world, still wary. 'And what'll happen to you, when I'm away home?'

'I must pay the tithe,' The Dreamer said. 'The Queen demands her souls. *Go*, Moira Jean. Be happy.'

'So you'll die?'

The Dreamer said nothing.

Moira Jean drew closer and peered at the mortal world. The clearing was empty, but for her own scuffed footsteps. Moonlight glimmered on a discarded whisky bottle. She had no way of knowing how long she'd been gone for – it could have been hours, it could have been months – but the sky seemed as if it was beginning to lighten. Whichever day she stepped into, it would be a new one.

She turned back to The Dreamer. He still held one hand raised in the air, but his shape was starting to flicker. Curling horns sprouted through his long, white hair. The skin of his raised arm was turning to bark. His eyes were iridescent again, shifting through more colours than she had ever seen. But still, he was beautiful. It was not his real shape, of that she was certain. But perhaps he would always be beautiful, when she was around.

The ground under her feet was starting to shake. Moira Jean picked up the shovel and tore off one of the sleeves of her shirt, winding it around the handle. She passed it to The Dreamer.

'Don't pay the tithe,' she said. 'It's Beltane. You can just go. Run. See all the things in your books. There's nothing worth staying for here.'

The Dreamer accepted the shovel gingerly. 'You do not have to pay for your freedom, Moira Jean. I shall give it to you.'

She considered him for a moment. Then she stepped close to The Dreamer and kissed him on the cheek, sharp and fast.

He stared at her.

'There,' she said. 'I'm not taking any chances.'

'Our last bargain,' The Dreamer murmured.

'Aye. The *last* one,' she replied. 'And now, it's settled. There's nothing more between us.'

The Dreamer raised a hand to his cheek.

'Goodbye,' said Moira Jean, and stepped into the mortal world.

There was a rush of noise and colour, a flash of The Dreamer's face, and then she was standing in the clearing.

Freezing air prickled at her skin. Moira Jean fell to the ground, her throat suddenly tight. She was home at last, and yet she couldn't stop shaking.

Moira Jean rolled onto her back and stared up at the sky. She wanted to laugh, to cry, to dance, to run. She did nothing. She didn't think she could. All the panicked energy of the past few hours vanished, leaving her flushed and tired and heavy as lead. The world would not be the same again, now that she had seen the Land Under the Hill. But the changes she had stumbled into would be ones she examined tomorrow. She was so tired.

Chest suddenly tight, she stared up at the stars until, at last, her aching eyes began to close.

Epilogue

It was warm. Too warm. That was the first thing she noticed. A lazy heat lingered in her face, making her throat dry and sore. Moira Jean tried to shake off the blankets, but they felt like they'd been weighted down with rocks. Even fidgeting took an effort.

'Open a window, would you, Ma?' she said. Or rather, tried to say. What came out did not sound like words but a cracked, dry whisper. The inside of her mouth felt like paper.

There was a shriek. The bed jolted. 'Moira Jean?' her mother cried.

Moira Jean opened her eyes.

It hurt. It was far too bright. But when her eyes grew used to the light, she saw her mother, perched by the door of Moira Jean's box bed, one hand reaching for her.

Her mother burst into tears.

Moira Jean was swamped in panic. She tried to sit up and comfort her mother, but she ached all over and her arms were shaking too badly to push herself upright. Not that she needed to. Her mother snatched her up and cradled her like a child, sobbing into Moira Jean's shoulder.

'The *scare* you gave me . . .' she said, when her tears had subsided. 'Here,' she said, raising a cup of water to Moira Jean's lips. The pain in her throat eased off.

Moira Jean leaned against her mother's shoulder. Her head was reeling. There were tears in her eyes, and a broad smile on her face. 'You're home,' she croaked. 'You're home.'

'*I'm* home?' her mother asked. She laid a hand on Moira Jean's forehead. 'You're still a wee bit warm, hen. I'll heat some milk up for you, and then you're to go back to sleep. All right?'

Her mother settled Moira Jean back against the pillow. Moira Jean tried not to wince; her back was sore just from lying on it. 'What happened?' she asked.

'Never you mind that now,' her mother replied.

'What *happened*, Ma?'

Her mother went to the fire and tipped some milk into a pan. She spoke into the flames. 'You've . . . you've had the 'flu, pet. You've been out for a few days. But you're through the worst of it now. So just you sit there and drink your milk like a good lass, all right?' Her mother tried for a smile.

Moira Jean tried to rub her eyes. Her hand moved slowly, like it was passing through treacle. 'You don't remember anything about . . .'

Her mother snorted. 'I'll mind these few days for the rest of my life, Moira Jean. Don't you talk to me about not remembering. Drink your milk, now.'

The next few days passed in a blur. Moira Jean slept through most of them. She was still too tired and sore to move much, but the heat of the fever left her, and soon she was hungry and restless, which her mother took as a very good sign.

Slowly, she began to tell Moira Jean what had happened.

According to her mother, Mrs MacGregor had arranged for Moira Jean to be taken to an asylum. Her mother had only found out when Fiona had banged on the door of

Drewitts, with half the village trying to hold her back. But the next day the driver had returned, saying that Moira Jean had gone, and had they seen her. Moira Jean's mother had screamed at him for a full ten minutes, demanding to know why he'd taken the word of a neighbour over a former nurse and Moira Jean's own mother, and he had staggered out of Brudonnock looking dazed and ashamed. Then, the search had begun.

They'd found Moira Jean in the woods after a week, travel-stained and in the grip of the 'flu. She'd been raving, her mother said, although when Moira Jean asked what she'd said she'd refused to tell her. Since then, she'd been wracked with fever, and until she'd woken her mother had feared the worst.

She told Moira Jean this in fitful snatches, and always when her hands were busy. It seemed easier for her to confess to the fire, or her mending, than to her daughter's face. This was how Moira Jean knew that her mother was telling the truth. Work was a burden, but it could be a shield, too.

She did not remember the Land Under the Hill.

Moira Jean didn't ask her. There was no point. The past few days had scored themselves into her mother's soul; Moira Jean could see it in the shadows under her eyes, and the new lines on her face. She didn't want to add to that burden. It was hard enough to believe that she'd really been gone for a week in the mortal world; her time in the Land Under the Hill had felt like hours. Better to leave it be. Her mother would only worry, if Moira Jean started asking about creatures from fairy stories and deserted villages.

Once, she'd come close. She'd cleared her throat – carefully, because the slightest cough made her mother flinch and pale – and said, 'When I was . . . I saw Da. Did you . . .'

Her mother's eyes filled with tears. She took Moira Jean's hand. 'Oh, love.'

She did not bring it up again.

The brownie did not return. Moira Jean did not see the glaistig, lingering in the door of the cowshed, or the cailleach, bent-backed and hobbling through the wind. One day she found the dry, brittle stalk of a rose crushed beneath her pillow, all the petals long since crumbled away. As she grew stronger Moira Jean began to wonder how much of what she had seen had been real, and how much of it had been the 'flu, lingering under her skin long before she'd felt it. If she hadn't found her friends in such strange places, she would've assumed she'd dreamt up the whole thing.

She would have asked them what they remembered, but that was complicated. Duncan was still recovering, as was Callum. Fiona had run away after her mother tried to have Moira Jean committed; she'd left a note saying she'd gone to Glasgow, wedged under an old iron horseshoe on the kitchen table. Jim had gone quickly, taken by an infection in his bleeding feet. Martha had succumbed to the 'flu, followed by her father not long after, and Mrs McGillycuddy was worsening by the day. A minister was coming down for the Galbraiths' funerals, and to finally give a service for Mrs Iverach. Moira Jean wanted to go, but her mother wouldn't let her.

'You're not strong enough to stand about in the cold, hen,' she said, as Moira Jean paced about the kitchen on legs shaky as a foal's. 'Besides . . .'

'Besides what?'

Her mother sat down. 'I just don't want you near them,' she said, her jaw set. 'They're bastards, every last one of them.'

Moira Jean couldn't repress a grin. 'You *swore*,' she said. 'You never let me—'

Her mother fixed Moira Jean with a look made of iron. '*You* try having your neighbours cart your youngest daughter off to the asylum and keeping a civil tongue in your head.'

'Sorry, Ma.'

They went quiet. Distant hooves echoed down the Aberdeen road. Moira Jean stiffened. She knew it was the minister; her mother had told her. But still she listened for the trundle of a hay cart, and felt sweat prickling on the palms of her hands.

She couldn't stay in Brudonnock. Not after what they'd done.

'Ma,' she said, her voice quiet, 'I . . . I want to leave.'

Her mother slumped in her chair. A smile quavered on her lips. 'Oh, Moira Jean. You don't know how long I've wanted to hear you say that.'

There was a lump in her throat. 'Not right now,' said Moira Jean. 'When I'm well again, and when it's safe. But . . . I want to *go*, Ma.'

'Where to, love?'

Moira Jean shrugged. 'Anywhere. I thought I'd write to Alastair, or to Aileen. See if they wouldn't put me up for a wee bit.'

It was not a good plan, and she knew it. Her siblings loved her, but none of them were in a position to support a wayward sister. But she had to get out of Brudonnock. How could she stand living alongside people who'd believed the worst of her? Could she ever forget the things they'd thought her capable of? She didn't want to find out. And then, there was the forest. It tugged at her thoughts like an insistent hand. If she stayed in Brudonnock, she'd spend the rest of her life turning over the past few weeks, until all the memories had been worn smooth. Who knew what she might do, if she only remembered the magic at her doorstep, and forgot how much it had hurt?

Her mother got to her feet and went to the old dresser. She took down the battered old tin that held their savings, and held it out to Moira Jean. 'Here,' she said.

'No,' said Moira Jean, at once. 'Ma, you've been saving for years . . .'

'Aye, years when I'd five children to feed and not just one. I'll make it up again soon enough.'

'But Ma . . .'

Her mother grabbed her by the shoulders. 'But nothing, Moira Jean! This'll buy you a ticket to Canada and there'll be enough left over to get you away to my sister's. There'll be work for you there. She and I planned this years ago, so don't let me hear any more "buts" out of you.'

Moira Jean took her mother's hand. 'But you didn't plan it for me, Ma.'

'Oh, love,' her mother said, squeezing her fingers. 'That doesn't matter. D'you think I'd ever leave you behind without knowing you were safe, and settled? I could've had that ticket in my hand and I'd have gone nowhere, if I thought you'd be in trouble without me. You're my own wee lass. You come first.'

Moira Jean's throat was too tight to speak. She pulled her mother into a hug, burying her face in her shoulder.

Her mother rubbed her back. 'There, now. Just you make sure to get my room ready for when I join you. I want a view, d'you hear?'

Moira Jean nodded, and didn't let go.

Moira Jean stood on the deck of the ship, pressed up against the railing. The sky blazed overhead, a brilliant blue. Crowds pressed in on every side, all of them leaning over the railing, waving and shouting at the tops of their voices. It was profoundly strange. Months later, they were saying that the danger had passed, but after so long keeping away from strangers, it was unsettling to be surrounded by so many people.

Still, Moira Jean smiled, and waved down at her mother. She was standing on the dock, waving a red and white handkerchief over her head. Alastair was with her; the only one of her siblings who'd been able to get away. Their mother had been on the verge of tears ever since they'd set off from Brudonnock, but the sight of Alastair was enough to keep Moira Jean's guilt at bay. It was easier knowing that her mother would not be going back to an empty cottage.

'I'll write!' Moira Jean called. 'I promise!'

'Mind you—'

The ship's horn blared, and the rest of her mother's words were lost. Ropes were cast off, the gangplanks were pulled back in. A band started to play. Moira Jean waved harder, nearly elbowing the woman she was standing next to. There was a great cheer, a slosh of water, and the ship began to pull away from the side.

'Look after her!' Moira Jean yelled to Alastair. He hadn't heard. He was waving and smiling, one arm wrapped around their mother's shoulders, but there was too much noise. They were already shrinking. Something twisted inside her as she watched them grow smaller. How long would it be until she saw them again?

The crowd began to move away from the railing, moving towards the bow of the ship to watch the open ocean. Moira Jean stayed watching the docks. She was in no hurry to stare at a vast stretch of open water. Her arm was starting to hurt, but she kept waving. She wanted to see her mother and brother for as long as possible.

Something caught her eye.

A figure was moving through the crowd. At first, she hadn't noticed them; there were too many people crammed together. But as the onlookers began to turn away from the docks, they stayed, standing at the edge of the harbour and watching the ship.

No. Watching her.

It was The Dreamer.

She almost hadn't recognized him. His long white robes were gone, swapped for a cream-coloured suit which seemed almost yellow against his skin. His hair was different, too – still white, but cut short, or perhaps pulled back. It was hard to tell from this distance. But he was still beautiful, still tall, still perfect.

Her hands tightened on the rail of the ship.

He'd found her. How? She hadn't been back to the forest since that night in the clearing. She hadn't seen any of his creatures. How had he known she was leaving? Her stomach swooped. He shouldn't have been able to find her. He'd never even left the forest before. She'd thought – hoped, if she was honest – that he might be stuck there, unable to follow her any further. How had he – could he get onto the ship? No, there was too much iron. Moira Jean took a deep breath. She was safe. He couldn't touch her.

Further back in the crowd, Alastair led her mother away. Relief flooded through Moira Jean as she watched them leave the harbour. The Dreamer hadn't come for them. He was standing as close to the water as he could get, his eyes still fixed on the ship.

Tentatively, he raised a hand. Moira Jean flinched. But nothing happened. The ship still pulled away from the harbour, the crowd still ebbed away from the water. The Dreamer gave her a small, sad smile, and lowered his hand.

At last, Moira Jean understood. He hadn't come to drag her back. He'd come to say goodbye.

She flushed. For a moment, everything she'd said to him had a cruel echo to it. He'd saved her life and helped her escape the Land Under the Hill, and she'd been too angry to thank him for it. He'd tried to be a good person, even if he hadn't succeeded. But then she remembered the fear, the doubt, all her frantic searching. He had tried to be a good person, but only when she'd bullied him into it. He'd still hurt her.

The iron rail was cool underneath her hands. Let him keep trying. She did not want to teach The Dreamer what it really meant to love someone, or the real value of truth and kindness. She had her own life to lead. Perhaps she had been foolish, to cast aside the power he had offered her, but perhaps it was the wisest thing she had ever done. She wasn't sure. The one thing she did know was that The Dreamer had finally given her something that she wanted: to be happy, without him.

Still, she was pleased that he was trying.

The harbour shrank into the distance until The Dreamer was a white pinprick against a dark mass of stone. When he was out of sight, Moira Jean let go of the iron railing. He might mean well, but she'd learned to be cautious, and her heart beat slower with iron in her hands.

The crowds on the deck of the ship had dispersed now, and she wandered up to the bow to peer down at the vast, blue sea. She'd have to get used to looking at all that water eventually; the voyage would be a long one. Still, she clutched the railing again, just to be sure. She wasn't going to forget meeting that kelpie any time soon.

The wind tangled in her hair. She could taste the salt on her lips already. The sky and the sea stretched out in front of her, blue as sapphires. She did not know what waited on the other side of the ocean. It would not be easy, to start her life again from scratch. But she knew that she could do it.

After all, she thought with a smile, she had iron in her soul.

A Fairy Bestiary

Baobhan sith. A female fairy known for seducing her victims and killing them. Commonly associated with blood, the baobhan sith either are drawn to the smell of blood or consume it as sustenance, similar to the vampire.

Bean nighe. A female spirit often seen near lakes and streams, washing the clothes of those about to die. Seeing her is an omen of impending death, although she is sometimes able to be reasoned with or to grant wishes. Similar to the Irish banshee.

Bogle. A malevolent shapeshifting creature that instils fear in humans. Bogles often frighten or confuse their victims rather than harm them.

Brownie. A household spirit that, if well-treated, will assist with basic domestic tasks. If treated poorly, it will cause problems. Small, hairy, and preferring to work at night so as not to be seen by humans, they can be set free or banished by giving them clothes.

Cailleach. A female figure, usually an old woman, believed to have control over storms and other bad weather, particularly in winter. Often featured in wider Celtic mythology, it is unclear whether she is Fae, a nature spirit, or a goddess. Sometimes referred to as the Queen of Winter.

Changeling. A fairy that replaces a human stolen by the Fae, usually a very young child. The changeling child often fails to flourish in its human home, being described as sickly. If the host family recognizes the changeling, it is possible to return it for the child the Fae stole, although this usually involves the application of fire or iron.

Cù sith. Translated literally, a fairy dog. Very large and often described as having a dark green coat, it is sometimes said to only travel in straight lines. Not always malevolent, but if heard barking three times before the listener finds shelter, the listener will die.

Each uisge. Translated literally, a water horse. Commonly found in the sea and lochs. Similar to the kelpie, but usually described as much more vicious.

Fae. Fairies. Many different creatures come under the heading of Fae, as Scottish folklore and mythology often uses the term 'fairy' (which this derives from) as a catch-all term to refer to a number of different creatures, including ones that have been listed here separately. Sometimes believed to have the ability to change shape, some Fae are seen as more or less human, with tales describing them as having homes, livestock, food, and pastimes very similar to those found in the human world. However, some Fae are decidedly more eldritch. The lore surrounding the Fae is rich and varied and could not possibly be extensively covered by one entry in a bestiary – however, a few common features the Fae seem to share are an association with the colours green and white, a love of music, an aversion to names, and a need to be respected.

Fuath. Malevolent water spirits, often with webbed feet and hands, and sometimes capable of shapeshifting between men and horses. This term is also associated with the each uisge and the kelpie.

Ghillie Dhu. A small male sprite, usually solitary, believed to live in forests and mountains. Usually seen wearing a cloak of leaves, moss, or bark. Appears to children lost in the woods and leads them to safety, although his interactions with adults are often less kindly.

Gigelorum. Believed to be the smallest creature in existence, allegedly inhabiting the ear of a mite.

Glaistig. A female fairy associated with tending cattle – usually described as blonde, grey-skinned, and with hooves instead of feet. Interactions with the glaistig vary depending on how she is treated.

If benevolent, she will protect cattle, often in exchange for milk. If not, she will lead travellers astray or lure men to their deaths.

Kelpie. This fairy is found in rivers and sometimes lochs. It can take the form of either a handsome man or a horse, both usually having dark hair and covered in water-weeds, although female kelpies have appeared in folklore. If the kelpie takes the form of an attractive person, their object is usually to win over a human and seduce them, sometimes taking them back to the bottom of their river afterwards. If the kelpie takes the form of a horse, they usually wait for travellers, act friendly until the traveller climbs on their back, and then bolt for the water, exuding a sticky substance from their skin which prevents the traveller from getting off their back. Either way, it doesn't end well for the human, who usually gets dumped or devoured.

Pech. A short, strong humanoid creature, a little like a gnome. Said to brew ale out of heather, the pechs are believed by some to have inhabited Scotland before the arrival of humans. However, it is possible that this is the result of some confusion with the Picts, a Celtic tribe (of humans) that inhabited Scotland from the third to the ninth century CE.

Sluagh. An extremely malevolent fairy horde believed to travel through the air. Sources vary on whether the sluagh is made up of fairies or the spirits of the unhallowed dead. Either way, the sluagh swoops down on unsuspecting humans wandering about at night, picks them up, and carries them through the air at phenomenal speeds, putting them down when and if they feel like it. They sometimes force the humans they kidnap to harm other people for fun. Humans rarely come out on top when encountering the sluagh.

Wulver. A creature halfway between a wolf and a man (but not a werewolf). Mostly humanoid but furry and with the head of a wolf, the wulver is not a shapeshifter and is not linked with the moon. Often known for helping lost travellers and occasionally feeding the poor, the wulver is surprisingly benevolent for a lupine monster – although, like all of the Fae, it will defend itself if it feels threatened.

Acknowledgements

As with a lot of my books, *The Thorns Remain* has been a long time cooking. The themes of grief, unhealthy relationships, and acknowledging who you are are all things that I've had to come to terms with myself – both when I was writing this book and when I wasn't. Luckily for me, that has been made infinitely easier with the help of the following excellent people.

First, I need to thank Rae, Ellie, and Moz, three people who I am unfathomably lucky to call my friends. Their help and support has meant the world to me, as have all the little book-related memes they've made me. I treasure all three of you and I am going to say so in public. Particular thanks must go to Rae, who not only read the early drafts of this book and helped me sound more Scottish, but also came to my house with food during my edits so I wouldn't have to think about cooking. Thank you.

My fantastic agent, Chloe Seager, also deserves a massive thank you and a massive cocktail, in whichever order she would like best. It's been so lovely working with such a talented and dedicated person. Really, the entire team at Madeleine Millburn have been fantastic and I can't thank them enough.

Speaking of the entire team being fantastic, it's time for me to talk about Magpie! I cannot tell you how absolutely thrilled

I am that *Thorns* is launching such a fantastic imprint and I'm so glad you picked it. Of course, a large part of this is due to my wonderful editor, Vicky Leech. Her championing of this book, her thoughtful suggestions, and her real enthusiasm for the story have been so encouraging, and they've helped to shape the book into something I'm proud of. Thank you also to Elizabeth Vaziri for indulging all my editorial requests; I really appreciate it. A huge thank you goes out to Caroline Young for her incredible cover – it is absolutely stunning. I'm also very grateful to Robyn Watts, Terence Caven, Sian Richefond, and Susanna Peden for the stellar job they did on producing and promoting the book.

I'd also like to take a moment to thank everyone who assisted me while I was researching this book, including the staff at the British Library and everyone who I pelted with questions on my research trip up to the Scottish Highlands – particularly, the staff of the Highland Folk Museum, who maintain an excellent museum with care and detail. I would really encourage anyone interested in the history of the Highlands to visit them – or if you feel able to, donate something. Also, shout out to the mechanics from Karen Yuill garage who came and rescued me when I had car trouble on the side of a motorway outside Glasgow.

Writing a book is a difficult and personal process, especially during a pandemic. Luckily for me, I have some great friends who made it a lot easier. To my housemates, Cath and Claire – thank you so much for all the support, and all the tea you brought me. To Fay, Ruaraidh, and Sam – thank you for letting me whine in the group chat, helping me justify all the takeaways I ended up ordering, and for telling me to just get on with my edits. Also, Sam – thank you so much for letting me turn up to your flat and straight-up steal your lunch out of your hands that one time. If it's any consolation, I'm going to feel bad about that forever.

As ever, I have saved the best for last. Throughout my whole life I have received nothing but unconditional love and support from my family; I value that more than I can say – which is a problem considering I'm a writer. Mum, Dad, Lucy: knowing that I can always, *always* count on you is one of the best things about my life. I love you all very much and I couldn't have done this without you.

JJA Harwood, August 2022